A PUFFIN BOOK

PROPERTY OF

_____

_____

PUFFIN BOOK

PROPERTY OF

Best known for his children's books, B. B. wrote and illustrated many books for adults under his real name, DENYS WATKINS-PITCHFORD. He was born in Northamptonshire, studied art in Paris and London (at the Royal College of Art) and taught art at Rugby School. But for most of his life he lived in Northamptonshire, developing a wide knowledge and deep love of the countryside.

B.B.

BRENDON CHASE

Illustrated by Denys Watkins-Pitchford

A PUFFIN BOOK

PUFFIN BOOKS

UK | USA | Canada | Ireland | Australia
India | New Zealand | South Africa

Puffin Books is part of the Penguin Random House group of companies whose
addresses can be found at global.penguinrandomhouse.com.

puffinbooks.com

First published by Hollis and Carter 1944
Published by Jane Nissen Books 2000
Published by Puffin Books 2016
001

Copyright © The Estate of Denys Watkins-Pitchford, 1944
All rights reserved

The moral right of the author and illustrator has been asserted

Set in 12.5/16.5 pt Sabon LT Std
Typeset by Jouve (UK), Milton Keynes
Printed in Great Britain by Clays Ltd, St Ives plc

A CIP catalogue record for this book is available from the British Library

ISBN: 978-0-141-36207-6

www.greenpenguin.co.uk

MIX
Paper from
responsible sources
FSC® C018179

Penguin Random House is committed to a
sustainable future for our business, our readers
and our planet. This book is made from Forest
Stewardship Council® certified paper.

The wonder of the world, the beauty and the power, the shapes of things, their colours, lights and shades; these I saw. Look ye also while life lasts.

Contents

Contents

If ye go thyder, ye must consider
When ye have lust to dine,
There shall no meat be for to gete
Neither bere, ale, ne wine.
Ne sheetës clean to lie between,
Made of thread and twine;
None other house but leaves and boughs
To cover your head and mine.
Lo, mine heart sweete, this ill dìète
Should make you pale and wan;
Wherefore I'll to the greenwood go,
Alone, a banished man!

1. Hatching the Plot

THE END of the Easter holidays was drawing very near; only two more days remained before five hundred odd boys, whose ages ranged from twelve to nineteen, would discard their carefree clothes to don the well-pressed trousers, the speckled straw hats and black tailed coats which, from time immemorial, had been the garb of all Banchestians. Farewells would be taken, some resigned, some sad, some even joyful, handkerchiefs would flutter down many a long platform, heads would cram many a window as the inexorable chuffing engine drew them away from their loved ones and all they held dear.

But to the three boys sitting together dreading the thought of another term at school, this did not apply. Their parents had gone abroad when the youngest boy, Harold, was only three years old, and they had been entrusted to the care of a maiden aunt who knew nothing of children, and never understood boys.

But their environment had one redeeming feature, namely the old Dower House, and its old fashioned garden, set snugly in a well wooded county with streams and river abounding. They escaped to the fields and spinneys whenever possible, bird-nesting, fishing and poaching with catapult and air gun, and, in general, getting up to all those tricks young boys love to play.

So that though the 'home' atmosphere was strained, the old house and grounds, the thickly timbered country and the adjacent Weald exercised a great fascination and they had come to love it.

Now the holidays were virtually over and only forty-eight hours remained, but to the young that is an eternity.

In a dim-lit loft, the three boys sat cross-legged among the onion skins.

Their council chamber was roomy, though one could only stand upright in the centre of the floor, because the sloping rafters came up on either side, festooned with cobwebs, and with dim lights showing here and there through chinks in the tiles. In one corner was a mass of drying onions, especial pride of old Rumbold, the gardener, the only other male member of the Cherry Walden establishment.

Robin sat facing the small window on an upturned flowerpot. From there he could see the ivy leaves shaking outside as the sparrows chirped and scuffled. Occasionally one would fly across the square of saffron light. He could also see the top of the lilac tree, masses of rich purple flower strongly lit by the low rays of the evening sun. The loft had a peculiar smell of its own. The scent of earth and the musty odour of rafters and plaster, all mingled into one exciting, fruity bouquet.

It was an ideal hideout. Rumbold rarely climbed the rickety wooden stairs. He kept the door below securely padlocked but the boys had found where he secreted the key, under a flowerpot on an upper shelf of the potting shed. No small wonder Rumbold kept the door to this loft carefully locked. Halfway down the stairs was his rook rifle of .22 calibre, fitted with a silencer, a glorious lethal weapon, with which he slew the grey wood pigeons when they raided his greens in the snowy winter weather. Naturally an Auntish decree forbade the use of firearms of any sort; even catapults were banned, though John possessed a good one, in the use of which he was extremely proficient. On this same stair was also the ammunition for the said rifle, fully a hundred rounds, in a heavy, red-labelled box.

As Robin sat watching the window a swallow passed now and again, the sun shining on its blue back and brick-red throat. He had seen swallows depicted in old Egyptian wall paintings and the red throat and forehead suggested the sun-baked lands of the Nile, pyramids and sphinxes.

The chirping of sparrows and twittering of swallows was strangely muted here in this dim chamber, as were all sounds of the sunny world outside.

The loft served not only as a council house where any important plots could be hatched, it was also a refuge from that strange drab world of grown-ups, those poor blind beings who had – apparently – no joy in outdoor life, and whose imaginations had long since been stifled and submerged.

When aunts and governesses became too troublesome, or 'visitors' threatened, it was to the loft the boys fled, to emerge timidly and fearfully, like rabbits, when their scouts pronounced the danger past. It was there they sought refuge when the Bramshotts arrived.

The Bramshotts were the prolific family of a neighbouring titled squire, who from time to time descended unbidden and uninvited, at least by the boys – in an open carriage – it was before the days of the universal car – driven by a wizened old family coachman. This vehicle reminded Robin of a comic turn he had once witnessed on the stage, when a never-ending stream of quaintly attired people descended from a dilapidated fly, to the accompaniment of rising squeals of hysterical laughter from a delighted audience.

As each Bramshott emerged they were counted and even when the last, a babe in its nurse's arms, had descended, the boys anxiously searched the interior of the carriage for yet another which might have been overlooked behind some cushion. As Robin once neatly remarked – rather coarsely perhaps – it was not a family, but a *farrow*, and such prodigality struck the boys, even at their tender age, as faintly disgusting.

Robin as the eldest – he was fifteen, John thirteen, and Harold twelve – was now unfolding a plan so daring and exciting as to give everyone a sudden warm ache in the pits of their respective stomachs.

'My idea is,' he said, 'that we should run away to Brendon Chase!'

'Run away!' exclaimed John. 'And not go back to school on Thursday?'

'Exactly. Why shouldn't we live in the forest like Robin Hood and his merry men?'

For the moment there was dead silence. The boldness of the idea was shocking.

'But how can we get enough food to keep us alive?' asked Harold after a breathless pause. He was always one for his stomach.

'There you go, you greedy little hog, always thinking of your stomach,' said Robin witheringly. 'Of *course* we should get enough to eat, we should go hunting.'

'I can't see how we can get enough to eat unless we have something to hunt with,' John said doubtfully, 'I've got my catapult but we can't rely on that.'

Without replying Robin got up and descended the stairs. The others knew what he was about. When he returned he had Rumbold's rifle in his hands. 'What about this?'

The rifle! They could kill all they wanted with that!

'Of course, by rights we should have bows and arrows,' said Robin, 'but we can make those when we get to the forest. In the interval we can use the rifle; it will keep us in meat and pelts.'

'Pelts?' queried Harold.

'Skins, silly. We should hunt for skins as well as meat, all proper outlaws do!'

'But if we go shooting about in the forest, somebody will hear us, keepers or somebody, and we should be caught and get in a fine old row.'

'Rot!' said Robin. 'Can't you see it's got a silencer? I saw Rumbold shoot a blackbird with it and it made no more noise than *that* –' he clapped his palms together.

They were suddenly aware of voices. In an instant each boy slid to the window with a warning whisper. Far up the kitchen garden was Aunt Ellen with two visitors, maiden ladies from the village. They were walking up the long cinder path by the lavender hedge and Aunt Ellen was pointing at the gooseberry bushes.

'It's only Aunt and the two Pug Westons,' whispered Robin, who had nicknames for everybody in the village. And after all the two Miss Westons *were* awfully like pugs. 'They're looking at the fruit trees.'

The boys could see their aunt, pince-nez on nose, her garden hat – which they hated – jammed down on her iron grey hair, earnestly talking to the elder Miss Weston and shaking a finger in front of her nose.

Robin turned from the window in disgust. 'Oh, it's all right, don't worry about them – women, women, women, that's the whole trouble. I'm just about sick of petticoat government. I've just about had enough of it. Even if you two don't come I'm going and nobody will ever catch me. If Father and Mother were here it would be all different and we shouldn't want to cut school and run away to the forest and live like Robin Hood. Anyway, Father told me once that when he was a boy his people let him go off every holiday with a gun and a tent and he walked all round the coast of Scotland living on what he shot and fished. But Aunt throws a blue fit even if we get our feet wet and we can't even ride the pony Father gave us, for fear we should fall off. I'm sick of it. What about you, John, will you come with me?'

'Come? Of *course* I'll come; I never said I wouldn't, did I?'

'And I'll come too,' said Harold.

The others looked at him doubtfully. 'I'm not sure you ought to,' said Robin. 'You might get ill or something, and then we should have to bring you back.'

Harold's face was a study; he was having a terrific struggle within himself to hold back the tears.

'Oh *please* take me, Robin, I'll do anything you want, all the camp work, I'll wash up the dishes while you and John go hunting. I shan't mind what I do! I swear I won't get ill or be a bother, really I won't.'

His elder brother looked at him doubtfully and his fate hung in the balance.

'Oh, very well then, there's no need to blubber, we'll take you,' said Robin grandly, 'but if you're a nuisance you'll have to come back and then you wouldn't have to breathe a *word* of where we were.'

'There's another way we can get food,' said John, whose mind had been busy, 'we can snare rabbits and things. Bill Bobman's boy showed me how to make a snare once, it's easy.' (Bill Bobman was the village poacher.) 'All you want is a bit of copper wire, a peg and a string; there's some in Rumbold's toolbox in the coach house, I saw it yesterday. Aunt Ellen wanted some wire to hang a picture and I saw him get it.'

'Well, we'll take some wire with us, that's a good idea of yours, John. All proper outlaws trap and snare.'

'And we can make deadfalls out of logs,' went on John, warming to his subject, '*you* know, a log propped up on a stick with a bait tied to it, and the wolf or beaver or 'possum comes along and pulls the string and down comes the log!'

'Like Bill Bobman's brick sparrow traps?' asked Harold.

'Yes, that's the idea, only bigger.'

'And then we shall want salt, and flour to make bread, shan't we?' asked John.

'Yes,' replied Robin, 'we can't take bread with us, it would be too bulky, and besides, it would go as hard as a rock. We've got to take as little as possible.'

'Why not oats instead of flour, and then we can make porridge?' suggested Harold. 'Nice stiff porridge you can stand your spoon up in, not Cook's sloppy stuff, full of lumps.'

'Well, that's not a bad idea, Harold,' said Robin, 'not at all a bad idea – for you,' he added grudgingly. 'We shall have to do without forks; for knives we can use our hunting knives.'

'What about plates?'

'Yes, we'd better take a plate each, the tin ones out of the picnic basket will do; we'll borrow the saucepan and frying pan as well, they're Father's anyway, though Aunt Ellen says they're hers, and we'll take the compass along, Father's old army one.'

'Kettle?' queried John.

'No, we can't take a kettle, too much to carry. Besides, we shan't drink tea, at least, not if we're going to be proper outlaws. We shall want a blanket each, we'll pinch those off our beds, and that's about all we'll manage to carry. Even that'll be too much I expect, when we come to escape. We'll take matches too; we can buy a whole packet at the post office.'

'I thought outlaws always made a fire by rubbing two sticks together,' ventured Harold.

Robin sighed wearily. 'I know they did, but it doesn't work, only in books, 'cos I've tried, ever so many times. There's a waterproof matchbox in the picnic kit; we'll take that along.'

'We shall want green stuff to eat or we'll get scurvy,' said John.

'Well, we must cook wild herbs, like all outlaws do. You don't suppose they eat cabbages and things, do you?' asked Robin scornfully. 'There's wild sorrel, and nettles and lots of things you can eat. It tells you in the Scout Diary Miss Holcome gave me on my birthday, and it tells you how to find your way by the stars, and all kind of useful tips like that.'

'We haven't got a tent,' said Harold.

'No, we shouldn't take one if we had. We'll have to make a hut or something out of branches; we'll soon find some sort of place in the forest,' said Robin confidently. 'And we must have proper names. I'll be Robin Hood, John can be Big John, and you, Harold, can be Little John.'

Suddenly from the garden they heard their names called, 'Robin! John! Har–old!'

'Not a word, the wicked Abbess calls,' hissed Robin dramatically, sliding to the window. 'The vicar's there now,' he groaned, 'I expect Aunt Ellen wants us to come and say goodbye.'

The vicar, known to the boys as the Whiting, was rather a pal of theirs. He was a keen entomologist and in the summer holidays they used to go butterfly hunting with him up on the Weald and in the woods. He also gave them amazingly good teas in his big creeper-clad vicarage, served by his cosy old pink-faced housekeeper. She had a goitre, a phenomenon which always intrigued the boys enormously and filled them with vague dread because Aunt Ellen once said it was 'catching'. In season the Whiting's table groaned with plates piled high with strawberries arranged in scarlet cones, plentifully laced with delicious cream and as much fine castor sugar as you wanted. Aunt Ellen banned strawberries from their diet as she said they gave you 'appendicitis' and 'rashes'. The Whiting, like many old bachelors, was extremely absent-minded. Many were the tales in the village of this weakness of his. Sometimes he would forget to preach the sermon or he would read the first lesson twice over. The best story about him was how once at a dinner party, when he was describing to the company present how a certain burglary had been committed, he demonstrated his story by putting the solid silver spoons and forks into his pocket and these had to be extricated by a tactful hostess before he left.

The Reverend Whiting's round jolly face was now partly visible over one corner of the greenhouse. Their aunt was looking towards the

Nutwalk – by experience she knew its green thickets usually held skulking braves – and she was clucking like a fussy hen.

No reply being forthcoming, they saw the Whiting smile, wag his moonlike face from side to side, and stick his thumbs over the pockets of his Norfolk jacket. Then they all drifted out of sight through the arched doorway by the ilex tree and their voices were stilled.

'The old Whiting isn't a bad sort and we might get a tip if we go and say goodbye,' suggested John slyly. 'He usually stumps up half a crown when we go back to school.' But even the lure of gold would not tempt Robin, whose imagination was afire.

'Let's go and say goodbye tomorrow evening. It'll be better without Aunt Ellen there, and we can see those white admirals he caught last year in High Wood. That reminds me,' he added, 'we ought to see heaps of rare butterflies in the forest. When I went there with the Whiting in his old car last summer hols he told me he had once met an old man called Smokoe Joe who lives in the middle of the Chase. He's a charcoal burner or something. He seemed to know quite a bit about bugs and things and he told the Whiting he'd seen a purple emperor in a certain part of the forest, though he wouldn't tell him where. The Whiting tried to get it out of him and even offered him half a sov if he'd tell, but he wouldn't. Smokoe told him all sorts of things about animals and birds; he'd seen goshawks and honey buzzards and all kinds of rare birds. He's lived there for years and years.'

'Won't he find us living in the forest?' asked Harold.

'It's doubtful; he doesn't get about much, he's too busy with his charcoal and his sight isn't good, so the Whiting said.'

'Aren't there any keepers or watchers who look after the place?'

'There used to be but not now. The Whiting told me that it's a Chase, and that means it was a hunting ground which belonged to a subject of the King and not to the King himself, though of course the King could hunt there if he wanted to.'

'It's a pity there aren't any boars and wolves now,' sighed John.

'Or deer,' put in Harold, tossing an onion from one hand to the other.

'There may be deer,' said Robin, 'though I've never seen one and the Whiting hasn't either. But old Smokoe Joe said he'd seen 'em, and I'll bet he's poached them too.'

'Who does the Chase belong to?' Harold asked.

'Most of it belongs to the Duke, I suppose,' replied Robin. 'He seems to own all the land round here for miles. Rumbold told me he even owns Cherry Walden. But the Crown owns some of it and I expect there are keepers there, but we needn't go near that side.

'As for the Duke, the Whiting told me he is an old man now and never goes near the Chase. At one time he was quite keen on butterflies and used to hang about the keeper's gibbets looking for purple emperors.'

'Well – *he* won't bother us much then,' said Harold.

There was a silence in the dim loft. Outside the little window the light was fading and the lilac crown was dark against the sky. Sparrows rustled in the ivy and hopped restlessly among the lilac leaves. They were thinking of bed already and were as restless as domestic fowls at roosting time. Then from below, the boys heard the sound of paws scrabbling on the potting shed door and suppressed whines.

'There's Tilly!' exclaimed Robin, and they all crept out of the loft and down the creaking stairs to be greeted by the boisterous welcome of the fat spaniel.

From bed to bed that night, Robin and John talked over their plans. It was strange lying there in the room where day still lingered, hearing the thrushes and blackbirds singing outside.

'It worries me a lot about Harold,' said Robin. 'I'm sure he'll crock up or something; he's too young to rough it and he'll only be a nuisance and get homesick and we'll have no end of bother. I didn't think he looked too well tonight, sort of flushed and bright-eyed.'

Harold had indeed seemed rather strange, so much so that their sharp-eyed aunt had made him sleep in the dressing room, next to her bedroom. She was terrified of even the commonest cold turning into something more serious, and she was one of those people who have a 'germ' complex. Every time she passed a bad smell in the street, or even the quite healthy smell of a farmyard, she would say, 'Spit, children,' as though the air was seething with virulent plague.

'Oh, I think it was simply excitement,' said John. 'I remember I used to feel just the same way before a party. Anyway, he'll have to come now; he'd pine away if he was left.'

Neither Robin nor John had any fear that Harold would ever split on their scheme, even if they decided he was too young to accompany them – they 'knew their man'.

It was some time before either of the boys could get to sleep and when they did it was to dream of nightmarish attempts to escape from Aunt Ellen and of vast green forests inhabited by strange and fearsome monsters which pursued them, breathing fire.

A letter arrived next morning which shook the boys up considerably. It was from their parents in India and the envelope bore the Simla postmark.

In effect it was to wish them well for the summer term at Banchester, and said that, if they worked especially hard, there was a chance that both their parents would be returning in the New Year as their father had been promised leave.

John could see by Robin's face that their bright plans were doomed. 'It's no good, John, we can't sneak off after this, we really can't. It's up to us to see the term through at any rate and then, in the summer hols, we might do it. The point is, Father wouldn't mind us taking to the woods a bit *in the hols*, I'm sure of that; he'd understand and Mother would, too, though, of course, she'd fuss no end. But they wouldn't agree to us cutting school. We can't let 'em down, old boy.'

John agreed, though his heart was heavy with disappointment. After all, they couldn't let their parents down. What a pity they had not thought of the whole scheme before, last summer, for instance, when they had had to kick their heels around Cherry Walden all through August and the greater part of September.

Harold, who appeared at breakfast seemingly his old self, was soon informed of the change of plan. Robin thought he detected a certain relief flit over his brother's features, but Harold affected to be as disappointed.

So, after all, the Last Day had dawned and tomorrow, for all the brave bold plans, the boys would be speeding back to school! They lay on the grass under the cedar on the lawn and heard, through the morning-room window, the voice of Aunt Ellen going over their school lists with Miss Holcome – erstwhile governess who was staying on as an 'Aunt's help'. 'Robin, three pairs pants,' and Miss Holcome's reply, like a response to a prayer, '*Robin, three pairs pants.*' 'Harold, one wool sweater.' '*Harold, one wool sweater.*'

After lunch the boys were summoned upstairs to superintend the packing of boxes. And then – Fate stepped in.

Harold, who earlier in the day had seemed quite recovered, again complained that he didn't feel well. Passing the schoolroom door, John saw him seated in a chair with a clinical thermometer sticking out of his mouth like a rakish cigar and Aunt Ellen and Miss Holcome poring over a gruesome medical book which gave coloured plates of all the various diseases common to those of tender years.

And when, later in the afternoon, the doctor's brougham was seen in the drive, it was obvious that something was really amiss. Robin and John, going their last round of the garden and visiting all the nests, were called indoors by Aunt Ellen. She was visibly upset, grey of face and tight-lipped.

'Harold has measles,' she said. 'You cannot return to Banchester tomorrow and I have wired Mr Rencombe to that effect. Both of you may catch it as you have been in contact with him. On the other hand, you may not. But it would not be fair on the school if you returned.'

'Then we can stay on here?' John asked, hardly believing his ears. 'We needn't go back?'

'Yes, you will stay on here, and on no account must you go near Harold's room. But though your return to school has to be postponed, I am arranging with the vicar to tutor you each day. You will work from eleven o'clock until one o'clock and from two-thirty to four-thirty, with the exception of Saturdays, when you will be allowed a half-holiday.'

'But, Aunt,' Robin began.

'Now, no "buts", Robin. I have arranged it all and you start tomorrow. The vicar, kind good man, has been most helpful; he is an excellent teacher. He tells me that before he entered the Church he was a schoolmaster, and he did quite brilliantly at Cambridge – he is a fellow of his college. Now, off you go and don't worry me any more; you must be as good and thoughtful as you possibly can as I have so much to arrange.'

'The old dragon,' growled John as soon as they were out of earshot. 'Isn't that Aunt Ellen all over, she can't bear to think of us not going back to school.'

'How long does it take to develop measles?' asked Robin, looking very thoughtful.

'Oh, weeks and weeks I think. I don't suppose we shall go back this term now, it won't be worth it. Why do you ask?'

'Well, I was just thinking that we might run away after all!'

'What, tonight you mean, as we planned?'

'Why not?'

'But supposing we found we'd got measles?'

'Pooh, we shan't catch it,' said Robin. 'Besides, outlaws don't catch measles; they're hard and brown and lean and never have a day's illness, not even a cold. And even if we *did* begin to feel a bit queer, well then, we could come back, couldn't we?'

'Aunt Ellen never said how *long* we were to be at home for,' said John. 'Supposing Harold gets better quickly, won't we have to go back?'

'No, stupid, he'll be in quarantine for weeks. Anyway I'm not going to kick my heels in Cherry Walden any longer. This place is all right; I like it, the house and garden and all that, but I can't bear another day of Aunt Ellen. I'm off tonight. Are you coming, too?'

'You bet I am,' said John with quiet glee.

*

After tea the two boys made a cache of some of the equipment in the Nutwalk. There was an old ivied stump, well hidden in the thickets, where once they had found a hibernating hedgehog. In this cavity they put the saucepan, frying pan and three tin plates from the picnic basket, together with a packet of matches and the Marbles waterproof matchbox. There too they put their hunting knives – surreptitiously purchased out of Christmas money – and five packets of Quaker Oats which they bought at the post office. A large tin of salt completed their supplies. The blankets and rifle they would leave until the moment of departure.

Tilly, sensing in that uncanny way dogs have that her gods were contemplating a journey to a distant country, stuck to them like a leech. Wherever they went she followed, with an enquiring look on her snub-nosed face.

It was a lovely soft evening, and the western sky a riot of daffodil, rose and blue. Their preparations complete, the boys strolled about the garden and then down to the tennis lawn. From the laburnum on the upper terrace a blackbird warbled richly and swifts clove the air like dusky crossbows, wheeling and screaming round the lichened gargoyles on the church tower.

This time tomorrow night the boys would be far away, beginning their new life, deep in the ancient forest; perhaps they would be setting out for their evening's hunt. Their hearts warmed at the thought.

With Tilly rushing alongside they jumped the ha-ha wall into the paddock and ran away over the shining grass – on, on, under the copper beeches, until they came to the still mirror of the Willow Pool. The trout were rising and this put the boys in mind of their fishing lines and snares. They had forgotten them, a dreadful lapse, which they would remedy when they returned to the house.

Along the shore of the pool rhododendrons grew right down to the water's edge and here Tilly put up a rabbit which she chased along the bank, puffing and panting far in the rear of the bobbing scut.

Robin looked back towards the old Dower House set among its cedars and limes. A light was already burning in Harold's room and as Robin watched he saw Miss Holcome gently draw the blinds.

'Pity about Harold. I bet he doesn't feel much like running away to the greenwood now!'

'It's the Hand of Providence,' said John with unwonted piety. 'We could never have taken him, you know.'

Aunt Ellen, all her plans laid with such efficiency and the unhappy patient safe in bed, was moving among the rose trees – she was a keen but ineffectual gardener.

'Poor old Aunt,' said John, 'she's not a bad sort according to her lights. I think she does her best for us in her own way.'

'Yes, I think we ought to leave a note or something,' said Robin. 'If we just disappear she might think we'd been murdered.'

So in the shadow of the rhododendrons they penned the following:

Dear Aunt,

John and I have decided that we would be better out of the way while Harold is ill, we might catch it.

We will be back sometime, but don't worry about us, we shall be all right and please explain to the vicar.

Don't try to find us because you never will.

Signed,
Robin (Hood)
John (Big)

'There,' said Robin, reading it through once more and folding it up, 'we'll put it on the card tray in the hall as we go out tonight. She'll find it in the morning.'

And so arm in arm they strolled back towards the house, where the bats were already hawking about the gables, not failing to notice their corded and labelled boxes still standing in the hall, a mute reminder that our destinies are ever in the lap of the Gods.

2. The Getaway

A HOUSE, even one so friendly and well loved as was the Dower House, is an eerie place at dead of night. Some miraculous change seems to take place when the last light goes out, as though a magic spell has been pronounced and every living moving thing frozen into immobility.

Familiar corridors and rooms, which during the daylight hours were full of laughter and bustle, the clatter of feet and merry clink clank of distant kitchen activity, are horribly silent, as silent as a vault – with shadows and vagueness everywhere.

The boys had no knowledge of this transformation. Their bright days were full of activity and sunlight. At nightfall, they, with other mortals, retired like fowls to their respective roosts, and left the old Dower House to its own ghostly devices.

So that when, with thumping hearts, Robin and John found themselves tiptoeing out to the landing, they sensed this new phenomenon and were momentarily appalled.

In some strange way they felt the hostility in their surroundings and for a few seconds they stood still, listening and watching like startled rabbits. But in all the old sleeping Dower House there was no sound, save for the *sotto voce* 'tick tock' of the grandfather clock on the stairs.

'Come on,' whispered Robin, startling John out of a trance, and they slid silently to the head of the front stairs. Aunt Ellen's shoes were outside her door waiting for the morning maid and there was light glowing dimly from Harold's sickroom, a long narrow strip of light between the bottom of the door and the curly black carpet on the threshold. But even the patient must have slept, his mind perhaps busy with feverish dreams connected with the escapade. He would not know what course his brothers had decided to take; perhaps he had guessed that now he had fallen ill with the measles they would carry out the original plan. It was easy to imagine his discreet probings the next day, his seemingly innocent enquiries as to what his brothers were doing. Knowing Aunt Ellen and Miss Holcome, and thereby knowing the ways of women, Robin and John realized that even when their disappearance became known, Harold would not be told for fear of heightening his fever.

Robin cocked his thigh over the smooth oak banister and the next second had plunged from sight into the dark well of the front hall with no more sound than that of a stealthy snake. John followed suit, landing silently beside him on the Persian carpet. For a moment they again paused and listened but there was nothing but the subdued 'tick tock' of the stair clock.

'John!' – this in a whisper.

'Yes?'

'We've gone and forgotten the blankets!'

'Oh Lord!'

'One of us must go back,' he whispered again. 'We'd better have them. Pop back and get them; it won't take a minute.'

Obediently, but with a quaking heart, John made to ascend the stairs but at the first cautious tread a board squeaked agonizingly and the boys shrank back against the hall curtains.

To John's annoyance he found his limbs trembling violently as though he had an ague. It was not fear but excitement.

'It's no good, we must leave them, we shall be warm enough! Besides they will be awfully awkward things to carry,' he said weakly.

'All right, leave them. Come on!'

They tiptoed down the stone-flagged passage to the kitchen door. Inch by inch Robin turned the brass knob. There was a loud click from the lock. Again they stood. In the silence of the sleeping house these sounds assumed titanic proportions.

Ting chimed the grandfather clock way back on the stairs and the boys jumped. One o'clock in the morning and they must make the forest before dawn! There was not a moment to lose!

It was unbelievably dark in the kitchen. John, feeling his way along the scrubbed white table, encountered a chair leg. It fell over with a hideous crash which seemed to echo through the house.

'Clumsy owl,' hissed Robin. 'Look where you're going!'

'How can I when it's dark?' he growled. The sweat was standing in beads on his forehead. 'Hist!'

They were both again frozen into immobility. From upstairs was heard the unmistakable noise of Harold's door being opened. It had a squeak which the boys knew well.

'Oh Lord!' groaned Robin. 'Somebody's heard us now. If they come down the front stairs we must bolt for it. Listen!'

But the guilty consciences were soothed by the sound of bold steps bound for the bathroom. It was Miss Holcome, or possibly their aunt, going to fill a water jug. They heard water running from the taps and steps returning along the passage. Then Harold's door shut quietly.

Perhaps the poor feverish patient was thirsty.

Breathing again they softly undid the bolts of the back door and the next moment were out in the garden and all the sleeping beauty of the early summer night. The stars shone clear and bright and the crisp bow of the moon in its first quarter was cocked jauntily over the stable roof.

It was the work of a moment to undo the door of the toolshed and secure the rook rifle and ammunition, scaring a rat as big as a rabbit which was sitting on the bottom stair.

And in the leafy Nutwalk they collected together their simple needs; the frying pan,

pan and plates, the matches and waterproof matchbox, the Quaker Oats and salt. John made sure that the fishing lines and snares were in his pocket and after feeling about inside the root to discover if anything had been overlooked, they jumped the ivied sunken wall and struck off across the fields.

They passed the churchyard, crammed with its glimmering white tombstones which made them avert their eyes, for fear of what they should see; they passed the ivied bulk of the old church tower framed against the luminosity of the sky.

A dog barked at them from Baldrick's farm and the noise roused every village cur within hearing. Worse still, from the direction of the Dower House, the boys heard Tilly uplifting her voice in plaintive howls. 'Blast the dog, she'll wake the whole place,' growled Robin as they hurried along in the shadow of a thick thorn hedge. 'I believe she knows it's us, doing a midnight flit.'

'By the way she's barking, she's trying to tear down the stable door,' said John. 'The sooner we're clear of the village the better for us.'

'It's all the fault of Baldrick's beastly cur . . .'

The barking dwindled behind them, fainter and fainter, until they could only just hear it.

They passed cows asleep among the buttercups, they smelt their sweet meadow breath and heard their subdued rustling in the shadows. Something of the eerieness of the silent Dower House lingered even here, out of doors. The landscape which, during hours of daylight, was so dearly familiar – they knew every tree and bush within a radius of a couple of miles about Cherry Walden – seemed now entirely changed and foreign. The big chestnuts along the lane, for instance, bulked large and forbidding, like couched monsters, yet in staring day they were friendly trees with many treasures in the shape of conkers and owls' nests.

Stealthy wildlife was revealed as they passed upon their silent way, the dim scut of a rabbit bobbed and wavered across the turf, splashings and ploppings sounded from the horse pond where Harold, in his happier days, used to fish for polly-woggles and nameless revolting worms – horse leeches he called them – and where even Robin and John had found much magic in the days of their extreme youth.

They felt like burglars or poachers as they nipped across the Brendon road and dived into the sinister shadow of the hawthorn hedge, and the dim ribbon lay vacant and horribly remote to right and left.

In early May the dawn soon comes and it was not long before the boys saw the sky paling to the east of them and trees and bushes becoming more distinct. And soon they heard the first lark singing over the Weald, its faraway music threadlike and cold, matching the silver light.

They took it in turns to carry the cooking utensils and the rifle, for they had not thought to make a sling for the latter before they started. From a blossom-smothered hawthorn a blackbird began to warble richly and soon birdsongs were echoing on every hand, from blackbirds and thrushes, chaffinches and wrens.

As the boys stood for a moment under the dim hawthorns, all the birds could be heard getting into their full stride and soon a cuckoo joined the chorus, dominating even the blackbird's rich warbling notes.

It was strange to think of Cherry Walden, yet asleep. Aunt Ellen's shoes would still be patiently waiting outside her door; everyone in the house and village would be wrapped in slumber. Yet in an hour or two their disappearance would be discovered and the hue and cry would begin.

It did not seem so very long before the boys caught sight of the Chase. It lay all along the horizon, a dense band of darkness against the dim sky. And when the sun rose at last over the rim of the Weald they were crossing the last field – where some cattle were grouped round a salt lick – for the shelter of the trees. Though it was now little after four in the morning – they had been walking continuously since one o'clock – the light was steadily increasing and they gained the forest edge not a moment too soon. For, on looking back the way they had come, they saw the first sign of life, a labourer with a rush skip on his back, cycling to work along a distant lane.

Robin turned in the shadow of the bushes and a strange expression passed across his face as he looked back at his brother, an expression of triumph and excitement.

'We've done it!' he exclaimed. 'We've done it, Big John!'

And then they capered and danced, Robin waving the rifle over his head like an Indian brave celebrating a victory, and as they danced they chanted curious half-formed words. 'No more Aunt Ellen! No more lessons, no more school!'

Carried away by their high spirits they even vowed they would never return to Cherry Walden; they would live in the forest, like outlaws, hunting and fishing like true wild woodmen, for ever and ever. The birds sang joyously, the scent of fern and leaf drove them nearly demented with delight. They rolled among the bracken and buried their faces in the dew-wet grass, they pelted each other with sticks and turned somersaults. They were drunk with the glory of living; they were the happiest beings in the world!

Meanwhile, the cocks of Cherry Walden were proclaiming to mankind in general that it was time to be up and doing. First arose the labouring men, the early birds in the country. They breakfasted heartily and sallied forth to work, some afoot, others on their bicycles, puffing their pipes of shag. A little later, the village domestics got up to light the household fires, and blue spirals of smoke began to curl from the chimneys of the Dower House, the vicarage and the Manor Farm, which made these dwellings appear to be awakening too, which in a sense, they were.

Hannah, the 'tweeny' at the Dower House, descended the back stairs with a heavy tread. It was

Hannah's first job to go all over the house and open the heavy white shutters. First in the kitchen, then in the dining room and drawing room, then in the morning room and finally in the hall.

It was then she saw on the tray – which stood on the Queen Anne table – a glimmering square of white paper. She was an inquisitive girl and immediately took it up and read it, at first hastily and then more slowly, four or five times. So, when Emma, the parlourmaid, in her stiff rustling print dress, knocked discreetly on Aunt Ellen's door there was a white slip of paper on the tea tray.

'Hannah found it in the 'all, 'm, on the tray. I think it must be from Master Robin and John.'

Aunt Ellen, as yet only half awake, pushed it on one side until she had finished her cup. 'Some rubbish from the boys I expect, Emma.'

But when she had read it through twice she put on her dressing gown and padded along the landing to the boys' room. It seemed strangely forlorn and vacant and the tumbled sheets were mute evidence of a midnight flit. Aunt Ellen, to give her her due, kept a level head. She went back to bed and poured herself another cup of tea, and considered in her mind her best course.

She never for a moment believed that the boys had really run away; it was some practical joke they were playing, a poor sort of joke just now, when she had so much to think about with Harold down with measles. She must think out a fitting punishment. Extra work with the vicar, that was the line to take, and no half-holidays this week. The whole business was very irritating just now; the boys must be taught to respect authority.

The Reverend Whiting was surprised to hear his front door bell ring a little after nine a.m. Like many bachelors he was a late riser. He had formed the habit of reading into the small hours and not retiring until long after midnight had struck from the ivied tower of his church, close by. He very rarely got out of bed before ten o'clock in the morning and his breakfast was taken when other people were beginning to wonder what was for lunch. To tell the truth, the tutoring of the Dower House boys was rather a nuisance because of this; it would mean that in the coming weeks he would have to alter his habits . . . Most distasteful.

Aunt Ellen, when she learnt from the vicar's housekeeper that he was not yet down, showed visible annoyance. 'Tell the vicar I must see him at *once*, it's most urgent. Tell him I will wait.'

She was shown into the cosy tobacco-scented study with its bachelor disorder, letters and papers lying on the mantelshelf, more papers and books piled on the chairs and table and – Aunt Ellen sniffed disdainfully – a tumbler and a half-empty whisky bottle, complete with siphon, reposing among the back numbers of the *Church Times* on his desk.

What a mess men live in when they have no wives to look after them, thought Aunt Ellen . . . the whisky, too . . . disgusting. If she were married to the vicar these things would soon be changed.

She paced about, unable to sit down. She passed her eye over his bookcase. There were the usual massive theological tomes and numerous volumes, mostly on natural history, butterflies, birds and the like, and from the top of the bookcase a stuffed stone curlew regarded Aunt Ellen with a glassy disapproving stare. The minutes passed and still the Reverend Whiting did not appear. Bumps and footsteps overhead gave her the impression he was frantically endeavouring to dress. She paced about, now to the door, now back to the window. She stared out with unseeing eyes at the sunny garden, where a spotted flycatcher was sitting on a croquet peg under the cedar, and a black cat was stalking it along the gravel path.

At last she heard footsteps descending the stairs and the Reverend Whiting appeared, with a red gash on his chin, which he was mopping with a bloodstained handkerchief.

'I must apologize for disturbing you at this early hour, Vicar, but, the truth is, I am in trouble.'

'Dear me, dear me,' said the Whiting, mopping at his chin, 'not Harold I hope? He is not dangerously ill?'

He motioned Aunt Ellen to a chair but she remained standing.

'No, not Harold, it's Robin and John; they've run away, in the night.'

'Run away! Run away! Dear me!' The vicar was so taken aback he forgot his cut chin and the blood ran down suddenly on to his white clerical collar. 'Tck, tck, I cut myself shaving,' he murmured apologetically as he applied his handkerchief.

'Yes, *run away*,' repeated Aunt Ellen severely, 'and I have come to you for advice. They left a note for me saying they'd be back "sometime". Of course,' she added, 'I have no doubt at all they will return in a few hours, when the novelty has worn off, and when they get hungry, but when they do come back they must be punished and I want your advice as to the best method. You see, Vicar, I am in charge of them. As you know, their parents are in India, and I naturally feel responsible.'

'I know, dear lady, it's very disturbing for you, but from what I know of boys I think you will find that the young gentlemen will be back at the Dower House before tonight. It's my belief that they are probably in hiding in the grounds, or even on the premises. I should not worry on that score. As to a fitting punishment, I should suggest extra work, extra homework I mean,' he added hastily. He foresaw that he might in a sense be punished too if Aunt Ellen insisted that they had longer hours with *him*, and though the extra guineas which he would receive for tuition would be useful, he was a man who valued his liberty as much as any boy. Indeed, he was very like an overgrown boy himself. Perhaps he secretly sympathized with Robin and John, and reflected that he would probably have run away too if he had had such an old dragon for a guardian.

He soothed Aunt Ellen as best he could and it was in a better frame of mind that she returned to the Dower House. She even half expected to find the miscreants sitting shamefacedly at the breakfast table.

Miss Holcome and Hannah – who met her in the hall – reminded her of two flustered hens. 'Oh, please'm, Rumbold's just been up to say his rifle's missing. He thinks the young gentlemen have taken it, he says they must have found where he kept the key to the pottin' shed.' Hannah seemed quite pleased about the whole affair.

Now, had Aunt Ellen known boys better she would have been uneasy at this latest piece of information. She still believed they would put in an appearance before the day was out.

In the meantime she tried to dismiss the subject from her mind and went to interview Harold who, so Miss Holcome said, had passed a restless night. She had decided to say nothing to him about the disappearance of his brothers. If he knew anything about it he would be sure to say something. But Harold, the unhappy Harold, felt too ill to talk, and after seeing that he had taken his medicine, and that the blinds were drawn, she busied herself about the house.

Lunchtime came and after a restless afternoon, during which she made several leisurely tours of the grounds, suspiciously eyeing every bush, she returned to tea. Her anxiety was growing with each passing moment. Rumbold, whom she found tying up the raspberry canes, was gloomily depressing.

'Ef you ask me 'm, they've cleared off somewheres an' we shan't see 'em back 'ere until they runs short o' food. They told me at the post office that Master Robin went and bought some packets o' porridge oats, five packets 'e bought! Looks as ef they mean to make a real do of it. Ef I was you, mum, I'd let the sergeant know, there's no knowin' what they may be up to with that there rifle o' mine, it's a dangerous weapon.'

The police! Aunt Ellen shivered at the thought. The whole village would soon know of the escapade, she would be disgraced, she would be made to appear foolish before everybody. She even visualized bloodhounds and Scotland Yard, headlines in the papers. 'Disappearance of two boys from Cherry Walden Dower House.' For the first time in her life Aunt Ellen felt she would like to have a good cry.

3. Gone to Ground

THE SUNLIGHT of late afternoon illuminated the tops of the oak trees. Every ride, every rabbit track, was wrapped in cool shade; scarce a breath of wind stirred the million, million leaves.

In the very heart of this magnificent forest which covered an area of eleven thousand undulating acres, in a little green clearing hedged around with fern and sallow, grew a massive oak tree. It was not very tall, indeed it was considerably lower than many of the other oaks round about, for centuries since its top had decayed away only the massive rough trunk remained. But thick healthy foliage grew from the gnarled and knotted crown, and these new branches spread wide like a vast, deep green umbrella for many yards on all sides.

The roughened trunk was covered with excrescences and bulges, its total outside girth must have been nearly twenty-five feet. At its base, on the western side, was a small aperture not more than two feet wide by three high, like the opening to a little black cave or a postern door.

In the quiet of evening the nightingales were singing, whitethroats were bubbling their merry woodland music from the depths of the hazels and sallows, and now and again a pigeon passed over, high in the sunlight, its breast lit by the low rays of the setting sun.

One of them, spying the thick crown of the oak below it in the clearing, closed its wings, wheeled round, and came to a clattering rest among the green leaves. It was amazing that so large a bird could alight so swiftly it seemed to pierce the wall of foliage with ease, almost as if it were an arrow.

After looking about it for a moment or two it puffed out its breast and began to 'Coo, Coo, Coocoo, Coo, Coo, Coocoo, Coo, Coo, Coocoo, Coo!' An amusing sound, very soothing, breathing the peace of the woods and ending abruptly with half a note as though the bird had heard something and had stopped to listen.

Other wood pigeons were answering from the surrounding trees; many no doubt had nests deep among the hazels. The bird had barely finished its song when the face of Robin Hood appeared at the opening at the foot of the oak. His eyes were rolled upwards showing the whites. He was searching the thick green coverlet of oak leaves overhead.

The pigeon which had already made quite sure there was no enemy below when he first alighted in the tree – they always look directly below them as soon as they settle – cooed again.

The face of Robin Hood emerged still further as cautiously as a fox. He could not see the bird, even though it was only just above him among the branches. Then, as he gazed round, moving his head slowly, he suddenly stiffened, paused, then withdrew silently into the intense black shadow of the tree. In another moment there appeared the barrel of a rifle. It wavered a moment, then steadied. A second's pause, then there came a muffled crack and a desperate fluttering among the oak leaves. A fat blue-grey body crashed through the branches to land on the short rabbit-nibbled grass below with a resounding thump.

'Got him! Got him!' ejaculated Robin triumphantly.

'Well done, Robin, first blood to you, a pretty shot forsooth!'

Robin Hood and Big John scrambled out of the oak like hens tumbling from a fowl house.

'What a beauty! *My*, what a beauty!'

'Fat as butter!'

'Shall we stew him or roast him?'

'Stew him I should think, 'cos we haven't got any fat to roast him.'

They picked the pigeon up, felt its breast and pronounced it a well-fed bird fit for any hunter's pot.

In a moment or two all was bustle and activity. Robin grabbed the saucepan and hurried away into the hazels. About twenty yards distant he came to a narrow path which wound in and out among the ferns. Following this a short way, he came to a small stream which ran between two low banks almost completely arched over with a tunnel of male ferns.

They had found this stream earlier in the day and had chanced upon it quite by accident. It was clear, fresh water and delightfully handy to their camp.

Meanwhile, Big John was busying himself with making a fire. He searched about among the bushes until he had collected an armful of dry grass and fine twigs, and a few paces from the entrance to their tree house he built the fire. First he rolled the dry brittle grass into a loose ball, and arranged the small twigs in the shape of an Indian wigwam all round it. Then he applied the match.

The grass flared up and in a minute or two the fine twigs caught as well. By the time Robin came hurrying back through the hazels with his saucepan full of water the fire was burning brightly. Robin seized the plump pigeon – with eager haste – and the blue-grey feathers came out in showers, to be carefully cremated in the fire. The boys were evidently old hands at plucking.

To Big John was assigned the business of 'drawing' the bird, an unpleasant job but one which had to be done. Outlaws cannot afford to be squeamish. It is wonderful how appetite acts as a spur on these occasions. He had many times watched Cook preparing a chicken at the Dower House and had noted how the job was carried

The outlaws' house

out. By the time he had finished, the result was quite professional and even Robin was impressed. The next moment the pigeon was popped into the pot with a spoonful of salt and it began to stew merrily on the fire. While this was going on Robin had been collecting firewood. There was so much lying about they did not have to go far to get it and soon there was a goodly stack which was stored inside the tree. They carried it under cover so that it should be in the dry, for even though the weather was fine, a heavy thunder rain in the night or the morning dew would be sufficient to damp it. Damp wood means smoke and smoke means advertising one's presence, and this was by no means desirable. Later they were not so particular about this precaution.

The doorway of the outlaws' camping place, or opening, in the oak was quite small. Inside the tree there was enough room to hold twelve fully grown men standing upright. Overhead was a mass of half-decayed wood and in the centre of this 'ceiling' a dark hollow, which no doubt passed right up inside the trunk like a chimney. No light showed from above, however, and as yet the boys had had no time to explore this wonderful natural cave of theirs.

It was by the merest chance they had found it. Truth to tell, the last few hours had been rather anxious ones. Since the outlaws had been capering among the bracken in the dim light of dawn, much had happened. Those high spirits soon evaporated, leaving behind a reaction, almost a depression. This was no doubt due to lack of sleep, for they had been marching all night. But after a nap they awoke hungry and refreshed and having stayed the inner man with two handfuls of porridge oats, eaten raw – not a particularly satisfying or appetizing meal for hungry boys – they had pushed on without delay into the heart of the Chase.

It was essential to find two things, water and a suitable camping place. Robin had heard the Whiting talk of a pool or pond, called the Blind Pool, which was somewhere in the forest and it was this they hoped to find. But the Chase covered so large an acreage the chances of discovery were small. It was with considerable relief therefore that towards the end of the afternoon, when they were weary with pushing through the bushes and the high bracken, Robin, who was forcing a path in front, came on the stream. They were so thirsty they drank deeply – how horrified Aunt Ellen would have been! – and having quenched their thirst they cast about for some promising place to camp. Robin had a vague idea of making a hut of branches and it was during their hunt for suitable wood for this purpose that they had chanced upon the oak tree in the clearing. It did not take much imagination to see at once that here was a permanent camping place already prepared by nature. In a very short while they had explored the interior of the old tree and found it ideal in every way. It was dry as an oven inside, though they had to clear away a quantity of decayed leaves and rotten wood which had fallen down inside the trunk. In doing so Big John found many beetle wings which puzzled them both. In addition to the wings they found curious oblong pellets, about the size of the worm pills which from time to time they had to administer to Tilly at the Dower House; later they discovered they were owl droppings.

There was plenty of room inside, room to store their few necessities, their pots and pans, the rifle and the meagre stores. They cut themselves armfuls of green bracken for a bed, the most delicious spring mattress imaginable.

In a very short while they had put their house in order and now their supper had obligingly arrived right on their very doorstep. So far then, the day had been a lucky one.

'My, but it smells pretty good!' said Big John, as he removed the lid from the saucepan. He was enveloped in a cloud of fragrant steam which made the inside of his cheeks tickle. 'I wish we had some potatoes to put in with it.'

Robin reached for the porridge oats. 'Here, stir some of these in, they'll thicken the gravy.'

So the oats were duly stirred in and after a while Big John – whose turn it was to cook – pronounced that supper was ready. He divided the pigeon into two equal halves – watched by the jealous eye of Robin Hood – and in a remarkably short space of time every trace of the luckless bird had vanished. When this was done they buried the bones under the bracken, washed up the plates and saucepan, and stowed everything away inside the tree. They were still hungry and they had, moreover, the uncomfortable feeling that there was nothing for breakfast but porridge. The somewhat wistful thought of bacon and sausages at the Dower House was courageously pushed aside. Robin slid back the well-oiled bolt of the little rifle and inserted a cartridge. 'It's your turn to shoot. We shall have to be quick, 'cos the light's going.'

'What about the fire?'

'Stamp it out, we mustn't leave it burning.'

'And we mustn't go too far away or we might lose the camp.'

'Pooh,' said Robin Hood scornfully, 'whoever heard of an outlaw being lost? The proper way is to blaze a trail as we go along.'

Big John took the rifle reverently; it was the first time he had ever had a chance to fire it.

'Don't blame me if I miss, Robin. I'll do my best.'

They stole off into the bushes, looking back once at their camp to see that no spark was burning in the dead ashes of their fire.

Sombre shadows were beginning to gather, for the sun had set and the whole forest was wrapped in fragrant gloom. Many of the birds had ceased to sing, though here and there a blackbird still warbled and the nightingales were making the dusky bushes resound with their rich full-throated notes. As the boys stole through the hazels and along the little mossy paths they broke a twig here and bent a grass there to mark their passage.

They crossed the stream and in a little while found themselves on the edge of quite a wide riding. Big John drew back with a little gasp. 'My gracious, look at that!'

Robin, who was close on his heels, stopped dead.

'What's the matter, have you seen somebody?'

'No, rabbits, *millions* of 'em!'

As far as the eye could see rabbits were dotted everywhere; on the riding edge, among the bushes, on the short green grass of the ride itself. Some were busy feeding, others sat up washing themselves like cats, or chased each other in circles. The boys had never seen so many before.

Not thirty yards distant a half-grown one was sitting up in the grass, eyeing them.

'Take your time,' whispered Robin, as the rifle muzzle edged up.

Crack! Even though the weapon was fitted with a silencer the explosion sounded dreadfully loud in the quiet forest – this was because the trees threw back an echo. Many of the nearer rabbits bolted for cover and those farther away all sat up like little question marks.

Big John's bullet sped true. A long apprenticeship with an airgun in the loft at Cherry Walden had stood him in good stead. The rabbit leapt skywards and fell back stretched out in the fern.

'Don't move,' whispered Robin, laying a restraining arm on his brother outlaw who, elated at his success, was about to leap out and retrieve his prey. 'Give me the rifle.'

The other rabbits, forty or so yards away, were still sitting up, listening. They had heard the crack of the rifle but did not know where the sound had come from; indeed as Robin raised the rifle, one or two dropped their heads again and began to feed.

He picked out a fat one which sat on the riding edge some forty yards distant. In the bad light he could only see his target as a dim blur in the 'scope and much of the sighting would have to be guesswork. He aligned the cross threads of the 'scope on where he judged the rabbit's shoulder to be and, holding his breath, squeezed the trigger. The crack of the report was followed immediately by the indescribable thud of the bullet going home.

The boys made a very triumphant return to camp with two fat rabbits for the larder and in the failing light the way was not easy to find even though they had blazed a trail. At last they pushed through the bushes into the little clearing and saw the old tree.

As Robin harled the rabbits – that is, threaded one back leg through the sinew of the other – and hung them up on a bough, there was a faint rustle in the oak tree top and a huge owl passed over their heads. A second later they heard its melancholy 'hoo horoo!' floating through the darkening forest.

They lit the fire and by its light prepared the rabbits for breakfast. Rabbit liver and hearts are exceedingly good, much better than sausages and bacon!

When these necessary jobs were done and the skins and refuse buried under the bushes they hung the flayed rabbits up again. The hearts and livers were put on a plate, after they had been washed thoroughly, and were stowed away inside the tree in case some marauding animal found them in the night.

Darkness came swiftly. Overhead stars shone out, quietly luminous, and from the inky black trees owls hooted near and far. Their dismal wailings put Robin in mind of a book he had lately been reading, Thoreau's *Life in the Woods*. He had learnt some of its more beautiful passages by heart. What was it? ... 'I love to hear their wailing, their doleful responses ... They are the spirits, the low spirits and melancholy forebodings of fallen souls that once in human shape nightly walked the earth and did the deeds of darkness ...

O-o-o-o-h that I never had been bor-r-r-rnn!
sighs one on this side of the pond, and circles with
the restlessness of despair to some new perch on
the grey oaks then – *that I had never been bor-r-
r-r-n* echoes another on the farther side with
tremulous sincerity, and – *bor-r-r-r-n!* comes
faintly far in the Lincoln Woods ... ' Walden
Pond! Yes, perhaps the Blind Pool was just such
another Walden Pond, a clear deep dish of
translucent water set down in the heart of this
English forest ...

The fire had sunk to a dull red glow, no flame
flickered or smoke rose up, and overhead the
leaves were magical in the dim illumination. The
boys lay stretched out on their backs with their
heads close to the dying fire, watching the still,
dark leaves of the oak against the stars.

'Wonder what Aunt Ellen's doing now,' murmured
Big John sleepily.

'I'll bet the village *is* in a stew.'

'Shouldn't be surprised if they aren't all out
lookin' for us with lanterns.'

'Don't worry, they won't ever find us here. We'll
stay in the woods forever I guess, or until our
cartridges run out.'

The Blindrush

'It'ud be grand fun in the winter too,' said Big John. 'Think of these woods under snow and all the leaves off the trees; bet we'd be as snug as badgers in the old oak!'

'We'd trap for pelts too, and have proper trap lines.'

'You bet.'

'I vote we never go back,' said Robin. 'We'll live here all our lives, like that Thoreau chap.'

'He didn't stick it more than two years though, did he?'

'Don't think he did . . . he lived alone though; it 'ud be a bit creepy in the woods all alone, with no one to talk to, not even a dog.'

'Pity we didn't bring Tilly with us,' said Big John. 'She'd have loved it – all those rabbits . . . '

'Oh, I dunno, she might have been a nuisance. She'd want to run home or something, or she'd get lost.'

Hoo Hoo Horoo! A big black shape swept overhead. It was the owl.

'I believe she's got a nest up in the oak,' said Robin, raising himself on his elbows. 'We'll have a look and see tomorrow. We might get a young one and tame it. Heigh ho! I'm for bed.'

'And so am I,' returned Big John.

They stamped out the last glowing embers and crawled into the tree. As they lay down on their couches of bracken, which smelt so sweetly, they saw the forest without, ghostly and dim.

'Goodnight, Robin Hood!'

'Go'night, Big John, sleep well. Don't forget it's my turn to cook the breakfast!'

4. The Hunt is Up

THE OUTLAWS were snug in their forest retreat, with the stars shining down benignly upon the spreading oak; the little green clearing in the bracken with the dark patch of the camp fire was now wet with the night dew.

Back at the Dower House, with every tick of the clock THE POLICE bulked inexorably nearer. After dinner Aunt Ellen could bear the suspense no longer; she went again to the vicarage.

The long-suffering Whiting met her in the hall with raised eyebrows and, 'Any news of the young rascals?'

'No, none whatever, and I have come to you again for advice. I feel like Job, Vicar; all my troubles have come upon me!'

She flopped down into a chair and heaved a desperate sigh. 'You see,' she continued, 'there's no knowing *where* they are or what they are doing. Supposing they develop measles? . . . Well, I mean to say, it's likely, isn't it? They've been with Harold right up to the time he went to bed and neither of them have had it.'

'Ah well, don't let us cross stiles until we reach them, dear lady. The thing is, we must find where they are hiding.'

'Yes, but how? Where can they be?' burst out Aunt Ellen. 'How will they manage to *live*? They have no money with them. I've at least been able to find that out; all their pocket money is untouched. They can't live on air.'

'I'm afraid there's nothing for it but to notify the police,' said the vicar, wagging his moonlike face woefully. 'We can't go out looking for them. After all it *is* a job for the police, you know; they should be able to track them down in no time.'

'Oh dear, must we *really* call in the police? It will all be in the papers, the whole village will know.'

'As to that, they know already,' replied the vicar, with a faint smile, 'everybody knows. They asked my maid when she went to the post whether the boys had been found. And if the village knows the sergeant must know. I'm afraid we shall have to call in the assistance of the Law.'

Sergeant Bunting was a pink mountain of a man with three double chins. His waxed moustache stuck out like two sharp needles on either side of his face. He removed his helmet and placed it gently on the hall table.

'Come in, Sergeant, come in,' Aunt Ellen fluttered at the library door.

'Thank you, ma'am.'

He stood fingering a notebook and pencil.

'I expect you have heard about my two nephews, Sergeant?'

'Well, I did 'ear something.' The sergeant had a very deep voice which rumbled like an organ, a voice which was all in keeping with his majestic bearing.

'The position is this, Sergeant Bunting. My two nephews have run away. They left a note to say that they would be gone for some time because they were afraid of catching the measles from my other nephew, Harold, who is now in bed upstairs. A flagrant excuse, I know.'

'Have you the note, ma'am?'

'Yes, here it is.' Aunt Ellen drew the now grubby scrap of paper from her handbag and passed it to him with trembling fingers. Sergeant Bunting read it slowly, half aloud, the ends of his moustaches moving slightly like the feelers of an insect.

'Dear Aunt,' he rumbled to himself, 'John and I 'ave decided that we would be better outer the way while 'Arold is ill we might catch it we will be back sometime but don't worry about us we shall be all right please explain to the vicar.'

'They mean by that,' interrupted Aunt Ellen eagerly, 'they wanted me to tell the vicar not to expect them for lessons. I had arranged with him to tutor them.'

'Ah, schoolin' eh?' said the sergeant, looking up.

'Yes, er – schooling.'

'I see, ma'am. Don't try to find us,' he went on, 'because you never will signed Robin (Hood) John (Big). Playin' at outlaws eh?'

'I beg your pardon?'

'I said outlaws, m'am, looks as ef they were playing at outlaws, Robin 'ood sort of idea.'

'Yes, yes, some rubbish . . . You see, Sergeant, I'm responsible for the boys, all three of them. They *must* be found. They may get ill; anything; I'm responsible.'

'I understand, ma'am,' rumbled the sergeant, 'you're their legal guardian like. Well, we'll see what can be done. They took a rifle so I'm told, a rook rifle, belongin' to your gardener?' Sergeant Bunting seemed well acquainted with the facts of the case.

'Yes, I believe so, at least the rifle's missing and we conclude the boys took it,' replied Aunt Ellen with a sniff.

'But you've no proof they did take it?'

Aunt Ellen began to get flustered. It was almost as if the sergeant was accusing *her* of taking the rifle.

'I think you'd better see Rumbold yourself, Sergeant Bunting. I'll have him fetched for you.'

'Sorry to give you the trouble, ma'am, but we've got to get all the facts.'

'Of course, of course.' Aunt Ellen touched the bell.

When at last Rumbold appeared, very red in the face and with beads of perspiration on his forehead, he wore a rather guilty defiant look. The reason for this was that the unhappy man had no gun licence. But Sergeant Bunting was a broadminded man.

'You know you oughter 'ave a gun licence to use that there rifle, Mr Rumbold,' he said in an aggrieved tone.

'That's right, Sergeant, I know I should, but I kep' it locked up in me shed and didn't often use it.'

'That don't matter, it's agin the law to shoot wi' a rifle o' that sort wi'out a gun licence. Point two two, wasn't it?'

'That's right.'

'Can't we go into that some other time, Sergeant Bunting? After all, it's the other matter which is most important,' said Aunt Ellen impatiently.

'Very good, ma'am, but 'e'll 'ave to get a licence to shoot wi' un all the same,' he added doggedly. 'Now, Mr Rumbold, wot makes you think the bo– the young gents – took your rifle?'

'Well, all I knows is that when I went to me cupboard this mornin' it 'ad gorn, clean gorn.'

'Was there any ammunition to it?'

'Ay, a bit in a box.'

''Ow many rounds would you say?' the sergeant was making notes in his book.

'Don't know exactly, 'undred maybe.'

''Undred rounds point two two,' rumbled the sergeant, writing laboriously. 'Took the lot eh?'

'That's right.'

'Well, Mr Rumbold, I think that's all I want from you.'

The discomfited gardener looked relieved and departed.

'I suppose you've no idea where they could 'ave gone to, m'am? Master 'Arold don't know nothin?'

'No idea whatever, absolutely no idea, and the boy upstairs is too ill to talk.'

'Mm . . . Well, m'am, I'll do all I can. An' don't you worry. From what I know of the young gents they'll look arter theirselves all right.'

'And you'll let me know if you have any news, Sergeant Bunting?'

'Certainly, ma'am, at once, ma'am.'

The sergeant made his heavy way to the hall and collected his helmet which stood on the table. He adjusted his chin strap under his first chin. 'Goodnight, ma'am.'

'Goodnight, Sergeant.'

He went away down the drive and Aunt Ellen stood at the door and watched the gentle summer dusk swallow up his massive broad back. How dark it seemed after the lighted library! Where could the boys be now? Sleeping out under some haystack like tramps perhaps! Why had she ever consented to take responsibility for someone else's children? She turned back into the library with a sigh.

The matter was now out of her hands, she thought; she had done all she could, things must take their course and she must wait developments. In the meantime, however, a little discreet questioning of Harold was suggested. He was already feeling better and the doctor had pronounced that he was on the mend. The rash had come out and there seemed no danger of complications.

But she found that young gentleman on his guard. He asked her naively whether his brothers had returned to school, and when told they had not, he asked what they were doing and when they would be allowed to come and see him. Aunt Ellen soon found that it was she who was being cross-questioned; he seemed to be cautiously pumping her for information. But he did it so cleverly she could not make up her mind whether he knew anything about the escapade. She eyed him suspiciously through her pince-nez but his face was inscrutable.

He asked, for instance, whether his brothers were 'having to do lessons?'

Aunt Ellen countered this with, 'I am arranging with the vicar to tutor them.'

'When are they going to start?' he asked.

'I don't quite know yet,' said Aunt Ellen crossly, 'I've had so much to think about.' She had an inward battle with herself as to the wisdom of telling him what had happened.

But Harold had other means of finding out. Hannah – who had had measles – was allowed to take him his meals. When she brought him his breakfast tray next morning he asked her point-blank where his brothers were. Hannah, who had been told that she must on no account tell him anything, was taken aback. She was a simple girl, unused to subterfuge. She stammered and looked confused and then told Harold to get on with his breakfast and not be inquisitive. This gave the game away; he knew then they had really gone, without a shadow of doubt they had gone, and he felt acutely miserable that by a stroke of ill fortune he was not now with them away in the greenwood. And yet, if he had not had measles they would all have gone back to Banchester. Fate was against him either way; he always missed the fun.

Hannah told Aunt Ellen that she had been cross-questioned and asked for guidance. And then and there Aunt Ellen had to make up her mind whether to tell Harold or not.

She thought out the matter carefully; she consulted Miss Holcome, and finally the vicar, and it was eventually decided that he should not be told. As the vicar wisely said, 'If Harold knows all about it you may depend upon it he had planned to go too; only the measles prevented him from accompanying his brothers.'

If he did *not* know, nothing would be gained by telling him. He was a sensitive child and in his present weak state it might worry him.

So when Harold asked his aunt once more when his brothers would be allowed to visit him, Aunt Ellen took the plunge.

Robin and John had gone away until he was better. She didn't want them catching measles. In a short time they would go back to school, she said, when the period of incubation was past. In the meanwhile, he was not to ask her any more questions, she had enough worry as it was. Harold could see his aunt was 'fabricating'.

The days passed. To poor Harold, still imprisoned in his room, the outside world seemed unusually attractive. The weather was fine and warm, the trees and bushes in the garden were in full green leaf. The Dower House seemed strangely quiet, the grown-ups broody and uncommunicative.

The glory of the young summer weather seemed to lap the Dower House round and Harold fretted at his forced imprisonment. He was allowed now to sit up in his bedroom, wrapped in a rug in an old nursery chair by the window. From this vantage point he could observe the summer world without.

A week after the disappearance of his brothers he was sitting at the window. The remains of his tea, dreggy cup and crumby plate, were on a tray close by and his favourite book, *Tom Sawyer*, lay face downwards on the floor. It was too glorious an evening to read; he longed to be out in the sunny garden where the shadows from the trees were already stealing across the lawn. White-rumped house martins dived and floated by, twittering happily as though they were riding the waves of an invisible ocean, and through the open window came the faint call of a cuckoo.

His aunt was downstairs writing in the morning room, Miss Holcome had gone out for a walk and Harold felt dreadfully alone. There was nothing to do but watch the garden and wish he was up and out.

He knew that his brothers had not returned; their continued absence only served to aggravate his unsettled state of mind. What a time they must be having away over there beyond the evening hills, deep in the greenwood, leading a Tom Sawyer-like existence unhampered by Aunts and fussy females!

Why had Fortune singled *him* out for punishment? It was just his rotten luck. If only he could get well and strong again he would go after them, he reflected. Then came a small cold fear. Would he? Would he have the courage to go alone all that way? Had he the courage to slip off at dead of night as his brothers had surely done and how would he ever find them?

In his heart of hearts he doubted it. And this made him all the more unhappy. Harold by nature was less self-reliant than his brothers. By virtue of being the youngest he had always laboured under an inferiority complex.

Out on the sunny lawn a wagtail was running up and down catching flies, moving so fast its legs were invisible. It seemed to glide over the mown turf – Rumbold had been mowing all the morning and the sleepy summery whirr of the machine had been yet another torture ... The smell of the newly cut grass came in at the open window in gentle puffs, bringing with it the scent of gilly flowers and the faint sickly perfume of wisteria bloom.

Round the church tower he could see the swifts wheeling; they had arrived only a week before. Now and again he could hear their threadlike screeches like a finger rubbed on a pane of glass. A fly buzzed fretfully under the blind. Poor fly, it wanted so badly to be out in the summer world, it had not the sense to crawl over the white wood of the upper window frame and buzz away. He was like the fly, he reflected miserably.

Then came Tilly the spaniel. She walked disconsolately from behind the trees and flopped wearily in the sun, stretching herself out. The little dog had been miserable since the boys' departure. She lay listening to all the sounds going on in the house. Like all spaniels, house sounds absorbed all her boring moments. Harold could see her pretending to be asleep, now and again snapping at a teasing fly and chasing imaginary fleas. But all the time she was listening; listening to the clink of pans and the hum of servants' talk from the kitchen, listening to the squeak of the pump at the top of the kitchen garden where Rumbold was filling a watering can. She was a sociable little dog; even hunting rabbits under the rhododendrons down by the Willow Pool did not lure her without human company. So she lay in the sun and listened.

Harold whistled the peculiar whistle by which they always called her. Tilly, who was pretending to find a flea above her tail – her nose snubbed up, little hissing sounds coming from her muzzle – stopped biting. She still kept her nose snubbed but she was holding her breath, listening. Harold laughed and whistled again.

She sat up suddenly with her long floppy ears fanned, looking towards the house. Harold waved his hand but she did not raise her eyes to the window. Then she went on catching fleas. Harold picked up *Tom Sawyer* again and read on:

'After dinner all the gang turned out to hunt for turtles' eggs on the bar. They went about poking sticks into the sand and when they found a soft place they went down on the sand and dug with their hands.'

It was no use, it only made him feel more miserable. Hullo, what was that? Tilly barking! He looked up. The spaniel was running on her fat legs across the lawn towards the front gate, fleas and boredom forgotten. She was barking lustily.

A man was coming in at the gate, a young man dressed in grey flannel trousers and a tweed coat, hatless and with what looked like a leather box slung on his back by a strap. Who could he be? What did he want? Harold saw him carefully shut the white swing gate behind him and then stop to speak to Tilly who, reassured, followed him closely up the drive smelling at his trouser legs.

Was he a traveller, one of those mysterious persons who, from time to time, appeared in sleepy Cherry Walden; beings from another world, with strange and sometimes fascinating merchandise?

He came up the gravel drive, but unlike the usual commercial traveller – he did not look like one, Harold decided – he did not go up the branching back drive but came boldly up to the front door below Harold's window, where the rough grey tangle of the wisteria branches hid him from view. There was a second's suspense – in which Harold pictured him pulling out the bright brass knob of the doorbell. It was like waiting for an explosion. It came – the rich alarming tones, pealing, pealing, through the panelled house. It was no timid ring, but bold and echoing, it brooked no delaying, an urgent summons to chattering serving maids.

Harold could imagine the sudden quiet confusion in the morning room where Aunt Ellen was writing – she seemed to be writing a lot lately – and then he heard Emma's steps clumping down the stone-flagged passage from the kitchen quarters. 'Clump, clump, clump, clump,' then silence as Emma passed over the turkey carpet by the front hall, then 'clump, clump, clump' again as she crossed the hall. After a pause he heard the front door slam. He flattened his nose against the pane but no figure reappeared. The stranger had been admitted. Was it a detective? Was it something to do with Robin Hood and Big John?

Tilly wandered back into the middle of the lawn – Aunt Ellen did not allow dogs in the house – and there she sat with cocked ears watching the morning-room window.

Who could he be? What did he want?

5. 'Under the Greenwood Tree'

Under the greenwood tree
Who loves to lie with me
And tune his merry note
Unto the sweet bird's throat.
Come hither, come hither, come hither,
Here shall we see
No enemy
But winter and rough weather.

Who doth ambition shun
And loves to live i' the sun
Seeking the food he eats
And pleased with what he gets –
Come hither, come hither, come hither,
Here shall he see

No enemy
But winter and rough weather.

Robin opened his eyes and stirred. Like a lazy shepherd he lay collecting his thoughts, which wandered between dreamworld and this.

In his drowsy ears there sounded heavenly music, the chanting of birds.

Now some say a forest is silent, that its birds are few and none sing save for the nightingales and pigeons. These people have never fallen asleep in an English forest in May, to awake at first light. As Robin lay on his bracken couch in the dim interior of the tree it seemed as if every bird in the eleven thousand acres of Brendon Chase was singing. Song thrushes, blackbirds, nightingales, wrens, tits, pigeons, blackcaps, whitethroats and finches, all singing as if their throats would burst.

He saw the dark walls of rotten wood framing the doorway and outside was a silvery green scene like the painted backcloth to a stage setting.

He could see the marks of their dead fire on the short grass, the strong new bracken fronds – like miniature tropical palm trees – and the motionless leaves on the bushes and distant oaks.

On the other side of the root lay Big John, fast asleep. He was curled round with his knees drawn up, his head pillowed on his crooked right arm in the way he always slept. He was breathing regularly and quietly in deep slumber.

Robin turned over on his right side and shivered. It was surprisingly chilly. The dew must have come in at the open door; his clothes and the bracken felt quite damp. He was aware of a strange depression which he could not analyse, a vague sense of uneasiness. As he lay there he tried to think out the cause. Suddenly he knew. He saw in his mind the white cloth on the long breakfast table, the silver dome of the bacon dish which was fluted in ribs and which, when closed, looked like a big silver Easter egg. He saw in his mind the crisp bacon rashers, the fried eggs sitting like half apricots surrounded by a flap of white which had uneven edges, a little crisp and brown in places. He saw the white steaming porridge in plates adorned with sprigs of blue lavender, the brown sugar and creamy milk, he smelt the coffee and the general breakfast atmosphere of the dining room at Cherry Walden.

Platoons of toast, crisp, brown and still hot, in rows on the silver rack – which had an ivory handle – golden marmalade, heaped and distorted through the glass globe of the jam dish. And he heard Rumbold 'pumping up' in the kitchen. The 'tunk-tunk' of the scullery pump was one of the morning sounds of the Dower House . . . All these things passed in procession through his mind and the disquiet within him was intensified. He found himself almost longing for Cherry Walden.

A week had passed since they had first come to the Chase, seven days . . . it seemed years. They had shot more rabbits, a pigeon or two, they had made two attempts to find the Blind Pool without success and in all that time they had seen no trace of man; their only companions had been the birds and rabbits. They had not even seen a fox, or a deer, and both boys were suffering from homesickness. Those days were the only vaguely unhappy ones they had in the forest. They had not reckoned on homesickness; their bodies had not yet become accustomed to the change of life and the novelty of the adventure had worn off. It says much for the character of both outlaws that neither even gave the smallest hint that they were homesick. Were it not for one another's company there is no doubt they would have gone back,

back to the security and the comfort of the Dower House, even at the expense of loss of liberty, unknown punishments from Aunt Ellen and lessons with the Whiting.

But Robin and Big John had bags of pluck; they were adventurous, self-reliant and very imaginative.

It is a good thing that this was so. Up to now, life in the forest had been a little tame, adventure was lacking, probably because they had not had the heart to seek it.

Robin got up out of the bracken and crawled through the door. He stretched himself, for his limbs were cramped. Then he set to work to make the fire. For breakfast they had rabbit legs and livers, stewed, and a little porridge. This had been their breakfast for the last seven days, and though Robin was hungry, the monotony of the diet had begun to pall. Above all things the boys craved something sweet – that, and bread. Robin felt he could have eaten a whole loaf at a sitting. These cravings were shown in the way the boys talked. At night, as they sat around their camp fire, they talked of nothing else but the sweets they used to buy in the post office, the peppermints, like little striped pillows, the chocolate marshmallows, the smell of the baker's shop in the main street.

Rabbit for breakfast, rabbit for supper, sometimes a pigeon or a blackbird or two, meat, meat, meat, everlasting meat. There were no fruits yet to be gathered in the forest; it was still far too early for blackberries, though later there would be millions, for blackberry bushes were everywhere. But even the blossom was not yet out.

On the third day Big John had had the brilliant idea of pigeon's eggs, and the eggs of the various songbirds – blackbirds, thrushes and even jay's eggs were eaten. These they boiled and found delicious, though the whites of the songbirds' eggs when cooked assumed a strange jelly-like appearance which was far from appetizing. But the yolks were as good as hen's eggs.

Another thing they craved was fat. Some of the pigeons were fat – they had yellow rolls of it just under the skin – but there was not enough of it. All their meat had to be stewed.

Now it is just possible that had this state of things continued for very much longer they would have been compelled to return to civilization and Aunt Ellen. The human stomach has a powerful influence over the higher spirit. And then, in a most miraculous way, their life suddenly took on the true adventurous quality of the wild.

Robin's first act after lighting the fire and putting some water on to boil for the porridge was to go and search under the hazel bushes where they buried their refuse, the bones and odd entrails and other rubbish from the camp.

Sure enough, he found, as he expected, that some creature had been prowling about the camp during the dark hours and had dug them up. For the last three nights this mysterious scavenger had been visiting them. Every morning now they found the same phenomenon: the ground scratched out, large hollows routed under the bushes and the bones and refuse gone.

This unknown nocturnal visitor was never seen. Once Big John had awakened in the middle of the night and heard strange noises coming from under the hazels; muffled grunts, scufflings and sounds of loud mastication. But nothing was visible. He had awakened Robin and together they had crawled to the cave mouth, listening and peering, but the moon was not yet able to give much light and the night sky was overcast.

It was also very creepy to hear those sounds. They even barricaded the mouth of the cave at nightfall with a large log. The puzzling thing was that the beast – or beasts – did not move furtively, but made considerable noise, and fed heartily with many muffled grunts and lip smackings.

'I can't make it out,' said Robin, when Big John at last joined him by the growing fire, 'that beast has been here again in the night. Whatever can it be?'

'Badger I expect,' said Big John. 'Badgers grunt like anything and they're big beasts.'

'Of course it might be a fox,' said Robin, stirring the porridge, 'though it makes too much noise for a fox. Perhaps it's a deer or a dog.'

'There wouldn't be dogs here.'

'I dunno. The old charcoal burner chap who lives somewhere in the Chase may have one. I wish we could pal up with the old boy, he'd maybe help us no end.'

'Not he,' said Robin with emphasis, 'If he found us here it would be all U. P. with us. We'd be hauled off to Cherry Walden.'

'What about waiting up for it tonight with the rifle? There's more moon now and we might get a shot.'

'All right, let's. I'd like to shoot a badger. We'd skin it and make a lovely pelt. We could make some skins to wear; my breeks are wearing out pretty badly.'

Big John exhibited his right trouser leg. The shabby old flannels he had worn since he came to the Chase were ripped to ribbons from the knee downwards. He had caught them on a briar. 'We shan't have any clothes fit to wear if we live here much longer.'

'By Jove! That would be fun,' exclaimed Robin, quite perking up, 'and we can save all the rabbits' skins and stitch 'em together.'

'How?'

Robin was nonplussed for a moment. 'I know,' he exclaimed, 'there's some string we've saved from the Quaker Oats packets – that would do. It's thick string and we can unravel it; it would make strong thread.'

'Well, if I bag the badger I'll have the skin for a coat,' said Big John.

'I'll shoot it,' said Robin imperiously. 'I'm the chief, it's my job.'

'But it's my turn to fire,' said Big John sulkily. 'You had the last shot.'

'Let's toss.'

'Righto!'

Robin produced a penny, his only worldly wealth.

'Call.'

'Heads!'

'Heads it is,' said Robin with rather bad grace. 'All right, Big John, you shoot, but if you miss I'll have two extra turns with the rifle.'

That night, after they'd had supper – pigeon's eggs and a squirrel, which was surprisingly good, as tender and white as a chicken – they turned in early.

Already the moon was rising over the forest trees and as the glow in the west died its new pale light shone down on the clearing. Owls hooted and they heard a fox barking, far away. Big John lay at the entrance with his rifle fixed on the hazels ten yards distant. They had sighted it in daylight and had wedged it into position with logs. Even if the light was bad they might hit the beast, for they had put the refuse in a small heap under the bushes and carefully aligned the sights on it. They had even tried out the experiment by placing a piece of wood behind the heap. The bullet had pierced it, right through the centre.

They had no means of telling the time for Robin's watch had stopped – he had forgotten to wind it up one night – and they had to guess the time by the sun.

As they crouched there waiting they felt like lion hunters sitting up over a kill.

The moon had already reached its zenith and had begun to dip down behind the trees. Soon all would be complete darkness for it was now an overcast night and a slight wind was blowing, rustling the bushes in a creepy sort of way.

Just when they thought their mysterious visitor would never come Robin gently touched Big John's arm. That worthy was almost asleep. He awakened with a start and nearly upset the rifle. 'Hist! It's coming!'

Big John's heart suddenly began to thump wildly, hammering at the base of his skull: *thump, thump, thump*. His mouth went dry. Some way off they heard sticks cracking. A heavy body was blundering through the bushes.

Then, peering into the gloom of the hazels he saw something moving. It was a large pale object and it grunted. 'There it is!' whispered Robin in Big John's ear, 'Wait till you can see it more clearly and take your time.'

'Whatever is it?'

'*I* don't know, it's bigger than a badger.'

At that moment the moon was obscured by cloud and when it reappeared it had slid behind the crown of a distant oak.

'I can't see a thing,' whispered Big John, nearly choking with excitement, 'but it's there, eating up the stuff. Shall I fire?'

'Yes, fire!'

Very gently Big John squeezed the trigger. There came the blunt report and a short sharp thud of the bullet striking a heavy object.

Instantly there arose the most blood-curdling sound the boys had ever heard. It was like a human scream but infinitely louder; it was a squeal, a grunt and a scream, all rolled into one. A terrific blundering and crashing followed in the bushes and then something rushed across the clearing right in front of the oak. It passed so swiftly that it looked like an enormous dog, but a dog with extremely short legs.

As it passed, Big John fired again, but they heard the bullet sing like an angry hornet away among the trees.

A terrified owl hooted, more distant cracking and smashing of sticks sounded, and then there was nothing but the wind in the trees and a complaining owl which called 'Eeewe-wip! Eeewe-wip!' in a penetrating urgent voice.

'I hit 'im,' said Big John excitedly. 'I hit him all right, but he's gone.'

'Serve him right, *he* won't come back!'

'But I didn't kill him; we shall never know what it was.'

Together they gingerly approached the bushes and Robin struck a match and examined the ground. All the refuse had gone. There was no sign of fur.

'I believe you missed him,' muttered Robin, trying to shield the wavering flame of the match with his coat, 'There's no fur or blood about.'

'I didn't miss him, I swear,' said Big John, 'I heard the bullet strike. I'll bet he won't go far.'

'Well, it's no use looking for him now, the moon's setting. We'll have a look tomorrow.'

Together they re-entered the tree and lay down on their bracken beds. For a long time they talked and argued. Robin said it was a dog; Big John insisted it was a badger, the grandfather of all badgers.

Next morning, at first light, the outlaws were out hunting in the bracken. A crushed fern frond here, a broken stick there, led them some way into the bushes and then for a time they found nothing. After a while the spoor petered out entirely and they cast about like baffled hounds.

'If only we had Tilly here with us, she'd find it,' said Robin.

Big John, who was on all fours examining the bracken, suddenly let out a shout. 'Here! Come here! There's blood!'

Sure enough, on a bracken stem was a spot of blood, and a little farther on, another. 'I hit him all right,' said Big John triumphantly, 'I told you so. We'll find him in a minute.'

And find him they did, not forty yards from the clearing. There was a deep ditch choked with bramble and fern which at one time no doubt had been cut for drainage, for the forest was very damp in places. And there, sticking out from under the bracken they saw a most amazing sight. It was a half-grown pig, a perfectly ordinary pig, like the one at Cherry Walden Bank Holiday Fête – the boys had bowled for it but it had been won by the vicar's gardener, much to their disgust.

'Well, I . . .!' Big John was speechless. They got hold of its curly tail and hauled it out, a perfectly beautiful pig! There was no need to 'stick' it, the bullet had performed that grisly operation for them. The crumb of lead had, by an extraordinary piece of luck, cut its throat.

'It must be a wild one,' said Robin after a pause, 'there's no reason why it shouldn't be. There's no farm within miles and no house in the Chase but the old charcoal burner's.'

'It must be his,' said Big John, rather sorrowfully looking at his victim. The pig lay on its side and seemed to be grinning sardonically.

'Well, we can't help that. It shouldn't come rooting about camp pinchin' things; serves him right.'

'What are we going to do with it, bury it?'

Robin turned a face of utter scorn on his brother. 'Bury it? Whoever heard of an outlaw burying wild boar? Why, Big John, where are your senses? Can't you see we've got bacon for breakfast? Can't you see we've got fat, we've got hams? We're in clover! It's the most amazing bit of luck that's happened since we came! Think of it, Big John. We come here, we find a camp ready made, a pigeon obligingly flies into the very tree we're camping under and makes our supper and now – a porker, a perfectly good porker, comes

Robin and the wild pig

and provides us with bacon! Here, give us a hand, we'll drag him back to camp.'

Robin grabbed the tail, Big John seized a leg, and together they lugged the pig back to the clearing.

Breakfast over, the outlaws then had leisure to examine their prize. Truth to say, each felt a little embarrassed, even a little like murderers. Pigs are such good-natured, hearty creatures; like domestic ducks, they have a keen sense of fun, they belonged to that other civilized world just outside the forest. Yet, as Robin pointed out, they are originally woodland animals and descendants from the wild swine which at one time inhabited all the larger forests of Britain.

There seemed nothing wild about this one. It lay on its side on the green grass as if it were peacefully asleep in Farmer Baldrick's sty at home.

Nevertheless, Robin and Big John could not help thinking of that globular silver dish at the Dower House and the exquisite smells which used to emerge from it at breakfast time.

'Well, Master Robin, what about this pig forsooth?' asked Big John, standing looking down at his victim. They had washed up the breakfast things and had taken off their coats.

'Well, don't ask me, *I* didn't shoot the poor porker.'

'I don't know how to skin a pig,' said Big John. 'I suppose one *does* skin a pig?'

'Dashed if I know. Wait a minute . . . ' Robin thought hard. 'No, of course you don't skin a pig! Don't you remember Rumbold's pig last Christmas holidays? He wanted us to come and see him kill it but we wouldn't. Don't you remember how we went out on our bicycles because the squealing was so awful? And we wondered how he could be such a beast to kill it after looking after it all the year and scratching its back and feedin' it.'

'Of course . . . and then after it had been killed it was scalded to get the hairs off and Rumbold scrubbed it on the table in the old laundry! We watched him do it.'

'Yes, and then what happened? He salted it, didn't he?'

'Yes, he salted it all over with saltpetre and salt.'

'Well, we haven't got any saltpetre and precious little salt.'

'Then we're sunk, old boy,' said Big John glumly. 'We shan't have bacon for many mornings; this old porker will pretty soon go bad, especially if the weather turns really hot, and – phew! – won't he smell!'

'We shall have to bury him then, cut off what we can eat and what we think we can keep and bury the rest.'

'It's an awful waste,' said Big John. 'We wouldn't have shot it if we'd known it was a pig. Besides, it's somebody's pig, it must be. If it was found out who'd killed it, we should be in for a fine old row. We might be accused of stealing and have to go to prison.'

'Wait a moment,' exclaimed Robin suddenly, 'don't you remember that when we were crossing that last field, just before we came into the Chase, we saw those cattle round a salt lick?'

'Well, what about it?'

'Why, there's our salt, you booby! There were several lumps lying about; the farmer wouldn't notice if we took one. We can pound it up and salt our pig with it, just like Rumbold did!'

'But we shall want something to salt it in, shan't we?'

'That's easy. We must find a hollow log, or hollow one out into a trough, and we can salt him in that!'

'Well,' said Big John admiringly, 'you are a bright chap, I shouldn't have thought of that.

We'll fetch the salt tonight. It's a long walk, but we'll find the field all right.'

'And meanwhile, let's look for our salting trough,' said Robin.

The boys did not take long to find the very thing, an old half-decayed ash trunk which lay upon its side not far from the clearing. They gouged out the upper side with their hunting knives until they had made quite a deep trench. Then they set to work to cut up the pig. Robin, who had a gift for carving, soon had the animal correctly dismembered. The fat hams looked most appetizing. It was lucky that the bullet had saved them the trouble of bleeding the pig, otherwise, despite the salt, the meat would have gone bad.

As soon as dusk fell they retraced their steps to the forest edge and speedily discovered the lump of rock salt. It was queer looking stuff, of a purple colour, but they ground and pounded it to a powder and hard work it was. Next, they fetched water from the nearby stream and filled the trough to the brim and after singeing the hairs off the skin they popped the pieces in, covering the whole contraption with boughs, to mask it from any prowling animal.

They left the pig to soak for seven days and then removed it from the salt. It smelt as fresh as the day they cut it up. When this was done Robin had another idea. Smoked pig!

'Big John, look ye here prithee, now we've cured this porker, we ought to smoke it; the flavour will be improved no end.'

'Isn't that a bit risky?' asked Big John. 'Won't someone see the smoke?'

'Yes, we can't smoke him during the day. We'll do it after dark. We'll bank up a good smoky fire and let the pig hang in it all night. Nobody will see the smoke. You see,' said Robin, 'the fire we have during the day doesn't show if we're careful, but smoking the pig will make an awful "smeech" as Rumbold calls it.'

So that night they built a fire of oak wood dust and rigged up a rough tripod of sticks to suspend the carcass and the hams. The thick blue-green smoke rose up in a column on the quiet air and ascended into the starlit heavens, unseen and unsmelt by anyone but the outlaws.

They smoked the pig for a week and at the end of that time it had turned a golden brown. Once the hams fell into the fire but were rescued by Robin. At last it was all done and ready for eating.

Bacon for breakfast would now be a regular thing. They had melted a quantity of fat from the pig and were well provided for some weeks to come. Fried pigeon's eggs and smoked bacon made a breakfast which would have satisfied the most fastidious palate and it was voted even better than the Dower House bacon.

And so, with a good deal of luck and a certain amount of pluck, Robin and Big John entered on their third week in the forest. No one had bothered them, they had not seen a soul and they had become accustomed to the fine outdoor life.

The curing of the pig and various chores about the camp had occupied all their time. But now the pig was done they would have time at last to explore, or as Robin said, 'begin to really enjoy ourselves'. There were so many things to find; Smokoe Joe's house for instance, Smokoe Joe himself – they had decided to observe him from afar, however; there were butterflies to seek – had not the Whiting murmured the magic words purple emperor? There was the Blind Pool to find, wherein there might be fish to catch; there were birds' nests and a hundred other delights which up to now they had had no time to seek.

Eight miles away was Cherry Walden and in Cherry Walden was Aunt Ellen and Sergeant Bunting! But the outlaws gave them no thought, they continued to rise each dawn with the birds and go forth into the greenwood to hunt and bird's-nest to their heart's content, living their brave new life among the ferny glades and mighty oaks.

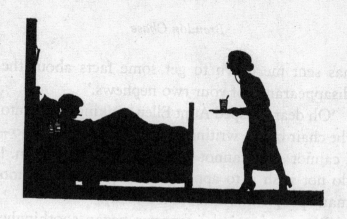

6. Harold

'PLEASE'M, there's a gentleman to see you.'
Aunt Ellen, looking harassed and flustered,
bundled up her letters into her desk and shut it
hurriedly. She had been in the middle of a long
letter to the boys' parents in India to acquaint
them with the news that they had run away.

'Who is it, Emma? What name did he give?'

'He didn't give no name, 'm, but 'e said 'e'd
come about Master Robin and John.'

'Show him in, Emma.'

Aunt Ellen felt a sudden hope rising in her
heart: perhaps the boys had been found.

A pleasant-looking young man entered and
introduced himself. 'My name is Hurling, and I
represent the *Morning Star*, madam. My paper

has sent me down to get some facts about the disappearance of your two nephews.'

'Oh dear,' gasped Aunt Ellen, sinking down into the chair by the writing desk, 'a reporter! No, no – I cannot ... I cannot give you any information. I do not wish it to appear in the papers – far too many people know about it already.'

'But, madam,' the reporter began soothingly; Aunt Ellen cut him short.

'I'm sorry, young man, but I have nothing to say on the matter; besides, it isn't of sufficient importance to be given such publicity.'

'I assure you, madam ... ' but Aunt Ellen cut him short again.

'Now, *please*, do not bother me with any more silly questions. I am driven almost demented as it is. I beg you not to mention the matter ... I ... I ... I could not bear it – the publicity ... ' Aunt Ellen shuddered.

Rumbold was pricking out lettuces in the kitchen garden when a voice said behind him, 'Good evening.'

He turned round. A young man was standing on the cinder path; he had a brown leather camera box slung on his shoulder.

'Good arternoon,' said Rumbold after a pause, straightening his back and eyeing his visitor with suspicion.

'Are you the gardener at the Dower House?'

'I am that.'

'Well, I represent the *Morning Star*. My paper has sent me down to get a story about the disappearance of the boys.'

'Ah?' Rumbold looked interested and began to feel important. 'Oh, so you're the *Morning Star* man, are ye? Takes it meself, allus has done.'

'Splendid! Now, Mr . . . Mr . . . '

'Rumbold's the name.'

'Mr Rumbold, can you let my paper have anything on the subject?'

'Why surely, surely. I tells you what, I'm just a'goin' up 'ome fer a cup of tea. Will ye come along, sir, an' I'll tell ye all I knows about the young devils, for devils they be, worritin' everyone be their pranks. An' the old lady, too . . . she's driven near crazy.' He led the way out of the kitchen garden and through the weed-grown stable yard to his cottage.

Next morning Hannah burst into the kitchen with the *Morning Star* which Rumbold had given her with strict instructions to keep it away from Aunt Ellen. 'There, Cook, wot d'you think of that, it's in all the papers now, and there's a picture of Rumbold, large as life, *an'* Mrs Rumbold, the Dower House an' all. Won't the mistress be in a fit!'

The paper was spread out on the kitchen table and even the superior starched Emma rushed to see.

There, as Hannah said, was a photo of the Dower House with Tilly sitting on the lawn, and close by, another smaller picture of Mr and Mrs Rumbold, the former in his shirtsleeves holding a spade.

Cook read out aloud:

'DISAPPEARANCE OF TWO BOYS
By our Special Correspondent.

'The two elder sons of Colonel and Mrs Hensman, who were staying with their aunt at the Dower House, Cherry Walden, Tilthshire, disappeared from the house on Monday night last, the seventh of May. They left a note to say they would return but since then nothing has been heard of them, nor has any trace been found of the missing boys. They were due to go back to

Banchester on the Tuesday, but, owing to a younger brother falling ill with measles, their departure for school was delayed.

'Considerable anxiety is felt in the village as to their whereabouts . . . '

And after a description of the boys there followed a long statement by Rumbold 'the gardener at the Dower House, an old family servant who has been in the employ of Miss Hensman for thirty-two years.'

'If the mistress sees this,' said Cook, ''e won't be 'ere another day' – and so on and so on until it came to the final passage.

'The police have been informed and the countryside is being scoured, so far without success. It is thought in the village that the two boys, who are of an adventurous disposition, may have taken to the woods and are defying capture. The position, if this is the case, is a difficult one, for Cherry Walden is in thickly timbered country with many large woods close at hand, including High Wood, the famous game preserve belonging to Sir William Bary, Bt, Master of Fox Hounds, of Handley

Hall. Farther to the west is Brendon Chase, eleven thousand acres of woodland, part of which is Crown land.

'It is believed that some disaster has overtaken them as no word has been received from the runaways. They had no money with them and, as far as is known, no food of any sort save a small supply of oatmeal which they purchased at the village shop.

'Search parties have been out and keepers and boy scouts have been scouring the countryside. The general opinion seems to be that they may be hiding, or in difficulties, in High Wood, as this extensive cover is within three miles of Cherry Walden and it is known the boys frequently went there after birds and butterflies.

'It is considered highly unlikely that they could have reached the Chase which is eight and a half miles from Cherry Walden, but a search is being made in that direction also.'

Then followed an account of an interview with the Reverend Whiting, 'the boys' tutor'.

'The vicar, who knew the boys intimately, told our reporter, "They are fine young fellows and I cannot believe any mischief has befallen them. Both are extremely self-reliant and well able to take care of themselves." '

'Well, I never,' gasped Cook, 'it takes the biscuit. Fancy it gettin' in the papers like this; what *will* the mistress say!'

'Won't 'arf shake 'er up,' said Hannah with evident satisfaction. 'I wouldn't like to be in Rumbold's . . . ' The kitchen door opened suddenly and there was Aunt Ellen. 'Cook,' she began, then her gaze fell upon the paper on the table. The startled maids had shrunk aside. 'Oh, ma'am, it's all in the papers!'

'What's in the papers?'

'You'd better look, ma'am.'

Aunt Ellen looked. 'I *knew* it, Cook, I *knew* it, I saw all this coming . . . I told the vicar so the first day . . . ' She took up the paper then crumpled it suddenly and threw it on the floor, her pince-nez trembling with passion. They fell off and she had to pick them up again. 'The impudence . . . the *impudence* of the man. Send Rumbold to me in the morning room at once, *at once* I tell you,' she screamed. 'Don't stand there like a lot of dummies!'

She flung out of the kitchen. Cook sighed and shook her head slowly. 'Dearie me, it'll be the death of 'er. Rumbold'll catch it proper. She'll send 'im packing, bag an' baggage.'

She collapsed on a chair her shoulders shaking, not with sobs but with uncontrollable laughter.

Sergeant Bunting's solid British figure was often seen about the by-lanes of Cherry Walden in the weeks which followed the boys' disappearance. He was most frequently observed in the neighbourhood of High Wood, especially at close of day and in the early mornings. Several wide-scale searches were made through this and other woods, much to the annoyance of both landlords and keepers, for the noise and bustle disturbed the pheasants. As Sir William Bary, Bt, MFH, remarked, 'There won't be a bird to shoot or a fox to hunt with all this trampling through my woods, just in the breeding season, too.'

There were certain reasons why High Wood was suspect. The day after the boys' departure Tilly ran away, a thing she very rarely did. In actual fact, she was searching for the boys whom she had heard leaving the Dower House the previous night. She was found roaming the fields close to High Wood where a keeper saw her coursing a hare. When the sergeant heard of this he put two and two together – as he thought – and believed that Tilly was trailing the boys.

He had also closely questioned the vicar.

'About these 'ere young gents, sir, did you ever go with them to High Wood after butterflies and sich like?'

'Why certainly, Sergeant, we often went and I know they frequently went on their own. I should say they know every inch of the place.'

'And did you go to any other wood where they might have gone?'

'Well, let me see, yes, many of the smaller woods close to home and last August I took the elder boy, Robin, to the Chase. We went by car.'

'Um,' the sergeant looked thoughtful.

'Personally I think it's highly improbable they would go so far,' said the Whiting, 'but it is possible, of course. My belief is that had they gone to the Chase they would have taken their bicycles.'

'Aye,' rumbled Bunting, 'but if we don't find 'em in High Wood the Chase will 'ave to be searched. I've notified the police that side so they are on the lookout and they'll let me know if they find any clues. It's a shockin' business for Miss Hensman, sir, ain't it? She's took it very bad.'

'Yes, yes, indeed, poor lady, it's most worrying for her.'

'We dragged the Willow Pool last night,' said Sergeant Bunting lugubriously, 'but all we caught was a pike as long as me arm. 'Ad 'im fer supper.'

After the visit of the reporter from the *Morning Star*, others arrived and filled the village – Cherry Walden had not had such excitement since Mr Baldrick's ploughman had hung himself in the big barn. As it was no longer possible to conceal the truth from Harold he was told everything and was subjected to third degree methods by Aunt Ellen, Miss Holcome, the vicar and finally the sergeant. But he gave nothing away and when asked outright whether he knew of any plan he declined to answer rather than tell a deliberate lie. His stubborn spirit refused to yield and not all the tears of Aunt Ellen or the threats of Sergeant Bunting would move him. He was so miserable that he decided that at the first possible moment he would run away, too, but for the moment he was still convalescent and he had to bear his cross alone.

The talk in the bar of the Woodman's Arms always turned to the same topic. 'Any news about they Dower 'ouse boys?'

'Bin found in High Wood, starved to death,' said one rumour-monger.

'Run away to sea,' was another version.

Sir William Bary's head keeper found himself in demand for the first time in his life and even the landlord stood him a pint in the hope of gleaning some fresh piece of news.

Rumbold survived the wrath of Aunt Ellen, but only just. In the heat of words he gave in his notice, but, much to his relief, it was not taken and Aunt Ellen sobered down. To lose Rumbold, such a good steady man, would be the final catastrophe. He was so useful in running messages and doing odd jobs.

But she forbade him to talk in the village of the boys' disappearance, an injunction he did not find hard to keep for he was a solitary, unsociable man and he did not drink. But he could not still the wagging tongue of his wife.

Harold's condition was improving rapidly. He was now allowed out in the garden but either Aunt Ellen or Miss Holcome always accompanied him; they haunted him like watchful shadows.

Aunt Ellen was terrified that if he were allowed out alone he too would disappear; she would have liked to have him on a lead if it had been possible. It was patent that he knew a good deal more than he said and his stubborn silences proved his guilt.

She even went to the length of locking his bedroom door at night – after she thought he was asleep. She was taking no chances. But this state of things could not continue; matters were coming to a head. The sooner he was back at school the better and the doctor thought that he was now well enough to go and would be better out of the way under strict school discipline.

It was the Whiting who had the unpleasant mission of breaking the news to Harold that, on the following day, he was to return to Banchester. Aunt Ellen thought it wiser that the vicar should tell him for she wanted to avoid a 'scene'.

She asked him to dinner and afterwards, as Harold and the Whiting were strolling round the garden, the bomb fell.

'I have to tell you, Harold, that you are returning to school tomorrow. The doctor considers you are now quite fit to do so and your aunt is in a very worried and nervous state. I did suggest that you should remain a little longer taking lessons with me but she feels it would be better if you went back to Banchester as soon as possible so that she should be relieved of the responsibility.'

Harold, pacing along beside the Whiting, felt a deep sinking of the heart. Go back to Banchester without his brothers! Why, it was unthinkable! He resolved to make a bid for freedom that very night. He would try and make the Chase before daylight and somehow or another find his brothers. He had a vague idea of the way, for he had pored over the map many times. It was pretty direct. He could not for the life of him think how he would find his brother outlaws once he reached the Chase but he would trust to luck.

He looked up to see the Whiting regarding him keenly, wondering, no doubt, how he would take the tidings. 'Well, if Aunt Ellen says so I suppose I must,' he replied meekly. 'I'd much rather have stayed and had lessons with you.' Harold affected to be not unduly worried.

'And I have no doubt,' went on the Whiting, 'that in a few days your brothers will be joining you.'

Harold did not reply. He was watching the martins circling about the gables of the Dower

House. They had already started to build their nests under the eaves, those cunning little mud castles which looked as though they were part of the masonry. The Whiting and Harold watched them for a while, then slowly paced on. 'And try and get me some chalkhill blues,' went on the vicar. 'You should find them on the Downs. I hope to get about soon; now June is in, the white admirals should be out in High Wood.' The Whiting looked at his companion with a sidelong quizzing glance. But he saw no sign pass across Harold's face.

Westwards the sun had set; the mirror of the Willow Pool shone out between the copper beeches in the paddock like a silver dish.

Harold was lying awake in his room watching the daylight die away and the tall limes outside the window grow ebon black. There was no moon now but the sky was clear of cloud. He could see the Milky Way over the dark-maned cedar on the lawn and in at the open window came the sweet scents of the summer night.

He had made no preparations for flight; it would have been too risky. He would go just as he was. The night was warm; he would not suffer from cold, but he had a horrid doubt as to whether he would be able to find his way in the dark. He had memorized the route; across the Cherry Walden road and fields, parallel to the Market Harrowby–Brendon main line.

People were still moving about the house. He heard Miss Holcome come up to her room and the maids going up the back stairs to bed and at long last Aunt Ellen ascending the front stairs.

His door gave a faint creak. She was coming in. He lay quite still, breathing heavily. He heard her listening and gave an extra loud snort as though he was turning over in his sleep just to let Aunt Ellen know he was there. Then the door softly closed again. A faint creak and click followed. Had Aunt Ellen turned the key on him? He could not credit her with such sound sense! After lying perfectly still for some minutes he very gently tiptoed across the floor and tried the handle. As he thought . . . it was locked on the outside. He tried to peep through the keyhole but all was darkness, she had left the key in the lock. This must have been so because there was a dim light under the door: the lamp was still burning on the oak chest on the landing.

Now he *was* sunk! Locked in like a common malefactor! Next he went to the window. In summer the big heavy shutters of his bedroom were always left open and the window too, though it was only open at the top. When he tried to push up the lower sash it made so much noise he jumped back into bed, his heart beating fast. But Aunt Ellen had now put out the landing light and had gone to bed. The house was as quiet as a vault.

Squeak! The sash was up at last and Harold looked out. It was a horrid drop to the gravel path and herbaceous border. It looked miles and miles. He couldn't face it. He was trapped. On the morrow he was to be delivered, bound, into the enemy camp.

The Banchester boys would know all about his brothers' escapade, they would have seen it in the papers. He would have no peace. He simply must get away. But how?

Tie the bed sheets together? A risky business, they might tear, though even a broken leg would be preferable to Banchester tomorrow without his brothers. But the drop was too great; he simply dare not try it.

What a peaceful night it was! A perfect June night. Below him he could see the pale blobs of a blossoming tree by the garage and the clipped yew hedge. Out in the paddock sheep were moving about; in the silence of the night he could hear them. One coughed once like an old man. Moths flew past; one came and buzzed round his head. Cherry Walden clock struck midnight.

Wearily and with a little shiver – for he had been standing at the open window in his pyjamas – he got back into bed. It was no use. Just his luck, he thought. At last he fell asleep.

It seemed to Harold that he had only just dropped off when he was suddenly awake again. Some sound had roused him. He did not know what it was. He lay listening, very still and rather frightened. A moth tapped on the window and an owl was screeching from the cedar but it was something else which had roused him from deep sleep.

Creak! The key was turning in his lock again! It was Aunt Ellen coming to see if he was really still in bed! He shut his eyes tight and then half opened them, expecting to see the faint light of her torch. But instead all was darkness. But the door *was* opening, very, very slowly. Was it some horrible dream? Was Aunt Ellen walking in her sleep? Harold had once seen in his dorm at Banchester a boy walking in his sleep and the horrible expression on his face was indelibly imprinted on Harold's mind.

Wider, wider ... and then the terrified boy saw a dim form, a shapeless dark form with a white blur for a face.

With something between a gulp and a gasp Harold buried his head under the bedclothes. This was some terrible dream. The figure at the door was not Aunt Ellen, it was not Miss Holcome ... it was a ghost!

7. Tally Ho!

HAROLD, buried deep under the bedclothes, felt something shake him by the shoulder. He was on the point of leaping from his bed and yelling for help when a voice, a familiar voice, said gently: 'Little John! Little John! Wake up! It's me! Robin, Robin Hood from the brave greenwood come to release thee, my merry man!'

'Robin!' gasped Harold, struggling into the air again and peering into the dim face of his brother. 'Why . . . what on earth!'

'Don't make a row,' whispered Robin. 'How are you, old boy; are you better?'

'I'm all right,' gasped Harold. 'They are sending me back to school tomorrow. I wanted to run away and join you tonight but Aunt Ellen locked me in.'

'Yes, I know. Well, you must decide quickly. We're only here to get more supplies' – Robin spoke rapidly in a whisper – 'we've run out of salt and we haven't had anything sweet for days, so we've bagged three pounds of sugar from the kitchen and some pots of marmalade. It's taken us since dusk to get here but we must be away before daybreak. We shan't have time to make the Chase before it's light so Big John and I thought of hiding up in High Wood until tomorrow . . . I mean . . . tonight. It's after three now so we shall have to be moving – there's no time to lose.'

Harold did not need any further urging. He dressed rapidly as well as he could in the darkness, while Robin sat on the bed and talked in whispers. 'Tilly heard us getting into the house,' he said; 'she barked like anything, I wonder you didn't hear her.'

'No, the first I heard was you opening the door. I thought you were a ghost. Where's John . . . Big John I mean!'

'Oh, he's packing up the stuff in the kitchen.'

'What sort of time have you been having in the Chase?' whispered Harold, as he frantically tied his shoelaces.

'Oh rippin'! Absolutely rippin'! We've killed a wild pig and smoked it and bagged no end of birds and rabbits, an' we've got an old hollow oak tree to live in. You'll love it. Are you quite sure you are fit enough to come?'

'Yes,' gasped Harold, 'course I am.'

'And free from germs?'

'Yes.'

'Big John and I don't want to get measles, you know, it would spoil the whole thing,' said Robin.

Harold stood up. 'I'm ready.'

'Right, follow me!'

They stole out of the room though not until Robin had slyly made up a dummy figure in Harold's bed by rolling up a rug. And he took care to lock the door again as they stole out. That would puzzle 'em!

They found Big John in the kitchen with two large cardboard boxes filled with sugar, salt, tea, flour and potatoes – new ones, Rumbold's pride – which he had found in the scullery.

It was a good weight to carry, but between them they managed it. Robin went first into the cellar, showing the way by the light of matches.

At the far end was a coal chute which gave access to the shrubberies. This chute had been discovered by the boys long before when hunting for a tame rabbit which had escaped.

There was just enough room for a boy to crawl up it. They replaced the iron grating which covered it – luckily it was not a permanent fixture – and in a short while they were across the paddock and heading for High Wood.

As has already been said, this extensive cover was only two miles from the Dower House. It would make a fine harbour for the fugitives. They had only to wait for night and then they would have comfortable time to reach the Chase.

Their way lay by the Willow Pool and as they passed it they heard a big fish jump among the weeds and a startled moorhen 'cruiked' in alarm.

The first birds were beginning to sing when they reached High Wood. They had not seen a soul. By the time they had found a deep thicket of privet, under which they crawled, the dawn was coming rapidly, and with its growing light Harold saw his brothers clearly for the first time. They were as brown as true Red Indians – his own poor pasty face seemed like a ghost's by comparison – and Big John was wearing a strange garment on his nether limbs which looked like a fur skirt. He explained that his grey flannel bags had been ripped to bits by briars and he had had to make himself this strange garment out of rabbit skins.

He had nobly endeavoured to construct some trousers but it had proved too much for him. He was not a great hand with a wire needle. As Robin said, 'This is where a fayre ladye would have come in useful.' Big John had waxed quite sentimental over this and had even run over in his mind all his girl friends. Unfortunately, he could not imagine any filling the bill. The only likely candidate would be Angela. Angela was the daughter of a doctor in Yoho, a dark-haired damsel who had taken Big John's fancy at a party last summer. Big John was sure Angela would play; she was eminently a sporting child and hunted regularly.

It rained that day and it was rather a miserable business lying up in the thicket. The outlaws filled the weary hours by telling Harold all the news and the latter told them in return how things had been going at the Dower House, how the police were after them and how Bunting had sworn to track them down.

'I'll bet the Dower House is buzzin' like a wasp's nest now,' said Robin gleefully as he sucked a leaf stem. 'Aunt Ellen is probably in a padded cell an' Bunting is talkin' of bloodhounds.'

My word, bloodhounds! That was an idea; it had never occurred to them before.

'Sure, they'll use bloodhounds,' said Robin. 'We'll very likely hear them bayin' soon.'

'What shall we do then?'

'Put pepper on our spoor, that's the right thing to do. The dogs snuff the pepper an' it makes 'em sneeze an' they don't like it.'

'What a lark! I hope they try it!'

Once, during the afternoon, they heard voices and sounds of people walking through the bushes. And once they thought they heard a terrier yapping somewhere. But nobody came near their retreat. The hours dragged on. Towards evening the rain stopped and all the bushes were ticking with falling drops.

After a while the blackbirds began to 'chink', sure sign that night was near, and stiff and cramped, the boys at last emerged from their lair.

There was still light in the sky. The west was ablaze with red and gold for the low rain clouds still hung about the setting sun. They scouted through High Wood until they came to the little lane which ran all along its western edge. In the distance was the tower of Cherry Walden church and a few scattered lights were beginning to star out; the wet foliage smelt delicious after the rain.

The lane seemed clear; nobody appeared to be about. Robin, who was the advance scout, judged all was safe. Once over the lane they would keep to the fields until they reached the Chase.

They heard the 10.40 express roaring along in the valley and saw the speeding jewels of the carriage lights.

'Come on,' whispered Robin, 'all's clear.' They dropped into the road. It was then that Robin's sharp eyes caught sight of something in the opposite ditch, something which gleamed dully in the dusk. It was a bicycle bell, and the bell was attached to a bicycle! He stopped dead in his tracks and put out a warning hand. And simultaneously there burst from the bushes twenty yards away the blue clad form of Sergeant Bunting!

'Hi,' he bellowed, 'Hoi! Come 'ere, you boys!'

'Into the wood,' shouted Robin at the top of his voice. 'They're after us.'

Sergeant Bunting came running down the road, dignity flung to the winds. Other figures sprang out of the trees; everybody was shouting. The sergeant roared, 'Don't let 'em get away!' But already the boys were plunging back into the dark recesses of High Wood. Terrified pheasants burst out of the trees, owls hooted insanely, the shouting and cracking of sticks died behind them.

Sergeant Bunting was like a baffled bull caught by its horns in a thicket. He drew his whistle and blew it loudly, his face crimson. His helmet had come off. It had rolled into the bushes and he could not find it. He had lost his torch, his hands and face were scratched and torn.

After a while panting figures came crashing towards him. 'They've given us the slip, the young devils, we 'adn't a 'ope in the dark.' It was Sir William Bary's head keeper.

Other men came up, puffing and blowing, grooms and gardeners, farm hands and even the postman from Cherry Walden. All were mopping their heated brows as they gathered round the towering figure of the perspiring Bunting.

'Don't worry, men,' he said, 'we'll get 'em in the morning. We'll picket the wood. They can't get away in daylight.'

'Allus said they'd be found 'ere,' said the postman, grinning. 'Wot's the time, Sergeant?' Sergeant Bunting peered at his watch. 'Half past ten.'

'Too late for a drink,' said the postman gloomily, 'I could put one back, I can tell ye, arter all that runnin'.'

'All three on them were there,' said an undergroom, 'the younger one an' all that got away last night.'

'Ah,' said Bunting, 'we'll get 'em come tomorrow.'

Meanwhile the three outlaws, still in possession of their precious supplies, had gone right through High Wood and out the other side like scalded cats.

High Wood, in the grey dawn of the morning after the boys had been so dramatically spotted by Sergeant Bunting, was a hive of activity. Figures were to be seen making their way towards the gloomy covert from every quarter of the compass. Sir William Bary, Bt, MFH, was there soon after it was light; he meant to be in at the kill.

'I'll chop these cubs,' he said. 'Gad, sir! I'll give them a taste of me huntin' crop.' These remarks were addressed to none other than the Whiting, who, strange to relate, was quite enjoying himself and had even foregone his late breakfast so as to be in at 'the death'.

'I've told every man on the estate to turn out,' said the Baronet. 'We'll have those rascals by the heels at last. It's a good sound beating they want and it's just what they haven't had. If their father was here things would have been different, I'll be bound . . . the – the young cubs,' he gulped as a pheasant, startled at the noise of the gathering multitude, flew cocking out of the wood. 'Shan't have a bird, not a bird this season with all this tramplin' through my covers.'

As the blear-eyed dawn grew, more and more people gathered. There were several newspaper reporters – including the man from the *Morning Star* – the postman was there and the village schoolmaster, keepers and grooms, undergrooms and gardeners, gardener's boys, farm labourers and shepherds; indeed, every able-bodied man in the parish had turned out.

Before they 'drew' the wood the squire addressed the men. 'A pound for the man who collars the first rascal,' he shouted. 'If I blow my horn, you know I've spotted them.'

'Old Squire be fair upset,' said Bill Bobman, who had had many a pheasant from High Wood and might even have another before the day was out. 'I pities them boys if he cotches 'em.'

'Ah, that I do,' replied an undergroom. 'He'll warm their tails I'll warrant.'

Some wit remarked to Sir William that it was a fine morning for cubbing and the squire turned away in wrath. 'All the riff-raff of the village is here,' he muttered to the Whiting, 'To think that three undisciplined kids could set the whole village by the ears like this!'

The Whiting said nothing but chuckled to himself.

What a day for Cherry Walden, *what* a day. Would it ever forget it? Sergeant Bunting was there and with him three more policemen. The sergeant looked sulky, for the head keeper had been put in charge of the drive because he knew the wood.

As soon as it was fully light Sir William blew a long note on his hunting horn and the beat began. Then the squire hurried down to the far end of the wood to act as a 'stop'. As each pheasant broke cover over his head he let out a new oath. He strode up and down, slapping his riding boots with his whip. Several of his men were mounted but Sir William had been forbidden by his doctor to ride since the early spring as he had taken a bad toss – on the last run of the season too – and he would not be able to ride for six months at least. This fact did not help to keep him in the best of tempers. 'If I had my horse I'd ride 'em down; Gad, sir, I'd *ride* 'em down,' he swore. Another bird broke cover and from the thickets came the terrified 'cheep cheep' of young pheasants.

'Here, Vicar,' bawled the squire to the Whiting who appeared from behind a bush, 'you go down the far end of the ride to see if the rascals break that way. Remember, if you hear me blow my horn you will know I've seen the boys.' At that moment a pheasant, which had been crouching, terrified, under the bracken, burst forth with a great bustle of wings and loud crowing directly overhead and it so happened that as it passed it misbehaved itself right on top of Sir William's cap. The spectacle was too much for the Whiting; he turned away, almost choking, his face quite crimson, to take up the position indicated. On looking back he saw the unhappy baronet trying to clean his cap on a bunch of grass.

The minutes passed. Sounds of approaching beaters came nearer and the sun, which up till now had been hidden by cloud, burst forth with full undimmed splendour. And as if by magic, butterflies began to appear in the ridings. Several pearl-bordered fritillaries flew by, looking like bright gold leaves as they danced along, dragonflies soared overhead, bees and wasps buzzed about between the trees. The Whiting took off his cap and mopped his forehead, then he produced a packet of sandwiches which his thoughtful 'old body' had put in his pocket at the last moment and began to munch with evident enjoyment. He had not had such a day out for years. As for the unhappy baronet, there were no sandwiches for *him* and he was very hungry. Not one of his many minions had thought to provide the master with any sustenance whatever. So he sat hunched on his shooting stick glowering at the rotund figure of the Whiting who, forty yards distant, was apparently taking no interest in what was going on but was devouring a thick ham sandwich. Blast the fellow, he hadn't even offered him one. 'Keep your eyes skinned, Vicar!' he shouted irritably, unable to bear the sight any longer. Then he resettled himself on his shooting stick and kept his gaze averted.

All at once a slight sound made him turn. He saw the Whiting hurl away his sandwich with a loud inarticulate shout and dive into the bushes, waving his cap about his head. He must have seen the boys! Sir William was a man of action. In a trice he whipped the hunting horn from his coat and blew a blast loud and long. Down the ride he had glimpses of the vicar dodging in and out among the bushes; he must be close on the fugitives' heels!

The notes of the horn had barely died away when two grooms came running round the corner of a ride and stood looking about them.

'This way, Perkins,' their master said briskly, 'this way, Shoebottom; the vicar's sighted 'em. After them! A pound for the first man to collar a boy!' Despite his hunting injury the squire hurried along the ride after the running men. Other beaters burst from the bushes and went pounding past him, urged on by more wild notes from the hunting horn.

He walked rapidly after the rest of the 'field' which, by now, had gone a considerable distance down the ride. Soon he saw a knot of men all together; they were crowding round the Whiting who was quite invisible, and all were looking at something he held on the ground. 'Old Whiting's caught one of them by Gad!' said the squire to himself. 'Dem it, I'll ask him to dinner tonight and give him some of my best Cockburn!' But when he came up to the group it seemed to melt mysteriously. Grooms and horseboys seemed to spirit themselves away into the bushes and only the Whiting remained, doing something with a small box inside his cap.

'Where have they gone?' roared the squire. 'What's happened?'

The Whiting looked up and saw the crimson face of his questioner. 'Too bad, too bad, Sir William, I'm afraid I raised your hopes.'

'What do you mean, sir, raised my hopes? Were you playing a joke on me, sir?' Sir William's eyes were glittering dangerously.

'No ... No, Sir William ... I ... I've caught the first wood white I've ever seen in High Wood. Look at it, a perfect specimen, a perfect specimen.' The Whiting proffered the little white box, like a pill box, with a glass top. Sir William did not even glance at it.

There was an awful pause, then the tornado burst.

'You're a disgrace to the cloth, sir, a disgrace to the cloth I tell you. A man of your age chasing after butterflies like a ... like a ... two-year-old. You did it on purpose ... I ... I ...'

'But, Sir William,' put in the Whiting mildly, 'I assure you I ... '

'Enough,' roared the squire. 'You and your ... butterflies. Pah!' With an angry gesture he turned on his heel and strode away up the ride, almost choking with wrath.

By midday the whole wood had been beaten through without result. I may say in passing that Bill Bobman had left early with his pockets bulging.

The unfortunate contretemps of the wood white became the principal joke of the day, and later the Woodman's Arms rocked with the gusty laughter of tired but jovial company.

But the fact remained – somehow the boys had got clear away; had they slipped like little silver fishes between the mesh of the net?

In actual fact, they had never been in High Wood at all during the 'drive'. After Bunting had spotted them they had gone slap through the cover and made straight for the Chase. At the moment that poor Sir William was vigorously blowing the horn with hope high in his heart, the prey had gone to ground in a very distant earth, namely, the old oak tree in the middle of a forest clearing in Brendon Chase, a point over eight miles away.

8. The Honey Buzzard's Nest

THE DECISION which had led to the raid on the Dower House for fresh supplies had been wisely taken. Big John and Robin had felt more and more the craving for sweet things; even such homely provender as bread and potatoes seemed food for the Gods. Furthermore, Robin, especially, lacked books to read. For a boy he was a great reader. Even though their life in the Chase was a busy one, now that their commissariat department showed signs of such great improvement and the necessity to hunt daily was not so pressing, there would be more time to read.

Robin had brought back with him from the Dower House his beloved Thoreau's *Life in the Woods,*

The Amateur Poacher by Richard Jefferies and *Bevis, the Story of a Boy* by the same author. Big John had chosen *Huckleberry Finn* and Little John, *Tom Sawyer*.

From this list it is easy to see in what direction their tastes in literature lay and to understand that perhaps it was not only petticoat government which first suggested to them the possibility of an outlaw's life in the woods.

Food for the mind and food for the body, these wants seemed now to be satisfied, and the boys embarked on their fourth week of liberty with renewed zest. In addition, the affair at High Wood had laid a false trail and for the moment the Chase was theirs in which to roam at will.

Even the smoke from their camp fire had not so far attracted attention and nobody had any suspicions that they were in the Chase. In any case smoke ascending from the Chase was not an uncommon spectacle, for the charcoal burner frequently burnt rubbish by his shack and his kilns, when newly lit, gave off a certain amount of smoke.

It was surprising how Harold took to the new life. The flight from High Wood had taxed his strength sorely and for a couple of days afterwards he found he had to take things very easily. But with an abundance of good food he soon recovered and was able to take his share in the daily work about the camp. The weather, which had been showery with overcast skies, took up and a settled spell was indicated.

In actual fact, the whole of Brendon Chase was not Crown property. A considerable portion of it, many hundreds of acres, belonged to the Duke of Brendon and it was in this portion of the Chase that the boys were hiding. There the trees were older and finer but the underwood had been neglected, and since the old Duke had died nobody bothered very much about it. Had it been Crown property it would have been doubtful whether the boys could have escaped detection for as long as they did.

When, on that eventful morning after the High Wood episode, they returned to camp, they found all in order. For safety's sake the rifle and ammunition had been hidden up inside the hollow oak and the smoked pig had been likewise concealed. They had carefully covered up the marks of their fire with dead bracken and turf and it would have taken sharp eyes to see that anyone had been there at all, still less living in the clearing for three whole weeks.

These were wise precautions. Had anyone chanced that way – it was very unlikely – and suspicious signs had been seen, it might have reached the ears of those in authority and the wonderful adventure would have come to a speedy end.

But luck was with them. Nobody came near, save the wild creatures of the woods: the foxes, rabbits, badgers and deer, and they, smelling before seeing, passed aside and shunned the spot.

Robin shut up *Bevis* with a snap and rolled over on his stomach and began to cut slices of smoked ham, preparatory to frying it over the fire. 'What about finding the Blind Pool tomorrow, you merry men? It's somewhere around and I fancy a bit of fishing.'

Little John thought it was a good idea. He felt ready for anything now and was as fit as his brothers.

'I have an idea that if we follow the stream we'll be bound to find it. The difficulty is that we don't know whether it's flowing from the pool or into it,' said Big John.

'Well, what about splitting forces?' suggested Robin. 'You and Little John follow it up and I'll go down. We're sure to find the Blind Pool then, if the stream really *is* connected with it. According to the map the Chase is about two miles across so the pool won't be too easy to find.'

'Bother,' ejaculated Big John, 'that reminds me, I meant to bring the map along. It was always kept in the hall drawer.'

'Never mind,' replied Robin, 'we can manage without it and I'm not sure it isn't more fun without a map. I rather like pretending I'm lost.'

'I shouldn't like to be lost in the Chase,' said Little John, 'wandering around all night without any grub. Besides, I shouldn't know where to make for and I might run into the old charcoal burner or a keeper or something.'

'Are those potatoes ready?' asked Robin. Big John nodded. 'Here you are, I've cut them up into thin slices – that's right, isn't it?' Big John held the plate up for his inspection. It was piled with potato rings about a quarter of an inch thick. 'They'll do. We'll cook 'em first before the ham 'cos they'll take longer.'

He dropped a lump of pork fat into the middle of the pan and it slid to the side, dissolving rapidly with faint spitting sounds. Then Big John passed the plate across and in a minute or two the bottom of the pan was hidden by a mosaic of potato slices.

'The trick of getting 'em nice and brown is to put in only a very little fat,' said the chef; 'if you put in too much they won't turn colour.'

Now and again he flipped each slice over with the point of his hunting knife and soon they were a crisp golden hue, the colour of ripe corn.

When these were cooked to his liking they were removed to a plate. Next followed the slices of ham, thick slices, with not too much fat on the upper edges. They skated about in the pan sizzling and spitting and gave out a delicious aroma. The pig had been a godsend to the outlaws and it certainly tasted better than any bacon they had ever had at the Dower House.

When at last the meal was ready, all set to with a will. Washed down with hot sweet tea, nobody could have wished for a better feast.

'My,' said Little John, as he inserted the last morsel into his mouth, 'that's about the best supper I've ever had in all my life!'

'You wait, young 'un,' replied Robin, 'we'll have venison steak yet. I'm sure there are deer in the Chase because the Whiting told me he had seen one. If we can shoot a pig with the .22 we can shoot a deer if we put the bullet in the right place. But I'm not so sure we aren't depending too much on outside supplies. After our sugar's gone and the jam's finished I'm not going back to the Dower House for more. It isn't my idea of living in the wilds. We must rely on what we can shoot and fish.'

'I think I should miss potatoes more than anything,' said Big John. 'Later there will be berries which will do for sweets.'

'How long are we going to stay here?' said Little John, after a pause.

'Why? Gettin' sick of it?' asked Robin Hood.

'No, don't be an ass, of course I'm not. I feel I never want to go back to Cherry Walden again. I'd like to live in the woods all my life! I was just thinking what fun it will be later on, in the autumn and winter, when all the leaves start to fall and the snow comes.'

'Well,' replied Robin, 'there's a lot to do yet, we've got to find the Blind Pool and the charcoal burner . . . and heaps of things. I vote we just go back when we're sick of it, or when Father and Mother come over . . . I'm not worryin' about it anyway. I don't think I ever want to sleep under a roof again. I should be like Mowgli in *The Jungle Book*, when they tried to make him sleep in the hut.'

Big John burst out laughing. 'I don't expect our people will recognize us when we go back to Cherry Walden. They'll come and shoo us away, firing off guns and beating tin cans like they did in *The Jungle Book*.'

A nightjar began to whirr some distance away. The strange sound rose and fell, exactly like an old-fashioned spinning wheel.

It was a beautifully still night. Across the clearing they could just see the first dog roses as little white blurs on a wall of green; even in the dusk they were visible.

And the sweet fresh scents of the forest in the warm night were unbelievably lovely. Honeysuckle was a very common plant in the Chase and at fall of night its strong scent was almost overpowering.

'What a life!' exclaimed Little John, throwing himself back with his arms behind his head and staring up and up until he seemed to be floating about like thistledown among the stars.

The soft rosy glow of the fire lit up the oak leaves and the great rough boughs. Dark shadows waved about mysteriously among the leafy caverns. 'I wish we could always live like this, I wouldn't care if I never saw a house again!'

He shut his eyes for a moment and felt the warm breath of the fire and smelt the reek of woodsmoke. Then he opened his eyes again and floated away among the stars. Some were larger than others and hung solemnly regarding him, others wavered and blinked. One small orange-coloured star seemed to jig up and down.

Little John began to think about the stars and planets, of how many were worlds and others were worlds to be or which were dead, like the moon. A foolish thought passed through his mind. They were like people, he was a God, seeing them all at a glance in various stages of creation. Then he began to feel frightened at the immensity of it all and his own littleness and at last he was glad to roll over and come to earth and watch the cosy flame-light playing about the faces of his brother outlaws.

But for a twist of chance he would now be sleeping in the dorm at Banchester with a dozen other boys all snoring round him like pigs! And tomorrow morning, as he lay on his bracken couch listening to the birds singing in the grey light of dawn, with the dew on the grass and the foxes and badgers stealing back to their holes, those other poor unfortunates would be making the most of their last hour or two of sleep in the long dark dormitory. Before him life stretched away, one long panorama of delight; his lessons would be in another school, he thought, the school of the woods. He would learn how to snare and Robin would teach him how to shoot. Up to now he had never had the chance.

Robin, also stretched beside the dying fire, had very much the same train of thought, though he was wondering what the Blind Pool would be like, if it was anything like Walden Pool. The owls were silent tonight, there was no mournful 'I wish I had never been bor-r-r-n' echoing across the dark and silent trees. All he could hear was the faint 'click tick' of the subsiding embers.

A moth flew into the flame-light and whirled madly round at an incredible speed. Then it fell down into the ashes. From the other side of the fire heavy breathing showed that Big John had dropped asleep.

It was time they went into the tree.

They started forth directly after breakfast to find the Blind Pool. Robin, by right of chieftainship, claimed the rifle. Big John and Little John had to make shift with the former's catapult. As Robin had suggested, they split forces when they reached the stream, which was only a few yards from the clearing, and after wishing each other good luck, Robin turned upstream and the others went in the opposite direction.

Like Big John's flannels, Robin's trousers had been torn to tatters and he had constructed a skin kilt for himself with the fur on the inside. It was held round his waist by a belt he had made out of the pigskin.

As he pushed his way along the course of the streamlet he kept his rifle unslung but not cocked as a twig might have caught the trigger.

It was very warm work for, after a while, when the sun rose almost vertically overhead, its burning rays shone directly down. Many butterflies appeared as the morning advanced, mostly speckled woods. These insects seemed to prefer the shady ridings where the undergrowth met in a tunnel overhead, but he also came upon them deep under the bushes. They were odd little butterflies, he thought, they flopped along in such a leisurely manner. Brimstones were common in the sunnier spots and wherever there was a knapweed in flower he noticed the brimstones were there too.

In places Robin came to dense thickets which barred his way. As I have said earlier, the forest had been very neglected, and though from the point of view of the health of the trees it would have been better if the underwood had been thinned, Robin revelled in the tangled masses of thicket and thorn.

In very many places he had to crawl on all fours like an animal, following the runways which were only used by the wild woodland creatures. In this way he found scores of nests which he would have otherwise missed. For, on looking up at the intricate green pattern of the leaves above, with the sunlight behind it, any nest or 'thickening' was immediately seen. The principal birds were whitethroats and lesser whitethroats. Before the morning was out he had found six whitethroats' nests, all with eggs. The bullfinch was another common bird in the Chase. Very often he could see the hen sitting, peeping at him over the rim of the nest with her round privet-berry eye, and her neat little black bonnet moving from side to side. Sometimes the eggs were visible. The bullfinch builds a very flimsy nest of rootlets and tiny lissom twigs, and lines it with horsehair, and the eggs show through the bottom.

Robin loved to feel over the rim of these nests and withdraw, very tenderly, the pale bluish eggs which were spotted and streaked with madder brown. These spots were nearly always arranged in a zone, or cap, at the larger end. The eggs varied in shape too; some bullfinch's eggs were nearly round, others oval, some pointed.

In the thick fern and underwood by the streamside he came upon a pheasant's nest. The hen burst from under his feet with a great clatter and startled him out of his wits. If he had had a chance to shoot the cock bird I am afraid he would have done so, even though it was the breeding season, for the outlaws had not yet managed to bag a pheasant and they had come upon several in the Chase. The big pale eggs were hard set and he did not interfere with the nest.

It was surprising how hot he became thrusting and battling with the underwood. The sweat ran down into his eyes and his hair was dank and wet. But he moved light-footed, like a true hunter and watched where he put his feet. He had no means of guessing how far he had come. The stream wound about among the fern and underbrush and it was difficult to judge distance.

He came upon one or two clearings among the trees. In one spot some ash poles had been cut down and stacked neatly at the side of a path. Robin went on one knee and examined the earth. Even in a dry summer these woodland paths remain moist for they are shielded from the sun, and the damp moss grows green and soft. He saw the marks of hobnailed boots, and they looked quite fresh. Somebody must have passed that way the preceding day. These signs made him move with extreme caution.

It would have been a lesson to watch him. By nature he was a born hunter and wild woodsman, and when he liked he could move as cautiously and silently as a fox. He was a dead shot too, and took a pride in the trim little weapon under his arm. He only wished it was his own. One day he would buy just such a rifle as this. It was wasted on Rumbold. The old man never cleaned it. He left it mouldering in the cupboard in the potting shed, never looking at it for months at a time. Robin had cleaned and oiled it and had adjusted the telescopic sight. The weapon now shot with great accuracy.

Now and again a rabbit crossed his path, or he glimpsed one bobbing away under the briars, showing its white beacon, but he did not shoot. The footprint on the path made him uneasy. He had an idea he was somewhere near the charcoal burner's dwelling. Now and again he fancied he smelt the curious fragrant smell of the 'pits'.

During the course of that morning he came upon several hedgehogs. One was a mere baby, not seven inches long, with little soft spines. He thought of taking it back for a pet but soon got tired of carrying it and let it go again. They had found many hedgehogs, at dusk, near the oak tree clearing, but truth to say, though they longed to sample one for the pot, they could not bring themselves to kill the quaint little spined urchins. They looked so comical when they ran along and their little eyes were full of intelligence. They looked friendly, lovable beasts.

As Robin stole forward he came to a small clearing surrounded by birches, the first birches he had seen in the Chase, and floating round these was a beautiful white admiral. This was by no means a common insect in the forest. The boys had once seen a single specimen in High Wood. They had gone with the Whiting the preceding summer and the excitement had been intense when the beautiful pied butterfly had been spied by Harold as it feasted on a blackberry blossom.

Robin had no net with him now and he wished he had. He was hatless too, so he could only watch it as it floated about enjoying the warm sun, now and again settling on some of the upper branches of the birch trees where it perched, opening and shutting its wings.

He spent quite twenty minutes staring at it. It looked like a lovely wrought ornament of jet and ivory. How excited the others would have been to see this rare insect! Here, at any rate, would be something to tell them!

With so much scrambling and crawling Robin felt desperately thirsty and he drank deeply from the stream. He longed for a swim. If only he could find the Blind Pool! At last he came to an open space in the forest where the bracken was up to his shoulders. The air was perfectly windless and heavy with the scent of summer. And at that spot the little brooklet had carved out for itself a fairy pool some ten yards long. It looked quite deep. He could see the spotted shingle on the bottom where some thick hazels overhung it, and knew it was no more than a foot or two. Tiny fish darted about. They were sticklebacks. Robin lay on his stomach and drew himself close to the margin of the pool, his face hidden in the lush sweet-smelling bracken. Pink 'milkmaid' flowers dropped over him and his back was partly shielded from the sun by the chequered shade of the leaves overhead.

What a beautiful spot! Could anything be nearer Paradise? The wood pigeons were cooing all about him in the trees, the whole forest was murmuring with their drowsy voices.

Robin was a strange boy, at least to many people he would have appeared strange. He loved best to be by himself in the woods. He liked to hunt on his wild lone and wander just like this, for a whole day, in some leafy secret place where nobody bothered to come. It was his idea of heaven. When, as now, he would come upon something which took his fancy, time would cease to be for him; he would be lost in a kind of ecstatic stupor.

As he lay looking down into this miniature pool his sharp eyes took in every detail, even the minute shadows of the sticklebacks were noted. Each fish had a shadow beneath it on the sandy floor. After a while, as he kept very still, they became bold and emerged from the shaded water under the hazel leaves and went about their business in their own watery kingdom.

He could see their minute fins trembling, and what perfect fins! These fishes in miniature were truly fascinating. The Creator must have had eyes like a watchmaker, thought Robin, to have made such delicate fishes, and he smiled to himself. The cock fish were very pretty with their bright blue backs and red throats.

They did not glide along in the water; they seemed to progress in jerks. Sometimes a cock stickleback would chase another away and then it moved with great speed, like an arrow, coming to a sudden full stop, opening and shutting its mouth, puffing out its lips.

On this same pool were water skaters or fiddlers. When Robin had come up to the pool these insects had all darted into the grass and ferns at the edge but as he lay quiet they emerged again and began skating about the surface. He saw the tiny dimple made in the water by their feet. They seemed to run about with as much ease as if they were on hard ground.

After a while a fly fell off the hazel leaves, a greenfly. It landed close to the edge but in a minute quite half a dozen water skaters had seized it and the largest bore it away in its jaws with all the others jumping after him.

Then a buzzing sounded in Robin's ear. It was a wild honeybee. He knocked it with his hand and it, too, fell into the water in front of him where it buzzed round making a circular fan of minute ripples. Several fiddlers immediately came skating up. They seemed at first rather afraid of the bee, but one, bolder than his fellows, darted in a rapier thrust. The bee's struggles grew weaker and finally its attacker began to run off with it wedged across his jaws. Robin had never realized what savage little insects they were; they reminded him of a pack of hounds.

The bee vainly tried to sting its captor but it was held fast. As Robin watched these fierce little creatures he noticed that some were fighting. Now and again one would fall over on to its back and show its silver underside. They skipped about each other like crickets.

It was delicious lying there among the cool bracken but the water seemed more inviting still. So he stripped off his shirt and the skin kilt and rolled off the bank. The pool only just covered his body when he lay down full length; it was a natural bath.

The water was warm in the full sun's glare, but when he sidled under the nut leaves it was quite chill. What a fairy-like little pool it was! Then he turned over on to his stomach facing upstream and watched the ripples hurrying round the bend towards him. He stretched out his arms – they looked blue under the water – and raised his fingers so that streams of silver bubbles came past his ears and nostrils.

He scrabbled at the stones on the stream bed and the water clouded for a second, but it soon ran clear again so that he could see his fingers showing bluish-white against the pied stones and silver sand.

Overhead a dragonfly passed to and fro, a bright blue dragonfly with dark spots on the ends of its wings like those he had seen by the Willow Pool at Cherry Walden. It settled on a reed in the full sun with its wings cocked high above its back. There were mayflies on the wing too, dancing up and down with their long graceful tails cocked up behind. When Robin was smaller he used to be rather afraid of them; he'd thought those long threadlike tails were stings.

It was so dreamy and cool and summery in that miniature paradise that Robin felt he could stay there for ever and ever. But at last he had to get out and lie on the warm bracken to let the sun dry him. The green fronds felt quite hot against his body after the cold embrace of the limpid water.

When he had dressed again he suddenly felt terribly hungry. You may have noticed that after a swim one often has a good appetite. And he had brought nothing with him to eat. They only had two meals a day, breakfast and supper. It was all they wanted and they were invariably ravenous for either.

It was quite an effort to tear himself away from this little fairy glade with its amber pool, but soon he was pushing down the streamside again, his body still tingling and delightful after the bathe. It had not been a *real* swim – he would have liked to strike out into deep water and oar himself along like a very fat carp and nose among green water plants. Perhaps he could do this when he found the Blind Pool, if there *was* such a place.

Then, quite miraculously, the trees thinned and he saw the object of his search. It was a long narrow pool, dark and very still, with beds of white water lilies growing near the banks. High oaks surrounded it on three sides. On the fourth were some tall and very gloomy pines whose tops were lit by the late afternoon sun so that their red branches seemed to be artificial, almost painted, or stained with blood.

At the far end, backed by the dark trees, stood a heron, its head sunk in its shoulders. It was standing on a mossy log which was protruding from the water. The pool was so still that a faithful reflection of the bird was visible, perfect in every detail.

Robin crawled through the bracken right up to the edge of the water and stared down into the depths. It was deep, so deep that he could see no bottom, and the water was a very, very dark green. By staring hard he could at last make out the steeply shelving sides diving down into the gloom. Robin saw his own reflection, curiously dark, so that his eyes were almost invisible, and behind his head an indigo sky, such as one sees in an old Umbrian painting, with the few white clouds which were passing slowly overhead mirrored very soft and dim. It was like looking at a richly coloured picture through a smoked glass.

As he lay screened by the reeds and fern, staring down, down, into the green depths, a dim movement attracted his attention below and a grave procession of massive bronze fish passed silently by, some five feet down. In weight and girth they were larger than any freshwater fish he had ever seen, with the exception of a pike. They were tench.

Robin was enthralled – bewitched! This place was even more magical than the tiny pool he had discovered a way back down the trail! He lifted his eyes again and saw that the heron had come to life and was walking rather awkwardly down the mossy log, clasping it with its long green claws and bobbing its head. It had not seen him, so well was he hidden in the reeds.

Several moorhens, which have the sharpest eyes of any wild bird, were feeding on a little grassy bank on the shore opposite to where he lay in hiding. They quested about like chickens, flirting their white tails. Moorhens are good to eat and so far Robin had shot nothing for the pot all day.

So he raised his rifle and took a steady sight on the nearest bird through the 'scope. It was not an easy shot for the moorhen was moving slowly forward, pecking as it went.

But Robin chose his own time and at the right instant the finger obeyed the brain and the crack was followed by the welcome thud of the bullet going home. The bird rolled over, flapped a wing once, twice, and lay still.

At the report of the rifle, muffled as it was, the heron sprang vertically into the air as if stung and came down again on the log. A moment before it had been hunched; now it was like a long slender grey reed and even from where Robin lay he could see its circular eye staring about it in the most comical manner. It had heard the muffled crack of the rifle but did not know from which direction it had come. Then it launched itself into the air and flapped away over the trees on wide cupped wings. One moment it was a grey bird against a wall of dark foliage, the next it was soaring into the sunlight and had vanished over the tops of the oaks.

All the other moorhens had run for cover when Robin had fired and now the pool was deserted, not a movement anywhere save some ripples on the water where a moorhen had dived. These came wheeling out towards him, breaking up the dark green shadow reflections.

He did not retrieve his bird at once. He still lay hidden among the thick reeds watching and listening. On the far green bank he could see the dark sooty spot of the dead moorhen. It would be delicious roast. Robin was so hungry he almost felt he could eat it raw with the greatest of gusto!

After a while he was aware of another bird moving among the sturdy reed swords at the far end of the pond, close to the sunken green log where the heron had stood. For some time Robin was puzzled as to what it could be and after a while he tried to see through the telescope of the rifle. At last he made out what it was: a mallard duck. Close behind her swam a lot of cheeping striped babies. She was threading her way in between the reed palisades.

What a heavenly place! How the others would love it! The white water lilies, so perfect and waxy, looked as though they were artificial. And those fascinating flat circular leaves! Strange fleshy leaves like dishes, how they seemed the very spirit of the water itself! There was a very faint smell of wild thyme and heated pond water. Earlier in the day the sun must have been shining full on the pool, for when Robin dipped a finger in it was quite warm. Another time they must come here and swim and fish. Alas! Robin Hood's day was nearly over. Why did the sun sink so soon? He had a long weary march back to camp. He must be starting. But as the sun dipped lower and lower behind the trees the powerful magic of the scene held him all the more. This place was surely far more lovely than Thoreau's pond he talked so much about. There was something mysterious, almost a little sinister about it. Why should it be set away in the heart of this ancient forest? The deer drank here perhaps, and all the woodland creatures — foxes, badgers, stoats and the like; pheasants, too, and all the wild forest birds. When Robin looked again in his magic mirror he saw no white clouds sailing, he saw a sky of rarest aquamarine and, as he watched, against that background a bird swam into view, a wide-winged bird, which wheeled and wheeled in vast circles.

Robin looked up at the sky above and saw the whole scene, only more distinctly and in clearer and more vivid colours. The bird was wheeling like a buzzard, the sunlight shining on the spread fingers of the wide-extended rigid wings. Could it be a honey buzzard? If so, perhaps it had a nest somewhere in the forest!

At last it soared from view behind the oak tops and was gone. He knew what he wanted to complete the picture of this dark green lake, set among the trees, starred with ivory lilies. Why, of course, it wanted this one thing, a moose, a huge black moose, pulling at the water lilies! He could imagine it so clearly, the loose pendulous lips dribbling sparkling drops, its echoing sloshings as it moved about in the shallow water of that remote and silent place.

Sadly Robin turned back upon his trail, the moorhen safely in his pocket. He took one last look at the Blind Pool. It was the loveliest thing he had seen in the forest, and he had enjoyed this day more than any other they had had so far.

He did not know then that years afterwards he would remember that picture; the dark pool set among the trees, so still, so calm, starred with those waxlike lilies, and the grey heron sitting on the log. Some things we see pass out of the mind, or, at least are forgotten; others, little things, little glimpses such as this never depart. And the memory of that first view of the Blind Pool would still be in his mind forty years afterwards, rather faded, perhaps, like an old photograph in an album, but still there, an imperishable masterpiece.

The glimpse of the wheeling honey buzzard, mirrored in the waters of the Blind Pool stuck in Robin's mind. There was a chance it was one of a pair and that its mate was sitting somewhere in the forest. But eleven thousand acres was a large expanse to search and finding the nesting tree would be like trying to find the proverbial needle. Robin knew that honey buzzards were late breeders, June being the usual month. He knew also that they were in the habit of using the old nest of other species such as crows and sparrow hawks, for he had made a deep study of the birds of prey; they were his favourite species. There was something fascinating about their fierce proud eyes and regal bearing; even the gentle little red kestrels which hovered in the wind over the Weald were lovely birds. Their rosy brown plumage was of a peculiarly beautiful tint.

It was some days before the honey buzzard was seen again. Then Big John brought news of a large barred hawk with rounded wings which he had seen fly into the top of one of the tall firs by the Blind Pool. It had swept up into the crown of the tree and Big John said that it made a noise like a spitting cat.

At the first opportunity all three boys paid a visit to the firs but Robin, sceptical of Big John's story, would not climb the tree. It was a tremendous height. Standing at its rough red base the topmost branches seemed a ghastly distance overhead. But there *was* a nest up there. Robin soon saw it, a mass of black sticks right in the tree's crown.

'Pooh, it's a pigeon's nest or a crow's,' he said. 'I'm not going to climb up there on the chance of even a honey buzzard; all Scotch firs have pigeons' nests in the top.' Robin was right, few such trees are without a pigeon's nest. 'If I could only see the bird I'd have a shot at getting up. Let's throw sticks and try and scare her off.'

So they gathered sticks and stones and bombarded the tree. But the nest was so high even Robin could not get a stone anywhere near it and Big John had foolishly left his catapult back in camp.

It was not very long, however, before proof was forthcoming. Robin, fishing in the Blind Pool the following day, saw the bird again.

It was a beautiful calm evening with not a cloud in the sky and the lowering sun lit the red trunks of the firs so that they were reflected in the still waters.

As he fished he heard a mewing note and looking up he saw *two* honey buzzards come over the tops of the oaks behind him. One of them carried a spray of green leaves in its beak; even though they were flying at a good height, Robin, with his sharp eyes, could see that at once.

The bird with the spray flew straight into the top of the fir and its mate followed!

The sight of those beautiful barred buzzards sweeping overhead against the soft sky was breathtaking. Big John had been right, they *had* a nest in the pine! Robin was so excited that he wanted to climb right away but the light was going and he had to curb his impatience.

That night he could hardly sleep for excitement and as soon as they had finished breakfast the following morning they all set out.

The pine was a difficult tree to climb for there were no branches for the first ten feet or so and their climbing irons were, of course, eight miles away in Cherry Walden. Robin was so keen to climb that he almost thought of going back that night to fetch them. He knew exactly where they were: in the white cupboard on the top landing of the Dower House, next to the schoolroom.

It was most tantalizing to stand there under the nest and know that up above a clutch of handsome eggs were reposing in a cup of beech leaves. Honey buzzards nearly always line their nests with beech.

Robin got Big John to stand against the trunk, with his head against it and his arms clasped round so as to give him a 'back'. But when he at last struggled upright, with his feet on Big John's shoulders, there was nothing to hold on to; the nearest branch was still beyond his reach.

He tried swarming, but the trunk was far too wide, and he slithered down, scratching his arms and knees.

'It's no good,' he said, 'we shall never get up this way. We shall have to get the climbing irons.'

'Let's try and find a branch to give you a start,' said Big John. 'If we can find a dead tree or something we might manage it that way.' So they searched about far and wide in the underbrush. At last Little John found a dead fir branch lying in some brambles near the pool. It was so big and heavy it took their united strength to drag it along, but after a terrific struggle they managed it, and reared it up against the rough trunk of the fir.

It made a precarious perch, but after some difficulty Robin got up among its topmost 'tines' and then, standing on the very tip, he found he could just reach the lowest branch. With all his strength he hauled himself up and the next moment the climb began.

The honey buzzard's nest

Robin had a bad head for heights. After the first twenty feet or so he had to take a rest. It was fairly straightforward work now, if he could only keep his wits, for the branches were plentiful, almost like the rungs of a ladder, going up and up above his head. He made up his mind that he would not look down. He said to himself, 'I *won't* look down! I *won't* look down!' But at last, exhausted, he reached a thick branch where he had to rest. Then he inadvertently glanced below.

Immediately he felt a horrible wave of sickness pass through him. Far beneath he glimpsed his two brothers, their faces absurdly dwarfed and white, gazing up at him, and behind them the Blind Pool – a bird's eye view of the Blind Pool – with the tops of the sallows and the green reed beds hedging it round.

Robin gasped and shut his eyes tightly. Then he looked above. He was not yet halfway up! He could never do it! 'What's the matter?' called Big John. 'What are you stopping for?'

Robin could not answer. He still kept his eyes tight shut, his cheek pressed tightly against the rough red trunk. The feel of that massive breadth of wood gave him comfort.

A small breeze was stirring among the tasselled needles and he felt the trunk sway ever so slightly. 'I'm all right, only a bit puffed,' he managed to gasp at last.

'You're nearly there,' called Little John to comfort him.

'Nearly there!' thought Robin, and he was not halfway! For quite five minutes he sat immovable, staring up at the nest above him. It certainly seemed much closer. He could see the individual sticks in the nest bottom and the tangled red boughs below it.

But no, he could not do it; he knew he could not. Yet if he was to come down now the others would know he was in a funk. He could never look them in the face again. He set his teeth and then continued to climb, vowing he would not look beneath him.

But as he climbed higher he could not help catching sideways glimpses of the forest below. Horror on horror! He was now looking down into the tops of some of the smaller oaks, and there, on all sides, stretched the unbroken surface of the Chase. It stretched away endlessly and beyond its outermost misty fringes he could see the open fields and yes, sure enough, there was Brendon away to the south, a cluster of red roofs and factory chimneys and over there Cheshunt Toller. He could see the tower of the church!

There was more wind up here now – he could hear it sighing in the pine top. He took another rest, fixedly gazing at the nest above. White clouds passed over against the blue sky; the fir needles whipped and tossed. He could never do it. 'How are you getting on?' came the voice of Big John. It sounded very far away. 'All right!' shouted Robin, without looking down. But he was *not* all right. His arms, hugging the trunk, were trembling, his whole body quivered as though he had an ague and his teeth chattered.

The nest was now some fifteen feet above. It looked a good deal closer. He could see much of its detail now. But Robin was all in. He could not climb another foot. His head swam and his mouth felt like an old boot.

For quite ten minutes he sat there motionless, not heeding the cries of his brothers below. Then he swung his leg over a branch. He was going to come down. It was no good, he could not go an inch higher!

At that moment the hen buzzard left the nest. There was an indescribable sound, a sort of blustering rush, and he saw the great barred bird sweep off the nest and she was gone.

'There she goes!' yelled Big John excitedly. 'There she goes!'

Robin, his eyes full of bark, and his hands and face scratched and torn, felt a sudden gleam of renewed enthusiasm. But it went as quickly as it had come. He felt like an amateur climber on a high mountain. He didn't care whether there were eggs or not; all he wanted was to get down again on to the ground, feel the firm earth under him and the yielding bracken brushing his bare knees.

'Go on!' called Big John again. 'You're nearly there.' Robin set his teeth. He reached up and caught the next branch above and for the next five minutes he climbed grimly and steadily, trembling so violently he could hardly grip the boughs. The great nest grew nearer and nearer; he could see it through his half-closed eyes. At last, Robin's grimy claw went up until it touched the rim. Even then he wanted to be back, back again on the good firm earth.

He gave another hunch and his hand felt over the rim. His fingers felt cold crisp leaves and then they encountered something hard, round and warm. 'EGGS!' he shouted.

'Good man,' shouted Little John. 'How many?'

'Can't say,' gasped Robin. His shaky fingers would not keep still. Only two! With a superhuman effort he managed to grasp one of them and without glancing at it he put it in his jacket pocket.

'Don't break 'em,' shouted Big John, 'put them in your mouth.'

'Silly little ass,' thought Robin. 'What did he think they were, robin's eggs?'

He looked below. And that one glance nearly sent him tumbling out of the fir. His brothers were standing at the base of the tree, little pigmies, their faces like white scraps of paper. Tiny particles of bark dust dislodged by his exertions wavered downwards into the giddy pit beneath. The Blind Pool looked no bigger than a duck pond. Robin gasped, his head swimming.

On all sides, like a vast green bowl, stretched Brendon Chase. Beyond were the rolling fields and the sunlit Weald. The little farms were like toy farms. He could see Brendon Park and the big red house standing among its many terraces with the lake to one side of it.

Ugh! It was horrible!

He shut his eyes again and then began to come down, taking care not to crush the egg in his pocket against a bough. Descending a tall tree is worse than going up because you have to look where you are putting your feet. The return to earth was a nightmare, indeed that climb of Robin's recurred for many years afterwards in the form of a terrible dream.

But eventually the worst was over, trees and bushes resumed their normal proportions and he no longer felt like a tiny fly perched on a precipice.

Down and down he came and at last he was at the final bough. His feet felt for the dead fir branch and the next moment he landed, both toes together, on the soft bracken. And what a sight he was! His knees and arms were red and raw, his eyes full of bits of bark and his face as black as the ground.

'Let's see the egg,' said Big John eagerly; 'do let's see it!' Robin put his hand in his pocket and drew out that round hard thing which had cost so much pluck and labour. There it lay, in the cup of his grimy claw, the loveliest treasure.

It was nearly round, with a white ground almost hidden by the most exquisite rich red-brown mottling.

'Phew!' gasped Big John. '*What* a beauty! Why didn't you take the lot?'

'Don't be an ass,' snapped Robin, 'there were only two and, really, we shouldn't have taken this one. But . . . after that climb I *had* to!'

He took up the egg and turned it over. Was there ever such a glorious prize as this honey buzzard's egg?

'My!' gasped Robin in spite of himself. 'But it was worth that awful climb.'

'Why awful climb?' asked Little John. 'It was an easy tree, wasn't it?'

'Easy tree,' replied Robin with scorn, 'I'd like to see either of you go up there! I thought I should never do it. You can see for miles from the top – you can see Brendon and the Weald and the whole forest.' Then he realized that his brothers, standing on the ground, could never visualize that staggering view, they could never guess what sickening agony he had been through up there in the pine top.

But there was a glow inside him which warmed him like a fire. He had overcome his cowardice and giddiness and by sheer pluck had won through. And this glorious egg had been worth it – it was a jewel beyond price. 'Feels pretty heavy,' said Big John who was holding it up to the light. 'We'll have a job to blow it.'

Robin took the egg. 'Here, give it to me, you'll break it. And if that happened,' Robin glared at Big John, ' . . . why I believe I'd kill you!'

Overhead they heard the mewing cry once more and saw both birds come wheeling over the oaks. They circled round in wide circles, barely moving their strikingly barred and spotted wings.

Robin watched them and suddenly he felt rather a mean beast. Pity there had been only two eggs in the nest! But honey buzzards do not lay more than three at the most. Perhaps that was why they were so rare! He looked at the egg again in his hand. It was a shame to take it, a rotten shame! Up there in the pine top the true significance of his act had not been apparent. Yet it was such a beautiful egg and to once more undergo that frightful ordeal by height was unthinkable.

He held it up to the sun as Big John had done. If an egg is new laid it is semi-transparent. But this blotched and clouded egg was difficult to see through. It certainly felt queer. Then he shook it against his ear. Immediately he knew that all was well. There would be no need now to contemplate returning this treasure – it was addled! As he shook it he heard the 'slop slop' of liquid inside, a sure sign that it was rotten.

He heaved a deep sigh, a sigh of satisfaction and relief. It was as though he had been rewarded for his pluck by a kindly Providence. He need have no qualms now about robbing those wheeling birds, whose hold on existence was as precarious as his had been a few short minutes ago!

When they returned to camp they blew the prize. The smell was appalling, but the job was safely done. Robin still has that egg in his collection and whenever he looks at it the memory of his great ordeal returns.

A week after Robin Hood's great climb, Big John came running into camp one morning, breathless with excitement. He had been out collecting firewood not far from the clearing when, so he said, he had heard a great humming noise and looking up he had seen a dark cloud of bees buzzing round the top of an old oak stump. 'There's millions of them,' gasped Big John, 'they're swarming, just like Rumbold's bees. Can't we take the swarm?' The others jumped up and hurried after him. In the glorious sunlight which flooded one of the many little forest clearings, Big John pointed to an oak stump. It was apparently hollow and all about its crown the bees darkened the sky like a miniature dust storm.

'I'll bet there's some honey in that tree,' said Big John, 'if we could only get it out. Honey will keep for years and years if the combs aren't broken. How grand it would be if we could get some!'

'There goes the swarm,' exclaimed Little John excitedly. 'The old queen's off and is taking her retainers with her. Let's follow!'

'Not a hope,' said Robin, 'they may go for miles across the forest until they swarm properly.'

But the bees did not go far. With a deep terrifying hum they passed over the clearing and all alighted on a sallow branch. Soon the great, brown, rather revolting looking ball of glistening insects began to weigh it down until it hung suspended, appearing not unlike a bulging shopping bag.

'If only we had a hive to put them in!' exclaimed Little John. 'Can't we make one?'

Robin was sitting deep in thought, watching the swarm as it hung there motionless.

'I have it! Let's make a straw hive like Rumbold's; they're easy to make. I saw him make one once.'

'But we haven't any straw!'

'No, but we can find some long dried grass, there's heaps of it along the rides. Come on!'

They soon found all the dead grass they required and they plucked armfuls of it. Robin began twisting it up into a thick rope, in the way he had seen Rumbold do at the Dower House. Soon they had a long length of it, firmly bound together. They coiled it round on itself, twisting it all the time, until they had made a sort of dome-shaped hat of hay. They bound each successive rope with cross lashings of briar and in a remarkably short time had constructed quite a professional looking hive.

'Now we've made the beastly thing,' observed Robin, 'I expect when we get back to the clearing the bees will have gone.' But they had not. The big glistening bag still hung suspended from the sallow, not five feet from the ground.

'It's all right,' said Robin, who knew something of the ways of those mysterious little creatures who work so hard and live in such disciplined communities. 'I don't think they'll go now. We'll wait until a bit later, just when the sun's getting low, and then we'll take the swarm. But first we must decide where we're going to have it. We mustn't put it too near our tree. We'll hide it away in a little open space somewhere, close by, where it will be handy to camp.'

With a little searching they found such a place within ten minutes' walk of their oak, and there, as though it had been planned purposely, was an ash butt which made a natural table. It was a stump, some four feet in height, with a fairly even top and on this they decided to place the hive when they had taken the swarm.

Robin took a little of their precious sugar and, mixing it with water, splashed the mixture inside the plaited grass hive. 'That's to make 'em feel at home,' said Robin. 'They always like the inside of the new hive smelling sweet.' It now remained to get the bees and it took some courage to approach that glistening crawling bag. There was enough poison in those little creatures to kill the boys many times over.

But they had often seen Rumbold take a swarm and had even helped him, and had never been badly stung. So when the sun set, they spread Little John's coat flat on the ground and placed the hive on top, raising the whole contraption a few inches on a levelled mound of loam.

They made a little door at the base of the hive and placed a flat piece of wood covered with a white handkerchief at the entrance, tilting it slightly so as to make a little ladder. Then, very carefully, Robin cut the branch above the swarm with his hunting knife, moving gently and smoothly as he had seen Rumbold do, and as gently the whole swarm was lowered to the spread coat in front of the ladder to the hive. The bees soon found this little bridge. First went the large queen and after her all her train. It took some while for all the bees to crawl inside, but they did so just as though they knew a house had been prepared for them. 'I can't think why they don't fly off again,' said Little John, 'they're awfully obliging little beasts.'

When at last darkness had come all the bees had retired to bed and they carried the hive – which boomed angrily within – to the little clearing and put it on the log. Robin was careful to leave a little ledge outside the entrance as an alighting board.

The coat was withdrawn very gingerly, but most of the bees had – as Robin had known they would – gone up under the dome of the nest.

Next morning when they visited it they found that the bees had already settled down in their new home and had begun work, flying in and out just like Rumbold's bees in the orchard at home!

'When shall we get some honey?' asked Little John. 'How long shall we have to wait for it?'

'Well, we ought to get some honey in August. She's an old queen and will lay plenty of eggs.'

'What's happened to the young queen?' asked Little John, whose knowledge of the ways of bees was obviously sketchy.

'Oh, she's still in the original tree. That reminds me, chaps. We'll have a look at the old nest. If only we could get inside that tree we should find pounds and pounds of honey!'

When they examined the oak stump carefully they saw that, as is usual in trees where honeybees hive, it was hollow. There was room for one person to stand inside the trunk and they could hear the humming of the hive above their heads. The wood seemed to be rotten so they hacked and poked until at last a lump of touchwood came away and several bees fell through from the nest above. One of them landed down Robin's neck and promptly stung him.

If they were to take the honey they must be quick, for the bees up above were beginning to be suspicious. The boys quickly built a fire inside the tree and piled on sodden leaves and moss to make a dense white smoke. This was soon seen issuing from the top of the stump above their heads in a thick yellowy-blue spiral and the bees, unable to stand the blind choking reek, began to leave the nest and fly off to the surrounding trees. Many, quite stupefied, fell down inside the tree and Big John was stung three times on the head and neck.

When all had ceased to issue from the upper hole, Robin again assaulted the mass of rotten wood above his head. Suddenly it came away, crumbling, and there were the combs, one on top of the other in tiers, every one symmetrical and perfect, cemented to the inner skin of the oak stump. The upper combs were a rich brown, almost a mahogany, tint. 'Those are the old combs,' said Robin, who was now dislodging the golden treasure and passing it down to his brother outlaws. 'The upper ones are always dark like that. These bees have been here for years and years. My gracious! There's nearly half a hundredweight of honey in this stump.' And indeed there was.

Even the old honey was as good as the new, though it had been there for ten years, possibly more.

Covered in bee stings and with honey all over their clothes, the outlaws went back to the clearing, carrying their spoils. They stored the combs in a large cavity in their oak tree and helped themselves whenever they felt inclined. There would be no more hankering for sweet things now. The forest had provided their sugar.

And as for the bees in the skip, they settled down well and would no doubt have provided the outlaws with another golden harvest in August had not some creature – Robin said it was a badger – broken open the hive one night and robbed them of every bee.

9. Bunting

THE MYSTERY of how Harold had escaped from the Dower House was quite baffling to Aunt Ellen and to the police. His bedroom door had been locked on the outside – had she not opened it herself that morning when he was due to return to school? – and close search below the window showed no trace of footmarks. Yet, somehow or another, he had got out of the house and, stranger still, had taken with him various commodities from the kitchen. Then, Sergeant Bunting concluded that his brothers had forced an entrance to the Dower House and it was they who had unlocked the bedroom door, and ransacked the kitchen cupboards.

He said as much to Aunt Ellen. Indeed, there seemed no other explanation. A search of all the windows and doors revealed no clue to the way the boys had got into the house. The coal chute had not been used for years and nobody suspected it was there. Hidden away under the shrubberies it was quite invisible, though I admit that Sergeant Bunting, had he been a little more thorough, would certainly have found it. But there we are. It was not found, and the mystery was a baffling one to everyone concerned.

Naturally, since the boys had been observed in High Wood, a very close watch was kept upon it and the adjacent covers. But the fugitives seemed to have disappeared as mysteriously as they had arrived.

By now Aunt Ellen had ceased to worry. She had become resigned and went about with the air of a martyr. Of course, since the chase at High Wood, the whole affair had become big news, not only in the local county paper, but in the London papers as well.

Various suggestions were offered in the readers' columns for the capture of the boys, some very original.

The *Morning Star* – with an eye to self-advertisement – then offered a substantial reward for any information which led to the discovery of the boys and this set every amateur detective on the 'qui vive'. The Woodman's Arms complained of lack of custom. Many of its regular patrons were out scouring the fields and woods. Sir William, in despair, went to the Riviera and tried to forget it all.

Sergeant Bunting, however, anxious to justify his reputation as a smart man, haunted the Dower House after dark. He decided that if the boys had come back for supplies they would come again, and it was only a matter of watching and waiting.

Many a weary vigil he spent doubled up in the shrubberies and in various stable lofts, his only companions owls, rats and mice. The days passed, and no word was brought by any of the voluntary searchers, and after a while the bar of the Woodman's Arms began to fill again at night, and other topics than 'Them Dower 'Ouse Boys' were discussed.

As for Sergeant Bunting, his name was mud. Everyone said it just showed how powerless were the police and how easy it was for criminals to hide. The boys had, of course, committed no crime in law, unless Rumbold wished to press a charge of stealing, which was of course untrue. The boys had not 'stolen' the rifle, they had 'borrowed' it and honourably intended to return it as soon as they became tired of living in the forest.

They could perhaps be arrested for vagabondage, for loitering even, without visible means of subsistence, if what Aunt Ellen said was true – that they had no money with them. As a matter of fact Little John had fifteen shillings in silver in his purse, so that charge would not hold good in law. It was very complicated.

However, they were minors, and Sir William, who was a magistrate, said he would like to have the boys well birched. He really meant it.

Truth to say, Aunt Ellen was a little relieved when she heard the news of the boys being seen in High Wood. At any rate they were well and had come to no harm. Of course it was very wrong of them to run away like that – in fact wrong was not a strong enough word – but she was nevertheless relieved.

The month of June dragged on in baking heat. Never had there been such a year for the hay. It was a record crop. Rain at nights had been ideal. And as the labourers took their midday meals under hedge and bank the topic of the boys' disappearance was still on every tongue.

'They'll be caught in 'Igh Wood, you mark my words.'

'I reckon they ain't there at all, but 'iding in some of the lofts up at the Dower 'Ouse.'

Nobody thought of the Chase . . . nobody, that is, save Sergeant Bunting.

Though Brendon Chase was off Bunting's beat he nightly contacted PC Cornes at Martyr Bar, four miles distant from Cherry Walden. PC Cornes, a cadaverous, melancholy man, had, on Bunting's suggestion, been snooping round the Chase. He had been to see Smokoe Joe the charcoal burner, but Smokoe had told him he'd seen nobody in the Chase, 'blame him if he had,' neither had he heard any shots or seen signs of fires. This was not surprising. Smokoe was getting on, his sight was not very good and his hearing worse. A whole tribe of outlaws might have been encamped within half a mile of him and he would not know it. He did not wander much from his little shack of pine logs, though every Saturday he trudged the three and a half miles into Cheshunt Toller, the nearest village – and braved the taunts of the village boys. There he purchased his meagre supplies. He lived alone with only a half spaniel, half terrier for company – if you did not count his hens and pigs. He drew his water from an old well behind the shack and occasionally he shot a rabbit or a pheasant when he wanted something for the pot. In hard weather he had even bagged a deer or two; these he sold to a butcher in Cheshunt Toller, one Samuel Snigg.

He was a wizened, whiskered little creature, who suffered from elephantiasis of the nose. At all seasons of the year he wore a leather jerkin, which he kept together with a broad leather belt about his middle, and wore a funny conical old felt hat shaped like an apple pudding.

In short, he was what one would call a very picturesque character, like something out of Grimms' fairy tales. All his life he had lived in forests, like his forebears for generations back; trees were 'in his blood'. They said up in the village that he was a wizard and could cure warts and wens, despite the fact he could not cure his appalling nose which made him look like a wrinkled old gnome. His dog he loved as a man loves a brother. It was his only joy and constant companion, he worshipped it.

During the summer months, when he was not working at his furnace, he did a little mowing along the ridings near his shack. He did not regard the forest with any wonder or delight, though he had a good knowledge of natural history, especially of birds and butterflies. Yet if – as was once suggested – he had left the Chase, given up his charcoal burning and settled down in one of the new council houses in Cheshunt Toller, he would have been wretched indeed. The trees were in his blood, as the sea is in a sailor's. Perhaps the Chase was like the sea sometimes. Smokoe often thought so, when on a gusty winter's night, he heard the wind booming over the forest, or in summer saw the massive oaks bending and roaring before a westerly gale. Some people said he was a man of considerable means and had hundreds of pounds hidden somewhere about his dwelling. Many speculated where the hidden gold was concealed; in the well, under his mattress – which consisted of sacks stuffed with bracken – or somewhere in the chimney.

Twice a year, in spring and autumn, he had a good spring clean. In some ways he was very like a badger. He brought out the filthy old sacks and pulled out the bracken of yesteryear, replenishing them with fresh dried fronds.

His gun was an old muzzle-loader, a wonderful weapon with a belled mouth, the barrel bound with brass bands to the scarred wooden stock. Once, 'twas said, it had been carried by the guard of the London–Brendon coach. How he came by it nobody knew.

Such was old Smokoe Joe, a bit of a wizard – who wouldn't be living all alone in such a place? – very much a character, a strange half gipsy, half poacher hybrid, who had no use for his fellow men – or they for him – set apart by the consciousness of his deformity, leathery as an old tortoise, wrinkled as an aged monkey, hard as nails and as some said, as strong as a man half his age. Nobody knew how old he was; Smokoe didn't know himself. He never bothered about the time but lived and ordered his days by the sun and seasons.

PC Cornes got no change out of old Smokoe. Very few people did. And Smokoe's dog very nearly took a piece out of the constable's leg. It ran off with one of his bicycle clips and Cornes never got it back. He was so angry that he nearly asked Smokoe if he had a dog licence but thought better of it.

Bunting, who had not much use for Cornes because he was so melancholy and never wanted to better himself, resolved to go to the Chase himself and take a look round. You never know, the boys might have gone there; Smokoe and Cornes wouldn't be any the wiser.

And so one day in early July the sergeant got out his bicycle and propelled himself out of Cherry Walden and headed for the Chase. It was unfortunate perhaps that he had chosen such a hot day; indeed, it was the hottest day of that very hot summer.

Behold him then, that square majestic figure, trundling away down the Brendon road, correct in every detail of his uniform, white gloves tucked into his tunic, his buttons shining, his blue cloth uniform – a little shiny at the seat of the trousers – neatly brushed by Mrs Bunting. Behold, that ponderous buttress of the law moving inexorably onward down the shadow-banded road under the limes.

In those days there was no tarmac as we know it now, no ferroconcrete highways beribboned with white lines. The Brendon road was little wider than a by-lane is today and it was white with dust which rose behind his back wheel in a little smoking trail like a powder train.

It is a 'give and take' road, the Brendon road; it flows up and down through pleasantly wooded country, skirting the foot of the Weald. It passes through two villages and over four canal bridges and finally, just before you get to Martyr Bar, which is four miles this side of the Chase, it passes over the Blindrush, the same stream which finds its origin in no more delectable a birthplace than the Blind Pool.

At Martyr Bar, however, it is already less impetuous. It flows sedately over its chalk bed, glassy clear, wagging as it goes the manes of waterweed and toying with sturdy reed beds where the village ducks, as white as snow, disport themselves with sparkling delight. After Martyr Bar bridge it flows on through pleasant meadows until it reaches Brendon Park, the seat of the Duke of Brendon. There the common herd may no longer gaze upon its tamed condition save on those rare occasions such as Conservative fêtes and Coronation Days.

When Bunting reached Martyr bridge he felt warmer than he had ever done in his life. He dismounted, took off his helmet and mopped his forehead with a very white handkerchief. As he stood there, looking at the cool waters of the Blindrush twinkling in the sunlight, he heard the sound of an approaching vehicle. At first he thought it was a traction engine, but in a moment there swept round the bend the ancient De Dion which belonged to the Whiting. It came thumping its way through the heat, shuddering and steaming, and swept past Bunting in a cloud of white chalk dust, which covered him from head to foot.

The vicar, absentminded as always, and whose whole attention was rivetted on keeping this amazing vehicle in the middle of the narrow bridge – no easy matter – never even glanced at Bunting.

The latter watched the coughing thumping machine whirl round the bend by The Martyr and then, after dusting down his tunic with his handkerchief, he remounted his bicycle. The time was a little after midday. The clock on the church tower advertised this fact. Bunting, in addition to being extremely hot, was also very thirsty. Though it is not permissible for police to take alcoholic refreshment when on duty, circumstances were different in this case. He would 'put one back' at The Martyr before going on to the Chase.

He leant his bicycle against the wall under the hanging sign, which depicted a bearded person in a nightshirt transfixed by arrows, and entered the cool parlour which smelt of beer. It was empty for it was yet early. This was excellent; he could have a drink. The landlord, who happened to be Bunting's brother-in-law, gave him a cheery welcome and when Bunting ordered a pint he went down into his little cool cellar behind the bar, where three small barrels stood in a row against the whitewashed wall.

The sound of beer trickling into a large tankard was heavenly music. Bunting pulled at his waxed moustache and gazed solemnly at the stuffed trout over the mantelpiece. Inside the taproom there was a curious reflected light which came upwards from the dazzling sunlit chalk road without. Flies were waltzing lazily around a fly paper which dangled from the gas bracket in the middle of the ceiling. He kept a strict eye on the village street in case anyone should see him quenching his thirst.

'It's a hot 'un today, Tom,' said the landlord, setting down the cold frothy tankard on the table and passing a cloth along the bar top.

'Ah, that it is, Ernie, 'ottest day o' the year.' Bunting took up the tankard and drained it rapidly. 'I saw a good trout under the bridge yonder.'

'Ah, they be some good fish there,' the landlord sniffed, and drew himself half a pint at his brother-in-law's expense.

''Bout the best thing to be on a day like this,' said Bunting, 'nice an' cool an' all, swimmin' around.'

'Ah. Well, Tom, 'ow goes it?'

'Oh, so, so, Ernie. Mabel's well and the kids are fit. She asked to be remembered to you, she ain't seen you since Christmas she said.'

'Ain't 'eard nothing o' the young gents from the Dower 'Ouse I suppose?' asked Tom. 'It's in all the papers o' course, as you know.'

'No, not yet,' replied Bunting, shaking his head gravely. 'It's only a matter o' time though, only a matter o' time, Ernie.'

'Shouldn't be surprised if they aren't in the Chase,' said the landlord. 'The missus says she reckons that's where they'd be. It's a big place.'

Bunting shook his head again.

'Cornes 'as been 'angin' about there a lot, but 'e ain't seen nuthin'. Smokoe Joe 'asn't seen 'em I suppose?'

'Smokoe Joe!' the landlord laughed. 'Smokoe Joe wouldn't see nobody not if a 'ol army were sitting on his doorstep! You goin' to 'ave a look round the Chase, Tom? You'll find it a warmish job today.'

'Maybe yes, maybe no.'

'I ain't tryin' to be inquisitive, Tom,' said his brother-in-law, 'but it might pay ye to take a look round. Between you an' me,' he added leaning over the bar, 'Cornes ain't what you'd call a keen man, you know what I mean, too easy-goin' like. Nice chap an' all that, oh yes! I got nothin' agin 'im, but too easy-goin' be half. Take His Grace's ricks fer instance in Yoho parish, which were set afire two years ago, well – I mean to say!'

Bunting had no intention of discussing a colleague, even with his brother-in-law.

'Ah well, Ernie, I'll be movin' along. I'm much obliged to you for you-know-what.' Bunting winked and nodded his head towards the tankard. 'I'll look in on me way 'ome.'

'Good afternoon, Tom, see you later.'

'Ah! Cheerio.'

Coming out of the cool bar parlour was like stepping into a greenhouse. Bunting blew out his cheeks and wiped his moustache furtively. He wished he'd come on another day when it was a bit cooler. It was a long pull up to the Chase.

He then mounted his bicycle from the step. He placed his left foot in the peg and punted with his right, and then, with impressive and even graceful dignity, lowered himself into the saddle. Soon there were no sounds but the gritty rustle of his bicycle wheels on the dusty road. His blue shadow moved along before him; the sun seemed to bore into his broad back. From Martyr Bar the road is, for two miles at least, treeless, until you reach the hamlet which rejoices in the whimsical name of Yoho. Cornfields come up to the road on either hand with low walls of stone, which is quarried locally. Somehow, these stone walls seemed to reflect the heat, and the road was truly like an oven.

Larks sang high overhead and corn buntings sat on top of the gateposts and jingled to Bunting as he went by with their maddening, reiterated apology for a song. Not a tree! Only a foot of blue shade from the left hand wall and that was on the dusty grass.

Bunting reached the foot of the long slope and dismounted. Now for it! The road stretched away, a white ribbon before him, bounded by its stone walls until it met the hard unyielding blue of the sky; the glare of the chalk dazzled him, his head swam.

His trousers were now grey, instead of blue, and the sweat, running down from under his helmet, made unsightly runnels down his well-shaved cheeks. But at last the top of the hill was reached and there below he saw the hamlet of

Yoho and beyond it Brendon Chase, a long low line of dark trees like a wall on his left. Before he entered the hamlet – there were only six houses besides the doctor's house, no church and no store – he reached a by-lane which turned off towards the Chase, close by a house which had a painted board announcing '*The Forest Retreat. Teas, Hovis Bread*'. And in a moment or two he had reached the outposts of the Chase.

This lane cut through one end of the Chase, right through, in a straight line for two miles. Along the white surface the air quivered and jumped; the trees seemed to waver up and down. Butterflies flew from one side of the road to the other. Far down the road, drawn up on the side, he saw a quivering mirage. Was it a gipsy van? A lorry? A steamroller?

Soon, as he pedalled nearer, he saw it was a car, and a little later, that it was the vicar's car. Well now, wasn't that a coincidence! If only Bunting had known the vicar was going to the Chase he might have begged a lift and been saved this terrible roasting ride. The vicar would be after butterflies no doubt.

When he came up to the car he looked over the gate and there, sure enough, was the Whiting. He was a long way off. He was running away down the wide grassy path making passes at an invisible insect. Bunting took off his helmet and mopped his head. He thought that the vicar might have found some more profitable hobby than running about after butterflies . . . golf for instance, he could understand that, but butterflies and bugs!

Well, he didn't particularly want to meet him. He would go on down the road until he came to the next ride, which, according to Cornes, led to Smokoe Joe's cabin. Bunting decided he would go and see Smokoe himself and try to get some information out of him. Cornes was only a common constable; the sergeant's stripes might impress Smokoe.

Bunting was not quite sure that this second ride was the right one. At last he came to it and he pushed his bicycle through the gate and leant it up against the hedge.

Had the ride been less narrow and not so rutty he would have cycled along it, but it was better to walk. Cornes said Smokoe's cabin was not more than half a mile along the ride.

Bunting thought that he would find it cooler in the woods but it was not so. In addition to the heat, with every step he took flies came joyously swarming round his head. They seemed to have been waiting for him to come along, killing time as it were, until he arrived. Now they teased his ears, his nose, they got caught in his moustache, they crawled up the short hairs of his neck. When he opened his mouth to puff and blow they were drawn down his throat. He cut himself a switch and winnowed vigorously and this, in a measure, gave some relief, but the flies still darted under his guard. Their maddening buzzings nearly drove him frantic. The ride became narrower and finally dwindled into a mere path, and not a well-worn path at that. Then it divided. He took the right hand fork; there was nothing to choose between them. Then it divided again. This could not be the path to Smokoe Joe's. He must go back. He turned round and retraced his steps; soon he was not quite sure he recognized the path he was on. Sallow and thorn hedged him round. He came to a sallow which had fallen across the path. *He had not been down this ride before!* Sergeant Bunting was lost, bushed, what you will, in the eleven thousand acres of Brendon Chase! He did not know in which direction his road lay. Only the sun was there to give him any clue.

Sergeant Bunting was very angry. It was all the fault of that silly idiot Cornes. Cornes should have come with him and shown him the way.

He might come on that old fool of a parson. He stopped, exhausted. Heaven knows where he was. The air was full of the low teasing hum of flies and a plaintive robin let fall a melancholy trickle of notes from the depths of the bushes. He smelt the hot leaves and dried grass and the shiny mounded oak trees.

A jay screamed; he just caught a glimpse of it as it bobbed about among the oak leaves. Perspiration ran down suddenly from under his helmet. Sergeant Bunting felt foolish. A fully uniformed policeman in the middle of Brendon Chase! My word, if he could only catch those boys! Instead of the sun's rays becoming less hot, as the afternoon drew on they became more torrid.

Never, never, never had Sergeant Bunting experienced such heat. He had expected a welcoming shade here, a pleasant ramble through the Chase to Smokoe's place, a useful chat and a nice ride home in the cool of the evening. He thought of the Blindrush. How he longed for a swim.

Bunting was a great swimmer. He had once won a cup for water polo in the Police Sports. He went on wearily. Sometime surely he must come to a road of some sort. His one desire now was to get out of the Chase. He hated the trees, bushes and the endless fern.

Some dark-maned firs appeared over the oaks and sallows. He certainly did not remember those!

Then the track he was following died away in a jungle of bracken and briar and – lo! – he found himself on the edge of . . . the Blind Pool.

This revelation was quite startling. He had heard of the pool, of course, as the source of the Blindrush, but he had never seen it. And suddenly here it was, a dark still water, looking incredibly deep and cool with its white lilies flat open to the sun!

Moorhens scurried into the reeds when he stepped from the bushes and a wild duck scrambled, quacking loudly, at the far end. It could not fly properly because it was moulting out its flights. It hurtled along the surface making a great noise and disappeared into some thick willows. The disturbed water calmed to stillness. Not a bird moved. He felt that many little creatures were regarding him.

But oh, the water, the dark green water, where the midges weaved and played!

'Oh frabjous day! Callooh! Callay!' he might have sung, had he known the classics. Here, at any rate, he would rest awhile, and he would swim. Yes, he would *swim*! In this forest pool all alone, unseen, Sergeant Bunting would become once more human!

In a moment his helmet was off, then his jacket and trousers. His shirt was pulled over his head, off came his underpants, vest, socks and boots.

Close by was a mossy log half in the water. It was trampled by the feet of water fowl. Feathers lay about, grey and white. He walked down it. His feet were bare, vast grimy feet, grimed with the dust of all those Cherry Walden miles, freed now from their sweaty prisons! The moss was yielding, cold, soft, like velvet.

Sergeant Bunting poised on the end of the log. Below the water was deep, so deep, a shoal of silver fishes darted, affrighted, by. Up went his arms above his head. He stood to attention there naked, white, pot-bellied – alas! The years had presented him with an ample waistline – in the hot sun, poised with arms outstretched. Then he sprang, and the icy water shut over his head.

He came up, some yards out, and shook the water from his ears and nose like a joyful spaniel, and struck out.

How glorious! How perfectly miraculous! The ride, that long ride from Cherry Walden, had been worth this! Yes, it had been worth it! He had not had a swim for years.

To enjoy swimming to the full one must swim naked. It is the natural way, it is therefore essentially right. From cradle to the grave we swaddle our bodies in clothes night and day.

Bunting swam right across the pool, overarm, then he turned over and swam breaststroke, slowly. The water lapped his mouth. He passed through a cloud of midges, he smelt the rare leafy tang of the woodland water. He skirted the lily beds – once or twice feeling the sinister snaky coils of their roots against his kicking legs. He turned on his back and floated like an upturned chubby boat, staring into the summer blue. Oh, it was heaven! It was *heaven!*

The sweat, the dusty road, the burning heat, the flies and briars, all had gone in this cool parlour. He floated dreamily, oaring quietly with his cupped hands like some woodland satyr, staring up, staring up.

A jay screamed again in the distance, once, otherwise a dreamy stillness settled on this place, this paradise. He drifted into the shadow where the water suddenly felt cold and the dazzle was shut away. Willows overhung him. A waterfowl complained nearby.

Oh! The keen clasp of the dreamy water! Oh! The cool embrace of the Blind Pool, bearing him up!

10. The Whiting

WHEN the Whiting's iron juggernaut came to a standstill with a final gasping hiccup, his first act was to rummage in the back seat for his butterfly net. It was a green one, jointed, Watkins and Doncaster's best. His second act was to sling across his shoulders the haversack containing (1) a bottle of pale ale, (2) a thick packet of ham sandwiches, (3) a hard-boiled egg and radishes, and finally, wrapped carefully in tissue paper, the leg of a chicken. His 'old body' he reflected, was a real treasure. Without her he would be in a bad way. Several people, including Aunt Ellen, had told him so, as if he didn't know!

The car was making strange gurgling noises in her intestines, so the Whiting went round to the front and looked at the radiator almost tenderly. She was boiling, poor dear, and no wonder, on a day like this! But later, he reflected, the nearby oaks would cast shade; the old car would cool down.

He climbed the gate and wandered along the ride, close to the bushes, his eyes – very sharp eyes they were – taking in every detail of leaf and stem. There was a fine sallow bush! Just the place for a purple emperor! Yet he had never seen one in this forest. It was his great ambition to do so. It was the one of the few British butterflies he had never seen.

He examined the bush very carefully with the close scrutiny of a treecreeper, pulling down the branches so that the pale soft undersides of the leaves were revealed to his penetrating gaze. But all he saw were beetles, strange hammer-headed beetles. He passed on, working his way very slowly, peering like a bird at every little leaf.

Now and again he scanned the oak tops until his eyes ached. What a fool to leave his green glasses behind. The 'old body' could not be expected to remember everything . . . How still and hot the forest lay under the burning July sun. Oh, for a purple emperor!

A tawny red butterfly appeared over the bushes and settled on a blossom of blackberry flower. It was a comma, quite a good thing. He made a pass at it with the net and missed, then he pursued it for some way down the ride until it eventually disappeared over some hazels. Bother! It had been a good specimen too . . . He went on, now down this ride, now down that. The meadow browns were hatching, they were bob, bobbing everywhere; nothing but meadow browns, drab meadow browns. They sat on the warm grass and seemed to look at him out of the cheeky painted eyes at the tips of their wings . . . He came to a junction of two main ridings. Here the oaks were tall and straight, fine trees. There was sallow too, jungles of sallow, everywhere. What a place for a purple emperor!

And then . . . he saw it, quite suddenly he saw it, the glorious regal insect of his dreams!

It was flying towards him down the ride and it settled for a moment on a leaf. Then, as he advanced, trembling with excitement, it soared heavenwards to the top of an oak. There he watched it, flitting round one of the topmost sprays far out of reach, mocking him, the unattainable, the jewel, the king of butterflies! It was well named the purple emperor – it was truly regal in form, colour and habits.

The old entomologists called it His Imperial Majesty! They were right, those old boys, it *was* an Imperial insect, and no mistake. The Whiting stood below looking up at it like a fox watching a pheasant in a tree.

But the maddening insect would not come down and after a while it floated from sight and he saw it no more. He heaved a sigh. At any rate he had seen it and could now tell the boys – if he ever saw them again – that *Apatura iris did* occur in Brendon Chase. Now – if only he had an old rabbit to hang up, that was the thing! Or if he could find a puddle or something. Emperors love moisture . . . If he was to come in the early morning he might have a chance . . . He pulled out his sandwiches and beer bottle and then found he had forgotten the opener for the bottle, so he had to prise it off with his knife. Oh dear! That old brain of his! It was getting worse, so his housekeeper told him. Only that morning he had come down to breakfast in two waistcoats. He finished his leisurely meal at last and then continued his search.

He left the main ride and wandered on towards the Blind Pool which he knew lay somewhere on his left. Like Bunting, who was also battling through the Chase not so far away, the Whiting began to suffer dreadfully from the heat. But it did not seem to take him long to reach the little path he knew led to the pool. Why shouldn't the purple emperor be there? He could imagine it in the hot sun, floating down like a large black and white leaf to drink at the muddy margin.

As he approached the pool he thought, once, he heard something moving in the underwood on the left of the path. The ferns shook as though some animal was making that way, but after a second or two all was still. A deer perhaps, or a rabbit . . . When at last he pushed out of the bushes he saw the pool, silent as usual and deserted, though many ripples came widening from under the willows. Waterfowl, no doubt, fleeing into hiding. But there was no fine emperor floating about in the hot sunlight, or drinking the dark green waters, so after a smoke on the bank and another pull at his beer bottle, he made his way back down the path by which he had come. Already the sun was westering. By the time he reached the car most of the butterflies had gone to bed.

He found the old De Dion awaiting him beyond the gate like a patient horse and she started up at

The roebuck of the Blind Pool

the first wind of the handle, shuddering and roaring and blowing blue acrid smoke from her rear. He threw his knapsack containing the remains of his lunch on to the back seat and his net followed suit. The knapsack fell off the seat on to the floor but he never bothered to look round.

Then he put her in gear and away he went down the straight white road in a cloud of dust. *He had seen a purple emperor!* He could think of nothing else. He would try and come again while the hot weather lasted. He would come with a very ripe rabbit and hang it up on one of the oaks!

The snorting chariot whirled along, and soon the Chase was left far behind. Martyr Bar flashed by, the shirtsleeved Ernie standing at the inn door, on over the bridge, up hill and down dale, whirling along through the evening air which was now so cool and soft.

White ducks flew quacking dismally almost under his wheels, hens, cats and dogs fled right and left, and the scented evening was tainted with the fumes of exhaust long after the ancient car had passed on its way. And at last he saw the tower of his old church above the sweet-scented lime trees and a minute later drove into the stable yard of the vicarage. It had been an interesting day, a very interesting day. But it was a pity he had not had time to look up Smokoe Joe.

His old housekeeper came bustling out to meet him.

'Well, sir, so you've got back safe and sound. I 'ope you've 'ad a good day and brought back all your things.'

'Yes, yes, a very interesting day, but hot you know, terribly hot.'

The 'old body' opened the rear door and drew out a haversack. Then her eyes popped out on stalks and the goitre seemed to bob up and down. 'Why, sir, whatever ... Whatever 'ave you got there?'

'Eh? Eh? What's that you say?' The Whiting came bustling to her side. On the back seat was a pair of blue serge trousers, a pair of socks, pants and vest, and a sergeant's tunic, *a police sergeant's tunic*!

'I can't understand it, I can't understand it,' repeated the Whiting in a feeble voice. 'I never put them there, I don't understand it!'

The housekeeper pulled out the tunic, the breast pocket of which was bulging with papers. A quick scrutiny revealed the rightful owner.

'Sergeant Bunting's tunic,' gasped the Whiting incredulously, 'I've never seen him all day. What on earth are his things doing in my car?'

'That's what I want to know,' said the housekeeper grimly. 'I expect it's some more of your absentmindedness, sir.'

And that also was what Sergeant Bunting would want to know, as soon as he returned to Cherry Walden, clothed in another man's trousers.

Bunting, floating under the willows of the Blind Pool, heard a cracking of sticks from across the water. He turned over like a big white porpoise and held on to a willow bough. Water beetles tickled his legs. He stared out from under the leaves. Good heavens! *Somebody was coming through the bushes!* And then, as his heart beat faster, he saw a green butterfly net waving over the underwood and a second later the squat figure of the vicar appeared. He saw him stand awhile gazing round; once he looked in Bunting's direction but did not see him. What a bit of luck! Though had the Whiting arrived on the scene a couple of minutes earlier, he, Bunting, would have been basking like a shark in mid-water. But what if the vicar saw his uniform and clothes? They were tucked under some hazels on that side of the pond not far from where the vicar stood. He saw the Whiting light a cigarette and sit down on the ferny bank. And all this while the unfortunate Bunting dared not move as, with every movement, ripples lapped outwards betraying his position. At last the Whiting got up and tossed away his cigarette and disappeared into the trees. He had gone! Thank heavens!

Bunting heaved a sigh of relief. How very awkward; he would have looked extremely foolish had the Whiting caught him there, swimming stark naked in the Blind Pool!

Bunting had been in the water for the best part of an hour and he was glad to get out. Bother the old parson. Fancy him coming like that!

He tiptoed gingerly through the ferns to where he had left his clothes. Then he stopped as if shot. His shirt was there, and his boots and helmet and white gloves, but that was all. The rest of his garments – his blue serge trousers, his tunic, his vest and pants – had gone!

The unfortunate man was so aghast he could not move. Wildly he looked about him, perhaps some animal had taken them, perhaps . . . he felt a cold clutch at his heart – perhaps the Whiting, in a fit of his notorious absentmindedness, had taken them! Feverishly he seized his shirt and put it on before that, too, was spirited away. He was shivering now, not with cold, for on such a day that was impossible, but with agitation.

He put on his boots and helmet and then began to search wildly all along the side of the Blind Pool, under every bush and tree, behind every reed clump. But no trace of the missing garments was to be found. It must have been the vicar. But why, in heaven's name, why should he have taken them?

Some cruel trick was being played upon him. What was he to do? How could he, a Sergeant of Police, return to Cherry Walden clad only in his helmet, shirt, boots and gloves? He would be looked upon as a madman!

The hapless wretch was beside himself. What was he to do? What *was* he to do? he kept repeating to himself.

Evening was coming; already the sun had lost its power, gnats played their fairy fountains above the still waters, ringdoves cooed sweetly up in the oaks.

His plight seemed more and more desperate. Should he try and find Smokoe Joe and borrow some trousers and a jacket from him? No, it would be all over the county. And he did not know which way to turn for Smokoe Joe's abode. There was nobody in Yoho whom he knew, besides – the shame of it! No, that was impossible . . .

He sat down on the bank and tried to think calmly. He thought of everything, a skirt of leaves or grass, a thick branch carried fore and aft, all these he thought of. At last he could only come to one conclusion. He must get out of the forest, find his bicycle, and go under cover of darkness to Ernie at The Martyr. Ernie would lend him trousers. But would Ernie hold his tongue? Would it not be better to go home as he was, clad only in his shirt, boots, helmet and gloves, all the way to Cherry Walden?

No, there would be a moon later. It rose soon after midnight. Once the moon was up he might be seen. No, it was Ernie or eternal disgrace. And first, trouserless, he had to get out of the Chase. A painful business.

A little after midnight Ernie, sleeping soundly beside his wife, was awakened by the rattle of a stone against his window. He grunted and turned over. Somebody wanting a drink, a drunken rustic perhaps. Again came the rattle of gravel. Ernie got out of bed. 'Who's there?'

A dim whiteness was seen below among the bean rows.

'Ernie, is that you?' came a husky voice. 'It's me, Sergeant Tom. Come down at once and let me in; summat's happened, summat bad. I've lost me clo'es.'

11. The Coming of Bang

NOW, AS you may have guessed, the author of this scandalous practical joke was *not* the poor absentminded Whiting. He had not even been aware that Sergeant Bunting had been in the forest until he was informed of that surprising fact by Bunting himself on the following morning.

I will not attempt to describe that harrowing scene or what passed between them. Suffice it to say nobody suspected the boys. I will qualify that statement by saying that, at least, nobody but the Whiting suspected the boys, but then, he also vaguely suspected himself. Nor will I attempt to describe, in detail, how the outlaws, bound for a swim in the Blind Pool, heard from afar the gurglings and splashings as of some large beast of the forest disporting itself in those sacred waters; or how Robin Hood, scouting forward with stoatish stealth, saw with his own eyes the never-to-be-forgotten spectacle of the Sergeant of Police bobbing like a bloated white walrus among the fair lilies. It would be tedious to recount the manner in which the neatly piled clothes were stolen with true Red Indian technique, or how the Whiting was also observed and the whereabouts of his car discovered. The placing of the sergeant's garments on the back seat was the work of a moment and both the departure of the Whiting and – best fun of all – the furtive-footed Bunting, were watched from the shelter of the impenetrable forest. It would be unseemly to describe how those three shameless villains had to roll among the fern to stifle their cries of mirth as the unhappy policeman pedalled rapidly away in the dusk of that summer night, his shirt tails flying, his white-gloved hands gripping the handlebars, and his naked hairy legs whirling madly round as he sped from sight.

In those far-off days there was little traffic on the roads after nightfall, but it is possible, nay probable, that some wandering lovers spied that apparition rushing by, as they lingered in each other's fond embrace among the honeysuckle.

The Chase had the reputation of being haunted by the Martyr. No doubt Sergeant Bunting would give renewed authenticity to the rustic legend, though it would take a deal of imagination to mount the Martyr on a bicycle, in place of the more orthodox headless horse.

July dragged on in sullen heat. The trees seemed to pray for rain; the little horse ponds outside the Chase shrank until only flaked and cracked hollows, like empty dishes, rewarded the maddened cows when they came to drink.

There were cases of sunstroke in many of the villages; the old people died like flies. Great heat kills quicker than cold. It was only natural therefore that the outlaws haunted the Blind Pool. Sometimes they slept during the greater part of the day and went by night to its magic shores and discovered a new ghostliness upon its sleeping waters.

It was there, under the full July moon, they saw their first badger and her farrow. They met her face to face down a riding and the little cubs scattered with urgent squeals. It was by the Blind Pool that Robin first glimpsed a purple emperor, drinking on the pond edge before the midday sun had topped the trees.

There it hovered upon the very margin, its wings widespread, showing all the glory of its purple sheen. And in the nearby sallows Little John disturbed the female, a vast insect like an outsize white admiral, but in her swift flight through the sallow wands she eluded him.

One disquieting fact was now apparent. Their ammunition was running low. There were still forty rounds in the worn red box which they kept hidden in a crevice of the oak, but they had to face the fact that the time was not far distant when there would be no more. And meat they must have.

There was no more ammunition at the Dower House and to make a journey into Brendon to the gunsmith's there would be fraught with peril. Besides, they only had fifteen shillings between them. 'No, chaps, it's no good,' said Robin Hood one evening as they lay discussing this very problem by their camp fire, 'the time is coming when we shall have to get our meat in some other way, by snaring or deadfalls or something. After all, the early outlaws hadn't any guns; they had to rely on their bows and arrows and their traps. We've got lazy – we haven't tried to snare any rabbits, though we've brought the snares with us, and we haven't made any deadfalls. It's about time we did something about it. Heaven knows what month it is, still less what day; we haven't any means of telling. We can only go by the signs we see. But by the look of the trees the summer's getting on. Banchester will soon be breaking up. It must be long past Speech Day anyway.'

'We'll set some snares tomorrow,' said Big John, 'it'll be fun too, and we'll make some deadfalls out of logs, though we shan't catch rabbits in those.'

'What's the use of setting 'em then?' asked Little John.

'Why, for pelts of course; there must be no end of good fur knocking around – badgers, foxes and stoats and things. After all, stoats are ermine.'

'Yes, but it's no use starting to trap yet,' said Robin, 'for pelts I mean. They aren't in good condition until the fall.'

'Well, we ought to start snaring anyway,' said Big John, 'or we shan't get much in the way of meat.'

'I'll go back to the Dower House and bring some more supplies, sugar, flour and things, if that'd help,' suggested Little John.

Big John fishing in the Blind Pool

'No you don't, my lad,' replied Robin, 'they'll have every door and window watched. I shouldn't be surprised if Bunting doesn't have a watch on the place all the time. You bet your boots they'll be expecting us to go back again for more supplies and we should be caught red-handed. Besides, Cook would be told to keep everything locked up, and anyway we ought to try and live on the country; that's half the fun of an outlaw's life.'

Next day the boys set to work to snare in earnest. They looked out the snare wire which had almost been forgotten and made neat wooden pegs for the snares, and set them in all the likely woodland runs, but without result. They next tried setting them in the mouths of the rabbit holes, but again no success greeted their efforts. They were doing something wrong. Once or twice they found a snare pulled up and gone but that was all.

Little John suggested making bows and arrows. They made a bow string from some of the pig's hide and bows from young saplings, but they soon found that a really successful weapon was beyond their ingenuity. Nor could they shoot their barbless arrows true. They did manage to kill a moorhen, but the wretched bird died of fright more than anything else. And all the time their stock of ammunition was dwindling lower and lower.

The smoked pig was nearly all gone – what a useful animal it had been – and endless rabbit and pigeon was becoming monotonous. They fell back mainly on fish. Every night, as dusk fell, the three outlaws set off down the woodland path for the Blind Pool. They fished by hand, for rods were too cumbersome. They lay with their faces close to the inky water fishing by touch. When the massive oaks grew black and still and the bats flittered across the surface of the pool they could hear the big tench rolling and sucking like pigs among the weeds, and now and again there would come a faint tremor from those abysmal depths as some sluggish monster fastened on the wriggling worm. The line would be jerked smartly upwards and a great bronze fish would come kicking on to the bracken, gasping and flapping, the fronds sticking to its scales. And what magical fish those Blind Pool tench were to be sure, with bold blunt lines, thick of back and sturdy of tail! Fried in pig's fat they were food celestial and never a night passed but they returned with at least half a dozen of these bronze beauties threaded on sallow twig.

One still and magic night, when the full moon shone down and its reflection hung like a great lantern in the oily water, Robin sat on the heron's log – the selfsame log from which Bunting had taken his fatal plunge – fishing in seven feet of water. Big John and Little John were somewhere down the far end of the pond and he was alone. Already he had caught three tench; the biggest weighed four pounds. They lay beside him on the bracken.

He lay flat on his stomach with his nose an inch from the water. Now and again a moth banged into him or a water rat swam across the moon's path to its hole under the willows. All at once something made him look up and there, twenty yards away in the moonlight, was a deer. It stood with the bracken up to its breast, gazing towards the far end of the pool where the other boys were busy over their lines.

Robin Hood never moved; neither did the deer. And after what seemed an hour the great beast moved silently out of the fern and bent its head to drink, half hidden by the willows. It drank noiselessly, but the widening rings went gleaming outwards and lapped the log on which he lay. A deer! So there were such things in the Chase after all. The Whiting had been right.

The rifle, alas, was back in camp, though even if he'd had it with him, it would have been a wrong thing to shoot in that dim, uncertain light. The animal might have been wounded and gone away to die a lingering death. Yet, given a good light and a clear shot, Robin was sure he could bring down a deer, even with so small a calibre rifle as the .22.

A muffled splash at the far end of the pool where Big John had just captured a large tench caused the animal to wheel lightly round and vanish like smoke into the fern.

They did not always visit the Blind Pool at night though the fish were easier to catch then. When the sun was hot the outlaws found the oak tree clearing windless and almost suffocating and then they would visit the pool for a swim, though they took the wise precaution of always having a scout on the watch. The sudden appearance of Bunting had been rather unnerving. And then there was that mysterious character, Smokoe Joe, whom they had not yet seen. If Smokoe found them the hunt would be up all over again. Sometimes when the wind set across the forest from the south they thought they smelt his fires but that was all. He remained an unseen potential enemy.

When the long summer afternoons grew unbearably torrid the boys would strip naked and slide off into the peaty pool, diving like dabchicks and chasing each other underwater. One of the things public school had taught them was to swim like otters. Sometimes Robin would drop his legs and hold his nose and let himself sink down and down out of the warmed upper layer of water into the icy depths below. He had glimpses then of a strange subaqueous world, of long-drowned pine trunks black and spiked and the dim green writhing jungles of the lily roots, which appeared uncommonly like the tentacles of an octopus.

And that underworld of water, where a green twilight reigned perpetually, revealed the fleeing forms of fish – some bulky, others small – which fled before him into the tangled forests of the weed.

It was always something of a relief to rise again to the surface, his body seemingly drawn by some invisible line as though he too were a captured fish; to leave below that icy cellar and break surface into the dazzling warmth of the sunlit afternoon.

Once Big John got into difficulties. He foolishly swam among the lilies to pick one of the attractive flowers – no wonder the ancients called the water lily the flower of the nymphs! – and the coiling pipelike roots wound themselves about his ankles and held him fast. The more he threshed and struggled the greater became their slimy grip so he wisely lay still and called for help.

Robin and Little John got him out, but for a long time he lay exhausted on the bank, white of face, and with a new cold fear in his heart. The Blind Pool was not to be trifled with, nor would it have its treasures stolen.

Robin was determined to persevere with the setting of snares. There was evidently something in their woodcraft which was lacking. So one afternoon towards the end of July he set out alone with some snare-wire snares in his pocket and set the near some burrows which he had found in another part of the Chase.

The others had said they were going to the Blind Pool to catch tench and had promised Robin they would be back before sundown to get the fire going in readiness for his return. He took the rifle with him and after telling Big John and Little

John to mind what they were about he set off into the fern. It was a gloomy afternoon, brooding and still, threatening thunder, which boded no good for the would-be tench catchers. Fish do not bite in thundery weather.

The flies were an intolerable nuisance. When the boys had first come to the Chase they had not been worried by them, but that afternoon they were almost unbearable. Hardly a bird sang for it was late summer, and they were worn out with family cares and perhaps they already felt the approach of autumn.

Already, on the blackberry bushes the blossom had begun to fade and here and there the berries had formed, hard and red as yet, but promising fine fruit later on. The nut bushes, too, showed tiny pale points which would, in time, be filberts. Robin carried his rifle at the ready but that afternoon not even a rabbit was visible.

It took him the best part of an hour to reach the warren and he began to search about for suitable runs. It was obviously no good setting the snares in the warren itself and he endeavoured to discover some well-worn run among the fern close by.

A sudden sound made him pause. It was a muffled whimpering as of some animal in distress.

It was some time before he located its direction. Not far distant was a large tree which had fallen and under its upturned roots were several holes. The whimpering seemed to be coming from there and after a time he tracked it down. Some creature was either trapped or in distress under the root. He lay at full length with his ear to the ground and listened carefully.

Then he found a broken branch and with this primitive spade he began to excavate. After a while he had removed a good deal of earth which he scratched out behind him like a rabbit. Then at last he saw the back quarters of a dog, a small dog, a regular lurcher's poaching cur. It had been caught by a snag through its collar and was unable to free itself.

After a little more digging Robin at last got it out. A more wretched animal he had never seen. How long it had been in the hole he could not guess, but its ribs were prominent and it was too weak to stand. Its rough coat was matted with earth and its claws worn down, the pads quite raw and bleeding. Robin took it up tenderly. It shut its eyes and trembled as it lay in his arms.

'Poor old chap,' said Robin, 'I'll get you back to camp; it's grub you want.' The poor little beast made a feeble attempt to lick his hand and dropped its head wearily on Robin's arm. It was evident that unless he got it back to camp without delay and gave it some food it would soon be dead.

When at last he reached the clearing by the oak tree he found the others had returned. They had had no bites, but this was not to be wondered at, as thunder was already muttering in the distance. They lit a fire and cooked some rabbit and soon the famished waif was eating ravenously.

'Why, he can't have had anything to eat for days!' exclaimed Big John. 'If you hadn't found him he would have been dead in the morning. What are we going to do with him, Robin?'

'We'll keep him I guess; he'll be useful to us for rabbitting and company for us too. There's no name on the collar; it's probably some poacher's dog.'

'What shall we call him?'

'Let's call him after Bill Bobman's dog, Whisky. It's a good name for a dog and it's short and snappy.'

'If we're going to use him for shooting we might call him Bang,' suggested Little John. The dog raised its head and looked enquiringly at Little John. 'Why, I believe that's his proper name. Is it

Bang, old boy?' Bang was too engrossed with finishing the rabbit.

After finishing his meal he lay beside the fire and feebly tried to lick the caked earth from his coat. He also licked his paws, grooming each paw in turn.

'Seems to be quite at home,' said Little John. 'It'll be fun having a dog. I expect he belongs to someone in Cheshunt Toller or maybe he's Smokoe Joe's.'

Smokoe Joe! They had not thought of that!

'We'd better keep him tied up for a bit,' said Robin, 'or he'll be going off again.'

But Bang at that moment seemed quite contented to stay where he was and after a while he curled up and fell asleep in front of the fire.

It was quite three days before Bang's claws were healed. They combed the mud out of his coat and soon he seemed a different dog. He went with them everywhere and it was not long before they found he was quite the cleverest poaching dog they had ever seen. He smelt out the rabbits under the fern and stalked them like a cat, pouncing on them as they lay in their forms.

And in addition to this they found he had an excellent mouth for retrieving game. When Robin dropped a pigeon into some thick cover Bang found it for them. He loved a gun and sometimes they would see him go up and lick the stock and wag his tail. As Big John said, he seemed to have twice the brains of Tilly, who was so fat; anyway she had never caught a rabbit in her life. The little dog was unhappy, however, and sometimes when they were sitting by the fire he would get up uneasily and wander about whimpering quietly.

But they never gave him the chance to run away and whenever for some reason or another they had to leave him behind, they tied him inside the tree. Evidently he had been trained not to howl when he was left because he never made a sound.

A week after his arrival he brought them a hen pheasant. The bird was alive and unharmed and Bang had evidently pounced on it as it sat on a nest. Either that, or he had smelt the bird as it crouched under the fern.

It was a most fortunate thing he was so useful in this way because Robin had to confess a complete failure with his snares. All he caught was one infant rabbit, which they had for breakfast with the bacon.

The pheasant, duly roasted, was delicious. Bang finished up the bones.

They found him perfectly trained for stalking. If Robin was worming his way among the underwood to get a shot at game, Bang would belly crawl five yards in the rear and if told to lie still he would do so and not follow until given a signal with the hand.

He brought them scores of hedgehogs which in some clever way he picked up in his mouth, without pricking himself. Most dogs will bark at a hedgehog but Bang was silent at all times. The only sound he had ever been heard to make was when Robin had found him trapped in the rabbit hole. He slept in the tree with them and the boys thus realized an ambition which they had always cherished, that of having a dog to sleep with them at night!

12. Mr Hawkins

'IT'S NO good, chaps, we've got to face up to it,' said Robin Hood one evening after supper. 'The pig's nearly finished and anyway it's beginning to taste mighty funny. I reckon it's because we didn't use enough salt in the curing of it. There don't seem to be any more wild pigs roaming around. We've shot up all the moorhens on the Blind Pool and it's too early for duck yet. We've got exactly one more breakfast of porridge oats, matches are short, the salt's gone; in fact, you chaps, we've got to rustle round a bit and do something.'

'You think it's too risky going back again to Cherry Walden and raiding the Dower House?' asked Big John.

'Yes, anyway, even if we could get into the house and we got what we wanted, it isn't my idea of livin' rough. Of course we've got the Blind Pool tench, we shall go on catching those for as long as the hot weather lasts and the perch will go on well into the winter, though they all seem to be small ones. But all the same, somehow or another, we've got to get some more cartridges. All I can think of is for one of us to go into either Cheshunt Toller or Brendon and buy what we want. We've only got fifteen shillings, but we could get a good bit with that, and we'll buy some more salt, sugar and porridge oats.'

'Looks as though we mean staying here,' said Big John.

'Well, why not?' asked Robin defiantly. 'So far we've got along all right and we've had a grand time. I vote we don't pack up until we're absolutely on our beam ends. Father and Mother will be back after Christmas and then we'll give ourselves up.'

'And take what's coming to us?' asked Big John grimly.

'Yes, and take what's coming to us,' retorted Robin. 'I don't care what you say, living wild like this will have done us just as much good as swotting away at Banchester all through the summer and autumn terms.'

'I don't expect Father will take that view,' said Big John. 'We shall probably be expelled from Banchester and our careers will be ruined.'

'Well, Father's sending you and Little John out to the colonies, isn't he?' asked Robin.

'Not before we've passed all our beastly exams; two terms is a lot of time to miss, you know. I've forgotten everything I ever learnt.'

'I wonder what Father will do to us,' said Big John with a certain morbid interest. 'It's so long since we saw 'em both I can't exactly remember what they look like.'

'I remember when he lammed me for cheekin' Mother once,' said Robin with fervour. 'I'll bet his arms are just as strong – stronger than old Batcham's.' Batcham was his housemaster. 'Well, as I say, we'll take what's coming to us,' said Robin again.

'I suppose we *are* doing wrong running away from the Dower House and Aunt Ellen; of course, it's wrong when you come to see it from their point of view. But as I say, if our parents were here we shouldn't have done it. We may have missed a good slice of Banchester, but we've been learning other things. It seems to me this idea of going to school and then into business isn't the natural way for a man to live, at least to my way of thinking. Don't you see what most people are missing? Something which is fine and grand. Living like we do, I mean out in the open air. They're getting farther and farther away from the natural life, nature and all that; they're creating a world which is ... Oh, I don't know ... I can't jaw properly ... but *you* know what I mean. Now for you, Big John, if you are going out to Canada, this trip will be the best thing for you. Latin and Greek won't be much good to you in the backwoods.'

'I dare say not, Master Robin, but what about you? You want to be a doctor, don't you?' said Big John.

'Yes, I do, heaven knows why.'

'Well, this sort of thing might not do Little John and me much harm, but I'm not so sure about you, Robin. Doctors have to be pretty brainy people, you know.'

'I know all that,' replied Robin, 'but look here, my merry men, I somehow feel this will be the best part of my life. I shan't ever get the chance again. When we've finished with Banchester, because, of course, we *shall* go back, if the school will have us, I shall go on to Cambridge, I expect, to Father's old college, and then it's bricks and mortar for me for the rest of my life. It's pretty awful when you come to think of it.'

'Well, don't let's think of it,' said Big John cheerily. 'We seem to have forgotten what we were saying just now about supplies. They've got to be got. I don't know about you fellows, but I'm dying for a nice big juicy cabbage. Salt's important, too. I don't think we can live without it. And the thought of rabbit makes me sick. We could do with a strong needle. And then there's the ammunition, too. We must get some more. How much have we left?'

Robin went into the oak and fetched out the box. He poured out the little brass cases on to the grass and they counted them. 'Thirty-one rounds, that's all.'

'Well, it looks like a journey to Brendon,' said Big John. 'One of us will have to go. Fifteen bob won't last us long either, by the time we've bought porridge oats, ammunition, salt, cabbages and . . . all the rest.'

'Well, we'd better toss,' said Robin. 'Toss for who's to go into Brendon tomorrow.'

Big John burst out laughing. 'There's no need to do that. Little John is the only one who has a pair of trousers! We can't march up Brendon High Street in rabbit skin kilts. Little John will probably be nabbed anyway. All the police will have a description of us and we can't go after dark because the shops will be shut.'

'Then Little John will have to do it.'

'I'll go,' said Little John at once.

'Right, well, that's settled. You'd better go tomorrow. Sneak out of the Chase before it's light and get on the road before people are about. It's only five miles. You'll be there as soon as the shops open and then you can come back and take your time over it. Don't try and reach the forest while it's light though. Hide up somewhere in a wood or a hedge. That's the plan.'

'I'll bet he'll get caught,' said Big John, eyeing their luckless brother outlaw. 'He looks pretty dirty and his jacket's torn.'

'Can't help that. He must take the risk. If you are caught, Little John, don't give us away. If you don't come back we'll know they've nabbed you.'

It was still dark when Little John set out. His brother outlaws had cleaned him up as best they could and they accompanied him to the edge of the road which cut through the Chase at the selfsame spot where they had witnessed the departure of the Whiting and the unfortunate Bunting. They watched his small figure disappearing in the half darkness and saw the first hint of dawn appearing in the east.

'I hope he comes back all right,' said Robin.

'So do I.'

'It would be awful if he was caught.'

'Don't worry, Little John can look after himself.'

It seemed a long time to Little John before he was clear of the Chase and all the while the dawn was coming up. Once he was outside he kept off the road and walked on the field side of the hedge. Men went past on bicycles and a few carts clattered by. As he neared Cheshunt Toller he saw a man driving some cattle. That meant it was market day in Brendon!

Then he had a brilliant idea. He would help the man drive them into the town; he would scoot ahead and pick them up in the village! By doubling along the side of the thick hedge he reached Cheshunt Toller well ahead of the drover. When the lowing brown herd came into view he pretended to be playing in the gutter. 'Mornin', mister,' he said to the drover, a big black-browed man with a red kerchief knotted round his throat. He looked like a gipsy. The drover did not reply; indeed, he scarcely even glanced at Little John, for at that moment one of the heifers, a small red animal, darted down a side road and the drover let out a torrent of original oaths.

'All right, mister, I'll get 'im for you,' shouted Little John. He tore after the heifer and stood in front of the poor mazed brute. It lowered its head, froth drooling from its mouth, and then clumsily turned round, slipping to its knees on the road.

'Well done, young 'un, that there beast is a —.' The drover used a word new to Little John. ''E's played 'ell wi' me all the way from Martyr Bar.'

'Goin' to Brendon, mister?' asked Little John cheerfully.

'Aye, I am an' all, worse luck.'

'Can I come along with you an' help you drive 'em?'

'Ain't you got to go to school?'

'No, I ain't,' said Little John.

'I'll gi'e 'ee threepence if you 'elp me drive 'em,' said the drover suddenly, ''Ere I ain't kiddin' – look.'

He held up three very grubby pennies. 'Threepence 'ef you 'elp me.'

'Righto, mister, I'll come,' said Little John, trying – very badly – to imitate the Tilthshire dialect. To add realism he spat and straddled with his hands deep in his pockets.

'You're a good boy, you are,' said the drover. 'One o' the right sort.'

'It'll be my good deed,' said Little John virtuously. 'I'm a Scout, you know.' I regret to say the last remark was true. Harold was in the Cubs at Banchester.

'Oh, ah.'

Little John quite enjoyed that tramp in the early morning with the sun just coming up and the lowing herd jostling along the lane before them. He scurried round the clumsy beasts like a little terrier.

'You're better'n a dawg, mate,' said the drover, pulling out a villainous looking pipe and lighting it. 'What's yer name?'

'Harold 'Awkins,' said Little John promptly.

'No relation ter Mr 'Awkins wot keeps the bakers in Cheshunt Toller by any chance?'

'Grandson,' said Little John glibly.

'I knows yer grandad,' exclaimed the drover. 'I've often looked in, when I've bin goin' past, for a crust o' bread. Bakes good bread, too, does yer grandad. Where d'you live, kid?'

Little John was rather taken aback for a moment. 'Lunnon.' That should be a safe card to play.

'Oh, ah, I thought you didn't look like a country kid.' Little John was not sure whether to take this as a compliment or not. 'I ain't never bin to Lunnon,' added the drover.

Conversation lapsed for a while, much to Little John's secret relief. They had been skating on thin ice.

'You ain't seen nothin' o' them boys 'oo ran away from Cherry Walden, I suppose?'

'What boys?' asked Little John innocently, though his heart gave a jump.

'Why, ain't you 'eard ... well, no, I don't suppose as you 'ave if you've only just come to these parts. But three boys – toffs they were – ran away from the Dower 'Ouse, and all the perlice ha' been arter them. Ain't caught 'em yet, neither. I bin keepin' a lookout; there's fifty quid fer infermation leading to their arrest.'

'Fifty quid!' Little John whistled. It was the first he had heard of it.

'Ah, fifty quid, some big paper offered it. But nobody's claimed it yet. I could do wi' fifty quid,

I can tell ye,' said the drover looking suddenly at Little John. 'Fifty quid's a lot o' money.'

'I expect they've run away to sea,' said Little John, 'like I've always wanted to do.'

'No, they reckon they're 'idin' somewhere in the woods. They've seen 'em once, up at 'Igh Wood, beyondst Cherry Walden. A rare old chase it was, by all accounts, 'undreds o' police and folks arter 'em, but they got away. Artful as foxes. Their old aunt's in a bit of a stew so I'm told.' The drover puffed at his pipe and hit a heifer a terrific blow on its angular hind quarters. 'Caao! Caao!' he bawled. 'Coup! Cauop! Cauop!'

Little John had never heard such a racket. 'Kiup! Kiup!' he shouted in unison, quite enjoying himself.

The sun was now well up, white dust arose in a cloud, dogs barked at them from farmyards, farmers rattled by in their gigs. They reached Brendon without incident and Little John helped the drover to take the cattle right down the hill past the grammar school and the Prince of Wales Inn to the cattle market by the station.

'Look ye 'ere,' said the drover, producing the promised threepence, 'I shall 'ave some ship to take back, mebbe this arternoon, fer Mr Hambro.

Ef you meet me 'ere at two o'clock and 'elp me take 'em back, I'll give another threepence. Wot d'you say, chum?'

'Right, mister, I'll be there!'

Little John was thankful for this drover. What a chance it had been! In his company none would suspect him and perhaps the man would help him carry his purchases for they would be cumbersome.

He went first to the gunsmith's and bought a hundred rounds of .22 – it was before the days of such things as permits. Then he purchased the cabbages, matches and salt, a pound of sugar and at the saddler's he purchased some cobbler's thread and a stout needle. The man behind the counter, an elderly person with a walrus moustache and steel-rimmed spectacles, looked so hard at him that he was glad to get out of the shop.

By the time he had completed his list it was nearly midday and he was ravenously hungry. He bought some chocolate and thought he had never tasted anything so delicious in his life. Laden with his parcels he made his way to the cattle market at half past one. A few police were wandering round and one seemed to be eyeing him suspiciously so Little John went up a back street. When he returned to the market the policeman had gone.

The market was an attractive noisy place, full of lusty-lunged men, swearing drovers, and loud with the bleat and moo of hundreds of animals which were crammed into iron pens, like sardines in a tin.

The heat beat down and the dust was choking. Little John wished the drover would come. And at last he saw him, guiding – or attempting to guide – a terrified flock of sheep up the station road. He ran after him, hailing him from afar.

'Ah, that's a good boy,' said the big man cheerily, 'thought you wouldn't turn up. It'll be the devil's own business getting these — outer the town wi'out a dawg.'

Little John thought so, too, especially as he had so much to carry.

'You bin marketing, too, sims to me,' said the drover, 'ye look like Father Christmas. 'Ere, let me carry yer big parcel,' he said good-naturedly. ''Ullow! Cabbages!' said the man, surprised, as he took them. 'Whatever's your grandad a'buying cabbages for? Don't 'e grow 'em on 'is allotment?'

'No ... no, 'ee don't grow many,' said Little John hurriedly, 'leastways he told me to get 'em for 'im, 'ee's very fond o' cabbages.'

'Seemingly 'ee is an' all,' said the drover, 'can't understand 'im buyin' cabbages.'

Luckily at this juncture several of the sheep decided to break away up Drum Alley and Little John had to head them off.

All went well until they reached the turning to Cheshunt Toller in the centre of the town. There a horse and van came trotting up behind them and the sheep had to be driven on one side. Little John heard the drover hail the driver. 'Ullo, Mr 'Awkins, I got a good shipdawg 'ere terday!'

'Got a wot?'

'A good shipdawg 'ere; yer grandson.'

Little John felt his heart turn to water. He looked round. There was the covered baker's van from Cheshunt Toller and on the side of it in curly gold and brown letters, the words, Thos Hawkins, Baker and Confectioner, Cheshunt Toller.

'My what?' bellowed the driver, a bearded, red-faced man, with a glass eye.

'Yer grandson, 'Arry. He 'elped me drive some 'eifers in this morning, and 'e's 'elpin' me drive these ship back to Cheshunt Toller. Don't mind, does you? 'Ere, 'Arry, 'ere's yer grandad,' said the drover delightedly, turning to Little John.

Little John looked at his 'grandad'; his mind was working quickly. The drover had the cabbages.

He must get them from him and then make a bolt for it.

'Wotcher mean, *grandson*?' said Mr Hawkins, eyeing Little John suspiciously.

'Why, 'ee's yer grandson, ain't 'ee, Mr 'Awkins?'

A slow recognition seemed to dawn in the red-bearded visage. A broad smile spread over Mr Hawkins's face, but not before he had caught sight of the policeman on point duty at the crossroads fifty yards ahead. 'Aye, aye, well, well, 'Arry, me boy, glad ter see you,' said Mr Hawkins. 'Climb up on the van, boy, climb up on the van!'

Little John was so thunderstruck he obeyed like a lamb. A strong – very strong – hairy fist grasped his arm like a vice and hauled up the unhappy outlaw on to the box.

'I'm afraid 'e'll 'ave to come 'ome along o' me,' said Mr Hawkins.

''Ere,' shouted the drover, 'can't 'ee stop and gi'e me an 'and?'

''Fraid not,' said Mr Hawkins briefly, ''is grandma will be worryin'.'

'Well, don't go without yer cabbages, 'Arry,' said the drover ruefully, passing up the brown paper parcel. Little John, still in a daze, took them from him.

'Gee up!' said Mr Hawkins and the horse broke into a trot. Little John's mind was still working. What was his captor's game?

'You don't want to go along o' 'im, boy,' said Mr Hawkins, clucking to his horse, and looking very hard at Little John out of the corner of his good eye, ''ee's a nasty rough man. I'll gi'e 'ee a lift along the Cheshunt Toller road wi' me.'

Little John did not answer but shuffled his feet.

'Bin doin' a little shoppin' eh?' said Mr Hawkins, benignly, looking at Little John all the harder out of his live eye. Little John did not know which eye to look at and so said nothing.

When they reached the policeman on point duty Little John noticed a strange thing. Mr Hawkins's hand which held the reins was trembling.

''Arf a mo', sonny,' he said pulling the horse up, 'I want a word with the bobby about summat.'

In a flash Little John saw Mr Hawkins's game. The man had recognized him and that trembling hand was already closing on fifty one-pound notes.

'All right, Mr Hawkins,' said Little John meekly. The sheep in the rear of the cart were making so much noise that Mr Hawkins had to lean down from the cart to attract the policeman's attention; at the same time his left hand wandered towards Little John's coat collar.

Then the latter acted like a whiplash. With all his force he drove his elbow in the side of Mr Hawkins and the next moment the unfortunate man lost his balance and reeled sideways. He fell from the cart almost on top of the policeman, who, turning suddenly round, caught the baker in his arms, grasping him as he would an enormous teddy bear. The next instant Little John had seized the reins and laid the lash along the side of the startled animal and Little John, horse and van went thundering away down the Cheshunt Toller road.

Cries, shouts and scufflings came to him, mingled with the bleating of sheep and the yells of the astonished drover. Looking over his shoulder Little John saw everyone was running after him down the road, sheep, drover, policeman and Mr Hawkins. Little John plied the lash. They were still in the centre of the town but the horse, terrified at the noise, needed no whip. The van swayed. Little John saw a fat grocer in a white apron rush heroically from his shop door and spread out his arms in front of them. The horse swerved, the van mounted the pavement and a large pile of wicker baskets full of new potatoes went tumbling in a cascade down the middle of the High Street.

Women fainted, boys – white of face – crouched against shop windows, a fat parson on a tricycle fell over, scattering books and parcels all over the pavement, dogs tucked in their tails and fled up back alleys, but Thos Hawkins, Baker and Confectioner, flew onwards, rocking like a stricken ship, spilling sacks of flour out of the back and leaving a white trail behind. A policeman at the end of Warburton Street saw the runaway van careering towards him. With great courage he spread wide his hands like a man endeavouring to field a ball. His eyes were staring, and his mouth was shut in a grim line as he jigged from side to side. But he, too, flashed by in a cloud of dust.

'Turump! Turump! Turump!' went the horse's hooves. Little John saw the foam-flecked neck and flying mane rising up and down in front of him like a piston. Never in his life had he travelled at such a speed, and neither had the horse!

Soon he found himself standing up, like one of the old Greek charioteers, yelling madly at the top of his lungs and plying the whip mercilessly.

The cries of men came in gusts. 'Stop 'em, stop 'em. Oi! Oi! Pull on the reins, boy! Pull on the reins!'

Never had Little John seen people move so fast! They seemed like puppets jerked on strings, or a film run very fast. They whirled and rattled past the Prince of Wales like a tidal bore. In front of him, down the street, everyone was standing staring. As he drew near they shrank aside into shop angles and corners or crouched behind lamp posts. When he had passed they darted out and ran after him.

Behind him in pursuit came a hardware van and a farmer in his gig; they, too, were plying whip and spur.

In the early part of the twentieth century, motor cars were not common as they are today. One or two motor vehicles were parked on the side of the road and just past the Prince of Wales was the magnificent Rolls-Royce belonging to the Duke of Brendon. Unfortunately it so happened that all these cars were facing in the wrong direction and in those comparatively early days of motoring it took time to manoeuvre a car round.

In a few moments all this noise, bustle and clatter was left behind and Little John, still lashing the horse, was thundering along the Cheshunt Toller road. The horse knew the way home and he was a young horse.

The hardware van was left far behind and on looking back Little John saw that pursuit had, for the moment, died away. The horse was now blowing like a grampus but it was still game; sparks flew from its hooves and the last sack of flour tumbled out on to the road. Little John helped its descent with his foot. Like a balloonist he was shedding all ballast. The sack burst on impact in a shower of white flour.

A mile from Cheshunt Toller he saw a cloud of dust with a black centre speed round the bend he had just passed. It was the Duke of Brendon's limousine!

Another bend in the road lay just ahead. Once round it Little John pulled his frothing steed to a standstill, leapt from the seat on to the grass and gave the horse a parting cut with the whip.

Away went the van again and the next moment Little John, still clutching his precious parcels, was in the ditch.

A cyclone passed him with a roar. It was the limousine. The smart blue uniformed chauffeur was crouched over the wheel, his face tense, and beside him sat a policeman! In the back, swaying to and fro in a most undignified fashion, was the Duke of Brendon, clutching a tasselled cord. He was shouting something to the chauffeur. And then . . . a beautiful peace reigned; the only sound was of a distant cowman calling in his herd, quite oblivious to the world-shaking events on the Brendon road, and a cloud of white dust hung in the air, to settle softly on the heads of the seeding hemlock in the ditch.

Little John wormed his way between two stout hawthorn stems, pulling his parcels after him, stinging his hands and face on some nettles and then, half hidden among the tall weeds and grass, he spied out the land on the far side of the hedge.

Exactly opposite to him was a steep dingle which seemed to be a rubbish tip. It was choked with elder bushes in full flower – their strong scent was almost overpowering – nettles and briars, a grand wild place abounding with good cover for a hunted outlaw.

It was fenced around with stout palings and on the opposite side were some allotments, evidently the village allotments, and there, not far beyond the fence, was a man in his shirtsleeves, digging industriously.

Little John knew that his pursuers might backtrack when they found the van was without a driver. He would be safer in the dingle. Even as he lay deliberating he heard the sound of a car returning slowly up the road. He must act.

He squirmed out of the ditch and crawled rapidly under the fence on top of the steep bank. The next moment he was slithering down, parcels and all, into the underbrush.

He lay there for some minutes without moving. Overhead a greenfinch was singing; he could see it sitting like a little green parrot among the elder flowers. 'Dreeezio! Dreeezio!' it sang, a curious, almost tropical song. The low light of the sun shone on the top of the elder bush making bird and leaves a brilliant green against the soft sky. But down in the dingle all was shade. In his nostrils was the sharp 'stingy' smell of nettle and the acrid scent of the elder.

Soon he heard voices on the road and a car engine purring. A man shouted, quite near. 'Hoy!' then 'Hoy!' again. The greenfinch flew off with a startled chirp.

Another voice answered from the allotments. Evidently his pursuers were on his track. Had they seen him go down into the dingle?

He peered through the thick leaves and saw the blue dome of a policeman's helmet bobbing along the fence in the direction of the allotment. For some time all was quiet, so quiet that a faint rustle below him made him turn just in time to see a large brown rat scurrying past a rusty tin.

Then the car started up and he heard it go off down the road in the direction of Brendon. Little John could breathe again. In a little while came the soft brushing of feet in long grass and peering once more through his leafy screen he saw the man who had been digging in the allotments come up to the fence. He was only ten feet away and the evening light shone full upon him. He was a stout, red-faced labourer, with bushy white eyebrows. He pulled vigorously at a stub pipe and the clouds of blue smoke came out like puffs from a silent gun, the air was so still. He leant his arms on top of the rail and looked down into the dingle; once he seemed to be looking directly at Little John. He bent his head and peered this way and that, still puffing at his pipe. Little John soon smelt the rank shag. Evidently the policeman had told him a wanted man was somewhere close at hand.

It seemed to Little John that the man *must* see him, crouching there among the bushes, but he did not do so. For, after remaining for quite three minutes with his strong brown arms resting on top of the rail, he slowly moved away towards the allotment. Little John's pulse slowed – it had been going like a mallet in his temples during that scrutiny – and all was quiet once more.

He glanced down the tangled bank, his eye roving over the rusty tin cans. There was a broken bedstead, an old tin bath, several bicycle frames and a dilapidated pushchair and hundreds and hundreds of tin cans. The inhabitants of Cheshunt Toller must have lived on tinned food, thought Little John. Now and again he caught sight of other rats, obscene scaly-tailed monsters, busy among the refuse. He had certainly chosen a very unsavoury place to hide.

Slowly the sun sank. The golden light left the top of the elder bushes and the rank smell of the dingle seemed to be intensified. It was somehow a very English smell, nettles, elder, grass and rubbish. The greenfinch came back to the bush and began to hop about, other birds with it, sparrows and chaffinches. They were thinking of bed.

Soon it would be time to move. All sounds of pursuit had died away. And then the first star appeared, faint at first, trembling like a tiny diamond in a greeny-blue sea, then becoming more brilliant.

The rats began to be noisy and bold. Cans clinked and he saw one old rat run along the top of the bedstead. He shuddered. If he stayed any longer they might set upon him; they looked fierce enough for anything. Very cautiously he crawled up the bank and peeped between the grass stems. The allotments were deserted, the labourer had gone home. Inch by inch he wormed his way under the rails. There was not a soul in sight. Somewhere to the right, beyond the allotments, lay Brendon Chase. In a few moments it would be nearly dark and he would make a move.

Bats fluttered by, and away in Cheshunt Toller he heard someone playing a mouth organ . . .

He gathered up his purchases, the porridge packets, the salt, sugar and the cumbersome cabbages. The last-named had been the most awkward of his shopping parcels. Yet he had hung on to them. It was surprising how they missed this vegetable. The wild sorrel and nettle tops which they cooked in the Chase only partly satisfied their craving for green food. Now, as Little John looked at those two large globes of green, his mouth fairly watered and he was glad he had not abandoned them in his wild flight.

With one last look round he got to his feet and set off across the field.

At that precise moment Robin and Big John were skulking by the gate which led on to the forest road waiting for his return. The dim ribbon of the lane, more dim because of its wall of trees on either hand, showed no sign of life save many rabbits, which went hoppitting across from one side to the other, as though propelled by clockwork.

'Wonder what time it is,' said Robin in a low voice, 'he ought to have been back long ago. It must be after eleven.'

'If we keep very quiet we may hear Cheshunt Toller church strike,' whispered Big John.

'Perhaps he won't come back this way; p'raps he'll enter the forest on the other side,' suggested Robin.

'He wouldn't know the way.'

'No, I don't suppose he would. But supposin' he was being chased, then he'd try to get back here any old way.'

'Let's go back to the oak; he'll turn up all right,' said Robin, but his heart was heavy with foreboding.

They reached the clearing and Bang, whom they had left tied up in the tree, actually gave a squeak of delight and pranced on the end of his pigskin lead. They let him loose and he tore round and round the bracken, tail down and ears streaming behind.

'Shut up, Bang, come and lie down,' ordered Robin, 'lie down!' Bang threw himself full length, panting. Big John stirred over the grey embers and found a few salmon pink cinders. And a minute later bright cheerful flames were jumping up and crackling merrily. They put on some tench to fry while Robin washed some new potatoes which they had dug up in a field outside the Chase.

After their meal they added some more wood to the fire and lay listening. Bang sat beside them licking his chops and yawning from time to time, for he had had some rabbit for supper and was content. Then they saw his ears prick and his muscles stiffen and they knew somebody was coming.

Robin gave the low double owl's note, their call sign, and the answer came back as softly. 'Good man!' exclaimed Robin. 'He's got back!'

The bushes rustled and into the firelight limped Little John. He was laden with parcels and his bare right knee was dark with dried blood. 'Phew!' he whistled through his teeth and flopped down wearily beside them. 'Gimme something to eat!'

They piled up his plate with fried potatoes and plump fish and watched him wolf it without a word.

'Well,' said his brother outlaws together when he had finished his meal, 'so you got the stuff all right!'

'Yes, it's all here: cabbages, cartridges' – Little John tossed them across – 'matches, sugar, porridge oats, flour, salt, thread – I think that's the lot, and I've six bob left too.'

'Looks as though you had to run for it, brother,' said Robin looking at the scratched knee. 'What happened? You weren't spotted?'

'Spotted! I should think I was! I cleared out of Brendon in a baker's cart, with the populace after me like a pack of hounds on bicycles, carts, gigs, motor cars and on foot. I'll bet it's the most exciting market day they've ever had in Brendon. And even *then* I gave them all the slip! Finished up by hidin' in an ash tip outside Cheshunt Toller!'

'Blast,' said Robin when he had heard the full story, 'I knew something like this would happen. Everyone will be on our trail like terriers after a rat. They'll comb the forest from end to end. They'll guess we're in the Chase. That fifty pounds reward, too ... phew! That'll make 'em all the keener. But they won't get us; they shan't ever catch us, they'll have to cut the Chase down first before they do. We'll be like rabbits in a woodpile. But there must be no more journeys to Brendon or anywhere else for supplies. When this lot's gone we shall have to manage.'

Little John wiped his knees tenderly. 'Got that jumping from old Hawkins's cart,' he said reflectively, 'Phew!' He opened his jacket and lay back. 'I thought I was collared good and proper. Wasn't it just my luck old Hawkins coming along then in his cart! Nobody would have been any the wiser if that hadn't happened!'

'I thought you'd get nabbed at the gunsmith's,' said Robin. 'I'll bet the police would have told them to look out.'

'A girl served me,' said Little John, 'otherwise they might have been sticky about selling the cartridges to me.'

'That was a bit of luck anyway,' said Robin. 'We've got enough now, if we're careful, to see us through. I'll bet you're ready for bed, Little John!'

'You bet I am!' said that worthy. 'I'll sleep tonight like a top.'

'You can have the next three shots with the rifle,' said Robin. 'You've earned them, brother!'

13. Smokoe Joe

IN THE weeks following Little John's escapade the outlaws knew that greater vigilance was needed. If any search was going on, however, they saw or heard nothing of it; the Chase covered a large area. Had they been nearer the road they might have seen weary, scratched men returning homewards at close of day, and you may be sure that there were some rare tales in the tap room of The Martyr at Martyr Bar. Even the story of Bunting's trousers had somehow got around in a weirdly distorted form, despite Ernie's solemn assurance to the victim that it should go no farther.

There was a new and subtle change in the forest. The boys noticed it especially first thing in the morning and late at night. Though they were barely conscious of it, July had come and gone – a sullen, sweating July it had been too – and it was now mid August. A strange silence was everywhere; the leaves seemed tired; no birds, save robins, sang in all that great tract of forest land. Another sign of the passing of summer was the tattered appearance of the silver-washed fritillaries.

In July these glorious butterflies had been met with down every ride. Robin, especially, had been impressed by their flaming swift beauty. They passed along the pathways and over the hot clearings like living flames and once he saw a bush smothered in blackberry blossom which was covered with these beautiful insects feasting on the white flowers. The white admirals had disappeared and only once again did Robin see the purple emperor flying round the same tree close to the Blind Pool.

The outlaws searched the sallow for the larvae of the latter but were unsuccessful, though Big John found the caterpillar of a white admiral on a spray of honeysuckle. It was a quaint little creature of a green which exactly matched the honeysuckle leaves. In his wanderings Big John also came upon a nightjar's nest. He had been walking through the forest and had nearly stepped on the bird which rose out of the laid bracken in a little opening in the trees. It looked quite unlike a bird, with its toadlike eye and strange spotted plumage. The two richly marbled eggs lay close together by his right foot; they seemed the loveliest things he had ever seen, like handsomely marked stones. He took them back to camp and tried to blow them but to his great disgust they were hard set.

Three days after Little John's thrilling adventure Robin Hood announced he was going on a hunting trip, as he put it 'into the interior' beyond the Blind Pool. He also said he was going alone and taking Bang with him.

Big and Little John pleaded to come but Robin was unwilling. He was rather a strange boy and seemed to be able to enjoy nature much more when he was alone. His discovery of the Blind Pool had given him a rare pleasure which he remembered with gratitude.

'I shall take the rifle,' said Robin, 'and I may be away for a night so don't get worried if I don't come back at dusk.'

'What's the idea?' asked Big. 'We're all outlaws, aren't we? We ought to keep together.'

'Certainly not. Robin Hood didn't always hunt with the band; he went off for days at a time by himself.'

'Are you going to find Smokoe Joe?'

'Maybe I am.'

'Is that why you're going by yourself?' asked Big John.

'Not exactly. I dunno that I'm going to find anything in particular. I just want to make a long trip into the "back of beyond".'

'Well, I *do* think we might come along too,' grumbled Little John, 'especially after I went into Brendon like that.'

'Sorry, chaps,' said Robin briefly, 'but you can't come and that's flat. Bang and I will be all right, we'll be back the day after tomorrow – before, if I find old Smokoe Joe.'

'I don't see much point in finding Smokoe,' said Little John grumpily, 'he'll only give us away if he sees us.'

'He won't see us, or rather he won't see me – don't worry,' said Robin with a grin, 'but he's such a character I want to have a look at him. After all, he's lived in this forest for years and years; he must know a thing or two. I think he'll be like old Rip Van Winkle to look at; the Whiting told me he was a wonderful old character with a huge nose, a reg'lar wild man.'

'You'll have to take some supplies with you,' said Little John whose mind was, as ever, running on food. 'There's still a little bacon left, though another day will see the last of it. What about something to drink?'

'Shan't bother about that,' said Robin, 'I'll find a stream or something. I can't go burdened with pots and pans. The lighter I can travel the better.'

'Where will you sleep?'

'That won't worry me either, I'll find some place.'

'What shall we do when you're away? We shan't even have Bang for company.'

'Try and catch some more of those perch in the Blind Pool. The more we can get now the more we shall have in the winter. If you salt and smoke 'em they'll keep all right, same as the pig.'

'I *do* think you might take us, all the same,' said Little John with an injured air.

'Anyone would think I was going off for a week,' said Robin. 'I'll be back the day after tomorrow.'

'Perhaps,' said Big John lugubriously. 'Supposin' you're caught and don't come back, we shouldn't know what had happened to you.'

'I suppose you'd go straight back to the Dower House and give yourselves up,' snapped Robin. 'The trouble is with you fellows you haven't got enough self-reliance.'

The others did not answer; they were sulky.

Robin set off early the following morning. In his pocket were six rashers of forest-cured bacon and twenty rounds of .22 ammunition. The parting was rather strained but the others grudgingly wished him luck.

He took the path to the Blind Pool. When he reached it there was no sign of life upon it. They had shot all the moorhens and the mallard had not been seen since their first visit. Very soon he was in a part of the Chase which was new to him. Here and there grew thick hollies, already covered in yellow berries. They were fine old trees, very tall and bushy, with curious black knobs and lumps, like boils, on their smooth green trunks. There were many pigeons in this part of the forest, possibly because they are very fond of hollies for nesting sites; later they would seek out the ripe berries, their favourite food.

The holly was always associated in Robin's mind with the Christmas holidays at Cherry

Walden and walks with Miss Holcome along the muddy winter roads. Underneath the trees were carpets of skeleton leaves. These make wonderful fuel for lighting fires. Also the thin dead twigs burn very easily, even in wet weather.

He saw many pigeon's nests, even though it was now late in the year, and he climbed up to one nest – Bang sitting patiently below gazing up at him with cocked ears – and therein he found two squabs, ready to fly. He took both of them, infant pigeon are excellent eating, and they went into his jacket pocket. Robin was pleased at this because he had not had to use a cartridge on them.

It was a curious gloomy day. The clouds hung low, but there was no wind. He saw little of interest all that morning beyond a few red squirrels and numberless jays, which made such a racket when they saw him moving through the bushes that Robin ground his teeth with anxiety. The jays are the forest watchdogs. Many a keeper has trailed a poacher by their harsh betraying screams. He came to several wide ridings. In one of them were the marks of wheels and the ground was rutted deeply. In winter it would have been a quagmire.

He made a halt under a clump of hollies and ate a rasher of cold boiled bacon. Then he was sorry because it made him thirsty and he could find no water. He wished now he had brought some with him, but they had no water bottle back at camp and he had not thought to make one out of the pig's bladder.

After a while the thirst subsided and when he came upon a few half-ripe blackberries – the first he had found – they helped to ease matters considerably, even though they were not quite ripe. Suddenly he noticed Bang seemed uneasy. He sat very upright with his ears cocked and now and again he sniffed the air. Robin listened very carefully but he could hear nothing save the gentle drip of rain for the sky was growing darker. Perhaps it was this gentle 'tick tick' of rain drops on the leaves which made the little dog restless.

Some blackbirds were making a great noise in the distance and a jay began to scream. Perhaps they had seen a fox or an owl. Robin called Bang and prudently retired under some nearby hazel bushes. He had been conspicuous under the holly. And then, without warning, he saw a fine red fox trot out from the bracken thirty yards distant.

It looked neither to the right nor left but went at a leisurely loping gait across an open space. When it reached the far side it looked back over its shoulder with one paw raised, the very picture of wild woodland grace. Robin had his rifle trained upon it but the fur was of poor quality. Fox's coats are not in good condition until later in the year. So the trigger was not pressed and a second later the fox had vanished into the fern.

Something had scared it, however, and Robin lay doggo. The next moment there came another movement among the bushes and a fallow buck trotted out from between two holly trees. Like the fox it stood motionless. It must have been upwind of Robin for it never glanced in his direction. This was only the second deer he had seen since he came to the Chase and he remembered that their pig was now devoured. It was a gift of a shot; he could not miss. Very cautiously he raised the rifle and drew a steady aim one inch to the left of its wide open eye which was as full of mystery and shadows as the Blind Pool.

Then he pressed the trigger . . . Robin swore out loud, for instead of the sharp crack, there was a deadened click. The cartridge had misfired. That tiny sound had been heard, however. With one beautiful arching bound the buck had gone; only a fern frond nodded to a standstill.

Bang, who all this time had been lying close behind Robin, let out a subdued yelp of excitement. He had evidently seen a deer before in the forest. Almost sick with disappointment Robin drew back the bolt and ejected the useless cartridge. It was one of those which Little John had bought in Brendon, an inferior brand. The copper cap had been dented by the striker pin but somehow or another it had not fired the powder.

With an angry gesture he threw the offending thing away and put in another, one of the original cartridges he had brought from Cherry Walden.

This great misfortune quite upset our gallant outlaw. To think that they had been so short of meat and he had missed such a glorious chance! There had been enough good venison within thirty yards of him to last them into the late winter!

Bang whimpered again and Robin, in an ugly temper, kicked out at him with his shoe and then – rightly – was sorry. Certain he was that the chances of ever getting such an opportunity again were very remote. He had been so sure of his aim;

had he fired he knew he would have dropped that buck in his tracks.

The gentle rain which had now been falling for some time had stopped and the sun tried to break through the clouds. Robin realized that the day was swiftly passing; he must push on.

After some time he came to a well-trodden path which wound about among the hazels. Indeed, it was so well used and the footmarks, hobnailed footmarks, were so fresh, that he thought it must be the way to Smokoe Joe's.

Bang began to be a nuisance, whining very quietly and trying to run on ahead. At last he became so impossible that Robin decided to tie him up to a tree. This he did, well back from the track. He must see where this path led to.

Very thick nut bushes hedged it in on both sides and it had many sharp corners with twists and turns, a dangerous place. He might meet anybody face to face round these sharp angles and the bushes were so thick he could not turn aside, indeed to do so would make considerable noise and might attract attention. In a short while Robin smelt woodsmoke and a little later saw a blue drift spiralling above the trees ahead.

It was now imperative to leave the path for this smoke could be coming from no other place than Smokoe Joe's abode. He crawled along among the bracken – the thickets of hazel were not so dense – and in a short while he came upon a clearing in the trees. In the middle of it were three curious mounds, like huge molehills, made of turf. One of them was not turfed all the way round and showed small faggots, some twelve to fourteen inches long, packed close together in the form of a cone. This heap was not smoking but the other heaps were, the blue reek emerging from a hole in the top, which showed the kiln had been recently fired.

Piles of faggots were stacked on the far side of the clearing next door to a very well-made shack of logs, built exactly like a Canadian log house. It was quite a large hut with a lean-to shed made of boards at one end. Smoke was also issuing from an iron pipe which protruded from the roof.

Behind the house the bracken had been cleared and there was quite a little garden. The dark rich soil had been tilled and rows of cabbages, lettuces and other vegetables had been neatly planted out. There was a covered well at the end of the garden, grown round with bushes.

Over the door of the cabin a pair of stag's horns had been nailed. But there was no sign of life.

This must be Smokoe Joe's place right enough, thought Robin, and he wished he could catch a glimpse of the man himself. He lay among the fern for some time and then, growing bolder, he wormed his way among the bracken until he was within thirty yards of the hut. He would dearly have loved to cut himself some of the cabbages and lettuces but that would have been stealing.

Evidently Smokoe was not at home. Only the blue smoke issuing from the chimney suggested the place was inhabited. Dare he crawl up to the window and peep inside? The temptation was very strong though he knew it would be a tremendous risk to take. But with every moment this urge to look in at the window grew stronger. Robin was quite startled to see a white hen appear from the back of the house followed by three others. They pecked about round the door and one of them went and drank out of a little pannikin of water. And from behind the house came the grunting of pigs. Smokoe certainly had a cosy little place here, thought Robin, quite a self-contained homestead. Compared with their own camp it was a palace!

Robin began to crawl forward very cautiously to the edge of the bracken. It was another ten yards to the woodpile. Once there he could approach the house on the blind side. Getting to his feet, with his rifle at the trail, Robin darted across the open space and the next instant he was behind the faggots. He rested here a moment, breathing rather hard. His heart was beating uncomfortably fast with excitement. Then he crawled round the angle of the house on hands and knees until he was under the window. Very cautiously, an inch at a time, he raised himself . . . higher, higher . . . another inch and he would be looking in at the window.

And then – Robin collapsed with a gasp. Someone had leapt upon him from behind. One immensely powerful and hairy claw gripped his right wrist and another seized him by the collar. He was thrown flat on his face and he felt a bony knee in his back. The horrible part of the business was that he had heard no sound, and even now, when his captor held him down, all he could hear was heavy breathing. There was a strong smell of birchwood smoke.

'Ach!' he gasped. 'Ah! Let me up! Let me go!'

'I've got you,' said a gruff voice in his ear. 'I've a-caught you, young feller. Gimme that rifle and no nonsense neither.'

Robin released his hold on the rifle, indeed, he could not help doing so for one blackened and knotted claw had gripped his little finger and was bending it back. He released his hold with a sharp intake of breath; the pain was agonizing.

'Now stand up, you,' commanded the voice.

Robin stood up, though a hand still grasped his collar. Then he saw Smokoe for the first time. He was a small wizened man, little taller than himself. He was dressed in old corduroy trousers tied in at the knee, a leather jerkin which had been ripped and cut by briars, a collarless shirt, and a curious conical hat was perched on the back of his head.

The face was wizened and crinkled like a monkey's. Two piercing grey eyes, as fierce as a hawk's, looked at him from under shaggy white brows and the lower part of the face was covered with a long white beard, and white hair hung almost to his shoulders. He couldn't have seen a barber for years. But it was Smokoe's nose which arrested the unhappy Robin's attention. It was the largest nose he had ever seen, a monstrous lump of a nose, purple of hue and horrible to behold. Robin Hood was very afraid.

'Wot's the idea?' demanded Smokoe. 'Wot's the idea, sneakin' round my shack a-pryin' on me? I saw yer come outer the bracken. I saw yer slip behind me woodpile. Wot's the idea?'

'Steady on,' said Robin, still fascinated by that ghastly nose, 'you needn't hang on to my collar, I won't run away.'

'No,' said Smokoe grimly, 'you won't get a chance. Is this 'ere rifle loaded?'

'Yes.'

Still keeping a hold on Robin's collar, Smokoe put the rifle barrel between his knees and withdrew the bolt a little way with his disengaged hand, just sufficient to see that Robin was telling the truth. Then he pushed the bolt home again, cocked the rifle and let go of his captive's collar, at the same time presenting the muzzle at Robin's chest.

'Any nonsense and I'll blow an 'ole in yer,' growled Smokoe. 'Now get inside.' He kicked the door of the shack open and jerked his head towards the opening. 'In yer go.'

Smokoe Joe

'Stand over there,' said Smokoe, nodding towards an iron stove in the corner. 'Play any tricks an' I'll plug a 'ole in yer.'

'You're Smokoe Joe, aren't you?' said Robin, who was now recovering his composure somewhat.

'Yurss, I'm Smokoe and who may you be?'

'I'm ... I'm ... Jack Robinson,' said Robin with a rush.

'Oh no you ain't,' said Smokoe, wagging his huge nose. 'Oh no you ain't. You be one o' they runaway boys wot the cops are after. I knows all about 'ee. They wus 'ere yesterday; they've been 'ere fer the last week huntin' ye, an' there's a reward fer you, Smokoe, they said to me, if you cotches them boys, or one on 'em. And I've cotched you, cotched you proper.'

'How do you know I'm one of the boys?' asked Robin lamely.

Smokoe's eyes were fixed on Robin's nether regions. The rabbit skin kilt had become dislodged in the scuffle and was in danger of dropping round his ankles.

'Ef you ain't one o' they boys they're arter, wot are ye doin' in that there thing?'

Robin saw it was no use bluffing. His eyes roved quickly round to the door which still stood ajar.

An inquisitive hen was peeping in making a querulous sound, and to Robin's astonishment he saw a white owl regarding him from the top of a cupboard in the corner. For a moment he thought it must be a stuffed bird until it winked prodigiously with its right eye. Smokoe saw Robin's wandering eye. 'Oh no you don't, me lad.' Still keeping the rifle pointed at his captive he edged to the door, shut it, and turned the key, putting it into his pocket. 'It's no good thinkin' you're goin' to gi'e me the slip, 'cos you ain't. You're a-comin' wi' me into Cheshunt Toller, an' I'll kip ye covered all the way there an' all. One little slip an' I'll plug you!'

'All right, Smokoe, I won't try and get away,' said Robin wearily, 'but for heaven's sake put that rifle up, it's got a hair trigger.'

And then any hope that he had of escaping vanished, for, as he glanced again round the room he saw through the window three figures in the distance coming down the forest path towards the cabin. One was the unmistakable form of Bunting and with him two men who looked like woodcutters.

Robin thought quickly. He decided to play for time. In another minute or two the men would be at the cabin door.

'Look here, Smokoe, I've been doing no harm, nor have my brothers; we're living wild in the forest and not harming anyone. We heard about you and wanted to meet you.'

'It's lucky fer you my Gyp weren't 'ere, 'e'd 'ave never let ye come nigh my cabin,' said Smokoe. 'Ef I 'adn't lost 'im like I did 'e'd 'ave 'ad ye be the breeches 'e would.'

'Your dog?' asked Robin eagerly. 'Have you lost him then?'

'Aye.'

'Is he a brindled dog, with a patch over his left eye?' said Robin quickly.

'Aye,' said Smokoe, 'that'd be 'im.'

'Then hide me quick, Smokoe, hide me somewhere, and when the police have gone I'll take you straight to him. I left him tied up down the trail. We found him trapped in a rabbit hole and saved his life.'

Smokoe's face seemed to undergo a strange transformation. 'You found my Gyp?' he said, scarcely speaking.

'Yes, yes, hide me, and when they've gone I'll take you straight to him.'

At that moment a sharp rap came upon the door.

'Smokoe, *please!* I'm telling the gospel truth, I swear it. Don't tell them I'm here and you'll have your dog back.'

Smokoe's face was a study. He was trying to make up his mind whether his prisoner was speaking the truth. Two more raps, more insistent, came upon the door and a dim featureless face crowned by a policeman's helmet, peered in at the window, the face of Bunting. It was dark inside the hut because the light was now fading. The policeman could see nothing.

In one corner was an apology for a bed. 'Get under there,' grunted Smokoe briefly. Robin did not need any further bidding; he threw himself flat on the floor and wormed his way under the bed. He heard Smokoe put the rifle up in the corner of the room and then unlock the door.

Heavy steps entered. 'Well, Smokoe, any sign o' them boys?'

'No, Sergeant, ain't seen nothin' on 'em.' Robin could have kissed Smokoe for that, despite his nose.

'Well we've searched the Chase all through and can't find no trace,' said Bunting, 'reckon they ain't 'ere at all.'

'The Chase be a big place, Sergeant,' said Smokoe.

'D'you think they're somewhere around?' asked one of the woodcutters, a little man with a face like a weasel.

'Don't know. They may be, mister, there's no tellin'.'

'Oh well, Smokoe, we'll be gettin' along. Goodnight to ye.' Robin heard steps clump outside again and the door was shut.

'Lie where you are,' growled Smokoe in a low voice, 'an' don't come out till I tells ye.'

'Righto, Smokoe, you're a white man,' whispered the relieved captive. 'Wait till they've gone and we'll go and collect your Gyp.'

'And no tricks mind,' replied Smokoe. 'Ef he ain't where you say 'e is we go right on to Cheshunt Toller and you'll be 'anded over.'

'Righto, Smokoe, that's agreed.'

The little room grew more dim as the light faded. Robin could hear owls beginning to hoot among the dark trees round the hut. It was rather noisome under Smokoe's bed and it was with some relief that he at last heard the gruff command, 'Out you come, you!'

The prisoner emerged. 'You're a grand chap, Smokoe, not giving me away like that.' Robin looked at the wizened little gnome who stood, still covering him with the rifle, by the stove.

'You're a desperate young rascal,' said Smokoe, 'blame me ef you ain't.'

'I'll never be able to thank you enough for this, Smokoe!'

Smokoe kicked open the door. 'Out ye go, quick march, an' don't forget I'm close behind you. One step off the path an' you're dead as a stuck porker.'

As they went down the now darkling track they made a quaint picture, Robin leading and with the muzzle of his own rifle in the small of his back.

As he walked along he could not help thinking how awkward it would be if Bang had got free. It was with a great sense of relief that at last he came to the tree where he had tied him up and saw Bang jumping and rearing on his string.

'Is that your Gyp?' asked Robin over his shoulder. But there was no need to ask that question. Smokoe had run forward and had fallen on his knees beside the prancing dog, which was licking the wizened little face all over, including the hideous plum-coloured nose.

Smokoe seemed to have forgotten Robin's existence. The rifle had been thrown aside into the grass and he was hugging his dog as if it were a prodigal son. And strangest of all, Robin saw a sight which almost awed him; large tears trickling down the monstrous nose into the long white beard!

'Well, ef you ain't the cunningest young monkey I don't know who is!' exclaimed Smokoe. He was sitting on the other side of the stove with Gyp's head on his knee, pulling his ears. 'Gettin' round me that fashion when one word from me would'a meant money in me pocket, more'n I get for a year's work on me kilns! Can't think wot I was about, being so daft.'

'Well Smokoe, if you had handed me over you wouldn't have got your dog anyway,' replied Robin with a grin.

Smokoe said nothing but continued to pull Gyp's ears. 'Yer see, Gyp an' me 'ave bin together fer ten years now, I've come to look on 'im as me own child. You see, 'e's the only company I 'ave, out 'ere in the Chase, an' the only one I've got to talk to, bar me old owl, Ben, up there in the corner. 'E kips to 'imself though, an' I can't talk to 'im like I can to Gyp. I've allus 'ad a dawg, but this one is the best I've ever 'ad. 'E ain't a dawg, 'ee's 'uman, the way 'ee thinks and talks to ye.'

'It was a bit of luck finding him down that hole, Smokoe; he was nearly a goner.'

'Not far from the Blind Pool you say? Blame me, the rascal! 'E's run off afore but 'e's allus come back. I knew summat 'ad 'appened to 'im. So you young devils 'ave been running wild in the Chase all this time, 'ave ye?' said Smokoe incredulously. 'You're sportin' kids I must say!'

'That's right, Smokoe, we haven't even known what month it is and we've lost all count of time.'

'Can't think 'ow you've managed to live,' said Smokoe, 'you look well enough I must say.'

'Oh we've shot plenty, rabbits and things, and a –' Robin stopped. He was about to tell Smokoe about the pig, but something checked him. 'We've caught some good fish in the Blind Pool too.'

'Ah, I knows the Pool, used to fish it when I was a nipper.' Smokoe opened the door of the stove and thrust in some sticks from a bundle which lay on the floor close by. 'Lived in the Chase all me life. You'll be campin' in Dukes Acres, as they call it. It's Crown Land across the ride yonder, you'll see notices up. Ef you'd bin campin' there the tenant o' the shootin' might 'ave got you. An' fifty years agone the Duke's keepers would a-netted you, but the old gent don't trouble about the Chase now.'

'D'you remember a clergyman coming after butterflies last summer,' asked Robin, 'a little round man with a red face?'

'Ah, the Reverend Whiting from Cherry Walden?'

'Yes, that's the man. It was Mr Whiting who told me about you.'

'Oh ah, we gets folks you know, now and again, arter butterflies and bugs, big toffs some on 'em. The Duke used to potter round arter purple emperors.'

'I saw one this summer,' said Robin, pricking up his ears, 'by the Blind Pool.'

'Up near the tall oak at the far end?' asked Smokoe.

'Yes, that's right, how did you know?'

'Why, that's an emperor tree. I've caught 'em there wi' an old rabbit for years. That there tree is a favourite place, but I didn't tell His Reverence that. I kips things to meself I do. Once it got about there were emperors in the Chase we'd 'ave 'arf the county 'ere arter 'em, tromplin' around. Like to see me collection?'

Smokoe got up from his rickety old chair and went across to a cupboard in the corner. From an upper shelf he reached down three glass-topped cases. 'The Reverend Whiting gi'e me these boxes,' said Smokoe proudly.

The butterflies and moths had been roughly set with big pins, but Robin saw three magnificent female purple emperors and two males; one of the latter was, however, slightly torn. White admirals, wood whites, pearl-bordered fritillaries and silver-washed, formed the bulk of Smokoe's collection. One high brown and two dark greens graced the cabinet.

'I don't bother much wi' the moths,' said Smokoe, 'though Mr Whitin' says there's some good 'uns in the Chase. But I don't like this 'ere sugarin'.'

Smokoe then shyly produced some carvings he had done in wood, and very fine they were. He carved them out of softwoods with his pocketknife and finished them with sandpaper. Some were really exquisite. 'Does 'em in odd times,' said Smokoe, 'in the winter evenings like when I've nuthin' else to do. It 'elps pass the time.'

When Robin had finished admiring them the old man glanced at the window where a dim light still entered. 'Well, we'd better light the lamp, young feller.'

Robin helped the old charcoal burner fill the lamp with paraffin from a cracked enamel jug.

'There,' said Smokoe, 'that's better. You'd better stay the night along o' me and go back in the morning.'

'You aren't going to give us away then,' said Robin.

Smokoe, whose face seemed all the more alarming in the steady yellow light of the lamp, grinned for the first time.

'No, sonny, Smokoe won't gi'e ye away, not even fer fifty quid 'e won't. I've got me Gyp back, that's all I wants, better'n any fifty quid.' Robin felt instinctively that Smokoe was telling the truth. 'But you mind they don't get ye,' added the old man earnestly. 'That Buntin' 'as been near worryin' me to death lately. 'E was a-saying, 'e wished they'd cut the whole place down, it 'ud make a lot er money, 'e said. A lot o' money!' Smokoe spat with unerring accuracy into the glowing stove. 'That's all some folks thinks about. 'Ark, don't it blow!'

Smokoe's shadow, thrown on the side of the hut by the lamplight, looked like some grotesque gargoyle. Outside the wind was rising and against the window came the gritty rattle of driven rain. Robin could hear the boom of the gale, the dull roar as each gust broke upon the thick trees around the shack. It was unbelievably cosy to hear the wild tumult without.

Smokoe's owl sat up in the corner, eating a piece of rabbit, gulping down prodigious pieces which nearly choked it.

'Where did you get the owl?' asked Robin.

'Oh, 'long in the old oak tree t'other side of the clearin'. Got 'im when 'e was nothin' but a ball of white wool. 'E's company 'e is and as wise as you make 'em.'

'I believe we've got a nest in our oak tree,' said Robin, 'we've seen the old birds going in and out; I'd like to get a young one too.'

'There's one thing I *would* like,' said Smokoe, who was now brewing some cocoa, 'and that's a rifle like your'n.'

'It isn't mine,' said Robin, 'I wish it was. It belongs to the gardener at the Dower House.'

'Little beauty idn'er?' Smokoe held it to his shoulder. 'Would it shoot a deer?'

'Maybe, considering I shot a –' Robin checked himself again. He had nearly blurted it out. 'It kills rabbits and birds well enough, I don't see why it shouldn't kill a deer. Do you ever get deer, Smokoe?'

The old man looked slyly at him and winked. 'Maybe, though I've got enough victalls 'ere wi' me 'ens and pigs.'

'So you keep pigs?' asked Robin innocently. 'I wonder there aren't wild ones in the Chase.'

'Yus, I kips pigs. I 'ad two, but one got outer the sty in the spring, a fine li'l pig 'ee was an' all, shapin' well. But 'ee took off into the Chase an' I ain't seen 'im since. Maybe 'ee's still around, there's plenty o' food for 'em, especially later on when the acorns drop. Seems ter me, young feller,' said Smokoe, 'it's a good thing ye be under a roof tonight, 'ark at it a-blowin', almost like winter, ain't it? Wot about some grub? Wot you say to a slice o' pheasant and some 'taters?'

'And I've got two squabs here,' said Robin, pulling the pigeons out of his pocket.

'Ah, they'll do for squab pie when they've 'ung a bit,' said Smokoe.

From an old cupboard in the corner he produced a cold bird and set it on the table. The potatoes he put on the glowing grate of the stove.

'This 'ere pheasant,' said Smokoe, passing his hairy claw over the plump heart, 'was one o' the foolish virgins, she cum strayin' roun' me chicken run one early mornin' last week, an' old Belchin' Bess put paid to 'er.' Robin had already seen Belching Bess and had thought how such a weapon suited old Smokoe down to the ground.

When the potatoes were cooked and the pheasant devoured – Gyp having the bones and crunching them under the table – the old man drew forth his pipe, one he had made himself out of hazel.

'Ain't you goin' to 'ave a spit an' a draw?' asked Smokoe.

'I've left my pipe in camp,' lied Robin, glowing inwardly at the compliment.

'That's no matter, I've plenty o' pipes, take yer choice.' Smokoe held out to him a handful of nutwood pipes. 'Made 'em last year, they smoke sweet.'

'I haven't any baccy either, I'm afraid, Smokoe!'

'No baccy neither! Well, I've got plenty. Live comfortable, that's my motto.' He passed across a tattered leather pouch full of a particularly tarry looking shag.

Robin had tried to smoke before but with poor results. And he didn't know whether to rub up the shag or smoke it as it was, so he watched Smokoe secretively to see how he managed. Smokoe cut himself off a slab of the plug and then sliced it up small with his clasp knife. When he had shredded it he passed over the knife to Robin.

''Ope you'll like this baccy,' he said, puffing a dense cloud of greenish smoke at the ceiling, 'it's strong, plenty o' body in it. Bosun's Plug they calls it, sixpence an ounce.'

Robin, having packed his pipe valiantly, lit up, and for a while they smoked in silence. Smokoe's baccy certainly *was* strong! This smoking was much more of an ordeal than the timid essays with Golden Mild behind the pavilion at Banchester. He was very soon aware of a curious feeling in his Adam's apple, as though he had a red hot cannonball stuck in his throat. He puffed a little longer, manfully imitating Smokoe, and then he felt as if all his insides were coming up. He coughed and spluttered and then retched violently.

'Ah! Ha!' laughed Smokoe rocking back in his chair and slapping his corduroys. 'I thought Bosun's shag 'ud tiddle ye up a bit!'

The tears were streaming down the unhappy outlaw's face. 'Phew! Smokoe, I'm afraid it *is* a bit too strong for me!'

'You'll get used to it, it's all right ef you don't swaller the smoke. You're swallerin' the smoke, that's wot you're doin'.'

But Robin could not finish the pipe.

They sat chatting into the early hours. Robin heard many a wonderful tale of the forest, including the legend of the Martyr who was supposed to haunt the road through the Chase. The fire burnt low, and soon Smokoe began to nod. The pipe fell from his hand on to the floor and this strange old creature with the enormous nose dropped asleep. Outside the wind continued to roar among the trees and the crazy casement rattled. Up in the corner Smokoe's pet owl, its eyes open very wide, regarded Robin with a peculiar penetrating stare and now and again it bobbed up and down and made strange serpent-like sounds. Without a doubt Robin Hood had fallen into strange company!

14. The Picnic

ONCE more to Cherry Walden, leaving Robin Hood and Smokoe Joe asleep on either side of the stove with the wind knocking at the window and Gyp – alias Bang – also lost in slumber before the dying embers.

Aunt Ellen and the Whiting, Miss Holcome and all the staff of that well-ordered establishment have almost been forgotten. Since the disappearance of Harold, Aunt Ellen had given herself up to despair: the boys were quite beyond her control and she had almost reached the stage when she dreaded their return. They would, no doubt, subject her to yet more ridicule.

The affair at High Wood had made her crimson with shame. When the Whiting told her about the episode, especially the incident of the wood white and the outraged squire, he had been unable to conceal his mirth. Aunt Ellen, without a word, had primly gathered her gloves with a 'we are not amused' expression and walked out of the house. Moreover, she did not go to matins the following Sunday, an unheard of thing for Aunt Ellen.

And then, after an ominous lull, there came the bombshell of the Brendon affair – the Bunting trouser epic did not, regrettably, reach her ears until years later. The headlines in the papers, more photographs, more reporters ringing at the bell – all these tortures had to be undergone afresh. To think that a nephew of her's, a Hensman, should have stooped to assault and battery, to say nothing of absconding with poor Mr Hawkins's van! Aunt Ellen, the family pride at stake, hired the village fly – she would not keep a carriage, though she could well have afforded it – and drove over to see the baker at Cheshunt Toller.

'But my good man, are you *sure* it was one of my nephews?' Aunt Ellen kept repeating, until the baker became, as Aunt Ellen said afterwards to Miss Holcome, quite rude and disrespectful. She

then made the mistake of offering him money –
no damage had been done either to his person,
horse or van. He, Thomas Hawkins, to be so
insulted!

It was a very subdued Aunt Ellen who returned
to Cherry Walden.

All her faults might have been put down to an
appalling insensitiveness and a lack of knowledge
of the ways of the world, but most of all to her
lack of a sense of humour.

On the very day of Robin's dramatic introduction
to Smokoe Joe she had a note from the doctor's
wife at Yoho.

> *Twelvetrees House,*
> *Yoho*
> *August 25*

My Dear Miss Hensman,
  We are having a little picnic for Angela's
birthday tomorrow and several of her little
friends are coming. She had intended to ask your
three nephews but since that is not possible she
is very anxious that you should come. I am sure
it would do you good, and it will be a change for
you, after all your dreadful anxieties. Your Vicar
is coming, too, and has kindly offered to bring

you in his car. He is so good with the children.
Do come if you can: forgive such short notice!
                                      Yours very sincerely,
                                      Elizabeth Bowers

'It will do you good, ma'am, I'm sure,' said Cook, when Aunt Ellen told her she was going. 'It will take your mind off your troubles. You haven't been outside the village for months.'

'The reason is, to tell you the truth, Cook, I dare not show my face in public . . . the shame of it all . . .'

'Still,' consoled Cook, 'you go, ma'am, it'll do you a power of good, especially if it's a nice day. I expect Lady Bramshott will be there, too, ma'am, and the children; it would be nice for you to see company.'

'I suppose it would,' said Aunt Ellen with a sigh, 'I suppose it would!'

The following day it rained in the morning and Aunt Ellen half hoped it would continue. But a little after midday the sun came out and the afternoon promised to be hot. Punctually at two-fifteen Aunt Ellen heard rumbling sounds at the gate and clouds of evil-smelling smoke advertised the fact that the vicar's car was awaiting her. She would have much preferred to go with Lady Bramshott, but she did not wish to appear rude to the vicar, who, after all, had been a very present help in trouble.

'Ah, Miss Hensman, here you are,' said the Whiting brightly, as Aunt Ellen appeared in motor veil and wrap, 'what a glorious day for the picnic!'

The Whiting was quite smart in a grey flannel suit and a white panama.

'Yes, so fortunate, Vicar, especially after the wet morning.'

'There we are, dear lady,' said the Whiting, arranging rather a grubby dust sheet over her knees as she sat down in the back seat. 'We are calling at the Hall for one of the Bramshott children and the nurse, as their wagonette will not hold them all.'

'Is Lady Bramshott going too?' asked Aunt Ellen, adjusting her veil.

'Yes, yes, I believe so, I believe so,' said the Whiting, grasping the starting handle and going round to the front of the car. The whole vehicle shook with his robust efforts at winding and the cherries on Aunt Ellen's hat quivered. A sudden hideous bolt-shaking roar suddenly burst forth and the Whiting climbed into the front seat. 'She always starts up so well,' he said over his shoulder, 'never any trouble!'

Aunt Ellen was thinking of a suitable reply when she was flung violently forward and her pince-nez fell down inside her veil. She gave a slight cry. Her dentures had also been badly rattled.

'Sorry,' grinned the Whiting, 'my fault, these gears are rather harsh, it's want of practice, you know, simply want of practice.'

'Please don't drive too fast, Vicar,' implored Aunt Ellen, 'I cannot bear speed.'

They turned out of the drive, where Rumbold was holding open the white gate, touching his cap and grinning as they passed. The Whiting noticed that many of the villagers smiled now when they saw him coming; they seemed much more friendly than they used to be. He did not know it was the story of Bunting's trousers which provoked the smiles.

As they bowled along, with dust clouds whirling behind them, the Whiting discoursed on the crops. They had ripened well with the hot weather and the rain and wind in the night had not been sufficiently heavy to cause any damage.

'Where is the picnic to be, Vicar?' asked Aunt Ellen, who was quite beginning to enjoy herself.

'Ah – Brendon Chase,' he said, 'I hope – ah . . .' There was an awkward pause. 'I hope we shall meet the others all right.'

At the sinister words 'Brendon Chase' Aunt Ellen made a small unintelligible noise. 'Oh dear, that's where the police have been hunting for my nephews . . . I . . . I think that Mrs Bowers might have chosen a . . . er . . . chosen another place for her picnic.'

'Oh, but it's ideal,' said the Whiting enthusiastically, 'so handy for Mrs Bowers, and the children will adore it.' Aunt Ellen noticed a green butterfly net sticking out of the Whiting's pocket and she sniffed. 'As a matter of fact it was I who suggested to Mrs Bowers that we should go to Brendon Chase,' confessed the Whiting.

'I suppose you did not think of the mosquitoes,' said Aunt Ellen severely. 'I suffer terribly from mosquito bites.'

They arrived at the gate which was familiar to the Whiting to find the magnificent equipage from the Hall standing in the shade with a cockaded coachman by the horses' heads. A squealing concourse of children, in their best clothes, was being herded by grown-ups and nurses into the green ride.

'Ah, here is our good shepherd,' said Mrs Bowers with unintentional profanity. 'So you've got here all right, Vicar; we thought something had happened to you!'

'Not late I hope?' said the Whiting, raising his panama. 'We started on time you know.'

'No, no, we've only just arrived,' said Mrs Bowers. 'Isn't it a *heavenly* place for our picnic, Vicar? The children will love it.'

The chattering, laughing crowd followed behind him down the ride, Mrs Bowers's chauffeur bringing up the rear, staggering under an ample wicker picnic basket full of good things.

It seemed an unendurable walk to the clearing which the Whiting had chosen for the party. One of the young Bramshotts stung its fat pink legs on some nettles and the forest rang with its cries. Lady Bramshott fanned herself delicately with a scented handkerchief and her red parasol trembled. 'Not much farther I hope, Vicar? The little ones . . .'

'Only a few yards more,' said the Whiting cheerfully, scanning the tree tops on either side of the ride as he walked along.

Aunt Ellen began to lag behind. She found herself among the camp followers, the nursemaids and infants.

'Oh dear, ma'am, I hope it isn't much farther,' gasped a fat nurse in grey, 'Master Jeremy is getting so tired and he's stung his leg so badly.'

'Boo! Hoo!' yelled Master Jeremy, 'I want to go home! I want to go home!'

'It's madness,' burst out Aunt Ellen, who was by now in what Rumbold would have vulgarly called a 'muck sweat'. 'I can't think why Mrs Bowers ever consented to the vicar taking charge like this. Bachelors cannot be expected to understand children.'

'Indeed no, ma'am, I fear Her Ladyship is feeling the heat dreadfully.'

By sheer British grit, however, shown, be it said, by children and adults alike, the party at last reached an open glade and the Whiting called a halt.

'Ain't it loverly though,' said the nurse to the chauffeur.

'It reminds me of a place I know in Burma,' said Lady Bramshott in rather a faded voice to the vicar. 'I never knew there was such a delightful spot so near to us.'

'Yes, yes, it's a favourite haunt of mine, Lady Bramshott, quite a favourite spot. Bless me!' exclaimed the Whiting suddenly. 'If that isn't a comma over there, on that blackberry bush!'

'I beg your pardon, Vicar?'

But the Whiting had already unshipped his net and was off in pursuit, with a party of children rushing at his heels. Lady Bramshott sighed. 'How the children love him,' she said to Aunt Ellen. 'Don't you think it's clever of him to find such a heavenly place for our picnic? It was quite worth that too, *too* tiring walk, don't you think?'

'I'm afraid your youngest must have found it very tiring,' said Aunt Ellen, 'the poor lamb has stung his legs *dreadfully*.'

'Oh, Jeremy *always* cries,' said Lady Bramshott – who was quite a good sort – 'he's really too small to bring out on a picnic but it will do him good. He'll be all right when they start to play. The children are still a little shy. How pretty Angela looks, Mrs Bowers. How old do you say she is?'

'Thirteen today. Yes, she's a pretty child.'

Angela at that moment was peering over the Whiting's shoulder at some object he was disentangling from his net. 'So fond of nature, don't you know, she *adores* birds and things. That's where the vicar is so good with children.'

There were cries of 'What is it?', 'Oh, let me look, please,' and, 'Comma, what a funny name. Why not call it a full stop!'

'I hope the little ones won't wander too far and get lost,' said Aunt Ellen.

'All my brats except the youngest can look after themselves,' said Lady Bramshott. 'My husband believes in them being self-reliant. A good thing, don't you think?'

'But surely, Lady Bramshott . . . if one of them *did* get lost, it would be a terrible experience for the poor lamb.'

Lady Bramshott, who had by now recovered from the hot walk, began marshalling the children for a game of hide and seek. The unhappy Whiting – who would have far rather been allowed to go off after butterflies – was called upon to organize.

Mrs Bowers directed that the picnic hamper should be carried into the shade. The time to eat had not yet arrived and the fish paste sandwiches might suffer.

'Where would you like it, ma'am?' asked the chauffeur, staggering under his weighty burden.

'Oh, anywhere in the shade; under the bracken will do, Burton, but see Master Jeremy doesn't find it.'

Master Jeremy, Lady Bramshott's youngest, was a fat and immensely greedy child, as greedy as a puppy. Mrs Bowers had not forgotten that on a former picnic in the Chase he had discovered where the basket lay and had helped himself, privily, whilst the other children and grown-ups had been otherwise engaged. And Jeremy had been rushed home, a dolorous journey, as he had been continually sick in the carriage all the way to Cherry Walden.

The grown-ups, who had not yet been roped in to assist with the children, now spread themselves in the shade, where they talked scandal and appraised each other's offspring.

The chauffeur soon found a nursemaid to entertain, the Whiting disappeared into the forest with the children at his heels – he reminded Lady Bramshott, so she said, of the Pied Piper of Hamlyn – and everybody seemed happy and to be enjoying themselves, all save Aunt Ellen, who had already been bitten twice on the neck by a mosquito.

*

Big John and Little John spent a lonely night in the tree. Without Bang and Robin for company they felt very depressed. They had caught no fish at the Blind Pool and the rain did not help matters. When, on the following morning, the skies were still overcast and the rain still fell in steady lines, they felt more depressed than ever. For the first time since they came to the forest they were bored and almost wished they could go back; even Banchester was better than mooning about doing nothing.

'Why *should* Robin have all the fun?' growled Big John, kicking the wood dust and staring out at the dripping trees. 'He's taken the rifle and if he *doesn't* come back today we shall run short of food.'

'I know. I vote we insist on keeping the rifle next time, if he wants to go off again by himself. Hullo! Big John, I believe it's going to clear up!'

It had stopped raining and very soon the sun gleamed forth and set the whole forest steaming.

'Hurrah! Let's go for a swim in the Blind Pool. Robin will just have to wait here until we come back!'

It was amazing how the coming of the sun brightened their spirits.

They reached the pool soon after midday. They stripped and had a delightful swim. Then they began to fish. Big John went up to the shallow end, where the stream trickled out of the pool, and the water daisy carpets grew. After the rain the perch were biting and he soon caught a dozen fine red-finned fish, the largest being well over a pound. It was great fun seeing the float move slowly away and down almost as soon as the worm sank to the bottom. A perch bite is decidedly bold and gladdens the heart of the patient angler. A large willow formed a comfortable seat for Big John and under it the water was some four feet deep. The glancing rays of sunlight revealed the bottom; he could see the dead leaves, and the rotten sticks embedded in them, he could watch his worms descending – even the perch were plainly visible as they moved out from under the willow roots to take his bait. Occasionally one dark thick-backed monster would glide up to the worm, examine it, and return to the shelter of the willow with injured dignity, as though to say, 'What *do* you take me for!' Sometimes as the worm touched bottom, Big John could see it wriggling to and fro like a little pink eel. And then a dark shadow eclipsed it and the float dived steadily.

Though these fish were smaller than the handsome bronze tench, they tasted even sweeter and, moreover, they were not so bony. Next to a trout, the perch is the best eating of all the freshwater fish. Very soon Big John saw a disturbance in the water, far out in the pool. At first he thought it was the head of a water rat and he put his hand in his pocket for his catapult. Water rats made good moving targets. But very soon he saw it was caused by a large grass snake. The creature came gracefully along, its head held well clear of the surface of the water, waggling from side to side. It came right in under the willow and Big John saw the long sinuous body waving like a green whiplash behind it.

The snake wriggled out of the water and began to glide away, with a faint rustle, through the fern. Big John, who wanted a snakeskin for a belt, dropped down upon it like a hawk and pinned it behind the head. The clammy green coils, with the black barred underbelly, writhed hideously round his hand in moving tight knots, but he held it firm.

He liked grass snakes. They were harmless creatures and usually the outlaws let them alone, but this particular snake was such a magnificent specimen it would make a fine belt, or even a scabbard for his hunting knife.

He was on the point of killing it when a thought occurred to him. Little John had never seen a grass snake at close quarters; he would keep it alive and show it to him. So he put it in his jacket pocket and a very unpleasant smell it made. Grass snakes when alarmed have this strange skunk-like power. But small boys are not so squeamish as grown-ups, so the snake went into his pocket as a matter of course. It writhed about a good deal and then lay still. It was dark in there and that quietened it.

Big John wriggled back down the willow and dropped into the bracken. He threaded his perch on a withy and walked back along the bank to join his brother. He found the latter in the act of landing a large red-finned perch of quite a pound weight, but as he drew it kicking and splashing to the side, the fish gave another plunge and tangled the line round a lily root. Their combined efforts failed to free it and a moment later the line came slack. 'Bother,' exclaimed Little John, 'it was a beauty too.'

They ruefully surveyed the broken cast and swore it was the finest perch they had ever hooked in the Blind Pool.

'Never mind,' sighed Big John, 'it was a beauty and no mistake, but I've got some good ones, enough for a fry. I've caught a snake too; I'll show it you when we get back to camp.'

They gathered up their rods and struck off through the fern in the direction of the oak tree. They had been walking for some time, Big John in the lead, when distant sounds brought them to an abrupt halt. Faint cries came on the air, children's voices! Children's voices in the Chase!

Their first reaction was to dive into the thickets but after listening as intently as deer for some considerable time Big John motioned his brother outlaw to follow and very cautiously they began to make their way in the direction of the sounds. The afternoon was so still that it was some time before they seemed to be drawing any nearer to these disturbers of their domain. But at last the clamour became so loud that both outlaws took to their hands and knees and finally their stomachs and at last, when they reached the edge of a glade, an amazing and disturbing spectacle met their startled gaze. For there, grouped about under the oaks, were clusters of children, chattering and laughing, some playing leapfrog, others playing tig and the rest clustered round no other person but the Whiting, who was apparently explaining the complicated anatomy of a caterpillar.

'Disgusting,' whispered Big John when he had recovered from his horror and astonishment, 'fancy coming into the Chase like this on a beastly picnic. Good gracious . . . there's Aunt Ellen!'

For a moment they gazed in awe at their unhappy aunt, it was so long since they had seen her. 'She's all dressed up like a dog's dinner,' whispered Little John, 'and she's got her Sunday hat on, the one with cherries in it.'

'That's because Lady Bramshott's there,' Big John whispered back, 'and look – there's that little hog Jeremy, wearing a ridiculous cap as big as a plate. Phew! What a crowd!'

'Yes, and there's Mrs Bowers *and* Angela,' said Little John, who had just caught sight of the latter on the other side of the glade. 'Let's get back to camp before they see us.'

But Big John's face was undergoing a change. A red tide slowly flooded his cheeks, his ears turned shell pink, ears which had not been washed for weeks. Poor Big John – he was suffering all over again the pangs of calf love. Angela was his ideal of the perfect woman. Now he was suddenly homesick. He wanted dreadfully to join that noisy, happy party and, more than anything, to talk to Angela. How she would love their house in the forest! How she would love to see the bird's nests and the butterflies! She was wearing a frilly white summer frock and a scarlet ribbon in her blue-black hair, and never, never, never had he seen her looking so adorable. But all this he had to bottle up and keep to himself. He would rather have died than betray these secret emotions. He must worship – alas! – from afar. Besides, what a sight he looked in his old rabbit skin kilt and his ragged clothes! His shoes, too, were wearing out, and the sole of one of them was tied to the uppers with thongs of pig's hide. An absolute tramp, in fact.

He was awakened, glassy-eyed, from his trance, by Little John's elbow jabbing him rudely in the ribs. 'Look, Big John, the picnic basket!'

'Oh shut up!' snapped Big John quite angrily. 'What about it anyway?'

'Why, can't you see they've put it under the bracken, over there? How about sneaking it? I'll bet it's chock-a-block with good things.'

Now it must be admitted that Big John was very hungry. Their breakfast had been meagre and they had just had a swim. In fact they were just about as hungry as growing boys can be who have had an enormous amount of exercise and have also been living rough.

'There'll be pies and cakes, sandwiches, and I don't know what,' said Little John. 'I'm off.'

'Here! Wait for me,' hissed Big John, Angela's charms quite forgotten for the moment.

The picnic hamper, a vast bright reddy-brown wicker one, was reposing close to the high bracken. Its guardian, the chauffeur, was flirting with a nursemaid under an oak close by. Certainly it was an opportunity not to be missed. It was easy meat for them, even easier than the removal of Bunting's trousers.

There was nobody on their side of the clearing; the picnic party had obligingly arranged themselves under the trees opposite to their hiding place, some on rugs – Aunt Ellen was sitting on two rugs because she feared the damp – and all were engrossed in small talk. The bulk of the children had now gone off with the Whiting, though they were not far away, as was borne out by the piercing screams of laughter and excited shouts which, to Big John and Little John, seemed sacrilege in this quiet forest retreat which they had come to regard as their own.

Had anyone been watching that happy picture, and especially the comfortable-looking picnic hamper, they would have seen a strange thing. The ferns moved ever so slightly close beside it and an extremely dirty claw appeared. Very gradually it felt towards the hamper, the fingers closed over the wickerwork and the hamper was mysteriously withdrawn an inch at a time, so slowly that the movement would have been scarcely discernible to the watcher.

Though the chauffeur and the nursemaid were only ten feet away they never heard a sound.

Big John gently pulled the wooden peg which held down the lid and, as gently, the lid was raised. There a wonderful sight met the gaze of those poor famished outlaws. A whole cold chicken! Blocks of sandwiches! Three large cakes, one iced with pink icing and in a box by itself; quite a dozen hard-boiled eggs! Ham! Honey! Pots of jam! And a hundred other mouth-tickling delights, including apples, oranges and chocolates!

In a moment or two every eatable had been removed, together with two aluminium kettles. The cups and plates they did not bother about but the kettles would come in useful.

'I don't think we ought to pinch the kettles,' hissed Big John under his breath, 'I've half a mind to put them back. It's too much like stealing.'

'Don't be a fool; remember Robin Hood. He robbed the rich to feed the poor, didn't he? We're outlaws, silly!' So the kettles were removed.

Then it seemed that Big John replaced something in the basket. Little John did not see what it was, he only caught a fleeting glimpse of some object being forced under the lid which was shut to quickly. Then the pin was replaced, the fern nodded once more and all was still!

'Ah, Vicar, you must be worn out with all your hard work,' crowed Mrs Bowers, when the Whiting appeared in a sea of hot red-faced children.

'Ah well, a little perhaps, but we've had a wonderful game of hide and seek, haven't we, children?'

'Yes! Yes!' they all chorused.

'And you must be famished too, you poor things. We will have tea at once, don't you think so, Lady Bramshott? It looks so cool!'

'Tea! Tea!' everyone shouted, dancing about. Some of the children turned somersaults with delight.

'I think I have brought enough for us all,' said Mrs Bowers, smiling at her guests. 'Now, Angela darling, you must look after your little friends and help to pass round the cakes and things.'

'Hooray!' shouted the children. 'Tea! Tea! Where's the tea!'

'Angela shall open the basket,' said Mrs Bowers, bridling, 'as it's your birthday, dear,' she added, 'and you may help your little guests to anything they like!'

'I feel Robin Hood and his merry men must be hiding somewhere in this forest,' said Lady Bramshott closing her sunshade. 'We must imagine we are in Sherwood preparing a hunting banquet. Come, children! Sit down anywhere!'

The hamper was pulled to the middle of the shuffling circle and every eye was fixed greedily upon it.

'This *is* a jolly picnic,' said Aunt Ellen – she had quite forgotten her mosquito bites – 'and how *kind* of you, *dear* Mrs Bowers, to ask us all like this!'

'The banquet is about to be spread,' boomed the Whiting, undoing the top button of his waistcoat. Mrs Bowers leant across and whispered something in his ear. He nodded his head rapidly, 'Certainly, certainly.'

'One moment, Angela darling,' said her mother, laying a restraining finger on Angela's arm, 'before we begin tea the vicar will say grace.' The shuffling and excited whispers died to silence as the party composed itself reverently with closed eyes.

'For what we are about to receive may the Lord make us truly thankful. Amen,' said everyone present – then – Angela lifted the lid!

The scene which followed is beyond my powers of description. For as Angela opened the hamper there instantly appeared over the side the waving head of a snake, its thin black tongue quivering malevolently, like the feelers of some obscene insect. Dreadful screams rang through the forest. There followed a moment of frozen horror, then the children scattered like rabbits in every direction. Aunt Ellen exclaimed, 'Oh! Oh! A serpent!' and fell back in a swoon, disclosing an unseemly length of thick woollen stocking and flannel underwear. Nursemaids and mothers fled, babbling incoherently between the trees.

Four figures remained. Angela, Lady Bramshott, the vicar and the chauffeur.

'It's only a harmless grass snake, I assure you,' the vicar exclaimed. 'There is no need for all this panic.'

Lady Bramshott, though white of face, seemed now rather amused – but then she had been used to snakes in Burma. And Angela, poor Angela, sat back on her heels, her head hung so that the dark curls fell forward and masked her crimson face. Glittering drops fell, like pearls, upon her knees.

'Fancy a snake in the picnic basket!' exclaimed the Whiting. 'I do declare it is a most strange occurrence! Come, children,' he said, gazing about him, 'come, everyone, it cannot harm you. It is no viper but a harmless grass snake!'

'But it's eaten the tea!' sobbed Angela, her shoulders shaking wildly. 'It's eaten the tea and spoilt my picnic!'

Mrs Bowers who, like the others, was emerging like a startled faun from the undergrowth, was speechless. Her eyes were staring at the empty hamper. The chauffeur now advanced upon the snake with a stick, but the vicar restrained him. 'Do not kill it, Burton, it is quite a harmless reptile.'

The harmless reptile was now coiling itself round the Whiting's arm, for he had taken it gently from the hamper, and was emitting a most skunk-like smell.

'Oh, Vicar, I'm sure it will bite you!' wailed Aunt Ellen.

'It's eaten the tea!' wailed Jeremy, who had now reappeared. The fact there was no tea was a far more dreadful catastrophe than the discovery of the snake.

'Nonsense, nonsense,' said the Whiting, 'of *course* it can't have eaten the tea! Grass snakes live on frogs and things, not cakes, and . . . '

'A *whole chicken*,' gasped Mrs Bowers, 'and there were cakes and sandwiches, everything. I superintended the packing of it myself!'

'Oh! Oh! Oh!' Angela collapsed again.

'My poor child,' said Lady Bramshott soothingly, 'it's *most* disappointing for you, dear, but never mind. The tea must have been left in the wagonette by mistake.'

'But the kettles have been taken too!' gasped Mrs Bowers.

'Are you sure nobody touched the basket?' asked Lady Bramshott, turning to the chauffeur.

'Perfectly sure, milady. I was sitting beside it all the time.'

'Most extraordinary, a most extraordinary occurrence,' repeated the Whiting, 'it is inexplicable unless . . . ' he swung round on his heel, his eyes glittering as he searched the inscrutable forest about them, 'unless those Dower House boys have some hand in it!'

Meanwhile, 'those Dower House boys', after waiting to see the result of their escapade, were now making their way swiftly and silently by devious paths to the oak tree clearing. Big John had taken off his ragged flannel coat and they had made a hammock of it, in which reposed all their booty. It was a heavy weight indeed, and every few yards they had to lower it to the ground and take a spell of rest. But at last they reached the tree and there found Robin building a fire. He looked up as they came into the clearing staggering under the weighty burden.

'Hullo, my merry men, what on earth have you got there?' he exclaimed, gazing in utter astonishment at his brother outlaws: Big John and Little John said no word but gently lowered the coat on to the ground and began to sort out the things. When all was spread they turned to Robin, whose eyes were now out on stalks. 'There you are, Master Robin, we've had good hunting. We've robbed the rich. There before you are the contents of a picnic basket, a very large picnic basket, as you can guess.'

Robin went down on his knees and undid the box which contained the iced cake. Reverently he withdrew it from its paper wrapping. The journey through the forest had rather crushed it and the pink icing was melting, but there, still legible, was written in sugar a name – ANGELA.

Big John's face, when he saw the cake unwrapped, underwent a complete change. A moment before it had been wreathed in smiles of triumph; now it was transformed into a face of someone much older, almost an old man's.

'Angela,' he gasped, 'I – I never knew . . . '

'Never knew what?' asked Robin, looking up at him, puzzled.

'Why . . . that must be Angela's birthday cake, it was her birthday picnic!'

'Well, what about it? What difference does that make?' asked his elder brother.

On a sudden impulse Big John sprang forward, snatched up the cake, and crammed it back into the box. The others watched him uncomprehending. Then he turned and made for the path, the way he had come.

'Stop him!' shouted Little John. 'He's going to take it back, he'll be nabbed!'

Robin went after the fleeing Big John like a panther. In a few yards he caught him up and Big John turned at bay, clutching the box. 'Leave me alone,' he said wildly, 'leave me alone I say!' Tears were running down his cheeks and Robin stopped, shocked beyond measure.

'I'm going to take it back to her, it was her party and we've spoilt it all!'

'Now, steady on, Big John, you can't do that you know, you'll give us away. You'll get caught.'

'I don't care,' said Big John desperately, 'I'm going to take it back.' He turned again to flee, but Robin grabbed him by the collar.

'You're mushy on Angela!' he exclaimed with scorn in his voice.

Big John struck him in the face with all his force; there was an instant of grunting and swaying. Then the box fell to the ground, shattering the cake to a squashy pulp. The two boys fought savagely, rolling over and over, punching and pummelling, until they stopped, like sparring gamecocks, from sheer exhaustion.

'What's all the trouble?' asked the astonished Little John, who had come up with them, drawn by the sound of fighting.

'I don't know,' said Robin wearily, 'he's mad I think. Here, take the blessed cake, it's not much good to anybody now.'

Big John sat among the fern. His nose was bleeding and the wild look was fading from his eye. Both Big John and Robin had just experienced strange primeval passions which neither understood. At last he got slowly to his feet. He came up to Robin and smiled wryly. 'Sorry, I . . . I . . . I've been a bit of a fool,' he muttered. And the three boys went back in silence to the tree.

15. Bunting Again

THE LATEST news of the doings of the Dower House outlaws soon reached Bunting. There was certainly something supernatural about Brendon Chase; it was haunted without a doubt, by other spirits than the Martyr and his headless steed! Else why should trousers, and the contents of picnic baskets, so mysteriously vanish into thin air?

Bunting remembered that cold and shameful ride of his, of how he had stood, like an escaped lunatic, in Ernie's garden, pleading to be let in. And now came news of weeping children, terrified out of their lives, of serpents, of ransacked hampers. It did not need a Sherlock Holmes to guess that the encampment of the outlaws was somewhere in the Chase. Bunting had blamed the vicar for absconding with his trousers. Now he saw he had been wrong. And there arose in his breast a great determination; he made a vow, by all he held sacred, that he would bring the boys to justice.

He organized quite an army of beaters from the Duke's estate. But the Chase was drawn completely blank. At least three of the 'hounds' passed through the very clearing where the boys were encamped, and even walked *twice* round the oak; they saw no signs of fires, or man. The outlaws, warned long before the drive began by the screeching of jays, had taken refuge with Smokoe Joe, who was now a firm and valued ally. They had cleverly concealed all traces of habitation. Even the marks of the fire had been covered with leaves and bracken, and nothing had been left within the tree to betray them.

The drive having drawn a blank, Bunting haunted the Chase by night and by day, though he saw nought but bats and rabbits and heard nothing but the quavering hoots of many owls. The only results were agonizing rheumatics and a bad cold. After all, how could a large policeman, quite unversed in woodland lore, utterly ignorant even of how to walk quietly in his bargelike boots; how could he hope to capture three desperate outlaws, whose hearing and sight was nearly as keen as the foxes with whom they dwelt, and who could move as silently as shadows through brake and briar?

He visited Smokoe several times – once all three boys had been hidden in the bushes close to the well behind the shack – but Smokoe shook his huge nose and peered at Bunting like a jackdaw deliberating mischief.

'No, no, Sergeant, there ain't no boys in the Chase or I'd 'ave seen 'em or 'eard 'em. I tells you they ain't 'ere! Ef I do find anything I'll let ye know, I've told you that.'

And Bunting would stride away, throwing defiant glances at the bushes about him as though daring them to mock him, and uttering oaths under his breath. He was no nearer, not one step nearer to their capture than he had been on the night Aunt Ellen had called him to the Dower House. He was like a bull trying to catch three field mice. Yet one day the boys would make some little slip, they would become overbold, and like foxes which have taken to chicken stealing, they would be brought to justice and the birch. So thought Bunting. And so thought many another in the surrounding hamlets, Aunt Ellen included.

But August mellowed into September, and at last came September's end, and no further sign was forthcoming, no little single clue which told that the outlaws were still at large. And then the good folk thought 'them Dower 'Ouse boys have gone away now, for sure, they won't be seen or heard of again'; besides winter was at hand. Winter was at hand! Ah yes, indeed it was, and with the shortening nights and misty mornings what a glory came to the forest, and what romance!

For weeks the trees had been heavy-laden with tired green leaves; every bird was silent save the robin, even the wood pigeons had ceased to coo. In the forest the air had seemed sometimes almost stale, if one can use such a word about nature, but now! What glory! What a colour ran riot in the underwood, how sweet and keen became the morning air which blew into the heated forest like a breeze into a stuffy room!

Those who have lived in the wilds, hunting for a livelihood, look forward to the fall. A new zest for living stirs within the blood, adventure beckons in every yellowing leaf. This is strange. Autumn is, in a sense, the negation of life; it is a season for death rather, and is associated in the mind with the aged. Yet what a spark runs through the blood of the hunter, both four-footed and two-footed! But what stirred the boys more than anything was to hear the fallow bucks challenging one another. All that summer they had seen only two, the one which Robin had seen beside the Blind Pool and the one he had missed with his rifle on that eventful day when he met Smokoe Joe.

But from the grunting roars which now resounded through the Chase it was evident that there were many more in the Chase than the boys had ever guessed. Big John heard a buck roaring close to their camp one evening but it was so dark he could not see it. Even the owls seemed to sense new adventure in the air, if an owl can do such a thing, and their loud hooting made merry music about their camp fire when darkness fell.

They missed Bang dreadfully, so much so they even contemplated another raid on the Dower House to fetch Tilly away. But Tilly was not half so well trained as Bang and she might betray their presence. At least twice a week they visited

Smokoe Joe. The latter was now their sworn ally. All the tales of his miserly ways were quite unfounded, as are most village rumours. Though there was a fat reward to be had – fifty pounds was a great deal of money to a poor man in those days – he never contemplated betrayal for a moment. It was enough for him that Gyp had been restored; he was their true friend now for as long as they chose to remain in the Chase. And more than that, for the very first time in his life he enjoyed company. With men he would have been stiff and sullen but these boys were after his own heart, they were unaffected, and he understood them. They never made rude remarks about his nose, though at first Little John, especially, had been awed and interested in the frank way boys have when they see anything unusual or abnormal, but after a while they never even noticed it. If Smokoe had possessed a tail the boys would have taken it quite as a matter of course. And what times they had in his shack! What feasts they had in that little dim room when the stove grew nearly red hot. Many a luckless pheasant was discussed upon the deal table, many a yarn was spun and many a pipe of baccy did Robin Hood and Smokoe enjoy when the day's work was done. Robin had acquired the art of smoking, but Smokoe's Bosun's Plug was too much for his brother outlaws.

They did not go near Smokoe during broad day. It would have been too risky. And since the time Bunting had called on Smokoe, and the boys had had to hide in the bushes by the well, the old charcoal burner had forbidden them to come whilst it was yet fully light. They were sorry about this because they loved to see him at work about his kilns. They would have liked to help him chop the faggots and stack them on the conical mounds and cover the whole with turf. But Smokoe was right: it was too dangerous.

The outlaws found him most useful in the matter of setting snares. He soon showed them why all their efforts had been fruitless. They had been making several mistakes. One was that they had been setting the snares in the wrong places. All through the forest the rabbits had their special runs, and the worn patches on the woodland moss showed where the animals rested as they 'loppitted' along. The wild rabbit will never travel far flat out even when he is pursued.

They set the snares between these bare patches and, as far as possible, took great care to avoid touching the snare wire with their hands. If any long grass had been trampled down or branches broken off, the rabbits never came near. Smokoe also told them how rabbits will sit on any little eminence, such as an ant heap or a molehill; sometimes the top of the heap would be found to be quite trodden down and worn, with telltale currants all about. A gin set there was sure of success, but the snares were a more humane method. Tree stumps and the tops of logs were also favoured resting places. Once they got the knack they caught as many rabbits as they required and thereby saved ammunition.

Smokoe swore that there were wild cats in the forest. It is doubtful whether what he said was true. The cats that were undoubtedly found, and sometimes seen, in the Chase were domestic cats gone wild and they grew as large and fierce as the true wild cat.

With the advent of autumn the outlaws turned their attention to trapping and snaring in earnest. They experimented with various springes, snares and even pits, covered with branches. The last were quite useless, though they did catch a hedgehog. Nor did they have any luck with the springes, even though Smokoe showed them how to set them. He had caught woodcocks, so he said, in springes. It was the deadfall trap which appealed most to the outlaws; there was a crude primitive look about the double row of stakes and poised log resting on its trigger. It was in this type of trap they caught their best skin and the securing of that pelt was destined to have many repercussions. So far, Bunting had haunted and lurked in the background, a blue shadow in the intricate forest, waiting to strike and pounce. He had sworn to bring the outlaws to book, and Bunting was a man of his word. Of all the Olympians who had suffered at the hands of the outlaws Bunting suffered the most, even more than Aunt Ellen.

His pride had suffered, his self-respect had suffered; no wonder that he cried for vengeance! And the knowledge that three young whippersnappers had so far bested him was more than he could bear. Outwardly he made no sign. He went about his usual business of administering the law in that rustic area, the inspection of dog and gun licences, sheep dip regulations and the like – all the everyday jobs of the rural policeman – with the same outward calm and dignity as of old, but it was the capture of the Dower House boys which secretly occupied his every thought.

Despite his unsuccessful ambushes he still went to the Chase whenever the opportunity arose; when normally he would have been digging in his allotment, he would sneak away to that reddening wilderness of tree and brake.

What worried him was that, so far, he had no real proof the boys *were* in the Chase! Indeed, the only time he had seen them in the flesh was that summer dusk at High Wood. But the fact that Little John had been seen in Brendon, and that when pursued, he had made for Cheshunt Toller; this was the most damning evidence.

One afternoon towards the middle of October, Bunting set out on what was destined to be the last time he ever dared to enter the Chase alone. Oblivious of what the fates held in store he mounted his bicycle, correctly garbed, and set his course along the now familiar road, feeling that at last success would crown his efforts.

It was one of those autumn days when the sun shines with a faded splendour which fills the distances with mysterious glazes. The ride to the Chase was a pleasant one, vastly different from that sweltering ordeal when he had toiled up the long hill in the merciless heat of July.

Bunting felt happy as he trundled along; he even whistled a little tune. Somehow he felt that today he would at last find some tangible clue that would land the boys in his grasp, to say nothing of the fifty pounds reward, which still held good. On the road the leaves lay in swathes, for exceptionally early frosts had stripped the ash trees as if with a knife. His bicycle wheel rustled quietly through them and there arose the fragrance of damp and decaying vegetation. Only the oaks retained the heavy green of summer. The chestnuts behind the inn at Martyr Bar were mounds of flaming gold, their splendour increased by the rays of sunlight which filtered through them from behind.

Out in the cleared stubble burnished rooks and jackdaws moved, glistening in the pale golden light as though they had been cast in metal and in one field a single magpie was perched on a sheep's back, digging into the wool for ticks.

When Bunting reached the Chase he found a very different picture from that which he had seen in the heat of midsummer. It was quite surprising how new vistas had opened out now the undergrowth was becoming bare; the ridings seemed strangely altered, almost unrecognizable. There were many horse chestnuts in the forest and as he made his way up the dew-wet path which led to the Blind Pool – he had left his bicycle, padlocked, under some nut bushes – the large spiny conkers thumped to the ground on all sides of him. Standing still, close to the riding edge, with the sweet aroma of the autumn woods in his nostrils, he could hear these resounding thumps coming from all sides. Some of the nuts crashed into the underwood, others bounced down on the grass beside him. He saw a little red squirrel under one of the trees eating a hazelnut, sitting up and holding it between its front paws, a pretty picture of wildlife, but one which was quite wasted on Bunting.

When he cautiously approached the Blind Pool – he knew his way now from painful experience – it was, as usual, deserted, save for three mallards which rocketed up over the willows with a great quacking. Now Bunting knew enough of woodland lore to know that had the boys been lurking anywhere near, those mallards would not have been on the pond. So risking the chance of getting lost he struck off between the trees in the direction of Smokoe Joe's.

The bracken was dying. Everywhere there stretched a sea of ruddy gold fronds and many rabbits bounded off as he pushed through it. Now and again he stopped to listen, and to get his bearings, but all he heard was the occasional thump of a chestnut and the faint cawing of rooks. He saw the latter at a great altitude above the Chase, wheeling about in wide circles in the way rooks have in fine October weather.

From their vantage point they must have been able to see the whole eleven thousand acres of woodland spread like a carpet below them, a multicoloured rug which every day assumed richer and more colourful hues.

Pigeon after pigeon clattered from the oaks about him as he went forward, their blue-grey bodies visible for an instant against the background of trees.

Even at this late time a few ragged butterflies were on the wing; red admirals and a tortoiseshell or two, flopping about as though drugged, looking, no doubt, for some cosy crevice in which to hide.

After much wandering Bunting smelt the reek of a fire and hopefully bent his steps thither. He was surprised to find himself stepping out into the clearing in which was Smokoe Joe's abode; he had not expected to find the place so soon. The old man was busy slamming the earth round one of his mounds or 'ovens' with the flat of his spade and he did not see Bunting until the latter shouted a cheery 'good afternoon'. Gyp came growling and barking from behind the shack, all his hairs on end.

Smokoe straightened his back and for a second did not recognize the sergeant, for the sun was in his eyes. Then he leant on his spade and spat. 'It's a grand afternoon, Sergeant,' he said at length. Bunting was thinking Smokoe's nose was bigger, much bigger, than when last he saw it. What a hideous old creature he was! Bet he knew something about the boys and wouldn't tell!

'You ain't claimed the fifty quid then, Smokoe?'

Smokoe spat again and countered with, 'No, 'ave you?'

'Not yet,' answered Bunting, taking out a cigarette and lighting it. For a moment or two he stood watching the smoke from the kiln going straight up in a blue, swiftly moving column, high above the forest trees. 'I just thought I'd take a walk through the Chase, it's such a grand day for it. Never knew it was so good in autumn.' Bunting indicated with a wave of his hand the rusting trees which hedged them round.

'Ah, it's all right,' grunted Smokoe, continuing with his work. 'You gets used to it yer know, livin' 'ere, year in, year out.'

'I suppose so. You 'eard 'ow one o' they Dower 'Ouse boys was seen in Brendon and 'ow 'e got away in the baker's cart, I suppose?'

Smokoe laughed. 'No, I 'adn't 'eard that; got right away did 'e!'

'Ah, a rare old hunt they 'ad. Those boys are in this Chase, Smokoe,' said the sergeant with sudden conviction. 'I've no doubt at all o' that. One thing, with winter coming on, they won't stick it long.'

'Mebbe they won't, if they are around anywheres.'

'You've got yer dog back agin then,' said Bunting, eyeing Gyp distrustfully.

'Ah, 'e cum back all right, cum back one day last August. 'E'd bin off huntin' I expect, the young devil. Well, I'll 'ave to be leavin' ye now, Sergeant; I've got some poles to fell in Duke's Acres.' Smokoe nodded to Bunting. He shouldered his spade and whistled Gyp who still growled low growls deep inside.

'Aye, aye,' said Bunting. 'Well, good day, Smokoe, don't ferget to kip your eyes skinned!'

He stood watching the old fellow go off through the trees and sat down on a log to finish his cigarette. The smoke from the fire had thinned to a faint blue column, like a very slender thread of moving vapour. He looked up and saw some midges dancing overhead. How quiet it was! How warm here, in this clearing among the trees! His eyes roved over the shack. A mean dwelling, not fit for a stable! No wonder Smokoe was queer in the head.

Humming a little tune Bunting got up and wandered carelessly round the hut. He glanced in at the window but the curtains hid the dim interior. Bunting stopped and looked in the direction which Smokoe Joe had taken. He felt as though he was prying indecently, but after all it was his duty.

He came closer to the window and peered in under cupped hands. He saw the stove glowing red and the little iron range against the wall. The deal table, well scrubbed, the tumbled apology for a bed in the corner. Up on top of the cupboard, right in the corner, he saw a whitish object sitting to attention, and saw with a little start it was Smokoe's pet owl.

Bunting went on whistling. Nothing suspicious there, nothing at all! Yet that old man knew something, Bunting was certain of it.

By now the golden afternoon was beginning to chill. A few cirrus clouds were visible, far up in the west, and from a distance he heard the ringing clap of an axe. Smokoe at work in Duke's Acre, no doubt.

He wandered away from the clearing, back the way he had come, his large feet brushing through the numberless leaves which lay thickly in the ride.

Then there came to him, as he walked along, a distant grunting roar, almost as if a wild beast, escaped from a menagerie, was at large. Bunting stopped in his tracks, puzzled. What a strange sound! It came again from among the trees on the left of the path. It was a sound between a cough, a bark and a roar, all rolled into one. How very curious!

Bunting decided to investigate. He pushed through the yellowing hazels, knocking off the polished brown nuts until he came upon a grassy open space. And there, in the centre of the clearing, a magnificent fallow buck was pawing the ground. Its eyes were rolling white, and it was thrusting its horns into the matted bracken and moss.

Bunting was interested. The animal was not more than thirty yards distant. He stood for some time watching it, not daring to move in case he should scare it. Then he whistled. The buck immediately raised its head and stared about it. Bunting was amused. Then it turned its full dark eyes and gazed directly at him, its muzzle held high in the air as it tried to wind him.

Bunting stood without moving, a cigarette in his right hand. How strange! He always thought that deer were shy of men, but this one was certainly not. Indeed it was far otherwise, for it actually took several paces towards him, grunting, roaring and stretching out its neck. Bunting thought it looked quite fierce; he even began to feel a little nervous. It was time to show the beast who was master. So he waved his arms suddenly, like the sails of a windmill, and shouted, 'Hey up!' Then all at once the buck charged. It came so quickly and so unexpectedly that Bunting was taken completely by surprise.

He let out a startled shout and dodged aside as the buck, which was almost on him, gave a savage sideways jab with its horns which missed him by half an inch. By Jove! Unless he got out of this pretty quickly it would be serious, for with a grunting bellow the buck had turned and was making ready for another charge.

Bunting, now thoroughly startled, made a leap for the nearest tree, a chestnut. He swung himself up into one of the lower branches and had barely got astride it when the buck came at him again. Its horns actually jarred the bough on which he was sitting. Bunting moved to a higher perch like a frightened fowl. And underneath the tree the buck stood, gazing up, grunting, pawing the ground, and now and again tossing up the moss and bracken. Then it walked rapidly round the tree as though on sentry-go. It had no intention of leaving his victim, no intention at all! Bunting, perched on his bough, deliberated on the best action to take.

The watchful buck still mounted guard below and there he looked like staying. Bunting thought of many things. He had better return to Smokoe . . . no, Smokoe might not be at home. At any rate, he wouldn't be back until dark. No, he must somehow get rid of this infernal beast, and make his way back to the road.

Already the sun was down to the horizon, the forest was growing chill. Up in his eyrie poor Bunting felt both cold and foolish. And still the buck made no move to leave.

Bunting shouted and bellowed. He broke off a rotten branch and hurled it at his tormentor – and missed. At last he called aloud on Smokoe to come and release him, for he had thrown all dignity to the winds. He did not care now if he was discovered perched up in a tree like a hunted cat, he felt he could not stay there much longer.

To add to his misery some mistle thrushes and jays, hearing the racket, came and perched on adjoining trees and scolded at him. They thought no doubt he was a new form of owl and regarded him as vermin.

He even desired that the boys might come to his rescue. But only the echoes mocked him. Owls began their melancholy hootings and in the west the sun had gone down, leaving a yellow flared sky against which the half-bare forest trees were thrown in sharp relief.

But that maddening beast still pawed and grunted below. It still did sentry-go round the tree. He stared down at its broad barrel of a body with the thick hair as dense as the pile of a handsome rug.

What was he to do? Drop to the ground and trust to his own speed? Impossible! He would not stand a chance!

Why had not Smokoe warned him that the wild deer, usually so timid and full of fear, behaved like this when the flames of sexual passion roused them?

He now recalled other tales of men treed by deer. A distant relation of his had been a keeper in Windsor Park and had, in like manner, been driven to desperate straits by a rutting buck. He remembered the story well, of how that unhappy man had been up in the tree for many hours and was only released when a fellow keeper shot the deer.

All about among the bushes little birds were hopping and peeping. They were preparing for the night but feared the monster up in the chestnut. Blacker grew the twisted branches of the trees against the sky, darker and darker grew the forest. Should he try and reach Smokoe? Would the buck see him when darkness came? Could they see in the dark? All these things he thought of as he watched the pacing beast below.

Bunting at last edged down the branch. It overhung some nut bushes. He might drop into those and get away under the thickets. But the buck saw the movement and came forward, grunting and roaring, its breath pluming on the cold air. Bunting edged prudently back. A crescent moon appeared over the trees, objects became indistinct, the stars came out, wide-winged silent owls flew by, hooting hollowly.

Then, from far away, Bunting heard another challenging buck. It meant deliverance. His guard below the tree pricked its large ears and moved slowly off. He could hear its indignant grunts as it trotted away through the trees. At last Bunting was free! Very painfully he scrambled to the ground. His limbs were so cramped he found he could barely walk. To try and find Smokoe would be to court disaster for there was little light now in the sky and one path looked very like another. But he thought he could find his way to the Blind Pool and so to the road.

He reached his bicycle at last and with half-frozen fingers unlocked the padlock. Why did such humiliating things happen to Bunting? This wretched Chase was alien, threatening him with evil. And it all boiled down to those unspeakable Dower House boys!

And that was the last time he ever went to the Chase alone.

16. The Badger Skin

THE GLORY of autumn in the Chase was not wasted on the outlaws. They had never dreamt it could look so enchanting. Even at midsummer a great forest can be rather monotonous in form and tone; there is no vivid contrast of colour, each tree and bush is very much the same shade of green. And in the greater part of the Chase the trees were of a uniform height; it was only in Duke's Acres, where the boys had their secret encampment, that there was any disparity in the size of the oaks.

But as soon as the first frosts got to work, each bush, each tree, was of a different hue. The brambles flamed a deep rose, the maples a clear singing yellow, the larches torches of amber flame – there were few larches in Duke's Acres, but many in the Crown forest adjoining – the chestnuts abundantly magnificent and generous of fruit. Besides horse chestnuts there were sweet chestnuts and filberts. The outlaws ate nuts until they were tired of them. Nuts are like chocolates, you can go on eating vast quantities until you feel you never want to see another. The boys dug a hole in the ground and stored therein, like squirrels, a large quantity.

The beech was uncommon in the Chase for it is a tree which delights in light soil and the soil of the Chase was heavy clay. This was curious, as not far away was the Weald where the subsoil was entirely chalk. Beeches grew there in profusion. Even in Brendon Park the beech was the predominating tree.

So the few beeches which were found in the Chase were much admired by the outlaws. The ground below was invariably thick with finches, which came after the beech mast. The boys saw some bramblings there at the end of October. They thought at first they were chaffinches but when they flew up they showed the white rump. They were colourful little birds, as richly patterned as the autumn leaves.

There seemed more to do in the forest now autumn had come. All the butterflies had gone and with them many of the summer birds, but other winter migrants came to take their place. And one of the most beautiful spots in the whole Chase was, of course, the Blind Pool. The sight of the solid carpets of gold and red leaves floating on the black water was perfectly enchanting. Robin would often sneak away to the pool, not to fish or shoot, but simply to watch, by the hour, the rich colours reflected in the water and those silent weeping trees. Sometimes the wind blew and showers of leaves filled the whole sky, and even in that sheltered retreat the dark waters were ruffled and the floating leaf rafts blown to one side. At other times it was deathly still, with the leaves wavering downwards softly and directly to earth, or maybe lighting with a fairy kiss upon the bosom of the pond.

It was at the Blind Pool that Robin saw one of the rarest birds which visit Britain. He had the rifle, loaded, in his hands, but he never dreamt of shooting, though he knew the skin would be worth a great deal of money.

One evening he stalked the pool, alone as usual, and on creeping among the dying bracken fronds and peeping along the surface of the water he immediately saw a dumpy grey bird standing on the bleached branch of a dead tree at the far end. It had much the same colouring as a heron but was far smaller and the neck was short and thick. Moreover, its back was a glossy blue-black; only the wing coverts were ash-grey.

Robin knew a lot about birds but this strange visitor momentarily stumped him. He half thought it might be an immature heron and then he suddenly realized what it was: a night heron.

He was not surprised that he should see so exciting a visitor in this lonely woodland pool, but all the same, the thrill of it was almost more than he could bear. He longed to rush away back to the oak and fetch the others to share his pleasure but he knew if he did so the bird would be disturbed and would probably never come back. For an hour he watched it standing there like a bird carved out of some beautiful grey and white marble or soapstone. When the day faded and the shadows gathered, the night heron seemed to wake up. It dropped off the dead tree into the shallows and began stalking about. No doubt it was searching for frogs. Very soon the light grew so dim he could barely make it out, only the wheeling ripples marked its position.

Then Robin stole back through the fern and ran back to the camp with the great news. Perhaps it would still be there next morning; it might even make the Blind Pool its home! There was something so essentially right in that secretive woodland heron living in such a place, all alone in the middle of Brendon Chase!

But when they went back next morning there was no sign of it and Robin even began to wonder whether he had ever seen it, or whether he had dreamt the whole thing. They never saw it again.

From the cover of the yellowing hazels Robin made some skilful shots at the shy mallards who now haunted the place with greater frequency. He had to wait until the unsuspecting wildfowl cruised near the bank before pressing the trigger and then, with a clean well-directed shot, he would turn them orange paddles up, to be retrieved with a true hunter's glow of satisfaction. Many an evening there was duck for supper, and appetizing and fragrant smells wafted from the clearing by the old oak. Perhaps it was lucky for the boys that Bunting had ceased to haunt the

The night heron at the Blind Pool

Chase. Of course they knew nothing about the episode of the stag.

So far their efforts to shoot one of these great beasts had been fruitless. They now occasionally caught glimpses of a white 'flag' bobbing through the rusty fern, but they never had a good chance of a well-directed shot and this, with their small-bore rifle, was of utmost importance. Had they a shotgun they could have no doubt bagged several but that was not to be thought of. Even Smokoe Joe's occasional poaching forays after the deer were risky for him. It is true that labourers in the field outside the Chase sometimes heard the roar of his old muzzle-loader but they turned a deaf ear and said nothing. Rumours frequently came to the Duke's ears of Smokoe's deer stealing activities, but he did not bother. He took no interest in game preserving and consequently employed no keepers, which was the luckiest thing in the world for the outlaws. Had there been keepers in the Chase the boys could not have lived there for many days without discovery.

As the cold weather came the tench ceased to feed and consequently the capture of one of these fish became quite an event. But there were still perch to catch and also pike which, now the temperature of the water had fallen considerably, began to show marked appetites.

With the help of Smokoe Joe, Robin rigged up some pike tackle. Smokoe lent the boys a big white pike float and some gorge hooks, and with small perch – from whose backs the spines had been snipped off – they caught some good ones. The pike bites were even bolder than the perch bites; the white blob of a float would suddenly vanish with a swirl among the golden leaf rafts and the feel of the big fish on the end of the line sent a tingling thrill through the angler.

They fished with rods – stout hazel wands – and sometimes when they struck their fish it felt as though they had fouled the bottom. Then the great, bronzy-green monster would be hauled in, fighting and splashing, until it was close to the bank and could be hauled ashore by its hideous shoe-shaped head. You can always grasp a pike firmly by the eye sockets. Perhaps the flavour of the pike was not so delicate as the tench and perch, but they were very good, especially if the boys took the trouble to remove the numberless tiny bones.

But it was trapping which occupied the greater part of their time. They did not trap for food but for pelts. Even Harold's clothes were now in ribbons and they made themselves complete suits of skins, with the help, I must admit, of Smokoe Joe, who took a keen delight in 'making do' as he called it.

Smokoe also allowed them free use of his vegetable garden and they had all the potatoes and cabbages they wanted, which made a great difference to their diet.

Indeed, had it not been for the old charcoal burner, I very much doubt whether the boys could have stayed on in the forest for as long as they did.

One evening, towards the end of October, as they sat around their camp fire, Robin broached a suggestion to his brother outlaws.

'I've been wondering lately about writing to Father and Mother and telling them what we're doing. You see, Aunt Ellen's sure to have written and told them all sorts of tales and they'll be in an awful stew.'

'But that'll spoil everything,' exclaimed Big John. 'They'll write back and tell Aunt Ellen, Aunt Ellen will tell the police and they'll search the Chase from end to end until they *do* find us.'

'Well, we've got to go back *sometime*,' retorted Robin. 'When they come home from India we

won't be able to stay out in the wilds any longer.
I was thinkin' that we might ease their minds; I
bet Aunt Ellen's painted as black a picture as she
can. What do you say, Little John?'

'Not a bad idea – it'll let 'em know we're safe
and well, and not murdered or anything.'

Robin got up from the fire and went into the
tree, emerging with a stub of pencil, a grimy sheet
of paper and an envelope.

'I got these from Smokoe when I fetched those
cabbages last night. I wasn't going to write
anything until I'd talked it out with you. Now,' he
said, squatting down in the firelight and wetting
the pencil stub, 'what shall we say?'

'Say we've run away to the woods and that
Smokoe's looking after us until they come back to
England. Say we've been awfully unhappy and
that Harold's been ill with measles.'

'Doesn't sound much of a case,' said Robin
ruefully. 'In her way Aunt Ellen's been good to us,
looking after us and having us at the Dower House.'

'I know, it's mighty difficult, but that's about
all we can say,' said Big John. 'Anyway, I think we
ought to tell them where we are.'

So Robin settled himself on his elbows and
began to write by the light of the fire.

Brendon Chase
October 20

Dear Father and Mother,

We expect Aunt Ellen's told you we've run away from the Dower House and all about Harold getting measles. He's quite all right again now, he's with us. We were awfully unhappy at the Dower House, Aunt Ellen doesn't understand us and we miss you both awfully. So we decided that when Harold went down with measles and we were told to stay on at the Dower House and have lessons with the vicar that we'd go off.

John and I ran away to Brendon Chase and later we went back for Harold when he was better. We've been living like Robin Hood, shooting all we wanted with Rumbold's rifle – which we borrowed – and we've made friends with an old charcoal burner called Smokoe Joe. He's a great pal of ours because we found his dog which had got stuck down a rabbit hole.

We've had a wonderful time. We live in a big oak tree right in the middle of the Chase. When you come home of course we'll come back.

We expect you'll be angry at what we've done. But we all decided that we'd write and let you know no harm has come to us and that we're

*longing to see you again. And we didn't want
you to worry about us or listen to any of Aunt
Ellen's tales.*

*You told us you were coming back in the New
Year. We'll come back then and you can punish
us how you like. We know we deserve it, but
we'd rather take our punishment from you than
from Aunt Ellen.*

This has been a difficult letter to write.

Your affectionate sons,
Robin
John
Harold

*P. S. We shot a wild pig in the forest and we've
found a lovely pool called the Blind Pool which
isn't very far from our hiding place. It's full of fish.*

'How will that do?' said Robin, when he had
finished.

His brothers read it in turn.

'Yes, that's about all we can say,' said Big John.
'It'll let 'em know we're safe and sound, anyway.'

Robin addressed the envelope, licked it and put
it back in the tree. 'We'll give it to Smokoe to post
in Cheshunt Toller; he's going there tomorrow for
his weekly supplies. Good old Smokoe, I don't

know what we'd do without him. We must ask him to supper one night. He can sleep here too, if he likes, though I don't expect he'll leave his kilns. He's never seen our camp.'

'Good idea – yes, let's!'

'And we'll have a special supper in his honour, and one for Bang – Gyp I mean,' suggested Robin.

The old fellow was manifestly pleased when he was asked.

'Yes, I'll come, Gyp an' me. There's a moon now and I can find me way.'

'Oh, we'll fetch you,' said Robin, in the tone of voice one might expect if he were offering to send a car for Smokoe. 'One of us'll act as guide. You'll never find us by yourself.'

And so Smokoe came, accompanied, of course, by Gyp. At first he was awkward and shy. Smokoe, away from his kilns and his shack, was like a fish out of water; he was as bashful as if he were dining off spotless napery with a footman behind his chair, but he soon forgot his self-consciousness. He admired the tree house and the cunningly made door of bark – which was always shut to at night, now the weather was cold – and he chuckled when he saw the deep bracken beds inside the tree. 'You'm be as snoog as badgers in this 'ere place, blame me ef you ain't. No wonder they couldna find ye 'ere!'

For supper they had for first course pike cakes, boned and fried, with fresh watercress, followed by a hotpot of squirrel and pigeon with mushrooms (dubbed by the outlaws Hunter's Pot) with cold roast duck to follow, and potatoes baked in the embers – Smokoe's potatoes, fresh greens – also Smokoe's, a savoury of infant perch on toast, and apples – Smokoe's – for dessert.

There was no wine but Blindrush water, but that didn't matter because Smokoe rarely drank intoxicants save at the festive season.

'Blame me, but there's nothin' wrong wi' that for a supper,' said the old man when the meal was over and Gyp had had his share. 'Live like fightin' cocks, you do, blame me ef you don't.'

'Of course,' said Robin, 'the vegetables and apples were yours. By rights we ought to grow our own.'

'You don't need to do that,' said Smokoe, 'I've plenty, more'n I need. Anything you want, ax me. That duck was a good 'un. Where d'you get 'im?'

'Blind Pool; they're coming there a lot lately.'

'Ah, nice and quiet, you see,' said the old man, 'nobody disturbs 'em like. Ducks allus goes to a pond like that, tucked away in the woods. I've seen otters there sometimes, an' once I sees a badger, as big as a bear; a beauty 'ee was, cummin' to drink.'

'A badger!' exclaimed Big John. 'D'you know, Smokoe, we've only seen one so far, and she had a lot of babies with her. They all ran off squeaking like little pigs when they saw us.'

'Ah, they would! There's no end of badgers in the Chase, but you don't see 'em, not often. But that there badger I sees, 'ee was as long as a gate, as long as a gate 'ee wur!'

'I'd love to trap a badger,' said Robin. 'Are they hard to catch, Smokoe?'

'I've caught 'em now and agin, in deadfalls.'

'We don't have much luck with our deadfalls,' said Little John, 'don't know how it is.'

'Mebbe you ain't baitin' up properly, or maybe yer trigger's not made proper. What d'you bait up wi'?'

'Oh, odds and ends, birds and young rabbits.'

'Ah, you ought to cotch 'em wi' young rabbits, they eat a lot o' they. Saw an old badger once, slit open, an' 'er belly were full o' baby rabbits, *forty-two on 'em*, all as long as me finger! They brutes'll eat most things they can master. Eggs too, they'll go for, eggs specially, them an' 'oney.'

'If you ever have a hen's egg you don't want, Smokoe, we'll try it as bait.'

'Ah – you can 'ave one, but ef you've got any o' that 'oney o' yours left try it, better'n eggs. I'd like to see yer cotch a badger, but it's getting' late now. They're still about though. They won't go down until the real 'ard weather comes along.'

'Where's the best place to set the trap, Smokoe?' asked Little John.

'Oh, somewhere near their sett, or 'long a ride somewhere. A badger, 'e 'ave a 'untin' path like a fox or a rabbit, reg'lar trod down.'

'We haven't found a sett anywhere near here,' said Little John, 'maybe that's why we haven't caught one.'

'I knows where there's a sett, leastways there used to be, an' that's purty close to the Blind Pool.'

'We'll go and find it tomorrow,' exclaimed Robin, 'and we'll set a deadfall there and bait it with honey.'

'Badgers be purty cunnin',' said Smokoe, pulling Gyp's ears gently, 'you'm 'ave to be careful like the way you 'andle the trap, same as ef it wur a snare. One smell o' you an' he'll give it the go by, that 'e will.'

'Smokoe,' exclaimed Big John, 'we'll get that badger tomorrow night!'

Smokoe laughed. 'I ain't so sure o' that, master. You'll very like cotch a rat instead.'

Then he went on to tell them of many wonderful badger hunts in which he had taken part as 'a nipper', tales of tongs and terriers, and of how once he saw a keeper have all four fingers taken off by an old boar badger. 'They bite wors'n a dog,' said Smokoe. ''Nother feller I see 'ad 'is 'ead down in the 'ole an' a badger cum up wi' a terrier arter 'im and the badger bit the chap's nose off, took the end right off, clean as a whistle!'

Robin's attention was, in consequence of the anecdote, directed to Smokoe's nose. As I have said, the boys were so much with the old man they had come to take no notice of his affliction, but as Robin looked at it in the firelight it seemed bigger than ever. Smokoe must have seen him looking at it, for he appeared uncomfortable. No mention had ever been made of this abnormally large appendage; the boys had not liked to appear morbidly curious and Smokoe had never referred to it in any way. But he did so then.

'I can see yer lookin' at this.' Smokoe pointed with his finger at the huge purple mass which was nearly as big as his fist. 'Ain't exactly a beauty, am I? And don't I knows it, when I goes inter the village! All the older kids make fun o' me, an' the tiddy totties runs to their mammies, squealin' and squallin'. Don't suppose you've ever seen a nose like mine afore?'

The outlaws certainly hadn't. They could imagine how Aunt Ellen would have drawn her skirts aside if she saw Smokoe in the offing, she would certainly have thought his nose was 'catching'.

'Has it always been like that?' asked Big John awkwardly.

'No, it ain't. Can't think wot's cum over it. P'raps the smeech from me ovens or summat. But I'd give all I 'ad to be rid of it and 'ave a proper snitch agin. But it's gettin' bigger. I know it is. 'Ave you noticed it gettin' any bigger?'

'No, Smokoe, of course not,' said Robin, lying deliberately. 'It's just the same as it always was.'

'P'raps it's wot comes o' livin' in the forest,' said Smokoe ruefully, 'all alone like, wi' the smoke an' the trees. But I wouldn't 'ave no other life, no, not ef you paid me an 'undred pound I wouldn't.'

'I believe a doctor could cure it, Smokoe,' said Little John. 'I know Doctor Bowers at Yoho is awfully clever.'

Big John shuffled uncomfortably and Robin kicked Little John's leg. Angela had not been forgotten and the doctor was her father. Strange as it may seem, none of the boys had ever met him. Aunt Ellen did not have Doctor Bowers for some reason or another, possibly because his surgery practice was rather far from Cherry Walden. But more likely because he was not what you would call a very impressive or prosperous-looking person and his patients were mostly among the poor. Aunt Ellen could never understand why he chose to live in so mean a hamlet as Yoho with no other 'gentry' in the place, unless it was because Twelvetrees House had such a lovely garden and, as everyone knew, the doctor was a passionate gardener. But for all that, whatever his manner or the way he dressed, he was one of the best doctors in the county; the poor loved him.

'Don't reckon Doctor Bowers nor no one else cud cure this trouble,' said Smokoe gloomily. 'I 'spect it'll grow an' grow until I can't see, nor yet eat me vittuls. I've sometimes wondered ef one day it'll drop off, same as a ripe pear. But I don't 'spect it will. No, poor old Smokoe won't never 'ave a proper nose. It's me cross, that's wot it is, an' I must bear it!'

Robin felt awkward, and to change the topic of conversation, he talked about the badgers again and the possibility of trapping that monster which, as Smokoe said, was 'as big as a gate from snout to bob'.

At last the old man got up to go and they gave him the letter to post, which he promised faithfully to do. They pressed him to stay the night in the tree with them, but there was no room; certainly it would have been a terrible squeeze, especially with Gyp. So they all went back to Smokoe's shack through the mysterious moonlit forest, along the paths which were striped like zebra's skins by the shadow of branch and twig.

Early next day the outlaws went to find the badger sett which Smokoe had told them about. It was some while before they came upon it, a huge mound of yellow earth scratched out under a bank of fern. The marks of his spoor were visible in the yellow clay, and quite a beaten track wound away under the hazels. It was a marvellous place for a sett, as cunningly concealed as the boys' own hideout.

It took them all the morning to make the trap, but at last it was done and baited with some of the wild bees' honey. They tried the 'drop' of the massive log, and adjusted the trigger until the slightest jar set it off. And then they left it, full of excitement as to the success of their primitive contraption.

'I expect he's deep asleep down there, under that bank,' said Robin. 'Sleepin' away tucked up in his ferns just like we hog away in the old tree.'

'Snoring too, I'll be bound,' said Little John. 'Never mind, if he does come out he'll go for that honey, I'll bet my boots.'

'We'll see,' said the less optimistic Robin. 'P'raps all we'll catch will be another beastly hedgehog. The next hedgehog I catch I'm going to eat like the gippos do; you roll 'em in clay. Anyway, it 'ud be something to say we've eaten a hedgehog. The numbers of people I've met who say, "Hedgehogs are good to eat, you know, you cook them in clay like the gipsies do," and when you ask 'em whether they've ever tried one, they say, "Oh, no, but the *gipsies* say they're awfully good." I hate that sort of person.'

For the next two days the trap was untouched. The boys took it in turns to visit it. Robin's turn was first, then Little John's, then Big John's.

When he pushed his way silently down the bank, the first thing he saw was that the trap was sprung; the big log had fallen straight and true between the palisade of oak logs, and it had not fallen quite home, which showed something was inside. And there it was. Big John could not believe his eyes, a magnificent silky-haired badger, so heavy he could barely lift it, and nearly as long as himself.

Badgers, like moles, are easily killed by a blow on the nose, even though some people say it takes more to kill a badger than to kill a cat. The heavy log had struck it fair and square; it had been killed instantaneously.

Big John drew it out by the back legs and stroked the thick pile of its fur. He admired the strong, incurved tusks, part of the comb of honey still fixed between them, and the vivid black-and-white head. What a skin, phew! What a prize!

It was a very exhausted but triumphant Big John who returned to camp, lugging behind him the heavy burden. They laid it on its back as soon as it was cold, and Robin skinned it by a method Smokoe had shown him, the way a deer is flayed, by slitting up the inside of each leg and rolling the skin back with the knuckles. He made no mess

about the business and soon the fine, thick pelt
was off, and every scrap of fat scraped away.

'We'll get Smokoe to cure it for us.' said Robin.
'It's too fine a pelt to spoil. He'll do it far better
than we can, and besides we're short of salt.'

Little John could not help picking it up and
stroking it. 'What a lovely muff it would make,'
said Little John, pulling at the bob tail. 'A muff
for Mother perhaps.'

'Pooh, she wouldn't want an old badger skin,'
said Robin. 'D'you think so, Big John?'

'Eh, what's that you say?' asked Big John, who
had suddenly become preoccupied.

'I said Mother wouldn't think much of this old
badger skin for a muff, after her lovely sables.'

'No, she wouldn't,' mumbled Big John, and
looked confused.

Robin looked at his brother puzzled. 'Wake up,
Big John, penny for your thoughts!'

'Oh, nothing,' said Big John, tossing a stick on
the fire.

'I suppose you think I'm going to bag the skin
for myself, is that it?' Robin demanded. 'Well,
you're wrong. It was your turn to visit the trap
and you brought it back to camp. So it's yours.
That's forest law.'

Big John brightened up somewhat. 'Oh, thanks, I didn't think you'd be so decent about it. It's mine to do what I like with, is it?'

Robin laughed. 'Of course, you silly chump. I know what you're thinking, you're going to make a waistcoat out of it. I know, you can't hide your thoughts from me! Well, we don't mind, do we, Little John? We'll catch some more badgers, won't we?'

'Rather, of course we will,' answered Little John, 'and Big John can have his rotten old badger skin and swank as much as he likes!'

Next day, they took the skin to Smokoe and laid it in triumph on the table in the shack. By the light of the oil lamp they examined it. 'Blame me! But it's a fine pelt,' said Smokoe, 'that'd be worth a bit, you know. They make shavin' brushes outer badger 'air.'

'Would it make a muff?' asked Big John, a little awkwardly.

'A muff? Wot, one o' they things ladies wear on their 'ands? Ah, it might do, it 'ud make a warm 'un an' all, blame me ef it wouldn't.'

'Big John wants to make a coat for himself,' said Robin.

'Ain't big enough fer a coat,' said Smokoe. 'Anyroad, I'll cure it fer you, I'll 'ave it ready fer you in a day or two, next Friday mebbe.'

'Then I'll call for it,' said Big John, eagerly. 'May I, next Friday? I've got some squirrel skins for you to cure, too. I'll bring them.'

'Yes, as long as you don't come until I'se finished me work, an' it's got darkish. I don't trust that Bunting. You never know wedder 'ee, or that other cop, ain't sneakin' round.'

Since the outlaws had made friends with Smokoe Joe, they had, in a measure, been able to take count of the days, but they still kept a stick, with notches on it, hidden in the tree, otherwise they would have lost their reckoning.

Big John seemed preoccupied during the next few days, even Little John remarked upon it and he did not usually notice things. The others would see him staring into the fire as though something was on his mind and when spoken to he would start and laugh it off.

At last came Friday, the day he was to fetch the skin from Smokoe's, and a wild autumn day it was, a day of equinoctial gales. November had come, first cloaked around with cold and clinging fogs, making more mystery in the forest. Now the north wind was roaring and tearing at the last leaves, and bringing with it fieldfares, woodcocks and wild geese.

That gloomy evening, when Big John, carrying the squirrel skins, set out from the tree and waved goodbye to his brother outlaws, seemed fraught with peril.

What was it about the oncoming darkness, the roaring wind, which told of dreadful things? On this night of all nights he would maybe meet the Martyr with a grinning skull for face, mounted on a headless steed – for so the legend ran – riding, riding, through the forest, a flaming cross borne aloft in his thin and bony hand.

The others had pleaded with him not to go on so wild an evening. 'Wait until tomorrow,' they said, 'the wind will have dropped by then. Go tomorrow night instead.'

But no, he must go. He would have gone had it been hailing molten lead. Big John had made up his mind on a bold course. He had determined that the badger skin, that soft rich pelt which he prized so much, which the forest, in a sense, had grown, should adorn a female form, the fayre ladye of his choice, the adorable vision, *Angela*!

For Big John had seen her, bowed, weeping over the empty hamper, not heeding even the green waving head of the snake, and this was to be his penance, aye, never a knight of old had purpose more high!

He would go through this turbulent night to her very door, and somehow or another she should have his offering. Doctors were accustomed to being called out at night. Had he not noticed 'NIGHT BELL' written on a little brass plate on the doctor's door in Yoho?

Someone would come, he would thrust the bundle into their hands and flee. It should be addressed to Angela, the donor should remain unknown. He might never get her thanks, but his honour would be saved. So had he planned it out. Many hours he had lain and pondered how to deliver the pelt. He might have got Smokoe to send it by post from Cheshunt Toller but that might serve as a clue and bring the hounds once more to the forest baying for their blood. Besides, that was the more cowardly way. It must be delivered in person.

Make fun if you will of Big John, that draggled scrap, clad in skins, black of face and scarred of limb, who looked like a gippo's child in his ragged wild attire. Even had he dared broad day to deliver his prize to his fair one it is doubtful if he would have been recognized, but he certainly would have been hounded from the door and the skin, his beautiful badger pelt, be carried in the tongs to the nearest dustbin.

Two pictures he carried of her in his mind. One of her at the party when she had danced with him, her straight dark brows which almost met – Robin once said they showed a bad temper, which was untrue, for Angela was a gentle child – her large green eyes with iris dark, dewy and limpid as a fawn's; the other picture, the bowed figure by the Blind Pool, weeping silently over her shattered birthday party.

An absurdly romantic child was Big John or 'mushy' as Robin once described him. Yet he was not 'mushy'. He was as brave as a lion as many of his grubby-necked schoolfellows in the Lower School at Banchester would have testified.

Some adults make fun of calf love. Perhaps that is the wisest thing to do. But to many children approaching adolescence it is very real and rather frightening, as are many other things about growing up.

As Big John sped down the woodland paths and dived here and there under the brakes and briars, the wind raved in the oaks. How it raved! The whole Chase seemed on the march, or engaged in some mighty wrestling match. The gusts came booming over the forest, bursting like combers on the creaking trees. The dim dusky night was full of whirling leaves that spun and eddied about him. Even the thickets stirred as if alive. Two things were rather terrifying about the forest when you were alone. The silence of night when no breeze moved among the watchful trees and everything seemed to be holding its breath, or a night such as this, when all the winds of heaven were up and out and every tree was pulling at its anchor.

A wild moon hung in the sky, a moon in its last quarter, over whose pallid face flying clouds were hurrying, hurrying, urgently, in flocks of wool. And across that fitful light, the whipping branches rocked and swayed, the numberless last leaves flew.

In Big John's ears there was the continual drum like a hundred rivers pouring over a hundred waterfalls, swelling to a crescendo, dying away to a low undertone of grief. He saw no beast or bird in his wild flight; no rabbits crossed his path, no slinking fox. Even the wild things seemed to have shrunk underground into their holes and hollow trees.

He felt he was the only living thing besides the wind in all that vast tract of groaning tortured forest. With uncanny light the moon shone upon some little clearing, or a wind-tossed bush top seemed like the mane of an ebon horse, rearing for an instant before it plunged once more into the welter of the fray.

Here might come some helmed knight, horsed and spurred, the moonlight winking on his armour, his foam-flecked steed breathing flames of blue fire; there a hurrying mass of grotesque bowed figures, hooded like monks, their faces invisible, seemed to vanish into the thickets carrying a body, foully done to death.

And at any time there might appear the dread Martyr himself, bearing the flaming cross on high!

Oh! Would he ever reach the shack and see the subdued glim of Smokoe's kilns defying the shadows of night! Oh, to see the gleaming window through the trees, the glow from Smokoe's cosy room beckoning him, a friendly beacon for the benighted traveller!

It says much for Big John's courage that, he, alone on such a night, should brave the terrors of this malevolent wilderness! No one must ever, ever call him 'mushy' again!

At last he came to a familiar bend in the path. Another yard or two and he must see Smokoe Joe's beacon and smell the reek of kilns.

But when at last he came out into the clearing the shack was silent, silvered in the moonlight, its single window blindly frowning upon him! A loose piece of corrugated iron on the tumble-down pigsty behind the hut was clanging dismally, clank, clang!

An unnameable dread seized him. Smokoe was not at home. Smokoe had forgotten and gone to sleep. Smokoe was dead! *Smokoe is dead! Smokoe is dead!* raved the wind, and the trees seemed to take up that maniacal shriek.

And then Big John heard a sound which turned his heart to water. It was a long drawn howl, dreadful, pitiful, full of the horror of the unknown, a lost soul wailing for its sins. He stopped, rooted to the spot. The wind caught that fearful noise and fled with it, shrieking with glee, until it died away. And then it came again, wailing, wailing, and Big John knew it was the voice of Gyp, alias Bang, mourning for his loved one, whom he would never see again!

It was the voice of a newborn thing which cries aloud to heaven because it does not understand, the same cry that a doctor sometimes hears from a babe which has not long to live.

And Big John, aghast, sank down among the restless leaves, his face covered in his hands.

17. Doctor Bowers

THE DISMAL howls were coming from the darkened cabin. Big John soon realized this. Why was he being such a fool? Smokoe had no doubt gone out, into Yoho perhaps, though the boys had never known him go anywhere but to Cheshunt Toller for his supplies and he had no friends in the adjoining hamlet. Besides, this was a Friday. Smokoe always fetched his provisions on a Saturday.

It was no good crouching here among the bushes. He must investigate. When he came up to the shack the howls ceased. He heard a scuffle from within – it was Gyp whining and blowing under the crack of the door. Big John knocked, but all he heard was another low whine. Then he opened the door and stepped inside.

Gyp jumped round him barking. At first Big John could see nothing save four squares of moonlight lying across the floor and one corner of the deal table on which lay the badger skin. The stove was nearly out.

He looked towards Smokoe's bed. Something dark was humped upon it. It was Smokoe, lying on his side as if asleep. 'Smokoe! Smokoe!' called Big John in a thick voice because his heart was thumping so hard. No answer! The wind moaned through the keyhole. Gyp was now sitting, motionless, watching him.

Big John thought he heard a drip, drip of moisture, and a little chill ran up and down his spine. He bent over the old man and put his hand out to shake him by the shoulder. Then he drew it back with a start. There was a snap and a hiss and a wing flapped. It was the tame owl. It was sitting on Smokoe's shoulder.

Big John turned swiftly and groped for the lamp. With trembling fingers he lit it from a matchbox which Smokoe always kept above the stove. And then, as he turned up the flame, he saw that Smokoe was not asleep for his eyes were open. He lay on his back, one leg stretched out awkwardly, and to Big John's horror he saw blood was welling from the knee.

'What's the matter, Smokoe? What's happened?' gasped Big John, sinking to his knees by the bed and taking the cold claw which moved feebly on the leather jerkin.

But Smokoe did not reply; he looked through Big John as though he were invisible.

Now Big John's first reactions were these. Someone had tried to murder Smokoe. Smokoe was not yet dead. Smokoe must be saved. Many boys of lesser calibre would have been overcome by the sight of that little old man with the monstrous nose, lying so still and sorely hurt, and a white owl perched upon his shoulder. They would have run back to the oak tree in a panic.

But Big John did none of these things. He bent swiftly and examined the wound in the leg. It was a deep gash, a very deep gash, and Smokoe had lost a great deal of blood as was evident from the state of the floor.

Big John had a Scout's knowledge of first aid and now it was to stand him in good stead. He cut open the sodden trouser leg with his knife to bare the wound and made a tourniquet from Smokoe's neckerchief. It was far from clean but it served well. He next fetched a faggot from the grate and wound it inside the cloth until it was drawn tight and the blood ceased to flow.

He made sure as far as possible that Smokoe was not injured in any other way, covered him with an old coat he found behind the door – a threadbare coat it was, green with age – and turning down the lamp, fled out into the night.

How trivial those other things seemed which, a few minutes ago, had so occupied his mind! The badger skin, Angela, his silly baby fears of the storm-tossed forest! It takes the big things to give true proportions. Smokoe was in deadly peril, perhaps he was dying; he looked it, and he felt so cold. Smokoe, their faithful ally and generous friend. Branches slashed Big John wickedly across the face, thorns tore at his jacket and tried to hold him back. The wilderness did not care! It did not care any more for him than it did for Smokoe. If a branch was to smite him down now as he ran along this forest path, the wilderness would not care. It would let him lie . . . He ran on.

Big John sped down the woodland paths

After what seemed an age Big John saw the lights of Yoho, like a little cluster of stars. He ran up the drive to the doctor's house and pealed upon the bell. Evidently the doctor had not gone to bed for lights showed in a lower window.

He heard steps approaching and there stood Doctor Bowers in his dressing gown, a pipe in one hand and a book in the other. A tall, clean-shaven man with bushy brows and grey hair.

'Yes, my boy, what is it? Is someone ill?'

'Are you Doctor Bowers?'

'Yes, yes.'

'It's Smokoe Joe, who lives in the Chase. He's badly hurt.'

'Smokoe!' exclaimed the doctor, 'The old charcoal burner?'

'Yes, and please come quickly, I think he's dying.'

With a few rapid questions the doctor had the details. 'Wait in there,' he commanded, pushing Big John into a room and shutting the door, 'I'll be with you in a jiffy.'

A lamp was burning on a desk and a bright fire flamed in the grate. Big John sat down on the edge of a chair. What a sight he was in his skin clothes, with his hair all matted, his muddy face bleeding from briar scratches, his shoes falling to pieces and bound with thongs! One thing was certain, the doctor would guess who he was. It meant the end of their stay in the Chase, the end of the great adventure, but that was one of the trivial things.

His eyes roved round the room, at the bookcase full of rows of learned-looking medical tomes and gardening books. *How to make a rockery*, *Rose growing for amateurs*, *Delphiniums*, *Practical Surgery*; his eyes ran over them rapidly. It was strange to be in a well-ordered house again after the rough cold forest. Then on the desk he saw a framed photograph of Angela, a recent one. He saw the straight black brows, the thick-lashed eyes . . . what was Angela to him now? Why didn't the doctor come? Why didn't he come?

Somewhere upstairs was Angela . . . what was Angela to him now? 'Come on.' It was Doctor Bowers' voice. He carried a leather bag and a motoring cap with flaps pulled down over his ears. He never seemed to notice Big John's strange attire. 'This way!' The doctor led him round into the yard and the doors of a coach house were flung back. The car was started and the next moment they were humming down the narrow lane for the Chase, the acetylene headlamps spluttering and jumping, filling the car with fumes.

What a drive that was! Flying along down the moonlit road with the leaves whirling and chasing across their path and the wind blowing and roaring in the trees!

'You don't talk like a gipsy's kid,' said the doctor, after a long silence, 'though I must say you look like one. I saw some vans by the Chase this afternoon; d'you come from there?'

'Yes,' lied Big John and then remained silent.

'I've never known a gipsy talk like you do,' said the doctor. 'Are you telling me the truth?'

'No.'

'Who are you then?'

Silence, save for the fluttering wind on the side panels and the throb of the car's engine.

'All right, you needn't say,' said the doctor, 'that's not my business. Smokoe's my business, that's it, isn't it?'

'Yes, sir.'

'So we'll say no more about it and ask no questions, eh?'

'I'd rather it was that way,' replied Big John, feeling very uncomfortable.

The doctor now asked him about Smokoe; how he had found him, whether he was bleeding badly, and many another question, which Big John answered as best he could.

'Hullo!' said the doctor, suddenly applying his handbrake. 'We shan't get any farther, there's a tree down.'

And, sure enough, a huge ash tree lay sprawled right across the road from hedge to hedge.

Half an hour later, stumbling and panting, they reached the clearing and entered the shack. The doctor went straight to the lamp, turned it up, and carried it across, holding it over the recumbent man.

Big John heard the doctor draw in his breath. 'Um, um, bad hæmorrhage. *Get out of it!*' this was to the owl which, hissing and snapping, flapped off Smokoe's shoulder to the corner cupboard, where it sat bobbing up and down.

'Can you get me a bowl of water? Anything will do,' said the doctor, after a quick examination of Smokoe's leg. 'I'm afraid we're too late, old chap,' he tossed over his shoulder to Big John as he unwound the tourniquet; 'he's lost too much blood and this tourniquet has been on too long.'

When he had bathed and rebound the wound and felt the old man's pulse, Doctor Bowers turned to the trembling Big John, who was fighting to keep back the tears which welled slowly from his eyes.

'Well, that's all we can do, young man; with care he may pull round. If you hadn't found him when you did he would have gone; your tourniquet may have saved him. Where did you learn your first aid?'

'In the Scouts at Banchester,' and then Big John bit his lip.

'Oh, so you're a Scout are you?'

'Yes.'

The doctor stood awhile in thought, looking at the still form of Smokoe on the bed. 'He'll want feeding up a bit; he'll need care you know, for a day or so. An old fellow like that can't afford to lose much blood. If you'd made the tourniquet any tighter he'd have lost his leg. As it was it just allowed the wound to bleed a little, otherwise he might have had gangrene. Will you stay with him tonight?'

'That's all right – I'll be around.'

'Your name's John Hensman, isn't it?'

A pause.

'Yes . . . I suppose that means it's all up with us now. Now you've found us, you'll split on us.'

'Where are your brothers, John?' said the doctor, ignoring the question.

'Somewhere out there,' said Big John, nodding vaguely at the door, 'away in the Chase. You'll never catch 'em. You've caught me because I can't do a bunk now; I've got to look after Smokoe. He's been a grand friend to us, one of the best.'

Doctor Bowers laughed quietly, his eyes roving over the tattered grimy object before him. 'You've set me a problem, you know,' he said, after a pause, and the twinkle vanished from his eyes. 'I *ought* to split on you. What made you run off like this?'

'Our people are abroad and Aunt Ellen doesn't understand us. She's a good sort in her way but we got fed up always being bossed by women. So when Little Jo – Harold I mean – went down with measles, and we couldn't go back to school, we decided to run for it.'

'And how long do you think you're going on with this madcap scheme?'

'Until Father and Mother come home after Christmas.'

'Um . . . I see . . . what will they say when they get back and hear all about it?'

'Don't know,' said Big John glumly, ''spect there'll be no end of a row.'

The doctor lit a cigarette and began packing some bandages into his bag. Big John sat on the edge of Smokoe's bed and watched him. 'I'll be back in the morning,' said Doctor Bowers. 'Give him something hot to drink if he wants it and I'll leave some brandy with you. And don't worry about me splitting on you. I'm the oyster, understand?'

Big John gulped and nodded his head. 'You've done a good job of work tonight, John; I'll find my way back to the road somehow, don't bother,' said Doctor Bowers as Big John got to his feet. He moved to the door.

'Doctor Bowers!'

'Yes?'

'There's something . . . there's something I wanted to ask you . . . '

'Yes, what is it?' Doctor Bowers looked at the grimy outlaw with a puzzled half-amused expression.

'I wonder whether you'd give this badger skin to Angela, from me; I was going to bring it anyway – I got it for her. It'll need dressing properly and all that.'

For a second the doctor was taken aback. 'Oh, so you know my Angela, do you?'

'Yes. I met her at the Bramshotts' dance last year and . . . and . . . well I wrecked her birthday picnic in the summer. You see, we were rather hungry and we sneaked the grub out of the picnic basket and bagged her birthday cake. I wouldn't have done it if I'd known it was her birthday treat.' Big John looked at the floor and wished it would open and swallow him up.

Doctor Bowers came over to him. 'That's all right, John . . . yes, I'll give her the skin. Shall I give her a message with it?'

'No, just give it her, tell her I sent it.'

'Um – d'you think that's wise, John?' asked the doctor, after a moment's pause. 'Won't it give the show away? It'll put me in an awkward position if I'm asked where you are. I should have to tell. No woman can keep a secret, as you'll find out one day for yourself. They aren't made like us, old man; they just can't keep a secret, poor dears. If Angela once knew where you boys were hiding the whole thing would come out. Supposing I just say a wild man of the woods sent it her, how would that do – eh?'

Big John nodded. The next moment the door shut softly and he was alone with Smokoe Joe.

18. The Trees

'BLAME ME, masters, but it wur a narrer squeak ole Smokoe 'ad.' Smokoe held up a mouse which he had caught that morning behind the stove and tossed it to the owl. It caught it deftly in its beak and huddled into the corner to eat it. 'I wur just a-cummin' back along the ridin' when wham! Down come a branch – near 'arf a tree – and dunts me on the leg. Knocked me over like a rabbut, wham! Like that!' Smokoe clapped his hand on his knee and his huge nose wobbled.

'Did it hurt?' asked Robin.

'No, never felt nuthin' till I gets up, didn't even know I wur 'urt. Then I sees the blood; bleedin' like a pig I was, ole feller like me, huh!' he laughed.

'What did you do then, Smokoe?'

'Tries to swab it, *that* weren't no good; tries to stop it wi' me 'and, *that* weren't no good neither. Then I thinks, Smokoe me boy, ef you doan't get back to the shack afore very long, you'll be growin' stooltoads.'

The boys laughed.

'I gets back, but on'y just. Gets to the bed an' then I doan't know nuthin' more till I wakes up next mornin' wi' doctor there an' all. Don't know where I'd bin all that time. But it's you, young master, wot saved old Smokoe. Smokoe won't ferget that neither; no, Smokoe won't ferget!'

Big John grinned. 'Oh rot, Smokoe, it was the only thing to do.'

The boys were sitting round the deal table in Smokoe's shack. A fortnight had passed since the accident. Outside the fog was thick, so thick that the trees on the other side of the clearing were invisible; a world of white opaqueness which smelt like a tube tunnel, a dank, rather thrilling wild smell. Doctor Bowers had thought that Smokoe would be better in hospital and two days after the accident he had fetched him away.

Smokoe had spent an agonizing eternity in a hospital cot. He had been washed all over for the first time since he was a boy, and he objected strongly to the indignity. 'I tells them nurses they oughter to ashamed o' theirselves washin' an' ole feller like me, as ef I wur a babby; told them straight I did . . . blame me! They said they could cure me nose fer me, cut it off or summat, but I'd about 'ad enough o' orspitals.'

'Never mind, Smokoe; you're back again now, and next time, don't go wandering about in the forest when it's blowing a gale. It's a lesson for you!'

'Ah, this ole forest is queer, you know, very queer.' Smokoe shook his huge nose again and his eyes glittered. 'I must 'ave done summat the trees didn't like fer them to serve me one like that. Don't know wot I'd done but I'd done summat.

'Livin' wi' trees you gets to know 'em, different from other folks. Trees be people, I sometimes think. They can't walk about, nor yet talk, but they breathe an' eat like people, ah they do!' The nose nodded up and down. 'And they *do* talk in a manner o' speakin'. Not like we do, o' course, but they talks togedder, sometimes quiet-like, all of a whisper like courtin' couples; next they're shouting an' cross, then agin they'll yell blue murder and get into a ugly temper, same as they wur that other night. You get a gale o' wind in summer when all the Chase be in full leaf. That's the time they let go full blast, so you can't 'ear yerself spik. Trees are allus more talkative-like in summer. They don't so much whistle then as roar.

'An' look at 'em tonight,' said Smokoe gazing through the window at one slender naked ash which was bowed and motionless in the fog, a flat, cutout tree, 'quiet as mice, quieter. That's when the trees be thinkin', for they thinks a lot, do trees.' Smokoe paused.

'Go on, Smokoe,' said Robin.

'You notice 'em in the spring when they begin to stir an' stretch theirselves. Why, I've 'eard 'em sighin', same as ef they'd just waked up from a long slip. And ef you cut a tree, then, master, they'll drop blood, fast an' thick, same as me old peg did t'other night – not red o' course, but clear, waterlike stuff. Aye, they'd bleed ter death I don't doubt. Then o' course, there're trees an' trees, as you might say. Some are shaller sort o' trees, like timid wimmin. Look at larches, one liddle puff an' over they goo, most o' the firs be like that. They pretend ter be very gloomy an' wise-like, same as me old owl, but they're soon knocked over wi' the snow or the wind. An' birds don't like the fir woods neither; no, masters, birds know a lot about trees. Blame me ef they don't.

'They won't sing in a fir wood. Only the pigeons goo there, an' all the rascally birds that don't want ter be seen, the 'awks an' jays, 'pies an' the like. Foxes like 'em too. But gi'e me the oaks, masters, them's the boys. Them's the trees to talk. An' their roots goo down an' down, an' they live us out. They'll live yer chillun out, and *their* chillun too, fer hundreds o' years. Aye, oaks see a lot o' life, more'n a lot o' grown folks do. Look at the old tree where you be camped in.'

'How old would he be?' asked Robin.

''Undreds o' years, maybe, a thousand very like, we don't know fer sure; though a Woods an' Forests man, a government chap yer know, told me once they can tell 'ow old a tree is by the rings on the trunk. Course I knew that, afore 'e told me. But wot we don't know is that when an oak be finished 'is growin' 'e don't grow no more rings, 'e just stands where 'e is like, and meditates, same as an old elephant. We don't know 'ow long 'ee's bin standin' there thinkin'. Mebbe 'ee's thinkin' wot stuck up fellers we be, pretendin' to know a lot more'n we do!

'An' then there's the birch, the Lady Tree I calls 'er. I use 'em fer me charcoal quite a bit. They're pretty critturs, pretty as a lass in their silver an' black. But they ain't like the oaks; no, masters, they ain't like the oaks. Yer see, a tree's like us. They got ter grow up from tiddy totties, an' then they 'ave their prime. An oak be in 'is prime when 'ee's a 'undred an' fifty years old. They don't grow an acorn even until they're seventy year old. A good big oak's worth anything up to six 'undred pund, but wot's money to a tree! Then, when they gets old like me, they grows all over knobs an' blobs, like me nose, only nobody wants to cut *those* off. An' they gets pot-bellied an' crabby, an' then they drop things on ye, like that ole tree in the ride. Get spiteful I suppose, an' irritable like. Oh ah, blame me! There's a lot to larn about trees.'

'D'you mind cutting a tree down, Smokoe?' asked Little John.

'Cuttin' 'em down, oh, dunno . . . never thought about it much. Yes, p'raps I does. I'll tell ye a story about a tree I knowed, an old oak 'ee was in the Chase 'ere, ef you'd like to 'ear it.'

'Go ahead, Smokoe,' said Robin, who was crouched forward with his elbows on the table, his sparkling eyes fixed on the old man's face.

'Well, when I wur a young man, an' 'adn't got this,' he pointed to his nose, 'I wur a fine upstandin' chap an' the strongest forester on the Duke's estate.

'The Duke then, the present man's farder, 'e'd just cum inter the property, an' 'e didn't take much account o' trees. One day 'ee cums up ter me, when I wur cuttin' poles in Duke's Acres. "Joe," says 'ee, "Joe, we're goin' to cut the Acres down; I wants to plant some firs, they're quick growin' an' makes money."

' "Yes, Yer Grace," I says, course I 'ad to do as I wus told.

' "Well," says 'ee, "wot d'you think o' that idea, Joe?"

' "Well," says I, "well, Yer Grace, o' course they're your trees, but it 'ud be a mighty shame to see 'em goo."

' "But a lot o' them ain't no good," says 'ee, "look at that old feller over there, 'ee's got a belly on 'im like an alderman an' enough boils fer a . . ." well 'ee didn't use a very perlite word. 'Ee was rough wi' 'is tongue was His Grace.

' "I don't allow 'ee's much good fer timber," says I, "but 'ee's a rare old stager, 'an ee's got plenty o' go in 'im yet."

' "That don't matter," 'e says, "'e's got ter cum down, an' a lot more as well, an' we'll make a start wi' that old feller first."

'To cut a long story short, I 'ears the trees a talkin' that night. An' didn't they roar! There was a fine old how d'you do! I don't know wot they was saying, but it wasn't very perlite. An' when I drops asleep they was still at it, a-roarin' like a lot o' lions at feedin' time.

'An' then I dreams a dream that night, which fair made me sweat in the bed. I dreams I stood under the old oak 'an all of a sudden 'e says to me, in a deep voice same as an old organ, "You tell 'Is Grace," 'e says, deep and rough like mind, "you tell 'Is Grace that ef 'ee cuts us down we'll cut *im* down," an' I feel all 'is big roots – like 'ausers they be, ye know – jump and shake under me as ef it was an earthquake. Well, I wakes up at that, in a fine old fright, an' I 'ears them still a-talkin' outside in the forest, but quieter like, more mutterin', ef you understand me. An' then, arter a bit, I gets asleep agin, and blame me, ef I don't dream the same dream all over agin! Well, next mornin' I was in such a state over this, that I thought I must goo up to the big 'ouse an' warn 'Is Grace. But the head forester, 'ee meets me goin' up, an' asks wur I be bound for. I didn't know wot to answer, an' looks a bit foolish like, I dare say, an' then I tells 'im straight out I was goin' to ax His Grace not to cut down the Duke's Acres.

'"You get back to yer work me lad," says 'ee, "or you'll be lookin' fer another job, an' it won't be on this estate. I don't wanter see the Acres down any more'n you do, but you've'a forgot yer place me lad." So I goes back ter me work, an' a little later, up comes the boys wi' the tackle and we set to on the biggun, cos that was 'Is Grace's orders. An' afore he cum down who should chance along but 'Is Grace 'imself to watch 'im felled.

'I would'a gone up then to 'Is Grace, but the head forester wur there, a-talkin' to 'im.

'Well, the last billet wur druv 'ome, an' then the old tree 'ee began to cry like a man, same as they do sumtimes afore they fall, an' the Duke 'ee laffed an' turned to a lot o' fine ladies standin' by an' says, "They ole chap don't like it, do 'ee?" an' they all laffs too. An' then, wop! Bang! Down cums the tree.

'Now the Duke, 'ee wur standin' a long way off, forty yards – more I dare say – but one lump of a branch 'ee fly straight fer 'im same as ef it wur a bee, and I sees His Grace goo down all o' a 'eap, an' the ladies too, like ninepins, only they was in a faint.

'We all runs up but 'ee was a goner, slap on the temple! Blame me, but I was scared! I ain't ever liked fellin' a tree since. I allus talk to 'em quiet-like, afore I do, an' pat 'em, an' tells 'em that it ain't my fault they gotter cum down.

'Well, masters, that's the story, an' it's a true one, as true as my name's Smokoe Joe, blame me!'

There was silence in the shack, only the kettle singing gently on the stove and the chirp of a cricket somewhere.

'My, you've made me quite creepy,' said Big John with a shiver, 'you might have told us that yarn some other time; we've got to go back to the oak tonight!'

Smokoe smiled. 'Don't you worry, my masters. The trees won't touch you. I'll bet that old oak you're under is chucklin' no end at the games you've bin up to, and mebbe 'ee'll look arter you fer lookin' arter me. They know I don't want to 'arm 'em, an' I wouldn't ef I 'adn't to make me livin' 'ere.

'But I still can't think why they wanted to deal *me* that crack on me leg, 'less it is they don't think I oughter let you stay around in the Chase.'

Smokoe came to see the boys off from the door. The fog had come down thicker than ever, but by now the outlaws could find their way almost blindfold to the clearing.

'They're very solemn tonight, Smokoe,' said Robin Hood, waving his arm towards the misty wall of forest.

'Ah, quiet as lambs they be. Thinkin', as I told you, or maybe just sleepin'.'

A minute later the door of the shack shut to and Smokoe went back to his fire. He got out his pocketknife and began carving a block of wood, and the chips flew sideways on to the floor, making Gyp prick his ears and hold his head on one side.

19. Robin Hood Goes Hunting

SMOKOE'S story of the oak made a great impression on the outlaws. They had now been long enough in the Chase to realize that there was indeed something about the trees which was strange; not exactly uncanny, that would have been too strong a word, but *personal*, in a sense, as though they were people.

It was now the first week in December and most of the leaves had fallen, but the forest was just as beautiful; indeed Robin thought he had never seen it looking so lovely. It was easy, he thought, to understand why primitive people practised tree worship; he felt sometimes he could almost pray to the trees himself.

But then, Robin was a strange boy in these matters. He felt things much more keenly and deeply than either of his brothers; he was more sensitive to beauty. Such people may suffer in the rough and tumble of 'civilized' life, but they also enjoy worthwhile things a great deal more than the unimaginative, so it may be said that one cancels the other out.

All three boys were highly imaginative or they could never have lived in the wilds – and had so few dull moments – for so long. They were of the stuff which makes our best pioneers.

Robin preferred to wander alone about the Chase, the rifle under his arm, not so much because he wished to kill things – they never shot animals or birds unless they were in need of meat or skins – but because it gave somehow an added excitement to his rambles.

He would sometimes come upon some specially lovely tree, an oak, or a birch, and he would sit down and feast his eyes upon it, just as he would go to the Blind Pool to watch the water and the floating leaves. There was something about the birches which was extremely attractive – their white bark was the colour and texture of kid – sometimes there was a beautiful golden flush on the smooth trunks which felt so soft to the touch. The delicacy of the tapering twigs and branches was exquisite. He had something in him of the true Red Indian's awe of nature. He would perhaps see a fine oak, still clothed in its dead garment of foliage – which was of that rich buff leather hue so characteristic of the tree in autumn – and he would sit and take in every detail of it. Or perhaps it was another oak which took his fancy, bare and gaunt with each little twig and branch naked to the winds. His eyes would begin at its sturdy rough base and dwell lovingly upon it, working up higher and higher, until he spied the very topmost twig of all, the 'King Twig' as Smokoe called it, and he would listen to the low hiss of the winter wind among the intricate network, which sang like wires in every passing gust. That sound of the wind in a tall bare tree often made his heart beat quicker. He would put his ear to the kindly grey trunk and hear that wild song much magnified; the whole tree would be pulsing, almost as though a heart beat there inside its rough body.

And then again, the smell of these winter woods gripped him, and he would lie with nose pressed among the dead leaves. No flower smelt as sweet he thought, and there was no more smell to the woodlands now winter had come.

Once, as he was coming home to camp by a new route, he found himself in quite a little coombe, where ash poles grew and masses of furze clothed the steep banks. The place might once have been a quarry or possibly a mine.

It was a wild autumn night; the sky was lowering and dark before its time, mad leaves spun high above the treetops and the ash poles squeaked and clattered, rocking like pendulums. Something reddish caught his sight, lying on a brambly bank. On going to investigate Robin saw it was a dead fox, a magnificent animal with a perfect coat and brush, apparently in its prime. It lay as if quietly asleep, the sightless eyes wide open, but grey and dull like unwetted pebbles.

Robin had never thought about death before. Somehow, as he stood there looking down at this wild woodland child, the mystery and the pathos of it arose and gripped him.

Those ears, once so finely tuned to catch every sound, were as deaf as wood; those eyes, which lately were as keen as a falcon's, dim and blind; that nose, which once conveyed to the brain all manner of exquisite scents, now no more than a hollow dead stalk. And he looked at the slim black legs, all sinew, built for speed, like a greyhound's, now rigid and still.

Was it the turbulent trees and blustering wind, the rocking ash poles and the darkling night in this wild place which made Robin think more particularly on these sad things? Was it the contrast between the movement of the bushes and the clouds and this still object, lying among the brambles, which brought the ancient mystery of death home to him?

Robin never had these thoughts when he shot a rabbit or a bird – why should he have them now?

There was no mark upon the fox, no sign of injury. Perhaps it had been raiding a hen roost and had been poisoned. He passed on, stumbling through the briars. But once again he looked back at that pathetic smudge of red down among the still green bramble leaves moist with rain.

And later that night, when he was back in camp and was lying in the oak with his brother outlaws, he heard the wind in the forest, surging and dying, and he thought of that dead forsaken fox lying motionless, away there in the dingle, alone in the heart of its secret world of trees and brake where it had spent all its conscious life. And Robin was afraid. He almost thought he should never again kill any wild thing by his own hand, and he hated himself. Yet, when next morning the sun shone and the clouds and wind had gone, he forgot the incident and his own puzzling thoughts, and was the same old Robin Hood once again, full of the zest for hunting and his wild free life in the 'greenshaw'.

Though all times of day and night were beautiful in the Chase, it was towards evening he loved the forest best. When Gyp had lived with them he had noticed the animal was also affected when night approached. The little dog would sit very still, save for his head, which turned to this side and that at every little twig's crack or rustle, the ears cocked, nose working, and eyes open wide with excitement. To hear the first blackbirds start to 'zink' made a warm surge pass through Robin, a curious wave of intense excitement, a feeling of breathless suspense.

Standing under some tree or thicket which he knew well, he would watch the soft grey winter sky flush to the pale sun's setting and the etched crowns of the oaks grow more delicate and minute against the dying light. He would see the pigeon flocks come home to roost. Now December had come they repaired each night to the forest in countless thousands; sometimes the sky was darkened by them. These vast flocks were not British-bred birds, but hailed from the pine forests of northern Europe. Though the home-bred birds were common in the autumn they seemed to disappear after November was out and their place was taken by the smaller 'foreigners'. He watched the big flocks settle all together with a great clattering and then, after they had digested the contents of their bulging crops, they would drop down one by one into the lower growth. Any oak which still retained its leaves was a favourite roosting place, and when dusk had fallen he could walk right under the tree and see their portly bodies puffed out above him. They were nearly blind then. But their cooing voices no longer filled the forest with sleepy sounds; they were silent now.

In addition to the pigeons, large flocks of rooks and jackdaws also roosted in the Chase, though their habits were different. For half an hour before sunset they made a great to-do, winging and bugling their way in large companies back and forth over the treetops before settling down for the night. Sometimes they held long conversations and noisy meetings in one of the taller forest trees. They never really settled down until it was almost dark. At first light they would stream away to the fields; they were nearly always the first birds to leave. It is beyond any writer's powers to do justice to that winter forest and the magic spell it exercised. So many things are beyond description, a mere string of words can conjure up only the faintest image of its beauty.

By now the bracken had died down, but where it was damp it lingered, buff and gold and red. The smell of it was as delicious as the spicy wet leaves which lay under every tree and brake.

It was a supreme experience for Robin to see the mysterious night settling slowly down, to watch the long vista of a ride shorten as the shades advanced and all the regimented trees so still and black arranged against the sunset.

Robin's sight was exceptionally keen, which was one of the reasons he was such a good shot. Not only was it keen, but it was sensitive to colour and colour harmonies. A mass of autumn leaves beneath his feet would pull him up short, and those soft blending colours would hold him absolutely spellbound. He found the way to appreciate the rich patterned tones of the leaf-strewn ground was to half close his eyes and then the pinks, golds and reds merged and blended; every outline was softened into an exquisite mosaic, enchanting and rare.

Towards the middle of the month the outlaws noticed many woodcock had come into the Chase. They flopped out from under the thick red-berried hollies and dodged away between the tree stems, but even Robin's skill with the rifle could not bring them down. The rifle was only used for sitting shots.

But the advent of the woodcock meant one thing – hard weather. The boys awoke one morning to find the forest white. They had suffered during the night from cold, despite their warm pelts which covered them, and their soft bracken beds. When Robin – whose turn it was to cook the breakfast – removed the door to the tree opening he was quite dazzled by the whiteness of it; the Chase was completely transformed. The snow was still falling steadily and unremittingly, each bough and branch was ridged with a white fur.

It was intensely exciting, more so to Robin than to the others. He remembered last Christmas holidays at the Dower House, how Aunt Ellen had forbidden them to go out of doors because it was snowing and they might have got their feet wet. He remembered the agony of that enforced confinement with the magic world of white, that fairyland, beckoning outside. Now they were as free as wild birds, to go where they listed. He exulted, the old warm surge of excitement passed through him. His first reaction was to grab the rifle and go hunting and when the others grumbled, he said they would have to 'lump it' and find something else to do.

'Visit the trap lines,' he suggested to them, 'that'll take you most of the day. You haven't visited the deadfall for two days. We may have caught another badger. And if we have, Big John, don't go and give the skin away to the doctor. I can't think why you did it!'

'Well dash it,' snapped Big John, 'he saved Smokoe Joe, didn't he?'

'Yes, I suppose he did,' said Robin grudgingly, 'but it was the best skin we've trapped; we shan't get another. Anyway, it's too late now, all the badgers will have gone to ground. I can't help it, chaps; it's my turn to shoot today, you know, and I like hunting on my own. I'll be back at dusk. If the snow's still here tomorrow you can go out together, if you like, *I* can always find plenty to do.'

So after breakfast he set out.

The first thing he did was to stalk the Blind Pool. Being so sheltered it was only partly frozen over. He sat for a long time watching the snowflakes descending on to the black water until he was quite dizzy and his toes and fingers numb with cold. The falling featherlike snowflakes wavered straight into the black water, snuffing out as suddenly as match flames. On the damp ice they glowed for a minute then faded; on the dry ice they lay fuzzy white and did not melt. There was a bunch of hardy starlings having a bath where the stream ran out at the far end. They were amusing rogues, covered with gay stars, very vulgar, always bustling and mimicking other birds.

Some were hopping about in the bare branches of the willows – they roosted there at night – shaking off the snow, powdering it down in showers, clapping their bills and mimicking every bird they had ever heard: jays, jackdaws, partridges and even the bleat of sheep. There were no ducks on the pond. Robin had hoped there might be, but the usual gaunt heron rose up with a loud 'Frank!' and sailed off into the blizzard, sending a jet of white droppings squirting out behind him in his fright.

So Robin turned left-handed and made towards the Crown forest. He soon knew when he was there because there were notices of 'FIRE DANGER' spaced out at intervals, together with the birch besoms, tied together, in case of forest fires in the summer heat. Moreover the Crown lands were fenced off from Duke's Acres by miles of fine-mesh rabbit netting. This fence was a deadly place for snares and the boys caught most of their bunnies there. Here and there the rabbits had made holes in the wire and there were plenty of well-trodden runs. Sometimes a woodcutter or a poacher found the snares and pocketed them.

The greatest danger to the outlaws lay in the fact that the sporting rights of this part of the Chase were let to a shooting syndicate, as was testified by the frequent remote pops of guns, and the sight of empty green and orange cartridge cases lying among the withered ferns. Now, in the snow, every track was plain: little green, melted patches, where the rabbits had relieved themselves, little black currants, and numberless pad marks of their back feet, crossed and recrossed in every direction. The outlaws wisely made it a rule never to shoot in this part of the Chase. But on this day Robin was in adventurous mood. It was unlikely that anybody would be about on such a day. Bill Bobman had once told him that a 'good old coarse day' was the best for poaching. So he went softly through the snow, just inside the fringe of the bushes, as stealthily as a fox. To have walked down the ride itself would have been to leave a clear imprint of his doings.

And very soon he came upon the slotted spoor of a deer. He trailed it far back into the Crown property and it was with a great sense of relief that he found that the spoor turned back towards Duke's Acres, for pheasants kept getting up with a great clatter from under the snow-weighted bracken and many jays screamed.

He trailed the spoor all that morning through the snow. Here and there he could see where the deer had stopped to bark a tree. Then he came upon a pile of smoking dung and knew his quarry could not be far.

The animal had evidently sensed it was being followed, in the uncanny way these creatures have, for soon he saw it had quickened its pace. The snow had been thrown out of the imprints in little white particles and balls; also, of course, he could tell from the way the spoor was placed that at times the animal had been trotting.

He followed on, however, full of expectancy. He could have shot a fine cock pheasant as it sat on a snow-covered log, but Robin was after bigger game. He now found himself well back into Duke's Acres, though exactly where he did not know. The Chase appeared strange under its deep white mantle.

And then, as he came soft-footed round a hazel brake, the snow squeaking under his hide moccasins, he saw his quarry forty yards distant, nibbling at an ash bole with its strong goatlike teeth. Against the blue-white snow the ruddy pile of its coat sang out as a warm spot of almost autumn colour. It was a fine buck and he carried an imposing head.

Robin was so excited he could hardly hold the rifle still. He sank down among the naked hazel wands and rested the blued barrel on a log.

It was of the utmost importance that he should wait for a 'dead' shot. In any case, he feared that the animal might go some way before it fell. Hit by a large-calibre rifle a stricken deer will frequently go some distance, even when shot through the heart.

At last the buck raised its head and looked steadily through the trees. It had spied a rabbit hopping along. Robin could see its mouth, which had been chewing, cease all movement. He aimed at a spot the size of a penny just behind the eye. In the 'scope it looked an easy target.

He held his breath – then squeezed the trigger! With one gigantic bound the buck cleared a bramble brake, sending the snow flying in a cloud. Boughs and sticks crashed, he heard the sound of horns striking a tree, and then it had gone.

In a moment Robin was across the clearing, running like a hound on the spoor. He had not far to go, a matter of a hundred yards or so. When he saw the buck, it was dead, lying stretched out in the snow between two birches.

Robin was embarrassed by the sight. So huge a beast! Far bigger than the pig! What was he to do? But he felt wildly excited; he could have executed a war dance!

The skin with its thick fur would make wonderful coats or even a sleeping bag and the horns a grand hunting trophy. Smokoe would show them how to skin the beast and set up the head.

The next thing was to get his magnificent prize back to camp. He kept on saying to himself, 'I've shot my first deer. I've shot my first deer.' He remembered St John's account of the Muckle Hart of Benmore.

As he stood beside his victim he caught the sound of chopping in the distance. Nobody but Smokoe used an axe in Duke's Acres. It must be he!

He slipped away in the direction of the sound and a few minutes later found himself on the edge of the cabin clearing. Smokoe had forbidden the outlaws to approach his house during daylight, so Robin worked his way through the snow-laden bushes until he was opposite the old man, who was chopping some firing near the ovens. Robin gave their signal, the long-drawn owl's hoot, and saw Gyp turn about and prick his ears. Smokoe was hard of hearing but when Gyp ran forward barking, he turned about and followed to see what all the noise was about.

'Blame me, master, I couldn't think who it was. Thought it must be that Buntin' a-snoopin' roun'. Well, what's wrong?'

'Smokoe, I've bagged a deer, a beauty!'

'You young rascal,' gasped Smokoe, 'bagged a deer 'ave you? What, wi' that li'l old rifle o' yourn?'

'Yes, he ran about a hundred yards then dropped as dead as mutton!'

'Blame me! Now I suppose you wants me to come and 'elp you fetch 'im in and gralloch 'im. Where do 'e lay?'

'Not far off – I'll show you.'

They went back, following Robin's footprints, until they reached the stag. 'Phew! He's a whacker!' ejaculated the old man. 'A whacker – slap through the brain pan too, eh? My – but that's a useful li'l gun o' yours. But look ye 'ere. We dursn't move 'im yet, we must wait until it gets dusky. There's a risk o' someone cummin' along right now. It won't be dark yet fer a couple o' 'ours so we'll let 'im bide wur 'ee lies. Seems to me we'll 'ave a good Christmas dinner, master.'

Christmas! Robin realized with quite a little shock the nearness of that festive time.

'My! Smokoe,' he exclaimed, his eyes shining, 'won't we have a feast? Venison for our Christmas dinner!'

'Aye, that'll be it, master, an' you must all come to the shack an' we'll 'ave it there ef you liked the idea. We shan't get anyone a-botherin' of us on Christmas Day.'

Across the snowy glade, where the flakes still fell thickly, Robin saw a holly decked with clusters of bright red berries. Thrushes and redwings were having a fine old feast, taking no notice of either Robin or Smokoe standing by the stricken stag. What a Christmassy picture it was! Christmas in the forest! What fun they would have with Smokoe, Gyp and the owl, and holly branches all round the room, and a big fire halfway up the chimney! Oh, how he wished the snow would stay and that it could go on snowing for months, the more the better!

'I hope we have snow over Christmas, Smokoe,' he said, voicing his thoughts.

'Ah,' said Smokoe, 'it'll be snowy all right, I feels it in me bones. I 'ate the stuff 'cos it makes the work so 'ard and it brings back all me old aches and pains. Well, master, you come back later, an' we'll 'ave that old stag skinned and gralloched in a brace o' shakes. Shot a deer afore?' Smokoe's eyes twinkled.

'No, Smokoe, the biggest thing we've killed in the Chase is a pig. We're afraid it was *your* pig, Smokoe! We ought to have owned up before, but it was just after we came to the Chase and he hung around our camp pinchin' things. We didn't know what it was because it came at night, so we shot off where we heard it moving about and killed it. If we'd known it was your pig we wouldn't have shot it.'

Smokoe, open-mouthed in astonishment, stood gazing at Robin. With his huge purple nose and funny little hat covered in snow, a red kerchief about his neck and his silvery beard, he looked more like a gnome than ever. Then he grinned from ear to ear. 'Blame me, I wondered where that pig 'a got to! I might 'a known you rascals 'ad 'ad 'im . . . Blame me! 'Ee was a fine li'l pig too!' he added dreamily.

'He was,' said Robin, with gusto. 'We salted him in a trough made out of an old tree trunk – we pinched the salt from a field outside the Chase where it had been put down for the cattle and we smoked the hams. They were about the best thing I've ever tasted, Smokoe!'

'You ain't tasted my smoked venison yet, master,' said Smokoe with a wink.

Later that evening all three outlaws foregathered at the shack and helped Smokoe skin the deer. It was hard work but Smokoe managed it in a remarkably short space of time. It was obviously not the first time he had done the job. When at last the skin was off and the stag jointed up, Smokoe straightened his back with a grunt.

'A grand skin that, master, better'n than that badger skin wot was give to Doctor Bowers. 'Ee told me about it. But don't go givin' this away. I'll cure it fer you and it'll make you a good mat to take 'ome with you.'

'An' don't forget,' said the old charcoal burner, as they said goodnight, 'you're all a-cummin' to me fer Christmas! You leave the venison with me!'

20. The Bells of Brendon

TO THE dweller in the wilds who has any understanding of nature, there is no such thing as 'bad' weather. Snow and frost may be nasty things in the great hive of a city – indeed, they are most unpleasant. If snow falls in the busy streets during the night it has lost its freshness in an hour or two and becomes like coffee pudding. But out in the wild woods it is very different. The only type of weather which can be termed in any way depressing in the country is when it rains steadily from a grey winter sky. Such rain in summer is often very refreshing and delightful, but when the skies are leaden and the air chill nothing attractive can be said of it.

These sparkling days of snow which now came to the Chase so seasonably were quite as beautiful in their way as the loveliest days of early summer; indeed the snow-laden trees and thickets were more picturesque. And after the heavy fall there came frost, hard glittering frost, powdering the snow into tiny crystals which winked and flashed in the pale winter sunshine.

Against the sunlit snow the trees and bushes glinted also; every twig and branch was covered in a film of ice. Each day was to a pattern now. Soon after eight o'clock the large crimson sun appeared, mounting in a low arc over the forest. Then, as evening advanced, and the sun reddened once again, the snow, where the rays caught it, likewise took on a rosy light. In the shadows it changed to blue. Few people realize how blue is the tint of snow. The dense thickets and brakes were purple-black against this dazzling background; the mystery of the trees was increased.

Yet men did not trouble about this beauty; not a soul thought it worthwhile to venture into the cold, silent Chase. Why should they? There was nothing to see there but endless aisles of oaks, twisting ridings and knee-high drifts which made progress wearisome. Those folks with town minds would have been acutely unhappy in the Chase, just as the outlaws would have almost expired if they had found themselves transported to the middle of a great city, with brilliant shops all about them and the din of wheels in their ears.

The smell of the Chase was more poignant now winter had come. As soon as the frost and snow arrived the old smells of damp musty leaves and sodden trees were replaced by an indescribable odour. That smell of the snow . . . there is nothing to describe it! It was a keen lung-shrivelling aroma; above all, it was a clean pure smell, like a disinfectant manufactured by nature. Just as the great expanse of sea gives off its own perfume, so the vast acres of that snow-covered forest land had their own particular essence.

The outlaws now presented a very pitiable appearance. Their underclothes would hardly hold together. Their stockings were useless. In a very short time after they came to the Chase they had had to discard the latter. The heels had worn through and they had no patient squaws sitting in the camp to remedy such matters.

Their coats made from rabbit skin answered well enough, but the kilts were not so successful. These they had now – with great labour and the help of Smokoe – converted into trousers which reached to their ankles. There was never any shortage of rabbit skins. And they had also made leather leggings which fastened with little hoops. Buttons defeated their ingenuity and though Smokoe had suggested he should buy some for them in Cheshunt Toller the boys found that the sewing of them to the leather was beyond them. It was not so much that they could not sew the buttons in place, but that they would not stay put and twigs and briars wrenched them off.

They had made themselves moccasins of fox skin and very good they proved to be. Their old shoe leathers served as a foundation, much patched and padded, but they could not devise waterproof footgear and now the snow had come they suffered agonies. But so healthy had been their life and so gradual had been the hardening process, they took no harm. Not one of them had had a cold since they had come to the Chase. Each boy possessed a fine pair of squirrel-skin mittens. All these articles of clothing were stitched with the cobbler's thread which Little John had brought from Brendon.

A great argument arose over the stag which Robin had shot, whether or not to use the skin as a rug – as Smokoe suggested – or cut it up for clothing. The latter course was decided upon and when Smokoe had cured it and made it supple – I am afraid the outlaws had been too lazy to cure it themselves – they constructed some very workmanlike moccasins which were much better than their old outworn makeshifts. Now that winter had set in they suffered from cold at night, despite the fact they had numerous pelts of their own trapping which served as blankets. But Smokoe procured them some old sacks stuffed with straw and these proved warm mattresses.

Somehow or another, despite all this glorious snowy weather and the sparkling days, the outlaws felt a vague sadness. They knew this idyllic existence could not last forever. It was all very well to lie on one's back and watch the firelight leaping like red and orange antlers, and say, 'We'll live here always, we won't go back to the old life.' Alas! They knew that in England at any rate such an ambition was utterly impossible. A 'civilized' people in a highly cultivated island had advanced beyond that stage. One had to work and work and not lead a selfish existence such as theirs. They knew that in the New Year their people were coming back, and then it would be goodbye, perhaps forever, to this free forest life.

But in the case of the boys their passion for hunting and fishing and – for Robin especially – their love of the open air and nature had got the better of them. Perhaps they were throwbacks to the time when every man and woman lived as they were living, hunting for food and dwelling in caves and holes in trees. There are worse things in life than that.

To these three boys had come the opportunity to live that wild savage existence for a while. They had seized it, rightly or wrongly, damning the consequences.

The Blind Pool was frozen over at last. Smokoe told the outlaws that in all the time he had lived in the Chase he never remembered it happening before, and he had seen some pretty severe winters. The outlaws bored round holes in the thick ice of the pond, and lowering wriggling red worms impaled on fish hooks, caught many red-finned lusty perch and one small jack of one pound weight. Even the wildfowl ceased to frequent the pool, for every particle of moisture was locked fast. All save the Blindrush, which still flowed gallantly under a roof of green ice. The outlaws broke open the stream to get their water and one morning Big John actually flushed a snipe from one of these water holes within fifty yards of their camp. And there was evidence in the snow that other creatures came to drink during the still and silent hours of night: deer and foxes, stoats and weasels, and other wild woodland creatures.

The nights were now so cold that after supper the outlaws usually huddled in the tree instead of lying round their fire. But they had a camp fire just the same and it was grand fun roasting chestnuts in the embers and watching the wonderful effects of the firelight on the snowy trees and bracken.

One night, exactly a week before Christmas, they were sitting thus in the tree after supper talking about the coming Christmas dinner at Smokoe Joe's.

'It won't be much good hangin' up a stocking,' said Little John, 'even if we'd got one to hang up, and there won't be any presents for anybody.'

'We've got plenty of Christmas trees, anyway,' said Robin with a grin, 'and I don't see any reason why Father Christmas shouldn't come along just the same to put something in your stocking, Little John, or anything else you care to hang up. My gracious, what fools we were to believe in Father

The Blind Pool

Christmas! When I learnt there was no such person I felt the grown-ups had played us a dirty trick!'

'I'd like to give something to Smokoe though,' said Big John. 'Can't we think of something?'

'No more going into Brendon thank you!' said Little John. 'I've never had such a narrow squeak in all my life. That reminds me, I think we ought to give Doctor Bowers something, he's been awfully decent not to give us away. But there you are, there aren't any shops in the Chase.'

'No, thank heaven for that!' exclaimed Big John with fervour. 'I'd like to give Smokoe a rifle like Rumbold's. He'd give his eyes for it. I've seen him looking at it often. But there you are, we can't give anybody anything this Christmas,' he ended gloomily.

'You're not suggesting that we go back to Cherry Walden for Christmas, are you, Big John?' enquired his elder brother.

'Heaven forbid! What do you take me for? Anyway, we should all be locked up and have bread and water instead of venison. *I'm* not worrying; we shall knock up some fun with Smokoe.'

Nobody spoke. It was an absolutely windless night, so still you could have heard a mouse rustle on the other side of the clearing. It was freezing again too and the snow was as deep as ever. As they lay there they were aware of a distant musical hum which came and went, and it was some time before any of them realized what it was. Then it suddenly dawned on Robin. 'Why, my merry men, those must be Brendon bells! Listen!'

Yes, indeed they were the bells, practising for Christmas! There had been no other time during their whole stay in the Chase that they had felt so homesick as they did then. Each boy was thinking of the lighted windows in the village, the brave display in the post office window at Cherry Walden. The usual rows of bottled sweets and picture postcards, *Cherry Walden Church*, *The Vicarage*, *The Willow Pool*, would have given place to brightly painted toys, yellow pop guns, toy soldiers, crackers and holly, and down four strings stretched from top to bottom of the window panes little blobs of cotton wool which were meant to suggest snow to the more imaginative minds.

They thought of the steaming turkey and the holly sprigs over the Roundhead's helmet in the hall, and the morning service in Cherry Walden church with the Whiting, redder in the face than ever, preaching his Christmas sermon.

And then the sentimental Big John fell to thinking of the wonderful dance at the Bramshotts', the breathtaking magnificence of it all, the huge Christmas tree with a present for everyone and Squire Bramshott talking to peppery old Sir William Bary about his pheasants. And then of course – Angela, and the dance. Ah me!

Little John's thoughts were busy with food, food of all kinds in such plenty that made mockery of the human stomach; turkeys, plum puddings, mince pies, pork pies, sausages, bread sauce – he was quite passionate over bread sauce – and, inwardly, he sighed too.

Robin was thinking of the Brendon pantomime. That had been the high spot last Christmas.

'I say, chaps, d'you remember *Jack and the Beanstalk* last year? My, but I enjoyed that. D'you remember the funny old red-nosed clown, dressed up as a tramp, who came and tried to sit next to Aunt Ellen and give her a string of sausages, and how everyone laughed?'

The clearing rang with mirth at the long-forgotten incident.

'Yes, when he moved off, Aunt Ellen had that "Spit, children" face!' said Big John, choking until his eyes ran.

'Yes, and d'you remember the fat lady who flew? It was the funniest thing in the show!'

'I liked the giant best,' said Little John. 'D'you remember how he brandished his big spiked club and roared? I thought that was grand!'

'Yes,' said Robin after a pause, 'and to think that it's coming to Brendon this week – why,' he exclaimed, 'it will be on tonight, the first night!'

'Ah well, don't let's talk about it,' grunted Big John, 'what's the use, we're poor outlaws, right in the middle of a forest, and we can't go in this get-up anyway; besides we haven't a penny left. Smokoe had the last shilling I had to get some bread with last time he went to Cheshunt. That fifteen bob lasted us jolly well though.'

'Listen,' said Robin. There was a pause. 'The bells have stopped now!'

'How quiet it is,' whispered Little John. 'I'm glad I'm not here alone!'

'There's the Plough up there,' said Robin staring up, 'and there's the Pole star up above him and Orion's belt. That's Orion's belt way to the right. I don't expect you can see it, Big John, from where you're sitting, but it's that little cluster of stars all close together.'

'If I look too long,' said Big John, 'I get scared and don't know where I am, or what I'm here for, or how I came here or anything. It's rather a beastly feeling. Hark! There's a fox barking, hear him?'

Far away they heard the 'augh augh' of an old dog fox.

'He's over in the Crown larch woods,' said Little John. 'We'll track him tomorrow and get his skin.'

Robin had relapsed into thought again. He was not thinking of the stars, but of that lone padding fox slipping along through the crusty snow looking for his supper. 'I'll bet Smokoe will see his hens are pretty well barricaded in this weather; the foxes'll go smelling round at night.'

'Yes, they do,' burst out Big John. 'Smokoe showed me their pad marks all round his hen house last time we were up there. He told me that he'd had one of his hens taken, too, during daylight.'

'I'll bet the old chap has been snooping about with Belching Bess just lately. I thought I heard it this afternoon. I shouldn't be surprised if he won't serve us up a pheasant on Christmas Day as first course!'

The others laughed. 'Yes, and he told me the deer had been at his winter greens, they broke the fence down. And, of course, the pigeons too. Smokoe was swearing away like anything about it.'

'Well, chaps,' said Robin, 'it's very nice sittin' by the fire like this, but I'm for bed.'

They stamped out the embers and smothered them with snow and a minute later the door of the tree was shut. It was cosy enough inside and each outlaw snuggled down under his fur pelts. They all slept close together now for warmth. And far away, over the snowy forest and bleak white fields, over the bare wold and the lonely shepherd's huts, far away in Cheshunt Toller, the village ringers were trooping out from under the old church tower, their glowing lantern making grotesque shadows on the snow-capped gravestones.

'Ah, it's a sharp 'un agin tonight, Tom!'

'Ah, it is an' all!'

21. The Christmas Dinner

I T WAS so quiet on Christmas Eve that Smokoe and the boys could hear the carol singers in Yoho serenading Doctor Bowers. They came from Cheshunt Toller and toured the district even as far as Martyr Bar.

Smokoe had promptly turned down a suggestion that they – Smokoe and the outlaws – should go round carol singing on their own. 'No, no, don't ye think o' anything so foolish. I ain't fergot Buntin' an' Cornes ef *you* 'ave. The perlice 'ave a way o' bidin' their time like, an' then reachin' out an' gettin' yer. Don't ye do it.' But the suggestion had only been made in fun by Robin to see what the old man would say.

'No, no,' said Smokoe again, 'our carril singers'll be the ole owls, 'ark at 'em!' And when they listened they heard them hooting all round the shack. 'Never known 'em make so much noise,' said Smokoe. 'P'raps somethin's disturbin' on 'em.'

'Maybe it's the cold that makes them hoot that way,' said Big John, tickling Ben under the chin until he winked his big eyes. 'Does Ben ever hoot back at 'em?'

'Aye, that 'e do, wakes me up sumtimes wi' 'is 'ollerin'. But 'ee won't ever do it while the lamp's lit, only when it's dark.'

The charcoal burner got up and poked the stove and a whole sheaf of bright gold cinders fell into the iron pan beneath. The little shack had been decorated with holly sprigs cut by Smokoe from the big trees near the Crown property. The wood pigeons and blackbirds had taken many of the berries; indeed, with the severe weather, Smokoe had found it quite a job to find enough.

'We thought we heard your old gun go off the other day, Smokoe. Were you doing a bit of poaching?' said Big John slyly.

'Poachin'?' asked Smokoe, with mock horror, ''Oo ever 'eard o' old Smokoe Joe shootin' one o'

'Our carril singers'll be the ole owls'

'Is Grace's pheasants? But 'Is Grace 'as given me a good Christmas box.'

'A Christmas box, Smokoe? What is it?'

Smokoe winked and went across to the bed in the corner. From under the mattress he pulled out a large bottle of port. 'Allus sends me that, my masters, every Christmas, *and* a sovereign as well.' He put his hand in his pocket and showed them the golden coin. 'When I goes up to Cheshunt to the shop it's allus there, every Christmas week, waitin' fer me!'

'That's decent of the old boy,' said Robin. 'It seems to me that we're the only ones who won't have a Christmas box. You're in luck!'

Smokoe smiled. 'Ah, 'Is Grace never fergets me, though I ain't set eyes on 'im fer – let me see – must be four years now. Ah – must be four years – all that.'

'Last time *I* saw him,' said Little John, 'he was hanging on inside his car, being shuttled about like a pea in a pod. That was when they were chasing me, when I went into Brendon in the summer.'

The others laughed. 'Ah,' said Smokoe, 'that wur a narrer shave, I must say, they nearly 'ad you then, master. It was smartish work gettin' away

445

like that. I 'eard all about it, o' course, when I went to Cheshunt Toller, they told me in the shop. The 'ole village was talkin' of it. One thing, they didn't never find ye. An' Doctor Bowers, 'ee'll 'old 'is tongue. 'Ee's the best feller that ever walked. An' ain't 'is little gel a pretty one! She cum to the 'orspital wi' some flowers fer me when I wur there. Doctor must a given 'er a badger skin, cos she was a-wearin' a muff made outer it. She weren't 'arf pleased about it and axed me if I'd sent it 'er. 'Course I didn't let on. I says "Yes."'

Meanwhile, during Smokoe's narrative, poor Big John had been turning a deeper red, and when the others looked at him he was matching the holly berries over the stove.

'Big John's going to marry Angela, aren't you, Big John?' teased Robin.

'Well, 'ee cud goo farther an' fare worse, blame me!' said Smokoe enthusiastically. 'So she's your gal, is she, master? Well, good luck to ye!'

'They're only teasing me, Smokoe,' gulped the unhappy Big John, when he had finished trying to strangle Robin Hood, much to the excitement of Gyp and the owl, which bobbed up and down and snapped its bill in fright.

'Just listen to them owls!' exclaimed Smokoe, after the noise had subsided. 'Never known 'em kick up such a racket! Wonder ef Buntin' is taking a walk!' He went to the door and opened it.

The boys could see him framed then against the background of moonlit snow. They could glimpse the dark palisade of bare oaks and the naked sallows against the stars. An icy breath stole into the warm little room.

Gyp, with ears pricked, scurried out into the snow and stood listening, a long blue shadow behind him upon the frozen trampled surface, for a shaft of lamplight streamed through the open door.

'Sick 'im, Gyp,' muttered Smokoe and the dog vanished. 'If anyone's sneakin' round Gyp'll nip 'em,' said Smokoe, 'but most likely it's that old fox agin arter me fowls.'

'We heard one barking in the Crown woods the other night,' said Robin. 'We shall have to shoot him. Hark! Gyp's found something!'

The outlaws crowded to the door and they all stood listening. Some way among the trees they heard furious barking.

'Treed a fox, I expect,' said Robin.

'Not 'e, it ain't no fox,' said Smokoe. 'Blame me, wot's up now!'

They heard Gyp give a piercing howl, and the next minute he came racing across the snow with every hair standing up like a bottle brush. He rushed past them into the shack and squeezed under the bed.

'Blame me,' said the mystified Smokoe, 'I've never known 'im do that afore.'

'It's hysteria,' said Little John. 'Tilly, that's our spaniel at the Dower House, she used to do the same thing.'

''Steria me foot, you gi'e me me ole gun,' said Smokoe briefly. 'I'm goin' ter see wot it is.'

Robin passed him his huge muzzle-loader and Smokoe rammed home a charge of buckshot.

Big John picked up their rifle and they all followed. Once outside the shack and with the door shut they all stood together listening. Massed clouds were coming up from the north obscuring the half moon, and on the faint breeze they heard Brendon bells ringing their Christmas peal.

'Doan't see nowt,' said Smokoe, 'but Gyp must a seen summat over there. Come on, masters.' They crunched across the frozen snow until they were among the trees. The light was too poor for tracking so they could find no clue, and a match which Big John struck was blown out.

'It ain't much good,' said Smokoe at last, 'wotever it was 'as gorn. I doan't 'ear nuthin' neither, but me 'earin' ain't good.'

They stood under the birches but only the low singing of the wind was heard among the bare branches and the faint, gusty peal of bells coming and going.

As they went back to the shack, something softly brushed Robin's cheek. It was a snowflake.

'We're goin' to 'ave more snow,' said Smokoe. 'Blame me ef we ain't!'

They found Gyp still under the bed, trembling.

On Smokoe's invitation the outlaws slept that night in his shack, lying round the stove on sacks filled with bracken. Before they dropped off to sleep, Big John poked Robin Hood in the ribs. 'Glad we haven't got to go back to camp tonight!'

'Why?'

'Dunno. It was a bit creepy, Gyp behaving like that. He'd seen something.'

'P'raps he'd seen the Martyr!' said his brother.

Big John gave a shudder.

'Merry Christmas, masters!'

'Merry Christmas, Smokoe!'

' 'Ere's a little summat in the way of a Christmas box,' said the old man shyly, producing an object wrapped in dirty brown paper.

'Oh, Smokoe, and we haven't got anything for you!' exclaimed Robin in quite a shocked voice. 'We talked about it, but we hadn't anything to give you and all our money's gone.'

'Bless ye, masters, you saved old Smokoe's life, didn't you? Isn't that about the best Christmas box I could 'ave?'

'Why,' exclaimed Robin who had unwrapped the parcel, 'what a lovely bit of work! You didn't do it, did you, Smokoe?'

'Aye, worked at it in me spare time like,' said the old man proudly.

It was a superb carving in walnut of a fox with a mallard in its mouth.

'But it's a *masterpiece*, Smokoe, the best you've ever done.'

'D'you think so?' said Smokoe. 'Thought it was good meself, blame me ef I didn't! I'm glad ye like it.'

The carving was put on the table. It really was a magnificent work of art. Smokoe had carved the fox in a position of tense action. It was crouched forwards, its head bent as it grabbed its prey.

''Ee's jist collared the old duck in the rushes,' explained Smokoe. 'Like I saw one do at the Blind Pool one day.'

'You've absolutely got it,' said Little John delightedly, 'you're a real artist, Smokoe. We'll always keep this, all our lives.'

'Well, ef this ain't a fine Christmas mornin', snowin' again!' exclaimed the old man, opening the door of the shack.

Instead of the sparkling, frosty snow and clear, cloudless sky, the forest was blotted out by a moving wall of snowflakes.

'We'll be snowed up soon,' said Big John, who could hardly tear himself away from Smokoe's present.

'Ah, we shall an' all, masters. There won't be any souls bother us today, I'll warrant!'

Starving blackbirds were hopping about outside the shack and on the trees round about magpies and crows sat hunched and miserable. While the outlaws threw out some crumbs for the birds, Smokoe took a shovel and cut a path round to his hen house.

In a few moments he came stumbling back in a great state of excitement. 'Masters, masters!' he was shouting, 'Summat's bin an' broken into me 'en 'ouse, two on 'em ha' gone! Feathers an' blood all over the place, an' the door o' the 'ouse broke right in!'

'The fox!' exclaimed Big John.

'Fox, me foot,' retorted Smokoe, 'it weren't no fox, there's pug marks like I've never seen afore!'

And sure enough, when the outlaws went back with Smokoe, they saw huge claw marks all about the hen house. They even discovered that the animal had been round the cabin during the night and, strangest of all, it had raked out all the old tins in Smokoe's ash pit. The fast falling snow was soon covering the spoor and when they tried to track it back into the woods it was lost.

Smokoe's 'blame me's' became more frequent than ever, and indeed, the mystery was quite unfathomable. But there were other things to think about.

Now all hands were turned to preparing the Christmas dinner. As the outlaws had expected, Smokoe produced a well-hung pheasant and tossed it on the table for the boys to pluck. Everybody grinned but nothing was said and the feathers were cremated in the stove. As Smokoe's small oven would not hold all the good fare, they lit another fire behind the house and cooked the vegetables on it, an idea of Robin's which worked admirably.

When at last the time for the meal arrived, Smokoe produced from the cupboard a box of scarlet crackers which he had bought in Cheshunt Toller. These were arranged on the deal table round the centre decoration, which was, most appropriately, the carved fox.

The pheasant was disposed of, then followed venison cutlets, with Brussels sprouts and roast potatoes. And like a magician, Smokoe marched in with a real plum pudding, also bought in Cheshunt Toller, with a sprig of holly in the top.

In a short while everybody, even Little John, was incapable of eating anything else. They pulled the crackers and Smokoe put an orange paper cap on his head. The boys thought they had never seen anything so funny in all their lives.

Gyp was given some venison bones which he took across to his mat in the corner under Smokoe's bed, but Ben the owl was drowsy and irritable and spent all his time asleep on top of the cupboard.

At last Smokoe broached the bottle of port. They charged their tumblers and drank toasts.

The first was to Big John for the part he had played in saving Smokoe's life. The boys had never had strong drink before and this port was no cheap stuff, as Smokoe said. Much merriment reigned. Outside the window they could see the soft flakes falling thickly and steadily.

'Drink up, masters, no 'eeltaps,' said Smokoe, who was sitting at the head of the table. 'I reckon this is about the best Christmas old Smokoe has ever 'ad. I ain't enjoyed meself so much since I wur a nipper! I don't know what I shall do when ye goo, blame me ef I do!'

'Don't let's talk of that,' said Robin, 'let's enjoy ourselves while we can.'

'Hear, hear!' said Big John, a little thickly. 'Le's all be jolly, le's all be jolly together! Goo' ole Smokoe! Goo' ole Robin Hood! Goo' ole Little John! We're the outlaws nobody can catch!'

'What about a song?' shouted Robin Hood, waving his glass above his head. 'Let's have a carol!'

'Ah, masters, let's have a carril,' piped Smokoe, and he began:

> *'Goo' King Wenceslas 'ee looked out,*
> *When then the snow lay crewel,*

> *'Eat was in the very sod,*
> *Which the . . .'*

Smokoe's quavering voice broke off in the middle, trailing away into a shrill squeak, and he dropped his head into his hands.

'What's up, Smokoe?' asked Robin anxiously. 'Not as drunk as all that, surely!'

Smokoe was mumbling, 'No good, too much port, Smokoe's seein' things.'

Big John, who at that moment happened to glance at the window, blenched visibly and looked wildly at Smokoe. As for Little John, he gave one hiccup and dived under the table.

'What's the matter with everybody!' exclaimed Robin. 'You all seem to be seeing things.'

Smokoe, who all this time had been peeping at the window from between his fingers, shook his head sadly. 'It'll pass, it'll pass!'

Then Robin was aware that the room seemed to be darkening, as though something was eclipsing the window. He swung round.

There looking in at them, its brutish breath fogging the cold glass, was a large grizzly bear!

Robin was so utterly taken aback he sat petrified. Certainly the Duke's port had been a vintage wine to produce so vivid an illusion! Then came Smokoe's voice, muffled in his hands.

'D'you see wot I sees, masters, a-lookin at the windy?'

'It's a ... a ... bear!' gasped the incredulous Robin Hood.

'Then I ain't the only one!' said Smokoe, triumphantly galvanized to life. His chair fell over with a crash, waking up Gyp, who sat up staring about him.

Then Gyp, who was certainly not under the influence of alcohol, proved beyond all doubt that what they saw was no phantom of the mind. His hair went up on end and with a desperate howl he fled under the bed. Smokoe jumped for the corner where his huge blunderbuss stood. He grabbed it and faced about. But the bear had gone from the window; all he saw was the falling snowflakes, and a little foggy patch on the glass. A silence ensued, save for heavy breathing.

A trembling query came from under the table. 'Has it gone?'

'Ah, master, 'e've agone all right. Smokoe's goin' to get to the bottom o' this; I ain't 'avin no bears aprowlin' round this shack.'

'But, hang it!' stammered Big John. 'We're living in Brendon Chase, not the Canadian backwoods. You don't have bears in England, at least, not running around in the woods.'

'Be careful, Smokoe, we don't want him coming in here!' exclaimed Robin, as Smokoe advanced, breathing hard, towards the door.

First he opened it an inch but the icy wind, whistling through the crack, made his eyes water. Then he cautiously protruded his huge nose, then his shoulder and looked quickly right and left. There was no trace of the bear. But the claw marks were there in the snow.

'He's gone round the back,' whispered Smokoe with a nod and a wink. And then Robin, whose sense of humour had always been strong, doubled up over the table, crying with laughter. The sight of Smokoe, the orange paper cap still on his head, his huge nose and the vast blunderbuss in his hand was too much for him. And the humour of the whole situation was too ridiculous for words. A real live grizzly prowling about their shack in Brendon Chase, and on Christmas Day of all days!

''Old yer rattle,' snarled Smokoe, angry for the first time since he had caught Robin spying on him, '"old yer rattle, can't yer?' But the sight of Smokoe angry only made Robin laugh all the more. He laughed until dreadful cramps seized him across the stomach and the tears were streaming down his face. With a muttered exclamation of impatience Smokoe disappeared outside. Big John and Little John stole out after, leaving poor Robin still weak with laughter, collapsed helpless on the table. When the boys got outside they saw Smokoe, treading very high because of the deep snow, his huge blunderbuss at the ready, and his eyes staring, half in astonishment, half in fright. He was going very slowly along by the side of the shack, hugging the wall. Then he reached the corner and knelt down. The blunderbuss came slowly up as he took a wobbly aim.

'Don't shoot, Smokoe!' hissed Big John. 'You'll only sting him up!'

But at that moment there was an opening mushroom of orange flame, a cloud of dense smoke and an explosion which rocked the old man back on his heels.

'Drat 'im, 'ee jist went b'ind me fowl 'ouse as I fired,' gasped Smokoe, scrambling to his feet.

'For heaven's sake don't try and get any nearer,' said Robin, who had now mastered himself sufficiently to join them. 'If you've stung him he'll come out and savage you, sure.'

Ominous growls were coming from behind the hen house, and as they stood watching, the bear came shuffling out on all fours, travelling very smoothly and easily through the trees, never looking back until he reached some birches on the far side of the clearing, when he stood up on his hind legs, his mouth slightly open and his paws hanging down against his brown, furry tummy.

'Why!' exclaimed Robin, whose sharp sight missed nothing. 'He's got a big collar round his neck! He must have escaped from somewhere.'

'Poor old chap,' said Big John. 'I hope you didn't sting him up, Smokoe.'

'Not I,' growled the old man, ''ee went be'ind the 'en 'ouse just as I shot off. ''Ow was I to know 'ee was a tame bear? Anyway, 'ee ain't any rights prowlin' round me place without as much as by your leave.'

'There he goes!' exclaimed Robin. 'He's had enough of us.'

As they watched they saw the big, brown form shuffling away into the forest, and a second later the whirling snowflakes hid him from view.

The big brown form shuffling away into the forest

Smokoe stood for some time with his mouth open, the bright paper cap on the back of his head and a thin trickle of smoke still issuing from the mouth of the huge gun.

'Go on, Smokoe, say it,' chuckled Big John.

'Blame me!' said Smokoe.

22. Run to Earth

THE KNOWLEDGE that a bear was loose in Brendon Chase, even though it had a collar round its neck and looked the most cuddlesome creature, was rather alarming. Besides, Smokoe's shot had peppered it, and a peppered bear might be indignant, nay, revengeful.

'I'm mighty glad we aren't going back to the tree tonight,' said Big John, when at last the lamp was lit and the door well barricaded. 'I don't mind going back in daylight, but it would be mighty creepy in the dark, knowing that he was somewhere around!'

'Maybe he'll come back,' said Robin, 'and have another shot at breaking into the fowl house. He was very likely trying to get in there for warmth and wasn't after the fowls at all. Bears eat berries and things like that, and they dig up roots in the woods and eat 'em.'

'*O* corse 'e was arter they fowls,' said Smokoe indignantly. 'It weren't no fox which 'ad 'em, 'is foot marks were there, weren't they, and blood and feathers all over the place? Why, it's as plain as a pikestaff!'

'*I* thought he looked a jolly old chap,' said Little John. 'P'raps if we'd made friends he'd have been all right.'

'Ah, maybe 'e would,' said Smokoe, with heavy irony, 'an' we could 'ave 'ad 'im in 'ere wi' us tonight, all merry like tergedder.'

The others laughed. 'Poor old bruin,' said Robin. 'I'm afraid he got a warm reception.'

'Ah, an' a warm tail, I'll warrant,' said Smokoe. 'I'll bet 'e'll be careful like where 'e sits 'im down tonight. It wur buckshot I give un, too.'

As soon as it was light on Boxing Day the boys were up and out to see if the animal had been back during the night. But there were no new tracks in the snow and no more hens were missing. The outlaws, after a vast breakfast of smoked ham and two eggs apiece, laced with crisp rounds of fried potato, set off to track the bear.

Even though more snow had fallen in the night, the old spoor was faintly visible in the deeper drifts, but after searching far back into the Crown spruce woods, all signs petered out and they had to give up.

It was nearly dusk when they returned to the shack, ravenously hungry and weary with walking through deep snow. Smokoe had an appetizing meal awaiting them; cold roast pheasant, venison cutlets and Brussels sprouts. He had also a surprising piece of information. During the day he had had visitors, PC Cornes and the bear's keeper!

It appeared that the bear had escaped from Brendon where it was taking part in the pantomime *The Babes in the Wood*. Somehow or other it had broken out of its quarters on the theatre premises two days before Christmas. After a chase almost as thrilling as the pursuit of Little John, it had been seen by a shepherd, entering the Chase.

'Cornes nor the panto chap didn't stay long 'cos I told 'em nowt about seein' the bear,' said Smokoe. 'Ef I'd a let on we'd 'ave 'ad everybody 'ere a-
in' fer 'im. I tells 'em that if the bear *did* come

inter the Chase, 'e'd make for the larch plantations in the Crown lands. There's spruce there an' it would be warmer than this side.'

'Lucky we didn't run into him, we've been into the Crown lands this afternoon,' said Robin, helping himself to a large spoonful of Brussels sprouts. 'We didn't see anything of the old bear there. We went into the spruce plantations too, but all we found was a dead jay lying in the snow.'

'Yes,' put in Big John, 'I've brought it back. I want to skin it, Smokoe, if you'll show me how.'

'You'll 'ave to look sharp, my masters,' replied Smokoe, 'there'll very likely be a lot o' folk roamin' around termorrer, lookin' fer the bear. Ef I was you, I'd stick close 'ere and kip yer eyes peeled. An' there's another thing you ain't thought on. You say you've bin to the spruce plantation, well, there's snow on the ground ain't there?'

'Yes, what of it?' asked Robin, with his mouth full.

'Well, I was thinkin' that ef Cornes, or other folks, go lookin' fer the bear they may cum across yer footprints, that's all.'

Robin lay down his knife and fork and whistl' 'My, Smokoe, you're right!'

'Ah, o' course I'm right,' said Smokoe. 'Three pairs o' footprints, small uns, not man's size, might cause some people to think a bit. You ain't bin seen yet be anyone but meself an' Doctor Bowers – in the Chase, I mean – so nobody knows fer certain you *are* 'ere. But ef the likes o' Buntin' should 'appen along, or Cornes maybe, they'll begin to put two an' two togedder like, see my point?'

'Oh, well,' said Big John, 'it's no use worrying. The forest is a big place. I expect other boys beside ourselves go mucking about the Chase, they won't know it's us for certain.'

But Smokoe Shook his huge nose and began to busy himself over his wood carving.

When supper was over the boys produced the jay and begged Smokoe to show them how to skin it. The owl flew down from its perch in the corner and alighted on Smokoe's shoulder, blinking at the dead body of the bird on the table and snapping its bill. The good-natured old man laid his work aside and took up the jay. It was a beautiful specimen with no mark upon it. Smokoe said the great cold had killed it.

He stuffed a small piece of wool into the bill an' turned the bird on its back, laying it flat on the ble. With a sharp knife he made a neat incision down its stomach, parting the feathers carefully so as not to cut them in any way. When this was done – he was careful not to cut into the flesh of the breast – he began to work his fingers under the skin on either side of the keel-like breast bone. Gently pushing and pulling, he loosened the skin, scraping with the blade of the knife at the fine binding tissues until he had rolled the skin back to the root of the neck. This he neatly severed, sprinkling flour on the damp skin and on any particles of blood which appeared.

Next, he felt for the junction of the wing and body and cut through the bone, repeating the operation on the opposite side. The old man worked intently and skilfully.

'Who taught you to skin?' asked Robin. 'You seem to do it so easily.'

'Taught meself mostly,' said Smokoe. 'I've skinned most things. There used to be an underkeeper who could set up birds; he larnt all 'e knowed from the old Duke, 'e larned me a bit. The secret is to take yer time an' not get 'urried like; ef you pulls too 'ard you'll tear the skin.

'There you are, masters,' said Smokoe, as he skinned round the second wing joint, 'now we'll 'ang 'im up.'

He tied a piece of string to the root of the severed neck, fastening it to a bacon hook which hung from the ceiling. The skin, now free from the neck and wing joints, hung downwards, and as Smokoe worked away, skinning carefully and gently down the back, the art seemed easy. He cut the thigh bones as he came to them and the skin was peeled down to the tail root, which he cut through, and the next moment the neat, floured carcass swung free like a pendulum and Smokoe held the jay's skin in his hands.

He laid it on the table and turned the neck inside out, until the base of the skull appeared. Very gradually he turned the neck skin inside out, cutting the tendons as he came to them and cleaning away all the flesh from the bone. When he came to the eyes and brain, he scooped these out with the point of the knife. At last he had cleaned the skull to his satisfaction and returned the skin over it. It was slow, delicate work, but the whole head suddenly pulled back over the skull and there was the completely cleaned skin, lying on the table.

'Be rights you should cure it wi' arsnic,' said Smokoe, stroking the soft feathers into place, 'but as we ain't got any, we'll use pepper; pepper'll cure a skin, though not so well as arsnic.

'An' you want proper eyes fer 'em, which we ain't got, so you'll not be able to set 'im up wi' a false body, but that's the way you skin a bird.'

'Marvellous,' said Big John, stroking the beautiful blue wing feathers which looked as if they had been painted, like blue ripples in a Japanese silk painting. 'It looks so mighty easy.'

Smokoe smiled and took up his carving again. 'You get an old starlin' and try out on 'im,' he said. 'Starlings be tough-skinned birds, an' pretty too. One day I'll show you 'ow to skin a squirrel.'

Robin filled his cob pipe and lit it with a professional air. He had now mastered the art of smoking. In a few weeks, he reflected, such luxuries would be forbidden; very soon now they must say goodbye to the Chase, and the oak tree and Smokoe too. He sighed ... Ah, but it had been a glorious time; these last few months had been wonderful ... the shooting and trapping, the fishing and birdnesting, the free, wild life and the incomparable companionship of Smokoe, who liked all the things they liked and could skin birds and carve wonderful beasts and birds out of wood. And finally, this glorious Christmassy weather, the jolly times they had had, and to cap it all a real live bear scaring them out of their wits! He let his eyes rove happily round the little shack. Smokoe was bent like a hideous but kindly old gnome over his carving. The owl, which was now hopping on the table, was gobbling up the scraps of meat from the jay's skin, and Big John and Little John had their heads together over Smokoe's work. Robin felt that in a moment or two he would wake up and find that it was all a dream.

Somehow, sitting in that cosy shack of Smokoe's, he felt that there would be little fun now in going back to the oak tree. The more he thought about it the more he disliked the idea. Why was it? Had they tired of their forest life?

The Easter term would be starting soon at Banchester; the time was slipping by. No, they must go back to the Dower House next week. Father and Mother were coming home in the New Year. They must be back by then; it would be dreadful to be away when they arrived ... dreadful. Yes, this great time was over, or nearly so. But whatever happened, whatever punishments were coming to them, this wonderful adventure would have been worthwhile, it would never, never be forgotten!

*

Why is it that there is always a sense of anticlimax in the days immediately following Christmas? So much seemed to have happened: the Christmas party at Smokoe's, the magnificent wintry forest wrapped so deep in snow, the excitement of the bear ... all three boys sensed it. In those last remaining days of the old year, the outlaws spent their time helping Smokoe with his kilns and visiting their trap lines. The great cold still held and the forest was a silent deserted wilderness of dazzling white snow with purple-black trees and underwood limned against it. Little John came back one evening with a pure white stoat which he found in one of the traps and Smokoe said it was the first white stoat he had ever seen. It was the continued Arctic weather which had made the little animal change his coat, so Smokoe said.

With his help they skinned and mounted it and for eyes they used boot buttons procured by Smokoe in Cheshunt Toller. As for the bear, no further trace was found nor was there any fresh news of it. Perhaps it had left the forest.

One night as they all sat round the fire in the shack, Robin made an announcement.

'We'll go back to the oak tomorrow and fetch away the rest of our stuff, the pots and pans and things.'

'Wot's the idea?' grunted Smokoe, who was, as usual, busy over one of his carvings. 'Ain't you goin' back there no more? I suppose you think it's more comfortable like, livin' wi' me 'ere, eh? Well, that's all right wi' me, I likes yer company!'

'The fact is, Smokoe,' said Robin, a little awkwardly, 'we think we ought to go back home the day after tomorrow; you see, our parents are coming back from abroad.'

'Oh, so you've got fed up wi' livin' in the Chase, 'ave yer?' said Smokoe, eyeing Robin keenly and spitting into the stove. 'Well, I can't blame ye.'

'It isn't that, Smokoe,' said Robin impatiently. 'We love this life but we can't stay here forever, not like you. We've got to go back to school. We shan't ever be free again, not like we've been these last few months,' he added mournfully.

Smokoe did not reply, but kept chipping away at his block of wood. 'Ah, I wuz fergettin' yer schoolin'. Aye, ye're right, masters, you'll 'ave to pack up sure enough, but I'll be main sore at partin', we've 'ad some good times in the Chase, one way an' another.'

'We have,' exclaimed the outlaws with enthusiasm, 'and you've been a trump, Smokoe; if it hadn't been for you, we don't know what we should have done.'

'Maybe you'll come an' see me sometimes,' said the old man wistfully. 'I shall feel mighty lonesome when you've gone, blame me, ef I won't. I reckon Ben an' Gyp'll miss ye, too.'

The following day brought a thaw. The outlaws awoke to find a world of mist; their feet no longer scrunched crisply on the snow. It seemed to Robin, as he gazed out of the doorway at the foggy, damp wilderness, that somehow such a change in the weather suited his present mood. All the jollity and sparkle of the snow was going, even the novelty of their woodland life was wearing thin.

Soon after midday a sorrowful procession set out on their last visit to the old oak tree. On all sides the bushes dripped; now and again a mass of snow fell to the ground with a strange, rustling rush which was quite uncanny.

In the dense fog it was no easy matter to find their way, and when at last they reached the clearing, something made them approach their old encampment with caution. Robin in the lead was brought to an abrupt halt. He said nothing, but pointed silently at the snow. For there, leading directly to the tree, were the footprints of the bear! The outlaws stood irresolute, poised for instant flight.

'He's gone into the oak sure enough,' whispered Robin, excitedly. 'What shall we do?'

'See if he's inside,' said Big John; 'it's your job as chief,' he added pointedly. Robin went stealthily forward. The opening to the oak tree was dark and yawning. The slab of bark which they had used as a door lay on one side; the bear's footprints led directly within.

Step by step Robin went forward until he was close to the door. At first he could see nothing, the gloom was impenetrable, but as his eyes became accustomed to the darkness he made out the shapeless form of some large, dark animal, half covered with the bracken which they had used as bedding. There was a strong smell of bear, and he could hear the sound of heavy breathing.

He tiptoed back to the others. 'He's in there all right, as cheeky as you please, and fast asleep too, I think.'

'That's pretty cool,' said Big John, 'making himself comfortable in our tree!'

'Who's been sleeping in *my* bed!' whispered Little John.

'Well, what are we going to do?' asked Robin. 'Fancy him finding our oak tree when there must have been plenty of other places in the Chase. It's the most extraordinary thing I ever heard of!'

'I think the best thing is to tell Smokoe,' said Big John. 'We shan't do any good by stirring him up. The poor old thing will be still feeling sore, anyway, after what Smokoe did to him the other day.'

'If we tell Smokoe he'll only want to shoot him,' said Robin. 'I vote we just don't say anything and let him sleep in peace. After all, he's as much right there as we have.'

'I'll bet he'll sleep there until the warmer weather comes,' said Little John. 'Bears do that, they go into their sleeping quarters under some brush pile and places like that, and hibernate just like hedgehogs, at least, that's what I've read in books. In Russia the hunters track them down to their sleeping quarters with dogs and shoot 'em when they come out.'

'But what about our pots and pans and things? Our fishing rods are in there too,' said Big John, in a plaintive voice. 'It seems to me it's a lucky thing we took the rifle over to Smokoe's place because, bear or no bear, one of us would have had to go in and fetch it.'

'Well,' said Robin, 'we'll have to leave the pots and pans; after all, we shan't want 'em any more. Of course,' he added, 'if either of *you* would like to go in and get 'em you can, they're up in the right hand corner, under the bracken.'

But neither Big John nor Little John showed marked enthusiasm at this suggestion, and after one last look at the tree which had been their home for so long, they turned down the trail for Smokoe's.

Their footsteps left ragged holes in the melting snow; there was a harsh, marrow-freezing chilliness in the damp air which seemed far colder than those other sparkling, frosty days which they had experienced before Christmas.

It was funny to think of their oak tree with another tenant, a hunted outlaw like themselves; the same thought occurred to each of the boys as they trudged onwards through the fog. 'I wish him luck,' said Robin, voicing his thoughts, 'and may he live in the Chase for years and years and never be caught.'

When at last they reached the cabin, early dusk had come, and the orange lamplight from Smokoe's window shone out at them in a cosy glow. No word was said as to the bear's hiding place; not one of the boys gave Smokoe the merest hint that they had found him.

After supper Smokoe took up his carving and began chipping busily. Gyp lay stretched before the stove, grunting and squeaking in his sleep – no doubt he was dreaming of the grizzly – and the owl flew out of its corner and came to Smokoe's shoulder, where it intently watched the yellow chips as they flew outwards from under the sharp knife.

There was a feeling of depression in the air, few words were spoken and the old man, normally so talkative, seemed unusually intent upon his task. Robin, watching him keenly, wondered what Smokoe was thinking about; was he thinking how lonely he would be when they had gone?

Robin thought of the day when he first came to the shack, of how Smokoe pounced upon him from behind, of how he hid under the bed in the corner, watching each movement of Bunting's huge, shiny boots not five feet from him. What a time it had been! How far away those dreamy days seemed when they swam in the Blind Pool and he had climbed to the honey buzzard's nest. It was that 'last night' feeling all over again.

''T'will soon be the New Year, masters,' said Smokoe at last, glancing at the battered alarm clock on the mantelshelf, which showed but an hour to midnight. 'An' ef I'd thought, I'd a got some booze o' some sort in, but to tell yer the truth, I clean fergot it! Now, if we 'ad some o' 'Is Grace's port, that *would* be something like!'

Robin went to the door and opened it. The light from the shack made a strange white wall in the fog but looking up he could see dimly, far above, a few stars. He heard the drip of melting snow from the log roof and all around the pat and tick of falling moisture. And clearly came the buzz of Brendon bells, just as they had heard them on Christmas Eve.

'Shut that door, you!' called Smokoe. 'We don't want that old fog in 'ere.'

Robin closed the door. 'The bells are ringing, Smokoe!'

'Ah, I 'eard 'em; ringin' out the old year, they be.'

Again there was nothing but the click of the chips flying from his knife and the muffled dream barks of Gyp.

It was so warm before the stove that Robin fell into a doze. His head nodded forward and soon he was asleep. The next moment, so it seemed, he was wide awake and his heart thumped madly. Gyp barking, barking with shrill, staccato yelps!

'Lor' luv us!' exclaimed Smokoe. 'Someone's a-cummin', either that or it's the bear!'

Then Robin heard the unmistakable sound of steps crunching outside. 'Quick, under the bed, you,' snapped Smokoe, 'it's someone a-cummin', Bunting, I'll warrant!'

The three outlaws dived under the bed and Gyp, his hackles standing up like a wire brush, and treading on the tips of his toes, was staring at the closed door.

The outlaws had barely hidden themselves when there came a loud double knock, which drove Gyp nearly demented. Smokoe advanced and slowly lifted the latch.

Two figures muffled in overcoats stood without. One Smokoe immediately recognized as Doctor Bowers and the other, a tall man with a tanned face, was a stranger.

'Well, Smokoe, may we come in?' asked Doctor Bowers. 'I've brought Colonel Hensman with me; the name will be familiar to you, I think,' he added with a wry smile.

Smokoe stood for a moment looking at his visitors. 'Come in, gentlemen,' he said at last. 'I reckon I knows wot you've a cum for. They're under the bed yonder, all three on 'em. We thought you might be Sergeant Buntin', so they hid up.'

Doctor Bowers stamped the slush from his boots and his companion shook the wet from his tweed hat. 'But don't be too 'ard on 'em, sir,' said Smokoe, turning to Colonel Hensman. 'They've bin good lads ter me, grand lads they be.' Smokoe looked towards the bed. 'Come on out, me young masters, you've bin cotched proper now, the game's up!'

There was a commotion in the corner and the relieved Colonel Hensman saw his sons emerge one by one. First Robin, then Big John and, finally, Little John; all dirty, with unkempt, tangled hair, scarred of knee and clad in skins. The outlaws of Brendon Chase had been run to earth at last, run to earth by their distracted father who had hastened home a month before his leave was due.

Epilogue

MY NARRATIVE is at an end, and what could be more fitting than it should end on this last night of the old year? What happened to the outlaws is now no concern of ours. I will not describe the just punishments and penances which they had to undergo before they had fully expiated their sins. It would be superfluous to tell of their return to the Dower House, and of the meeting with poor Aunt Ellen. Even the story of how, later, Smokoe was persuaded to go into Brendon Cottage Hospital and was cured of his 'nose' has nothing to do with this story.

Much water has flowed down the Blindrush since those far-off days. Big John married his Angela and holds a responsible post in the

Department of Woods and Forests, Robin is now a prosperous country doctor with a practice many times larger than that of Doctor Bowers. Little John is sheep farming in New Zealand and grows some of the best mutton you ever tasted. All this is by the way.

And as to the bear, it was never seen or heard of again! Whether or not Smokoe's charge of buckshot put a lingering termination to its career, or whether, as I like to fancy, it still secretly lives in Brendon Chase, I do not know. But the oak remains, little changed since that lovely summer day when the outlaws first came upon it, though its only occupants are now brown owls.

I am told that it is still possible to trace the site of Smokoe's kilns in the Chase, and the ruins of his shack, but the old man has long been gathered to his fathers, and the incense of his fires ascends no more upon the windless air.

With what more fitting lines could I conclude my story than those of the immortal Keats?

> *On the fairest time of June*
> *You may go, with sun or moon,*
> *Or the seven stars to light you*
> *Or the polar ray to right you;*

Epilogue

But you never may behold
Little John, or Robin bold,
Never one, of all the clan
Thrumming on an empty can
Some old hunting ditty . . .

A PUFFIN BOOK

Extra!

Extra!

READ ALL ABOUT IT!

B.B.
BRENDON
CHASE

B. B.

1905	*Born 25 July in Lamport, Northamptonshire*
1930	*Having studied at the Northampton School of Art and the Royal College of Art in London, teaches art at Rugby School for seventeen years*
1939	*Marries Cecily*
1942	The Little Grey Men *is published and wins the Carnegie Medal*
1944	Brendon Chase *is published*
1948	Down the Bright Stream, *the sequel to* The Little Grey Men, *is published*
1957	Bill Badger and the Wandering Wind *is published, which is followed by* Bill Badger and the Pirates *and many other Bill Badger titles*

1958	Monty Woodpig's Caravan *is published*
1976	Lord of the Forest *is published*
1990	*Receives the MBE*
1990	*Dies aged eighty-five*

INTERESTING FACTS

B. B. was a sickly child who was educated at home, unlike his twin brother Roger, who was sent away to school. His most famous book, *The Little Grey Men*, was inspired by seeing a creature he believed to be a gnome in his attic at the age of four.

B. B. lived in the country for most of his life and loved animals, as well as traditional field sports – hunting, shooting and fishing. He based his pen name on the size of the lead shot he used to shoot geese.

B. B. wrote books for adults as well as children, and was renowned for his illustrations, which he published under his real name, Denys Watkins-Pitchford.

WHERE DID THE STORY
COME FROM?

B.B.'s inspiration for Brendon Chase *came from his love of wild places and his imagination. As he was often ill as a child he had not been permitted to play with other boys, so did not experience the sort of adventures Robin, John and Harold relished.*

GUESS WHO?

A 'Whoever heard of an outlaw burying wild boar?'

B 'Gad, sir! I'll give them a taste of me huntin' crop.'

C 'I've caught the first wood white I've ever seen in High Wood.'

D 'Well we've searched the Chase all through and can't find no trace.'

E 'Well, ef you ain't the cunningest young monkey I don't know who is!'

ANSWERS: A) *Robin* B) *Sir William Bury* C) *The Whiting*
D) *Bunting* E) *Smokoe Joe*

WORDS GLORIOUS WORDS!

*Here are some **words** and **meanings** from the story. You can also look them up in the dictionary or online for fuller explanations!*

inexorable *impossible to stop or prevent*

virulent *highly infectious*

quarantine *a time during which people or animals are kept away from others if they have an infectious disease*

poacher *someone who hunts or catches fish or game illegally*

miscreant *someone who has done something wrong or unlawful*

sotto voce *in a quiet voice*

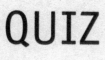

QUIZ

Thinking caps on — let's see how much you can remember! Answers are at the bottom of the next page. (No peeking!)

1 **Which butterfly does the Whiting hope to spot on his lone trip to the Chase?**

a) *Wood White*

b) *Purple Emperor*

c) *Comma*

d) *Brimstone*

2 **What did Big John find inside a hollow oak stump?**

a) *a swarm of bees*

b) *a bird's nest*

c) *a pig*

d) *a hornets' nest*

3 Where does Harold go in search of ammunition?

a) *the Dower House*

b) *Rumbold's potting shed*

c) *Brendon*

d) *Martyr Bar*

4 What did the boys call the dog they found in the Chase?

a) *Tilly*

b) *Gyp*

c) *Whisky*

d) *Bang*

5 What did Smokoe Joe give the boys for Christmas?

a) *an owl*

b) *a wood carving*

c) *a case of butterflies*

d) *a dog*

ANSWERS: 1) b 2) a 3) c 4) d 5) b

IN THIS YEAR

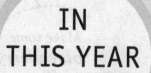

1944 Fact Pack

What else was happening in the world when this book was published?

1944 was the year before the **Second World War** finally ended.

6 June 1944 was **D-Day**, when 155,000 Allied troops landed in Normandy, France.

In August the hiding place of **Anne Frank** and her family was found and they were sent to concentration camps.

Food in Britain was **rationed** and people were encouraged to **grow their own** vegetables.

The famous volcano **Mount Vesuvius** in Italy erupted for the last time in March 1944.

MAKE AND DO

Make some **blackberry muffins** to share with your friends!

YOU WILL NEED:

* A 12-hole baking tin and 12 muffin cases
* An adult to help you
* 55g butter (plus extra to grease the tin)
* 100g caster sugar
* 2 eggs
* 100 ml full fat milk
* ½ teaspoon vanilla extract
* 200g plain flour
* 2 teaspoons baking powder
* 110g fresh blackberries

1 Ask an adult to preheat the oven to 200 °C/160 °C fan/gas mark 4. Grease the muffin tin and line it with muffin cases.

2 Put the butter and sugar in a large mixing bowl and beat them until they are light and fluffy. Beat in the eggs, one at a time, until blended. Then beat in the milk and vanilla extract.

3 Sift the flour and baking powder together into another bowl. Mix and add to the muffin mixture. Add the blackberries and stir until they are mixed through evenly.

4 Divide the mixture between the muffin cases. They should be two-thirds full.

5 Bake in the preheated oven for 25–30 minutes, until the muffins are well risen and firm to the touch.

6 Remove from the oven and allow to cool before serving.

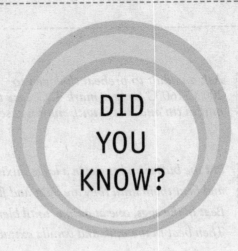

DID YOU KNOW?

Robin, John and Harold love reading and took with them books to read, as well as supplies. These are the books they took.

Life in the Woods *by Henry D. Thoreau*
This book – also called Walden *– is an account of the time the American author spent living simply in a cabin he built himself in Walden Pond in Massachusetts between 1845 and 1847.*

Bevis, The Story of a Boy *by Richard Jefferies*
This novel is based on the author's childhood adventures in the countryside around his father's small farm in Wiltshire during the 1850s and 1860s.

The Adventures of Tom Sawyer *and* The Adventures of Huckleberry Finn *by Mark Twain*
These two American children's classics were published in 1876 and 1884. They are adventure stories set along the Mississippi River, with a big cast of characters.

PUFFIN WRITING TIPS

Change your scenery and go see something you've never seen before.

Two heads are better than one! Find **a writing buddy** to test ideas on and develop ideas!

HOW MANY HAVE YOU READ?

stories that last a lifetime

Animal tales

- ☐ The Trumpet of the Swan
- ☐ Gobbolino
- ☐ Tarka the Otter
- ☐ Watership Down
- ☐ A Dog So Small

War stories

- ☐ Goodnight Mister Tom
- ☐ Back Home
- ☐ Carrie's War

Magical adventures

- ☐ The Neverending Story
- ☐ Mrs Frisby and the Rats of NIMH
- ☐ A Wrinkle in Time

Unusual friends

- ☐ Stig of the Dump
- ☐ Stuart Little
- ☐ The Borrowers
- ☐ Charlotte's Web
- ☐ The Cay

Real life

- ☐ Roll of Thunder, Hear My Cry
- ☐ The Family from One End Street
- ☐ Annie
- ☐ Smith

A Puffin Book can take you to amazing places.

WHERE WILL YOU GO?

#PackAPuffin

stories that last a lifetime

Ever wanted a friend who could take you to magical realms, talk to animals or help you survive a shipwreck? Well, you'll find them all in the **A PUFFIN BOOK** collection.

A PUFFIN BOOK will stay with you **forever**. Maybe you'll read it again and again, or perhaps years from now you'll suddenly **remember** the moment it made you **laugh** or **cry** or simply see things **differently**. Adventurers **big** and **small**, rebels out to **change** their world, even a mouse with a **dream** and a spider who can spell — these are the characters who make **stories** that last a **lifetime**.

Whether you love animal tales, war stories or want to know what it was like growing up in a different time and place, the **A PUFFIN BOOK** collection has a story for you — you just need to decide where you want to go next . . .